Special Delivery

by

Tommy Coletti

Published in the United States by HW Publishing, a division of House of Walker Publishing, LLC, New Jersey
Copyright © 2010 by Thomas Coletti
Library of Congress Control Number: 2010927217
Cover design by:
Jennifer Coletti-Harren and Tommy Coletti
Cover illustrated by Dawn Phillips
Special Delivery/Thomas Coletti
ISBN-978-0-9818652-6-3

For my wife Donna Jean

*With thanks for your patience and all your encouragement
while I struggled with my first attempt at writing*

Table of Contents

SPECIAL DELIVERY

Another Day

Sunday, June 29, 4:10 a.m. -- the fifth hot day in a row. It hadn't gone below 75 degrees during those nights. Sleep was out of the question unless you were fortunate enough to capture a whiff of the elusive breeze that passed through every so often. As luck would have it, this night was not one of them. Even the mosquitoes, who did manage to get through the tiniest hole in the bedroom window screen, seemed to exercise the least bit of energy biting and sucking the blood out of us. I managed to get bit only about a dozen times during the night. I sluggishly got out of bed. The sheets stuck to the small of my back and felt damp and heavy as they peeled away. My wife didn't move but I could see her eyes were wet with tears which dampened the pillowcase enough to indicate that she had been laying there crying for some time. She asked if I was going to try again. I told her that I would see what the news predicted before I attempted another truck run.

As I sat on the end of the bed I could see the apprehension in her eyes. Another failed attempt would mean that we would be out of diesel fuel and the rig could be stuck on the side of the road. The cost and effort to get fuel was almost impossible. If you ran out before you could get in line, a minimal road service fee of $1500 could break us. With diesel fuel costing $13.90 a gallon, this almost guaranteed six to eight hours of waiting in line. Besides, if they didn't run out, the rogues that roamed the waiting lines were always looking for spare cash or food compounded the problem enough to make the fueling effort a major decision any morning. A chill ran down my back for a second thinking that I had left my Colt .357 Python out on the truck's seat again. That could invite vandalism. I didn't need, nor could afford that. But then I remembered that I did lock it in the cab's glove compartment for safety. I didn't want her to

1

see it again. I especially didn't want her to know that I still brought it with me when I went out for fuel. The rogues could get a little aggressive at times. The police looked the other way most of the time because they had enough to do to maintain law and order in the major areas of town where government still tried to function enough to keep the utilities working.

The .357 magnum was a revolver that I had purchased years ago but hadn't fired in five years. I always made sure I had ammunition on hand for my son and I to use when we went pistol shooting and this Colt served us well. Who would have thought I would need it for self defense these days. I was pleased that I had maintained an adequate amount of ammunition because gun shops had ceased to exist. The federal government had seen to that a few years ago. There had been too many shootings over fuel, food and basic commodities. Firearm licenses had been revoked despite the constitutionality issue of freedom to bear arms. You could bear arms only on your own property. If you got caught off your property with any type of weapon you were arrested. If you were caught with one drawn out, even for self defense, you were considered a rogue and shot on sight by the police or military. *Shit, this was America 2014* I thought, *not the Wild West. Or was it?* It wasn't southeastern Connecticut anymore and it would never be again. *I wasn't going to contemplate that*, I thought, but then I considered the evidence. We were down to the basics, getting food and maintaining shelter like the Puritans had done four hundred years ago. They had the indigenous Indians to deal with and we have the rogues. Then my mind began to wonder about what the winter was going to be like this year. I erased the thought from my mind. I decided that I had to deal with today and I'd worry about winter some other day.

She got out of bed, and even though she was in her early 60s, she still had a nice shape. It was nice enough to bring about a little arousal in me. She noticed that and with a little gleam she began to smirk.

"What's that? You've got to be kidding. We don't have time for that today. It is too hot, the sheets are sticky and just forget

2

it," she said. I pulled her close and held her long enough to feel her relax, hug me and then pull away to put on the TV. The local weather report had just finished. We both sat at the edge of the bed waiting to hear what the news had to offer.

It began with the usual information that we'd been hearing forever, it seemed. Fuel was still going up; only a few gas stations in the area were expecting to receive fuel deliveries this week and people were still getting hurt or robbed for just about anything that the rogues could steal from them. The police made statements indicating that they were in hot pursuit of these criminals and that it wouldn't be long before they were apprehended. The usual bullshit we were used to hearing. Everyone knew that the police didn't have time to catch these small time criminals. The main purpose of the police now was to make sure that the city government buildings, that still functioned, were protected. It was reported that the local unemployment and social services building was damaged yesterday and one social worker died from injuries sustained from someone throwing a bottle that unfortunately struck her in the head. It took over two hours for emergency services to respond to her needs due to the hostile crowd. It was difficult to comprehend that a social worker, trying to help people, was killed. They never mentioned whether she had a family or not. I guess there wasn't any time to find that out. News reporting, these days, just covered the basics. Even CNN just reported the basics. Everything was usually bad news anyway and it was getting worse. I guess there was no need to go into any details. People only wanted to know what gas stations had fuel, what food stores had any deals and what transportation companies were still running and to where.

She looked at me and noted that there wasn't any news about fuel availability. I told her not to worry because I had talked to someone a few days ago and he had given me a tip that there would be fuel available across town at the Shell station on West Town Street today.

"Who gave you the tip?" she asked. I explained that I had broken up a fight between some rogue and a trucker who was

3

being hounded by the rogue for some spare cash while we waited to see if we could get fuel. The fuel attendant at the station was grateful for my assistance and he gave me a tip as to where the first delivery truck would be tomorrow. He said he would pass on my license plate number to the attendant at that station so that he could identify me, put me at the head of the line and fill up my truck. The fuel attendants at the stations usually knew the schedule so that they could fill up their station tanks and then announce a day or two later that they had fuel. They thought it would keep the lines down. It usually never worked because most of the time, aggressive truckers working for the big hauling companies slept in their trucks near the fuel stations in order to see when the delivery trucks would arrive. They'd use code language over their CBs to their co-workers to announce where the fuel was being delivered. It was something like the 'Wind Talker's' of World War II. *God, I thought, this country had been degraded in such a short time.* The little guys like me had to rely on sheer luck for tips like that.

My wife asked about the altercation at the fuel station and I explained that it wasn't anything to be concerned about.
"Did you get in a fight? What happened? How'd you stop the guy that was causing a problem?" she almost demanded. I said that I just shoved him around and he left the fuel station to probably go hassle someone else. She looked at me and said, "At five foot, eight inches tall, one hundred ninety five pounds and with that cute round old face, how could you shove some jerk around without getting into a fist fight? You're not the intimidating kind and most guys like that would have attempted to hurt you right away." She gritted her teeth. "You scared him with your gun, didn't you?" she asked, raising her voice. "You're still carrying that damned gun around and you scared the shit out of him right?" Her voice got an octave higher. "I can only imagine if he had taken the gun from you," she said, as she burst into tears and walked out of the bedroom. She had a point. The rogue could have probably killed me. He

was a big bastard and probably could have wrestled the gun from me. She didn't know that he had really pissed me off that day and I had put the gun right into his mouth. He knew better than to screw with me while in that position. I only hoped that I didn't run into him again because I would probably have to seriously hurt him or even kill the piece of crap.

I forgot about that scenario and walked out of the bedroom to catch my wife and put my arms around her. Too late. She was already in the bathroom peeing and wasn't in the mood for any of my affection. She just looked at me with those swollen eyes and asked me to stop putting myself into predicaments that could get me hurt or even killed. I smiled and said that I would be careful and keep out of harm's way. I knew I was lying to her because these days, since the Gulf hurricane and the Saudi jet crash, we were now in the new Wild West called the U. S. of A.

I washed quickly. I dared not to use any hot water because I didn't want to risk using any of our furnace oil. We had almost a full tank and God only knew when I would be able to get another home heating oil fuel delivery. The oil company we did business with in the past had burned down. Too many people had been unable to pay their bills on time which led to credit problems for the company. The oil company refused to honor any more contracts they had from their customers and would not deliver oil unless there was cash paid up front. They needed the cash to secure deliveries to their oil storage tanks. Needless to say, someone torched the place one winter evening. The owner's night watchman was burnt to death in the explosion of one of the tanks and it took five local fire departments to extinguish it. We were now down to two fuel oil companies in the area and they would not deliver to anyone at this time. They were stockpiling, under heavy armed guard I had heard, as they waited for the winter months to approach.

Bridgeport and New Haven, Connecticut were the centers for oil storage for New England. The local oil companies stockpiled fuel oil there. Diesel and gas storage was also centralized there since the Crescent Tug Company, CTC, of

Bridgeport, Connecticut had come into existence in the last five years towing oil barges in and out of those ports to supply New England with the liquid gold. Since Hurricane Angel on May 30, 2010, when all the refineries in Texas were basically rendered inoperable, we were lucky to get any fuel oil at all for the 2010 to 2011 winter months. The first hurricane of the season had reformed out in the Caribbean after hitting the Yucatan Peninsula as a category one storm. Hurricane Angel developed into a category five within five days before she blew into Houston. For the winters that followed, getting fuel and paying the price was nearly impossible.

A few months ago I was lucky enough to do some bartering and get some oil delivered during the middle of the night. Because it was early summer, none of my neighbors had noticed. Burning wood helped in heating your home but it was difficult to get it now. The farmers and land owners were constantly fighting off rogues and even the common people to keep them from deforesting their property. I did have some opportunities to get wood from some of the friends I grew up with that still had land. Bartering usually was the main source of exchange. When I did get some wood, I stored it in my basement under lock and key. I had to put some bars over my cellar windows to keep out potential thieves. Driving out to get wood was always pleasant a few years back, but now, the lots and fields were becoming decimated. It looked as if World War I, which had been fought 100 years earlier, had just been fought yesterday in Connecticut. There were no trees of any considerable size to be found, just stumps. All the brush had been used as well. Land owners who still had wooded areas, attempted to use those areas as protection to raise food crops. The area was patrolled at times in order to protect the wood as well as keep people from seeing what food crops they were growing. The land owners and farmers kept those new fields close to their residence. I had witnessed this way of life develop over the past few years as I sometimes was contracted to pickup harvested crops and deliver them to the market under armed guard. The guns were never exposed but everyone,

6

including the rogues and police, knew that these people would protect their produce.

As I dried myself, she approached and wrapped her hands around my waist. She asked what I would like for breakfast. I laughed and said that I could not stand another steak and egg breakfast again. I was so tired of eating that every day. She smiled and pinched my butt.

"You're a real jerk. You have two choices, tea and some Instant Breakfast or Instant Breakfast with tea. There is no milk so you have to mix the Instant Breakfast with water," she said.

I thought, *thank God we still have electricity so I can boil some water to make a hot cup of tea.* I had been lucky enough to get a case of the Instant Breakfast at the central artery terminal, as we locals called it. There had been some left on the dock and I threw it into my truck on my way home one night. I had stolen it but I felt no guilt. We were down to the basics now and someone else would have taken it if I hadn't. Stealing food was a way of life now and my excuse to be exonerated. We hadn't seen any fresh eggs in over three months and even then they were $12 a dozen. I never would have believed that one day, a lone egg would cost one dollar. If you were lucky enough to live near someone who had chickens that were laying eggs you might get away with a dozen for $10 if you had something to barter that they wanted. But you usually couldn't get any eggs from the farmers because they relied on eggs as their main source of food. They sold or bartered only when absolutely necessary and a dollar for an egg was an easy system of trade to keep account of.

It had been six months since the Saudi crash of February 15, 2011 and coffee was non-existent. Tea was also getting scarce. People had more tea bags on hand, I guess, and made them last longer. We used them twice at home for hot tea and let the old bags soak in water to savor what flavor could be extracted for iced tea.

The Iranians orchestrated a "peace flight" from Tehran to Baghdad. They used this opportunity to introduce the newest and largest airbus they had purchased. This was how they were going to make their new mark in the world. This so-called peace flight from Tehran to Baghdad was highly publicized and the terrorists listened and plotted intently to ensure that they did not miss their mark. Unbeknownst to the Iranians, a group of terrorists managed to get onboard. The entire world watched in horror as the 300- ton passenger jet plummeted into Saudi's main mid-eastern oil storage facility killing everyone on board as well as completely rendering the facility useless for the next two and a half years. In all, 700 people had lost their lives instantly that day. The refinery is still only producing 30 percent of its capacity and it will take several more years to produce what it used to according to the latest news updates.

Saudi Arabia blamed Baghdad, Baghdad blamed Tehran, and Tehran blamed the Saudis because the terrorists who had piloted the jet had been Saudis just like on 9/11/2001. The United States had just withdrawn from Iraq the previous year after almost seven years of war to stabilize the country. The Iraqi people had been able to elect a government that represented the three major factors in the country but that all went to hell after the crash. The oil production from Iraq had begun to pay off for the people there and assisted in adding much needed oil to the strained production coming from Saudi Arabia. After the crash, there was complete confusion in the entire Middle East, causing a complete shutdown of oil production because the world's demand over exceeded production. It became a real nightmare for Europe and America and eventually the world.

I finished my tea and stared at the flicker of sunlight that came through the window and lit up the kitchen table and my half drunk Instant Breakfast. My wife had finished hers and reminded me that I should finish the rest of mine because it would be a long day again unless my tip was a good one and I got the fuel I needed for our truck. I had bought the truck when I retired from cross country trucking five years earlier. I was planning to use it part time to make a little cash to offset medical expenses and keep a small stash for when we needed

8

it. I thanked the Creator, every day, for helping me make the right decision to sell my big rig and start semi-retirement. I couldn't imagine driving cross-country today in a rig that needed thousands of gallons of diesel fuel to operate it.

She had made me a lunch. A can of King Oscar Sardines in olive oil was a nice surprise. I didn't know that we had any left. My wife just smiled and said she planned to make sure my breath was stinky enough to keep the ladies of the afternoon away from me while I was busy delivering anything I could manage to get paid for at the central artery terminal. She knew that too many rogues pimped women free around the truckers to get access to their delivery goods while they were occupied with the ladies of the day as they had become known.

I looked at my watch. It was 4:26 a.m. and I needed to be at the Shell Station in about 30minutes. If I got there about 5 a.m. and the tip was good, the attendant would recognize my license plate number and wave me on to the nearest diesel pump. The only thing that I had to worry about now was carrying $1400 on me to pay for 100 gallons of diesel fuel. No credit cards were accepted anymore for fuel because most of the credit card companies were non-existent. Nobody could pay any of their fees and the legal system was so backed up with credit card bankruptcies that the system almost completely failed. The legal system was using all of its resources to take care of the increasing number of hard criminal cases. The rogues knew that the system was failing and that is why self protection was fueling the Wild West atmosphere here in New England and in most places of the U.S.

I opened our little safe and drew out 14 new $100 bills and some assorted notes just in case the price had changed in the past 24 hours. Most cash settlements were done to the nearest five dollars because one dollar bills were useless. Nothing could be purchased for a dollar bill anymore except eggs maybe. I looked over the cash in our safe and it was evident that I needed another delivery job. We were down to about $1500 in cash in the safe after this fill up. Groceries for the two of us next week would eat into a quarter of that and after that we'd be in trouble if I didn't get a delivery contract soon. I always did manage to keep ahead to feed my wife and myself but it was hard helping the kids and making sure that they were getting by with even the basics. I figured that I would stop by my daughter's house if my deliveries brought me close to it. It was a slim chance but I usually could find a way to go by her house and check in on her and her family. Occasionally, I timed it right and was able to catch all of them at home. I didn't want to chance seeing them in the evening because the rogues would be out in strength and I didn't want to attract attention to their house especially if I had some deliveries for them. Rogues usually knew if a delivery truck had been to someone's home during the day. To them, that usually meant something they could steal and sell. All of the neighborhoods were having this problem.

I was ready to start the day. With my money in my front pocket, my hope that the tip was good, and the anticipation of getting a delivery contract to help make it through another day in the wild west, I headed out the door. The clock read 4:38 a.m. as I slowly opened the door, peered out, and looked cautiously in both directions. I walked around the truck and double checked it to make sure my two gas cover locks had not been tampered with. They looked fine and there was no visible damage done to the truck. I had, on occasion, found the truck tires missing or the fuel tanks tampered with. Quickly, I learned to install locks on my wheel lugs as well as locks on my tanks. The cost of those items alone had us eating pasta and parmesan cheese for two weeks. I didn't want to go through that again especially since we couldn't get the parmesan cheese anymore.

The truck started. I checked the right tank. Shit. I forgot it was empty. The left tank had about three gallons of fuel left in it though. That was more than enough fuel to get to the Shell Station. It was probably enough fuel to keep in line long enough to get the fuel I needed, depending on how long the line was. All would be great if the tip that I had received was good and the attendant remembered my license plate number

10

and waved me on to the nearest pump. I tried to blank out that it was a lot to happen in only a few minutes. If all went well, I'd be in and out of there and up to the artery terminal in a few minutes to take on any new deliveries. I knew that I could make some good money if I got one of the early deliveries. They usually paid the best and were usually close by in the area. That could mean a double. Not in the sense of baseball talk but in trucker talk. I mean a second delivery could be possible and the amount of fuel I used on the first one would be insignificant if I could get a second one in the same day. I started doing some finances in my head then decided that I could do that when and if I got the second delivery. *Shit. I'm getting way ahead of myself and I need to concentrate on my driving and keeping my wits sharp*, I thought, as I slowly pulled out of the yard.

When I looked back at the kitchen window, she was there, as usual, watching her not-so-shining knight off to do battle in the concrete wilderness again. She'd be leaving for work at the hospital in an hour or so. I hoped that she would be in a better mood when I returned in the evening. I thought about the old days when I left in the morning and took the Colt out of the glove box and slid it between my belt and the small of my back. The old days weren't so long ago. Three-to-four years ago, I could park overnight on the street. Any truck was safe in those days. I didn't need to be in the yard overnight. The truck could have been full of canned goods or building materials or anything imaginable that needed to be delivered. If I did that today, I would have needed the National Guard to hold off the rogues as well as my desperate neighbors. Anybody would steal you blind these days. You just couldn't be street smart as the old saying was; you had to be paranoid and think of as many ways people could think of to screw you over and you had to improvise accordingly. Street smart had turned into survival intelligence.

Despite the hard times in the second decade of the 21st century, Americans tried to still be Americans in their values and way of life. The rogues in America saw it differently. Do unto him before he could do unto you was a way of life now for the new lowest class. In the world of the rogue, doing anything and everything to survive was acceptable. America was trying to deal with the rogue problem but outside forces were taking advantage of America's weakness. Those outside forces controlled the majority of the local fuel deliveries and most of the major hauling companies that I had to compete with were now buying up the independent tug and marine shipping companies to control that commerce.

Fourteen Hundred Bucks

The sun was coming up quickly this Sunday it seemed. It was 4:53 a.m. as I rounded the corner. I could see the Shell Station sign up ahead. "Shit!" I blurted out as the line of trucks appeared before me. I'd probably be 20th in line based on the vision I processed through my head. That would mean 40 to 50 minutes in line waiting to get fuel. That is, if fuel was available after some of the big boys sucked up 200 to 300 gallons of diesel at a time. I don't know where they got that kind of cash these days. Carrying $3000 to $4000 in cash in your pocket was something I didn't want to ever be in a position to have to do. Most of these guys had strong arms with them. They paid them good money for protection. *Still,* I thought, *who's to say that these guys didn't go sour occasionally and take all the money the trucker had before he had a chance to buy the fuel.* Some of these characters made the rogues look like hospital candy stripers when you heard stories of how they screwed over some trucker, took his cash and left him for dead after the beating they gave him. There were wore horror stories about female truckers in the same predicament. I had not seen any female operators in almost two years.

I decided to take a chance and not get in line right away. I figured that if I drove my truck by slowly, maybe I could get the attendants attention and he would recognize my plate number and wave me in front of some of the first trucks in line. But where was the attendant? They were usually right out in front. If my decision was wrong, then I was really in trouble. I'd end up 30th or even farther back in the line. I would have to go home with another opportunity missed. I couldn't bear to see Jean's face when I returned home empty handed again after the encouragement I gave her on the good tip I had received.

"No balls, no blue chips," I mumbled. I slowly drove parallel with the line of trucks. Surer than shit, the attendant came into sight. I honked my horn. He looked up and for a second and

13

looked puzzled. *Oh shit,* I thought. He has no clue who I am. But then, as all is holy, he smirked, waved me to a spot next to the lead truck and jumped onto my running board. "Where, the hell, have you been?" he asked. "I figured you'd be out here earlier than five a.m. And don't do that shit again if you get another tip for my station. You are a lucky bastard that I gave you a few more minutes and the only reason you got it is you saved my brother-in-law's ass a few days ago from that rogue." He blurted it all out in one breath. I noticed the tattoo on his left forearm. It was a U.S. Army veteran tattoo at that. I just looked at him and said, "Thanks." I knew better than to say anything else. I learned over 45 years ago to keep my mouth shut at the army fuel terminals. The depot sergeants were real dickheads and ran a tight operation. Fuel up quickly and get out the same way. I had mostly forgotten about my tour of 'Nam in '68 and those days of convoys on the highways there. The thought of the times when some gook would take a pot shot at my duce and a half as I drove through a village had almost disappeared until a year or so ago when the whole country began to become a third world country like Vietnam was then.

He guided me in so that I was probably third in line to fuel up. The guy I cut in front of really got pissed off. He bumped my truck enough to almost dislodge the attendant from my running board. The attendant got pissed too. He caught his balance, jumped off my truck's running board and was in the face of the other truck driver in an instant. I kind of felt sorry for the guy for the verbal abuse and threats the attendant gave him. I would have been a little pissed too but I knew better. The attendant had the power to make or break your day and he let the young driver know that. The attendant had a heart though. He must have been a regular army lifer because he looked like he was training this kid to shape up when he was at his station. The attendant's mannerisms brought back memories of another time in my life.

The attendant finally quit his tirade and reassumed his position of authority. He waved me to the pump where he yelled, "Give me the tank keys and how much?"

14

I said, "Fill them both. They should take about fifty gallons each."

He nodded as he gave the pump attendant the keys and the filling process began. It ended quite quickly.

"Okay, thirteen hundred and ninety bucks," he said while putting out his hand next to the window. He was looking down to make sure the fuel attendant locked up the tanks. I looked at him while he gave me my keys and began to correct him that the attendant had only put in about 98 gallons. He looked at me and smiled.

"Are your tanks full? Didn't you get a break in line? Thirteen hundred and ninety bucks or the price goes up." The pump attendant began to slowly move toward my truck as he heard the conversation going on. I handed the station attendant the cash, smiled and started my truck. He smirked in acknowledgement. I set the trip odometer to zero miles as I always did after I filled. It was 5:11 a.m. and all was right in the world. Well almost all. I had gotten hosed for two gallons of fuel. I figured that I'd make that up getting an early delivery and possibly getting a double before the end of the day. That station attendant had made a few bucks off me but he also risked getting some shit from the other drivers. *Those few bucks I lost weren't worth thinking about,* I thought.

The day was really beginning to get hotter. The temperature was now at 81 degrees according to my cab thermometer. It was not even 5:30 a.m. yet as I entered the artery terminal parking lot. Not very many local delivery trucks like mine were waiting so it looked like a good day was about to develop. I turned off the truck, slid my Colt out from my belt and into the glove box and jumped out and locked the truck. The terminal foreman was talking and handing out assignment sheets to a few of the drivers that were gathered around him. He looked up as I approached.

"Sprague, you made it today."I smiled and nodded. He handed me an assignment sheet and I glanced at it. It was across town and I probably would be able to deliver whatever it was in a relatively short time. Maybe I would get that double after all.

15

He instructed me to get into my truck and get to the loading dock for my delivery quickly. I had the truck in position in a few minutes. The loading process took a short time. According to the assignment and delivery document, it indicated that it was farm machinery parts for the International Harvester, IH,Dealership across town. It paid okay and was a piece of cake delivery. A double was really possible today.

The terminal foreman yelled out that I was all set. He yelled again and asked if I knew the details of the delivery or did I need directions to get to the IH dealership. I put my left hand out the window with my middle finger extended as far as I could in acknowledgement of his sarcasm. He laughed and waved me away.

Wow, 6:10 a.m. and I'm on my way. It would take about 15 to 20 minutes to get to the dealership. I drove along very alertly. I actually put on the AC in the truck because it was almost 82 degrees now. I figured that I could afford to burn up just a little more fuel on this run with the AC on. I only had a short ways to go anyway. The ride was routine and on a well driven road. The route actually brought me by the police station. I guess it was too hot for any rogues to even think about attempting to case out my truck using that route. Then I realized that they probably knew what I was carrying anyway. Farm equipment parts weren't anything that they could quickly get rid of in the black market. Dry goods, frozen and fresh meats and any type of clothing articles were dangerous deliveries to have. I usually stayed away from those types of deliveries even though they paid the best. My wife had wanted to kill me for taking on an assignment like that once. The rogues attempted to take a load of canned goods off me a few years ago. That convinced me of staying away from deliveries like that. That delivery had earned me a four inch cut on my left forearm, a black eye and some damage to my truck. The Python played an important equalizer in that altercation. I never fired it but the sight of it was enough to back off the three goons that attempted the hijacking. I wouldn't try that now because the criminals out there are packing and they would not hesitate to use weapons these days. If I ever had to draw my Colt again, I knew that it would be discharged in the direction of the rogue who was trying to rip me off. I hoped that it would never have to come to that. I had managed, in my life, to keep from killing anyone so far. Even in the army, I never had to shoot anyone. I had guys riding shot gun in my army trucks shooting at people but I didn't have to pull the trigger. I only had to keep driving as fast as I could.

I arrived at the IH depot and dealership in Franklin about 6:30 a.m. There were a few guys standing at the dealership entrance door as I pulled up slowly and rolled down my window. I knew that deliveries at the depot were in the back but I just wanted to let them know what I was doing there. They could have given a shit because they just looked up for a brief second, made some inaudible sounds and kind of waved me on as if I was annoying them. *Screw them,* I thought. I thought I was doing them a favor for letting them in on why I was there that early. You never knew these days when some security guard or night watchman would get trigger happy and do something stupid to ruin your day or maybe end your existence. I had heard of delivery truckers being shot at because they failed to identify themselves when approaching an establishment in the off hours. *But 6:30 a.m. wasn't really off hours,* I thought.

Most businesses, like the IH depot, opened up early to avoid running their air conditioning as much as possible in the summer months to keep costs down. This way, they could also release their employees in the early afternoon hours. Most day jobs were from 6 a.m. to 2 p.m. Weekends had melted into the normal work week these days. Most employees liked that arrangement and they were happy to get eight hours of pay any day. For awhile, after the crash, if a business was functioning, it only kept the doors open for six hours a day and usually for no more than four days a week. Night shifts in the summer were better for use of utilities but you risked the possibility of inviting criminal activities. With fuel and food costs skyrocketing in those months after the crash, 24 hours a week

17

paychecks weren't making ends meet for most blue collar workers yet people seemed to adjust. How? I don't know, but I'm sure dogs, cats, squirrels and rabbits made up for some of the food sources. I know we ate some dog food once that I was fortunate to get. My wife and I had diarrhea for two days. It was bad enough that I thought I would have to get medical attention for the case of hemorrhoids I developed. We almost gave some of it to the kids but we realized the consequences before we were able to. Thank God. It wasn't the best food for human consumption. We don't see or hear of stuff like that happening around lately because most of those types of food were eaten up quickly by the rogues and their so called underground food suppliers. I hope a lot of them got the shits like we did but I'll never know.

I pulled around back and began backing up to the loading dock. I gave the customary horn while I docked and assumed I would see somebody as soon as I came to a stop. I hadn't noticed that there were six of them waiting for me. As soon as I put on the emergency brake, one of them opened my driver's door and asked to see my delivery document. I noticed he seemed in a hurry. He was a large guy, very well tanned with mammoth hands that he extended to take my paperwork from me. He closed my door and told me to stay in the truck. No "please," no courtesy of any kind, no nothing. I thought I recognized some kind of accent but I didn't give it a second thought. I wanted my truck unloaded, my paperwork verified and signed so I could get back to the terminal and collect my fee. The chance for a double looked even better now. I figured that I'd be out of here by 7a.m. but by the way this guy seemed to be in a hurry, maybe I'd be out even sooner.

I started to fantasize about how my wife would react when I got home tonight with cash money from two deliveries. I thought about this morning and her swollen eyes and thought that maybe, just maybe, I could put a big smile on that face and put her at ease for a little while. We could put some money back in our little safe and relax knowing we would be okay for a few weeks.

18

I also realized that I still had the Colt in between my belt and the small of my back. It was beginning to irritate my skin so I decided to put it back in the glove box. No need to have it exposed. I already had fuel and was almost unloaded and would be able to get back to the terminal to get another load. I didn't anticipate any trouble for the rest of the day. Things looked good so far.

I relaxed as I shut the glove door. The truck rocked a little due to the unloading being performed. I couldn't see what was going on but didn't really care now. No problem. I usually was able to bullshit with the dock hands and pass the time while I was being loaded or unloaded but the tanned guy wasn't being too friendly so I just sat there and waited for the unloading to be completed and the paper work to be signed.

I thought that I might pick up some wine on the way home but realized that there weren't any liquor stores open around here anymore. Most liquor stores folded within a year of the storm and crash that happened. No one could afford wine or beer because most suppliers went underground. The fruits, hops, grains and stuff that made booze were needed for human food consumption now. Food was tradable for fuel and was accepted as money in many places. Bartering for food was commonplace again. It was a nice thought though as I closed my eyes, bored from the unloading and rocking of the truck.

I was startled when I heard a loud noise and felt the effect of something dropping in my truck. I heard a few men yell and the tanned guy was really pissed off and also yelling at someone. I jumped out of the truck and immediately got screamed at by the tanned guy who noticed me coming around to the back of the truck. As he came to me in his irritated state, I noticed that my truck had been unloaded but there was a large covered unit in the truck that had been loaded on. It took up half of the loading space available in my truck. I looked at the tanned guy as he grabbed my arm. He was yelling and pulling me back away from the loading dock. He was starting to piss me off. I tried to steady myself but his strength and size kept me off balance. I started yelling myself.

"What did you load onto the truck? What is it? Where is this going to?"As the tanned guy continued yelling at me, I felt someone grab me. I could hear someone behind me. As I turned to see who it was, it all went black.

The Missing Pieces

I could hear noises, inaudible garbles, as if someone was turning the tuning knob on an old fashioned radio in search for a clearer channel. Then I began to hear names being called out that were strange to me. Someone was holding my hand. I finally opened up my eyes to see my wife Jean's pretty brown eyes moistened with tears, just smiling at me. Her face blurred and I tried to focus my eyes on her again. The noises became more audible now and I realized, before she could speak, that I was in the emergency room at the Backus Hospital. The hospital PA system rang out again for some doctor to report somewhere.

Jean leaned over closely to my ear and said softly, "I love you." She then said, as she moved away, still looking straight into my eyes as they adjusted to the light, "You have a cut on your head that needs to be stitched up before I can get you home."

I started to speak when the attending doctor said, "Welcome back to the world Mr. Sprague. You're a lucky man."

"Doctor, Mr. Sprague's vitals are normal now," the nurse said.

"Good, move him to the prep room and you can stitch him up. Nice to meet you Jonathan," he said as he turned to leave. I didn't have a clue of who he was but I figured that Jean would tell me that later. All I knew was that I had one hell of a headache and I could just about lift my head off the very uncomfortable pillow they had under my head and neck. Jean watched as the two orderlies that were summoned moved me from the bed to a gurney for a ride to the prep room.

Jean turned to the emergency room nurse and said, "Thanks Katie, I appreciate it." She smiled, nodded and carefully watched the orderlies wheel me away. As the orderlies moved me onto the table, I remembered. I looked a Jean, with what looked like terror on my face, and before I could speak and ask what happened, she grabbed my hand and held my forearm to inform me that the truck was fine and it was in the hospital parking lot.

"Jon, relax. When your head is clear, I'll give you the details of what happened," she said softly.

"My goddamn head is hurting but clear," I blurted out. "What happened?" I was almost yelling now.

She told me that the foreman at IH said I had walked right in front of them loading a unit into my truck. I had gotten struck on the head from one of the fork lift blades. The IH workers had rushed me over to the hospital. She continued to fill me in on what had happened.

"They delivered your truck to the artery terminal but then they were nice enough to get the truck delivered to the hospital parking lot." She then looked at me, smiled and said, "I have the money for the delivery and a little extra to cover your medical treatment." I just took it all in and did not question her any more. I figured that all was good for now. The only thing that passed my mind was that I missed that double and a chance to make a few extra bucks today. I was still trying to put together the whole sequence of events when one of the orderlies began cleaning up my scalp. It hurt like hell and he didn't seem to care about that.

My wife watched Katie don some sterile gloves as she informed the orderly that she would clean and prep the wound for stitch up.

The orderly looked at her, said nothing and left the room. *A real Mr. Personality,* I thought.

I asked Jean, "Who was that guy?"

She said he was a very over worked orderly who had another shift to complete before he could go home. She continued to tell me about this guy who had to work as many hours as he could to keep his family fed. The thought of him working those hours, I realized he's no different than the rest of us. That allowed me to excuse him from his rudeness when he left the room.

"Okay Jon, that's the last one," Katie said. Twenty-one stitches was my record now. My last record had been broken today.

The last time it had taken 15 stitches to close my cut arm a few years ago. As she flicked off the gloves, she looked at Jean and instructed her to keep it exposed, but dry. She told her I could wash my head in a few days, but until then, she wanted the site to be kept clean and further instructed her to make sure I kept my baseball cap off for a while. She didn't want the dirt and sweat from the cap band to irritate or to infect the wound.

"There is no need to see you back here again. Jean can take it from here," she said. "Your wife can pull the stitches out in seven to ten days from now when your wound has sufficiently healed" was the last instructions she gave to me while looking at Jean.

"Take care of yourself Jon and be careful," Katie said as she walked out of the prep room. By her look to Jean and the expression on her face, I felt she was thinking that I needed some reminder that I was too old of a man to be getting into situations where I could get hurt. The first thought I had was that I didn't like the look she had given my wife but then I realized that she had treated my wound well and that her expression was probably right. I chose not to say a word because Jean had already thanked her for both of us for her time. She looked at me and said, "Okay old man, let's get you home." Damn, she was thinking the same thing as Katie was all the time. Maybe they had mental telepathy or something. Or maybe I was really just too old to be getting into situations like this.

It was under a similar situation that I had met the mother of my two children over 40 years ago. She was a 21-year-old nurse working in the Post emergency room at Fort Bragg. She was the cutest second lieutenant I had ever seen. My buddy, who needed stitches in his hand, really didn't notice her because he was going on and on as if he was going to die. You would have thought that 12 months in Nam would have toughened him up a bit but he was whining. While he whined and whimpered about the cut he needed stitched up from an accident that occurred at the motor pool, I got a chance to begin small talk with her. I asked her if my buddy was going to be all right and would she be the one to sew up his hand and advised her that he was a little scared about needles and things like that. I didn't have enough backbone to ask her out that day. All I could say when she asked questions was, "yes lieutenant" or "no lieutenant." I envied the medical staff that worked with her every day.

About one week later I ran into her at the Post Exchange. I was with a medic buddy of mine who knew her from working with her at the Post hospital. He introduced her to me. We hit it off. We were both from New England and that gave us some common ground. Our relationship grew from that initial meeting even though the army fretted about officers fraternizing with enlisted NCOs. Our dating continued for a few months until my term of enlistment was up. I then did the damndest thing. I extended for another year so I could be with her at Fort Bragg for her last year in the army. Uncle Sam fixed both our asses. I got my second tour of Vietnam and she got her first. I ended up in Saigon in the south and she was stationed at DaNang which was almost on the DMZ in the north. We couldn't have been farther apart. I got to see her for one week of the whole 12 months we were there. One good thing about Nam was the South China Sea beaches. If I ever wanted to go back to Nam, it would be for that reason only. I've never seen beaches like that since. Maybe it was just being there with her that made them seem that they were the greatest beaches in the world. The warm sun, slight breezes, bleach white powdered sand, deep aqua water and the prettiest round eyed girl in country was more than any G.I. could ask for.

My mind came back to reality when I heard her say, "Are you up to driving?" I realized we were out in the parking lot and approaching the truck. The heat from the parking lot made the 90 degree day seem even hotter.

"Yes" as I got out of the chair and slowly began to walk around the truck when Jean asked where I was going. I told her I just wanted to check things out to make sure the truck was the way I had left it. She told me that everything was alright because the IH depot foreman had told her so. I ignored her and continued around the truck taking a visual inventory on areas I had known to look for problems. But all was well as I took the keys from her and stepped up into the cab. I immediately turned the ignition on to see what the fuel tank gages indicated. There was only a slight indication from the left tank that some fuel had been used. That tanned guy at IH was an honest guy after all I began to think. Everything checked out until I checked the trip odometer. It indicated that the truck had been driven 187 miles but yet the tanks seem to indicate only 20 or so miles had been driven. *That wasn't the approximate mileage from the terminal to the Harvester place and to the hospital* I thought, but I had seen something in the truck seconds before I was rendered unconscious. Where did that go? It had to be somewhere in that mileage. I turned to Jean, looking confused. I began to present my findings to Jean.

She looked at me and said, "Jon, they had to go to the terminal before bringing the truck here so that's probably where the extra miles came from." I almost butted in but waited for her to finish.

"There were only instructions on the shipping document that I was going to return to the terminal with a load from the Harvester depot," I said.

She stared at me. "It doesn't matter. You're safe, the truck is safe, and we got paid." For a few seconds she paused and asked again, "Are you okay to drive home?" She said that she didn't want to drive the delivery truck. I realized that she was going home with me. She was leaving the hospital early. She'd lose about four hours of pay to babysit my ass at home. I didn't protest because it would be nice for her to be home early and with me. We didn't usually see each other until after our 12 hour days had passed. But today, we would be home before three in the afternoon. Maybe we could spend some quality time together. Then it hit me.

"How much money did they give you for the delivery?"

She looked at me and answered that she had received $300 from the terminal and $400 from the IH foreman. One hundred dollars of that money was to help cover any unforeseen

25

medical expenses. She produced $700 in cash. As I slowly drove out of the hospital parking lot, I told her that I could have made a lot more money today if I had gotten that double. She smiled and just looked over at me.

"Let's go home," she said.

"How much is the emergency room visit going to be?" I asked as I began rolling down Washington Street and away from Backus Hospital.

"The foreman had indicated that IH would be paying that bill."

"Good," I said. "I don't know how we would have been able to pay that expense."

"Jon," she said, "I don't even want to think about that so let's not talk about it." It was bad enough that she copped a few pills for my type-two diabetes and high blood pressure problems almost every day to keep me functioning. Without those medications I would be really sick in about a year and worm food in probably five years.

When I was a cross country trucker, I had decent medical coverage that paid for half of those prescription medications. After Hurricane Angel hit Texas and the terrorists caused the Saudi crash, insurance companies began to fold like a lot of other businesses. Eventually, the only medical coverage around was Medicare, Medicaid and the Veterans Association. They didn't pay for much these days because government funds to run them were reduced considerably.

We arrived home and parked the truck in the yard. We made sure to park close to the kitchen entrance as we usually did to keep an eye on the truck. My head was really pounding by now and my neck and shoulders muscles seemed to be stretched and aching. Even stepping off the running board caused each muscle to seize in pain. I slowly walked behind Jean to the kitchen door. She stepped aside and watched me enter the house. We were home, safe and tired. I looked forward to some rest. Jean needed to relax and she indicated that by throwing herself onto the couch and closing her eyes. I moved her feet a little so I could sit on the couch next to her. I closed my eyes. I was home, safe and okay. My eyes began to get heavy.

Whether it was the heat, the drugs or the sheer tiredness from the accident, I didn't care. I was sleepy, had a chance to lie near my wife and that was a good thing for the time being.

I woke up about two hours later or so to the sounds of Jean in the kitchen making dinner. Something smelled good. Was that hamburgers? We hadn't had meat in several months. It had been too expensive to buy. She was mixing it with something in a pan. As I slowly got off the couch and gained my balance, I made my way into the kitchen. She was making Mexican tacos.

"Where did you get the meat?"

"Ed sent it over to us about twenty minute ago. He said that he wanted you to recover quickly and this was just a little something to get you there sooner."She told me that he said was he wanted us to enjoy it. Ed McAuliffe was a great friend. He'd always been a nice guy and a good friend.

"I'll make sure to say thanks for the favor when I see him tomorrow at the terminal," I said. Jean stopped cooking and looked up at me. Her eyes were almost black now.

"Jonathan Joshua Sprague, you are not leaving this house until I tell your old ass when it can leave. Do I make myself clear?"

I couldn't help but laugh a little, even though it hurt the stitches in my head and the stretched muscles in my neck. To look at this pint size woman, glaring at me, with both hands on her hips. If she'd had her army nurse uniform on, I would have leaped to attention. I just smuggled her up, squeezed her and softly whispered into her ear that I loved her for taking such good care of me. She relaxed enough to listen to me tell her that we would see in the morning how I felt and take it one day at a time. She knew, and I knew, that I would be up before the crack of dawn to get an early Monday delivery at the terminal. When you got work, you were judged on how quickly and efficiently you handled the job. You were judged like this because there was no overtime, no unions, and no rules. We just hugged each other and settled down to a nice dinner we both anticipated would be one of the best meals we've had in months.

The aroma that filled the rooms as she cooked was no match for the excitement my palate experienced as I bit into the taco. Just as we had expected, the ground beef aroused my taste buds that had been dormant for many months. Jean smothered the taco in a few sweet tomatoes she had managed to barter, for that substituted the salsa we hadn't seen in months as well. It wasn't what we had experienced on the vacation we had in Cancun before it all changed, but the flavor we experienced did inspire us to reminisce about that trip. We glanced at one another at almost the same time knowing immediately that we would save some for the kids. I'd bring the rest over to my daughter's tomorrow after work so that her family could enjoy some of our good fortune. I checked the freezer to make sure we had enough ice to pack in the cooler so I could keep the meal cold enough through the day.

Ed McAuliffe was sitting at his desk when the phone rang. "McAuliffe here," he said before the second ring.
"Is Jon Sprague okay?" the voice at the other end inquired.
McAuliffe's stomach turned. "He had some stitches in his head but there was no concussion. He'll probably be back driving Monday morning. He won't take anytime off unless he is dead."
"If Sprague is not available then you'll have to drive the next shipment to its destination. Do you understand?"
McAuliffe swallowed and responded, "I do." This was all he replied before the line went dead.

Paranoia

My head was sore and my neck stiff but my 65-year-old body still had a little youth left in it to get me out of bed and prepare me for another work day. It probably wasn't youth, it was probably being scared enough to motivate me to get out and compete for the deliveries I needed to have to maintain what we still had. Despite all the chaos, the bank still wanted the mortgage payment; the credit card people still wanted their monthly fees even though you couldn't use cards much these days. Everything, or mostly everything, was cash and carry. Utilities were outrageous and nobody, not the President, not the Congress nor any business entrepreneurs had come up with a way yet to wean us off crude oil. Car pooling had caught on and some municipalities were even ticketing people who didn't have more than two people in their car when driving down the road. That wasn't enforced very well because the rogues still kept the police too busy with their shenanigans. Truckers were an exception, obviously, but the long haul truckers always had protection with them. The term, "shotgun" that had originated in the 1870s, was a reality and a necessity in 2014.

As I quickly dressed, I thought about that hamburger meat that Ed McAuliffe had sent over last night. That was nice. I'd make sure that I would quietly seek him out at the terminal and thank him when I saw him. I didn't want to make too big of a deal about it because people got irritated easily these days about things like that. What people didn't know was good for them. I needed to ask Ed a few questions about the Harvester depot shipment and their foreman just to satisfy some final details I was curious about.

Jean was still sleeping when I opened the fridge to get the taco meals out for the kids. As I began putting ice into the coolers, I felt her presence behind me. *The noise had awakened her*, I thought. I told her that I was sorry for waking her up. She didn't answer me but proceeded to walk around me to observe the stitches in my head.

"You aren't going anywhere until I clean up that cut."

"Jean, please make it quick because I want to be at the terminal as soon as possible," I said while continuing to load the cooler. A few minutes later, after she had checked and cleaned the stitches, she gave me a litany of instructions: make sure I keep my baseball cap off, make sure I take my Tylenol every four hours to keep the pain away, and to keep my dirty hands off of it even if it began to itch, not to let anyone convince me to cover it and put any type of salve or cream on it and so on. I eventually tuned her out and began thinking of some more questions I would have for Ed McAuliffe at the terminal that still hadn't been explained yet. She grabbed me by my belt and asked, "Did you hear a word that I said?"

"Yes Jean, I did," I said and began to repeat the first few things that she had said to me. That was enough for her to smile a little, kiss me on the cheek and tell me to be careful.

"Call me on your cell phone sometime this morning and let me know how you're doing."

"Okay, but it will be a short call because we're running out of cell phone minutes quickly." It was very expensive for any minutes you went over on your contract. I didn't need that aggravation again.

I finally got out the door. It was getting hot again, almost 80 degrees according to the cab thermometer. I checked my truck, started it and proceeded to the terminal. I noticed someone standing on the corner of Park and Main Streets. That's an odd place for someone to be waiting this early in the morning. It was too close to my home at 4 Main Street. *That's two houses away from the corner.* Whoever he was, he risked becoming a target for the rogues who roamed the streets early in the morning. They'd roll you in a heartbeat for any small change you might have on you. People usually didn't come out from their homes until after seven in the morning for just that reason. He looked away as I passed by with the truck. If he had been a resident of the neighborhood, I would have seen him before. Also, he would have waved because most people in the

30

neighborhood knew me by my truck and knew that I had a delivery business.

I called Jean immediately on my cell phone. "Hey, look out one of the front windows."

"What?"

"Look out one of the front windows and see if you can see the guy that's standing on the corner."

"Yeah, I see him, so what?"

"You ever see him before?" She was quiet for what seemed to be minutes but was only a few seconds. I was starting to feel uneasy now. She came back on the phone and said, "He looks like one of the guys that were with the IH foreman when he dropped off the truck at the hospital, yesterday." My head began to ache immediately. Why is this son of a bitch hanging around my neighborhood? I began to have disturbing thoughts and I could only imagine why he would be there at this time of the morning alone.

"Hey, is there a car or truck nearby?"

"You want me to go outside and check because I can't see him anymore."

"Damn it Jean! Stay in the house and just look out the window will you," I said forcefully. "Do you see him anymore?"

During the conversation I had managed to turn the truck around. I was almost at the house when Jean said, "I see a truck like yours now."

"Jean, it's me."

"Oh."

She walked out the front door but stayed on the front steps. I parked the truck across the street. I rolled down the window and yelled, "That was strange! I wonder why he was hanging around here!" I instructed her to be careful when she left to catch the bus this morning on her way to the hospital. She looked a little puzzled but yelled back that she'd be more observant. She now looked a little uneasy and I explained that it could have just been a coincidence. I yelled over and said, "I'll see you tonight. I love you."

"Love you too," she yelled back just as I noticed a slow

31

moving car coming up the street. I motioned to her to get back in the house as I opened up the glove box and drew out the Colt Python. I double checked the chamber to make sure it was still loaded and rested it on my lap. As the car approached, I could see that it was probably some rogues on a last minute tour to see if they could find something to steal and sell. As they approached my truck in their silver Honda Hybrid, they didn't see me sitting in the driver's seat because they were watching Jean as she was turning to get into the house. She was still in her thin bath robe and that cute little shape was keeping their attention.

They almost came to a stop when the driver noticed me in the cab holding my Colt that was resting on my left forearm in the open truck door window as they approached the truck. I didn't have to say anything because he immediately accelerated the Honda and drove off. They both locked eyes on me as they sped past. I noticed that Jean was looking though the window as I watched the two of them drive off. I contemplated taking my wife to work to ensure her safety when she came outside again. She asked if they had gone.

"How about I wait for you and take you to work in the truck?"

"You'll miss out on getting good hauls today if you are late and you know it. I'll be fine on the bus. Go to work," she said and smiled.

I let it go because I knew she hadn't seen the gun because if she had, I knew that I would have received some shit for it. She began to turn and head back to the house when she stopped and said, "The passenger in the car looked like the guy I saw at the corner." She asked if I thought everything was alright now. I assured her that it was but for her to make sure she locked the doors and put on the air conditioning.

"Why the AC?"

"You know that is expensive to run."

"I know, I know, but I want all the windows locked and make sure that the security system is on okay?"

"Alright, I'll see you tonight, bye."

I really wanted to see Ed McAuliffe now more than ever for

32

information he hopefully could give me about the Harvester people. I needed to know why one of them was walking around in my neighborhood. I still felt uneasy about what had just happened and my stitches were aching as I drove a little faster towards the terminal. I began to question myself. Was I becoming paranoid or were my instincts really in touch with the situation and there was something really wrong? The whole frigging world was wrong right now but this was now a personal wrong and I didn't like the fact that Jean seemed to be involved somehow. I didn't want her involved in any way with the IH people or the terminal boys. There were a lot of unanswered questions on my mind.

I drove past the same Shell station where I had filled up at the previous day and noticed that there was already a line of about 25 trucks. The station still must have fuel from yesterday or they received another delivery. They were doing well. Usually, the tankers spread the deliveries and most stations didn't get them every day. I pondered that thought when I noticed that the same silver Honda that passed my house was behind me now, about 50 yards back. I approached the turnpike and signaled onto the entrance way to head for the artery terminal. The silver Honda Hybrid followed.

"Okay," I mumbled to myself. "You bastards want something?" My head was really pounding now where the stitches were. I still had the Colt on the seat and I took it and rested it on my lap. A thought did go through my mind though. I didn't want to get careless and shoot my own balls off while I rested it there but then reality set in. I knew how to handle a gun and that seemed unlikely. The Honda stayed in back of me even when I slowed a little to edge him on to pass. I looked down and realized I was doing 55 miles per hour and these morons still hadn't passed me. They definitely were following me. *No need to panic,* I thought. I'd be at the terminal in three more minutes or so and if they were dumb enough to follow me in amongst all the truckers there then I would challenge them there in front of all those guys. The advantage was mine I reasoned.

As I turned off the turnpike exit, I could see the artery terminal and all the delivery trucks lined up. I realized that my delay in the neighborhood made me later than I wanted to be and I would definitely be on the tail end of getting any local deliveries today. I pulled in and immediately placed my truck in the line. I noticed that the silver Honda continued to go on down the street and disappeared as it turned down one of the side streets off the terminal artery boulevard. I put the Colt in the glove box. No need to keep that out. I realized that I had taken it out too many times in the last 24 hours and that made me very uncomfortable. I got out of the truck and locked it. I noticed Ed McAuliffe coming directly towards me. He had that shit grin on his big Irish face that indicated that he either just got laid or some good news had come his way.

I'd known Ed and Beth since I got out of the army and began driving trucks. They were one of the first trucker families I'd met and I really valued their friendship in those early days. Ed drove rigs until he crashed one year. It almost killed him. Driving too fast under sever conditions was the police charge, but all who knew him, knew too well the real story. He was on a suicide run because his wife Beth had died of breast cancer a few months earlier. They had no kids and he was left all alone and really couldn't take the loss. So with a full load of timber, speeding down Laurel Hill, he rolled the rig with all its contents into the Shetucket River. Lucky for him some boaters who were fishing saw the whole thing and got his unconscious ass out of the truck in time before he drowned.

Jean knew his wife Beth very well. She had been a lab technician at Backus Hospital even before Jean started working there. Jean helped her through the dual mastectomies, the chemo and radiation she needed. In less than two years, Beth succumbed to the cancer. Jean also treated Ed at the Backus ER the day he came in. She was influential in getting Ed the mental health assistance he needed to get him through the grieving process and put him on a path to try to live a better life. Jean was an angel. Ed worshiped her. He always told me that Jean would be the only woman that could ever replace his

Beth. The accident had changed Ed and he never had any desire to get back on the road. He went on to work as a dock hand which allowed him to stop by the local pub and drink until he could just about walk home. That helped him forget about Beth in the evenings and at bedtime when the memories of her were too much for him to cope with. When he would wake up in the morning, the hangover was enough to keep him from thinking of her until the end of the day when the whole ugly process would begin all over again. This went on day after day for a while until Jean got him into an AA program at the hospital. He straightened out enough to work his way up to terminal foreman and he still remained one of my best friends today.

As Ed was approaching, I thought of Jean and immediately speed dialed her number. A few seconds later, I heard her voice.

"Is everything okay?"

"Yes, everything is fine. I'm on my way out the door and off to work. There are several people at the bus stop and I know all of them," she said. I relaxed a little, wished her a great day and closed the cell phone. Ed approached and said to me, "I heard that you had a little accident. Good thing that you only hit your thick head. It's like iron. That's the only thing that probably saved your sorry ass. Was that my little angel you hung up on? Did you get the hamburger meat?"

I nodded at all the sarcasms and questions.

"Thanks," I said. "I need to talk to you in private. You got a second?"

"Sure Jon," he said as his facial expression changed and his voice went into a lower octave.

"Come with me, we'll use my office. It's private enough. What's up?" he asked as we entered the office.

After I had finished my story, he looked at me and said, "You are the most paranoid guy that I have ever known. What kind of dope are you sniffing these days? That is about the most concocted story that I have ever heard. You aren't drinking, are you?"

I assured him I was straight and not on anything except Tylenol for my headache. He told me to sit down and he began to explain that the paperwork I had received the previous morning needed to be updated after I had left the terminal. But I was on the road and he figured he would get in touch with me when I reached my IH destination. He couldn't remember my cell so he dialed ahead to the Harvester office. He had reached Tommy Lupinacci, the manager at Harvester, to give me the update on the shipment and to advise me that I would be coming back to the terminal but with two Harvester shipment units. Tommy failed to tell his terminal foreman, Sid Owlia, in time.

"You were already being loaded when Tommy and Sid attempted to keep you from you getting clipped by the forklift carrying the second unit."

I explained to Ed that I had an extra 185 miles on my truck and wanted to know where that came from. He looked at me and said, "Your truck didn't come here while you were at the hospital. It was unloaded and your load was put on another truck at the Harvester dock according to Sid. They made all the arrangements. Tommy and Sid were scared shitless that you were going to die or something. They drove your truck to Backus Hospital when they got a chance. They called to tell me that and I sent them to see Jean. After that, they gave the truck keys and cash to Jean with a little extra in it that they collected to help the medical costs. As far as seeing one of Sid's guys at your house and then following you here, that's probably a coincidence. Sid lives about four blocks from you. He's on Sturgeon Avenue somewhere. I've been to his house a few times. The quickest way to the Harvester place from your neighborhood is right by here. You know that as much as I do."

Ed was almost out of breath after giving me one fact after another and had made me feel stupid but a little relieved.

"What about the extra miles?"

"Maybe you set the trip odometer wrong, Jon. You had a shitty day yesterday and maybe you thought you did but you probably didn't. I have a contract here for you to pick up and take material to and from IH depot daily. You want the contract? You can see it pays well."

I smiled and nodded, "yes."

"Okay, I'll contact Tommy Lupinacci but I will fill you in on some of the dos and don'ts of working with IH. One of them is to stay away from their forklifts," he said while grinning. I then asked where he had gotten the hamburger meat.

"Never mind," he said. He made a signal by putting his fingers to his lips that the question wouldn't be answered. We left his office and my day had now turned for the better, or so I thought. I looked at the shipping documents and noted that I would be dropping off machine parts to IH and returning to the terminal with some completed machinery units. Their destination was unknown to me but I didn't really care. It was a good shipping job and most of all it was going to be steady for a while. I couldn't wait to call Jean at the hospital and update her on my new daily run for IH. I wanted to call her now but I knew she would be on the bus on her way to work. Even though she had a cell phone she usually didn't have it on most of the time. She never really felt comfortable with a cell phone. We had cell phones for better than 10 years and, even today, she refused to text. Many times I would check her cell phone when I got home at night to find out that she never answered any of my calls or messages because she never turned the damn thing on. I thought I'd call her hospital number.

Sid Owlia dialed the cell number he had memorized.

"Makel here."

"The units are shipped."

"Good. Keep me informed." The line went dead.

The Breakdown

I headed for the IH depot loading dock as I entered the facilities' parking lot. It had been an uneventful trip from the terminal and my headache seemed to be going away. It was probably going away because I was a little more relaxed, my blood pressure was probably normal now and I had some steady work to be grateful for. I looked down at the passenger matt and eyed the cooler. I was also pleased that I would have a chance to see one of the kids tonight when I dropped off the meals that Jean had prepared last night. In all, I thought, it was going to be a good day.

As I pulled up to the loading dock and began to position my truck to be unloaded. I glanced at my passenger side rear view mirror to see that silver Honda just pulling into one of the empty parking places near the loading dock. It looked like the same two guys that Jean and I had seen earlier this morning. They both looked in my general direction but then disappeared into the loading dock office. I felt the urge to go over to them and see what their reason was to be in my neighborhood at that time of the morning but then I remembered the conversation I had with Ed about being paranoid and all that stuff he accused me of and decided to just keep them at bay and see if Ed was right. I still had an inclination that I was right, though. I began to reason that they hadn't done anything and if they really wanted to be a pain in my ass they could have reported me to the authorities for pointing a pistol at them. That could screw up my steady deliveries with Harvester and even my business. I thought, *maybe they didn't see the gun and I'm thinking way too crazy.*

Sid Owlia came over to the cab and asked for my paperwork. "Oh, you're the guy we took over to the hospital yesterday. How's your head?"
I thanked him and assured him I was alright.
"You will stay in the cab, right?"

"Yeah, no problem," I said. I was about to thank him and his boss for the collection they had given my wife. I also wanted to thank his boss personally for paying for the emergency room bill. He gave me a look as if I was some kind of child who had just been reminded to behave himself. I decided to wait for a better opportunity to talk to him and sat back and felt the truck moving back and forth as the dock workers unloaded my delivery and then began to load up the shipment that they wanted to send to the artery terminal for shipment out of state somewhere.

Sid came back and told me to pick up a second load at the terminal. I was to return from the terminal and bring it straight back. He also told me he would have a second shipment for me by the time I returned again.

"Great, I'll see you when I return," I said. He handed me a signed docket for Ed McAuliffe to review and gave me some more paperwork to identify the cargo I was carrying back. Some farm machinery equipment I quickly noted.

"Hey Sid, I'd like to thank you and your boss Tommy, for all you did to cover my medical expenses. Is Tommy around? I'd like to thank him personally."

"No problem man. He's not available but I will tell him," he said while walking away. I thought he was an odd duck but I just decided to ignore him. I started the truck, looked in both rear view mirrors, acknowledged the signal wave to go ahead from a dock worker and slowly moved the truck to head back to the artery terminal. I glanced at my watch and it was a few minutes past 7 a.m. My headache had gone away. I went to put my baseball cap on but remembered Jean's explicit instructions. I picked up the cell phone and dialed her at the hospital. I noticed the Silver Honda was moving out of the harvester parking lot again. Was it another coincidence? Jean's friend Alice answered the hospital phone.

"Emergency Room Triage."

"Hi Alice, put Jean on for a second please."

"How are your stitches?"

"Okay, for a lucky old man."

"You're never too old for me sweetheart."

"Thanks honey, but put Jean on, I'm in the cab and in a hurry."

"You're always in a hurry Jon but I understand that you take your time when it really counts."

"Put Jean on," I requested again.

"Sure big guy. I see her down the hall. It'll take a few seconds," she said with not so much banter in her tone as before.

"Thanks," was all I could say.

Alice was a great nurse, according to Jean, but she had more quills stuck in her than a porcupine as the saying goes. She had three failed marriages in less than 20 years as I recalled. A submariner from the base back in the '90s was her first one. I think she scared him off. He was a mid-western kid and real nice. She was too hot for him to handle, I guess. She married some hospital technician a few years later. He got fired for groping a candy striper in the x-ray lab about six months after Alice and he were married. That led to a quick divorce. I guess he was too hot for her. The third guy was a previously divorced emergency room doctor who came to Backus Hospital on the rebound. Alice pushed his buttons enough to land him for a few years. She was too much for him. They divorced last year. She made a few bucks on that one and received a small cottage on the beach as part of the settlement. I hear that she entertains there often enough. Even as old as I am, I probably could get invited. It scared the hell out of me even thinking about Alice and me bumping uglies in the cottage. The scariest thought was Jean. She always told me that even a dog never shits where he eats. Screwing Alice was something I didn't even fantasize about. Jean would probably kill us both. Anyway, Jean was my soul mate and the only woman I have ever wanted since I saw her in the Fort Bragg Post hospital.

"Hello, Jean Sprague speaking," she said coming onto the phone.

"Hi honey. Guess what? I got a contract with the IH depot and it looks like it will last a while. Ed McAuliffe set us up."

"Oh Jon, that's great. Are your stitches okay? Do you still have a headache?

"Jean, all is fine. Did you hear what I said?"

"Oh yes, that's great. Tell me all about it tonight when you get home. Jon, just take care of you. Don't push it today, okay?"

"I won't. I got to run. I love you."

"Bye, me too," she answered and hung up the phone.

I put the cell phone back into my pocket as I entered the turnpike on my way back to the artery terminal. I hadn't driven a mile on the turnpike when I noticed the silver Honda coming up behind me at a quicker speed. I was going 65 and the Honda was doing at least 80 based on the way he was gaining on me. I looked at the glove box and hesitated for a second. *Should I get the Colt,* I pondered. Just then, the Honda passed me. I first thought that he would be getting off the next exit up ahead because his right blinker was on. I then noticed that a box delivery truck similar to mine was on the side of the road just past the exit ramp with its emergency flashers on. Were they going off the exit or were they stopping in back of that truck? I began to slow down. I began to feel uneasy again and thought it best to get the Colt. The Colt gleamed in the light. I set it down on my lap and watched to see what these guys were about to do. "Damn," I mumbled. These guys were stopping in back of that delivery truck. I slowed and began to pull in behind them and the truck. They had gotten out of the Honda pretty quickly. The driver of the truck was now visible. He had come around to meet these guys from the right side of the cab. As they were approaching the driver I pulled right up and almost touched the rear bumper of the Honda. My air brakes must have startled them as they turned around quickly to see me already standing on my running board outside my truck. I had the driver's side door in front of me as protection if needed. They didn't see the Colt pointing down and closely positioned at my side. I recognized the driver of the truck. It was George Woodbridge. He was a trucker I knew from the terminal. Our paths always crossed as we worked together hauling stuff for different companies for many years. We used to hang out socially but as the kids grew up and school events took up our time, we grew apart. But we were still friends and would still do anything for each other.

George was about to speak to those two guys when he saw me standing on the running board of my truck. He yelled out, "J.J., is that you?"

"Hi George, yeah it's me. Do you need help?" I yelled back.

"Yeah, I blew a right front tire but these guys from the Harvester company have come to help me change it and get me back on the road for Newport," he said as he approached my truck. The two Harvester guys were moving towards the front of George's truck and had ignored me. As George came up, he saw me put the Colt back in the glove box. His eyes widened and I noticed his facial expression.

"You look a little jumpy J.J."

I glanced back at him as I put the Colt away.

"You can never be too cautious these days, George." I explained to him that I thought maybe these two guys were turnpike rogues looking for a quick score. He said that he knew both of them and they were okay. He had actually called the Harvester depot people on his cell phone to send someone out to help him. He told me that they were the guys that Harvester had sent. They didn't talk too much but they were harmless and he was glad that they got there as fast as they did. He told me that he too, had thought about the rogues cruising on the turnpike looking for old bait like him.

The two Harvester guys returned and asked George for his keys to unlock the spare tire cage that held the tire they needed. George obliged. One of them looked at me and said, "Shouldn't you be on your way to the terminal with that load you're carrying?"

I was surprised for a second. "Well, you're probably right, but I just wanted to make sure George was okay."

"He is."

I looked at him and was going to ask him if he was the same guy who was on the corner near my house earlier this morning, but I stopped and just smiled.

"Well George, it looks like you are in good hands," I said and began to turn towards my truck. I quickly spotted the same type of units I saw yesterday just before I was knocked cold by that forklift. One of the Harvester guys or George had mistakenly left the roll down truck door up just enough for me to see the two units securely strapped down in the back of George's truck Why it wasn't shut completely, I didn't know, but it was open just enough and I took advantage of it. The other Harvester guy who had told me to move on casually pulled down the roll down door and secured it so the units were hidden from sight again before he went to assist the other guy.

"Hey George, how is Anita these days?" I asked. Before he could answer I asked, "What are you hauling to Newport, RI?" He smiled and said, "Anita is sassy as ever and I don't really know what they are … some kind of a unit that IH is loading onto a big barge near the Naval Base. When I get up there and unload, I'll get a few minutes to look at that new aircraft carrier that is docked right across from the barge. The Navy docked it there a few months ago and she is a beauty." He then whistled to indicate how beautiful she was.

He told me that the ship was the U.S.S. William Jefferson Clinton. According to George, she was the biggest flat top the Navy had built by Northrop Grumman of Newport News, Virginia. The Navy had ported her at Newport, Rhode Island to assist in using her four reactors as extra utility power plants for the Naval Base and surrounding communities. She was ready to leave port at a moment's notice according to the official Navy releases but while she was docked there she was a godsend for the locals to maintain electric power needs and keep the grid level constant during power surges. According to George, there had been too many brown and blackouts in the area. The greater Boston-Providence area utility companies welcomed the Clinton. Her reactors kept the grids on line when the overstrained power plants were low on fuel that was always in short supply. The Navy was doing that type of assistance all over the country these days.

The Harvester guy saw us still talking and started to head for us. I shook George's hand and said, "Look, I got to run. I got to complete this run and I still got another one to complete for Harvester before I go home." George garnished a big smile. "Good luck man and thanks again for stopping and checking on me."

He looked down at his wrist watch that he always hung off his belt to check the time. I remembered that wrist watches use to bother the skin on his wrists. As he looked back at me, he said, "J.J. this is my only run today. I got to do only one hundred and eighty five miles round trip and then I am done for the day. Someone else had to take yesterday's run because I had trouble getting fuel in time enough to make the run but they were able to get a quick replacement." *My odometer hadn't lied*, I thought, as George ended the conversation.

"I got to make time and you take care, J.J." We waved to each other as I engaged my truck, moved back onto the turnpike and I was on my way back to the artery terminal. I put my baseball cap on and then remembered that I was supposed to keep it off. My head didn't hurt but putting the cap on irritated my stitches that now began to sting a little. I realized that my truck had been used by these bastards to go to Newport, RI to deliver the units I had seen just before I got knocked out. They seemed to be the same type George was hauling for them now. That was no big deal, but why all the secrecy to make sure my fuel tanks were refilled to almost exactly where they should have been? And based on that, the bastards should have paid me more money that they gave to Jean. A trip like that would have been another $600 or $700 each way. They gave me $100 extra for my medical expenses and never mentioned that they went to Newport and back. The more I thought about it, I knew I had to run this by Ed. I knew sometimes he thought I was a nut case ever since I got clocked at the Harvester depot but he understood that people shouldn't screw with your truck. Especially in these hard times, a truck was like a horse in the old west. People got hung sometimes.

I realized I was thinking too much about the fuel, tanks, and mileage. My head was beginning to ache again but there was the fact that someone had covered up the use of my truck.

44

Why? I was going to run this by Ed McAuliffe when I got to the terminal. Besides getting paranoid again, I was a little pissed that I hadn't been compensated for wear and tear on the truck. I was going to go slow on this because I didn't want to screw up my new and steady contract with the IH people. I worried about George being with those two Harvester guys but he was a seasoned trucker and could take care of himself.

I remembered, as I drove, that George Woodbridge had been one of the first African Americans to break into the trucking business up here back in the mid '70s. He too had been a trucker in the Army for two years. He had been drafted from his home town somewhere in New Jersey and had spent most of his time hauling army loads in and out of Fort Dix. He dated a girl from Philadelphia who he met through a buddy. They ended up getting married before he was discharged and he got a job as a dock hand at the terminal. Through hard work and luck, he was able to break the color barrier. He purchased an old truck and began doing any and all local deliveries that most of us didn't want because they didn't pay enough. That guy worked his tail off until he was able to purchase a better truck. He stayed with the local runs and made a good living. He was well liked and was a good friend to all who knew him. He was one of my best friends.

He and Anita raised five kids. Anita seemed to get pregnant every two years like clockwork. They had four boys and finally a girl, which I think was their goal. I kidded George when we were alone at the hospital looking at that beautiful baby girl the night she was born that he must have had really good sex that night, nine months ago. But George was the bashful type and really didn't get the pun when I explained that he had gone too deep and knocked the balls right off that fifth boy. When he did get it, he punched me in the arm. It hurt for a few hours. I think I embarrassed him more than making a joke. We use to tease them all of the time when we got together. We'd ask if they knew what was causing all these kids to be born. There wasn't anyone in town who didn't know about the Woodbridge kids. Every one of the boys played football, basketball and baseball for our high school. A few of them played with my son Joshua. George and Anita kept them in line, too. They all went on to college where some played sports and all of them graduated. I did know one boy was an officer in the Navy assigned to one of those super carriers. I guess that is why George enjoyed getting a firsthand look at the U.S.S. Clinton docked at Newport these days. I'd make sure Jean called Anita soon to set something going for the four of us one of these days. It wouldn't be fancy but good company was always relaxing. *We all needed some relaxation these days,* I thought.

I could see the terminal up ahead and began slowing down to take the exit. I checked my mirrors to make sure I was clear to exit when I saw the silver Honda again. I didn't think much about it because the two guys had helped George and they looked harmless now that I had firsthand experience with them.

Ilea Adel's cell phone rang in the silver Honda. He answered it on the third ring. He sat quietly as he listened to the instructions for his and Mohammad Owlia's next assignment. Before he could ask questions, the line went dead. Mohammad asked who had called as he drove the silver Honda.
Ilea answered, "Makel."

Curiosity

I entered the terminal parking lot at approximately 9:10 a.m. and pulled up to the unloading staging area. There were a few trucks ahead of me but I figured that I could run over to the breakfast truck I had seen setting up about 50 feet from the unloading dock. That guy came daily and sold the best egg sandwiches you could get. I was hungry and looking forward to that $7 sandwich and a soft drink, which was way too expensive these days. I secured the truck at an idle and scooted over to buy them. Jean would be pissed that I bought this stuff often because she always packed me some fruit when we could get it or something healthy. But old habits were hard to break. Besides, what could one egg sandwich really do to me? I quickly picked up what I wanted and headed back to the truck just in time to see Ed McAuliffe whistle to me to bring my truck up to the undocking platform. He moved his arms a little quicker than usual so I knew he was probably running behind schedule.

As the unloading began, Ed appeared in my driver's rear view mirror. He waved. I waved back and then stuck my head out the open door window and yelled to him.

"When you get a second come by so I can talk to you." He acknowledged me but continued to look at the men unloading my truck. I guess when he was pleased with the progress they made he walked to my driver's side window, jumped onto the running board and said, "What's up?" I explained what I thought had happened. I explained that even though I couldn't prove it except for my odometer being the only truth teller, IH had used my truck to go to Newport, Rhode Island to deliver some of those units that they guarded so secretly to a barge near the Naval Base. Ed looked at me and I thought he was going to rip into me when he said, "Yeah, Tommy Lupinacci's guys are a little too protective of their shipments, especially those units you are talking about."

"So you don't think I'm some paranoid nut after all."

"Well, let's all keep an eye on them. The money they are paying us to make sure we stay on schedule is real good. They are paying much more than any other client around in this area would these days." Half-whispering, he continued, "I wouldn't think that farm equipment was in a big demand these days but maybe I could be wrong. When you finish your run for them this afternoon and come to get paid, stick around for a few minutes, I want to talk to you about something you said this morning that made some sense." He almost mumbled as he spoke. He stopped and looked puzzled and said, "I didn't know George Woodbridge was hauling for them." He looked at one of the dock hands who indicated I was ready to run.

"Okay, see you later and keep your eyes and ears open and your mouth closed until we can get a better feeling about these guys. I don't want to screw up a cash cow but I am curious about a few things."

I acknowledged his last words and reassured the signal from the dock hand that I was ready to roll. I felt a little strange now. First I was paranoid this morning, then felt stupid for the ass chewing Ed had given me, then delighted that I had some steady work, then apprehensive about meeting George on the turnpike with those two Harvester guys. Now, the guy that had chewed my butt off and then put me at ease, and got me a great contract this morning, was now doubtful about the whole situation himself. My stitches, neck and head began to ache as I started back to deliver my second IH delivery.

I kept thinking of what I had learned from George this morning. I was surprised to learn that the Navy was docking major ships in specific ports on the coasts these days. It made sense though that they would be concerned about the electric power problems that our communities were dealing with. Whoever thought of stationing nuclear powered capitol ships to support the country's electrical grid needs was a genius. George had also said that the Navy had made sure that the American citizens knew that these ships were in constant readiness to leave the docks and be somewhere needed at a moment's notice. This was a comforting thought, but I realized in most cases, the U.S. Navy wasn't going anywhere these days. I did know that some of the subs that came into New London were hooked up to the grid to assist when the area needed it but I also thought that we were the only ones that needed assistance. I don't know why I thought that but I guess I was too busy worrying about day to day deliveries and income to be concerned about other parts of the country that needed the same grid assistance as we did.

According to George, most militaries worldwide, including in the United States, were supporting their country's needs to keep the power grids running as efficiently as possible. In the last few years, the major countries that could have instigated a nuclear attack couldn't have cared less about initiating one now that their navies were in direct support of supplying power to their countries. I thought a little more about that. The navies of the world had a different assignment now. The governments of the world needed them to maintain peace and order at home. Supplying electrical power was one of those major assignments that did that after the two catastrophic events. The only country still sending out ballistic missile submarines on patrol grids to ward off the threat of nuclear attacks was the US Navy. I wondered about that too but then but I thought that was a good thing as I continued driving to the Harvester depot.

My conversations with George fueled more thoughts as I continued to drive. The terrorists that had hoped to destroy the industrial non-Muslim nations, had actually in fact, united them more now than ever before. I didn't care for religious fanatics whether they were Christian, Jewish, Buddhist or Muslim. Extreme anything had always been bad for the world, I believed. Organized religion was still being practiced. People attended services to pray for things to get better. There wasn't much monetary support anymore and the clergy didn't ask. They understood. It was surprising that most congregations and parishes were still functioning but only due to volunteerism.

I thought about how Jean helped out at St. Patrick's free clinic when she could as all her fellow nurses at Backus Hospital did in other churches, temples and mosques. Occasionally, when

Jean returned from mass, she would be upset because the cathedral was in need of repairs but no one had any money to help the monsignor repair it. I told Jean that people were trying to take care of themselves these days and generosity at the level it once was wouldn't be seen for a long time to come. If the church needed money, maybe they could sell some of those gold artifacts that they kept in Rome and sell them on the gold market. That seemed stable these days even though few people had gold. We argued about that sometimes when she would look at me and state that no one would be sacrilegious and sell a cross or a chalice. I reminded her that those items could be melted down and sold in bar form and nobody would be the wiser as long as it passed the gold standard authentication tests they had.

I realized that I was coming up to the turnpike exit for the IH depot. My solving world problems would have to be put on hold now that I was going to be unloading and loading up again at the depot. As I turned into the Harvester parking lot I noticed that George's truck was back in the loading dock. I was waved off by Sid Owlia. He then yelled and said that I was to wait until the truck at the dock pulled out. I acknowledged his request but couldn't understand why. There was plenty of room available for me to park parallel to him in the docking area. I looked for George and didn't see him as I waited. Eventually George's truck began to pull away from the dock. I still didn't see George and didn't recognize the driver who was pulling his truck away from the docking area. The driver pulled by me and never glanced in my direction which I thought was odd. All truckers acknowledged each other whether you knew the other guy or not. I thought that maybe George was still inside and that he had a dock worker move his truck to make way for me. I was the next truck to be serviced. It wasn't unusual for things like that to happen in the old days but most truckers today didn't allow anyone, especially a stranger, to move his truck for any reason. As I watched the truck go by, I assumed that the driver would park George's truck and wait for him to come out and drive it to its next destination. The driver kept right on going out of the parking lot and heading for the turnpike. If he headed east he was probably going to the terminal or to Newport. If he turned west he was heading to New York. He went east. I made a mental note to ask Ed McAuliffe if George Woodbridge's truck ever came into the terminal that afternoon. I positioned my truck in the loading dock area. I stayed in the truck and waited for Sid or someone to take my load documents. I had gotten into the IH routine.

The unloading and reloading was completed. I was given my paper work and was signaled to begin pulling away from the docking area. The silver Honda was nowhere to be seen as I pulled out of the IH parking lot. At least I didn't have to deal with that on my return to the artery terminal this afternoon. Because it hadn't taken long to do the two complete deliveries, I had time to pick up some fuel this afternoon. Even if it took a while, it would give me an advantage to be ready first thing in the morning to continue my double deliveries without worrying about fuel concerns. *Today had been a good day,* I thought, as I headed for the final run to the artery terminal. I was still going to see Ed for an exchange of information on the stuff that we had experienced today with these new employers. I was more determined than ever to find out some more answers to the questions that I had about these people. My head and stitches didn't hurt very much now so I thought about putting my baseball cap on then I thought about Jean and decided not to.

I reached the terminal docking area and immediately saw Ed on the dock. He motioned me to line up and get ready to be unloaded. He walked around to my driver's side and just moved his head in the direction of his office for me to follow. I got out of the truck and gave my keys to Dan Kelly. He was Ed's assistant and I trusted him to move my truck and lock it when it was unloaded. I followed Ed to his office. No words were exchanged. When we entered the office and closed the door, Ed turned up the volume of the radio and spoke as the music blared.

"I called Brian this morning," he said.

"Who?"

"Brian McAuliffe, my nephew, you remember him?"

"Of course I remember that kid."

"What kid? He's thirty six, a chief in the shore patrol, actually a senior chief and up for master."

"I asked Brian to check some things for me."

"What things?"

"Jon, just listen to me for a few minutes. I asked Brian to find out anything he could about Tommy Lupinacci who lives in Newport and is working at the IH plant down here. He said that he would get back to me when he got a chance. I also told him to be very careful and not let anyone know what he was up to because I didn't trust Tommy. Brian asked me why he needed to investigate a civilian in the Newport area but I pushed off the question a little and just said that something wasn't right with this guy. I told him that he had too much access to goods that most people only dreamed about getting their hands on during these troubled times." Ed looked around to make sure no one could hear us.

"I still don't follow you on Tommy Lupinacci."

"Look, I hear he is friends with Donnie Costello. I need Brian to find out if Lupinacci is tied in with the Costello family. I want him to find out if there is a connection without asking for it directly."

When I heard the name Costello, I sat back and listened more intently to what Ed was saying. I was hoping Brian could find out some more information on these people who were constantly associated with crime. Ed and Beth had practically raised Brian when Ed's brother was killed in a trucking accident when he was a child. Brian's mother had remarried about ten years later when Brian was about 16. During those adolescent years, Brian had a decent stepfather to raise him but it was Ed and Beth that guided him. Brian graduated from high school with distinction in academics and sports and could have gone to any college he chose to but joined the Navy instead. He had been taking college courses over the years while he was in the Navy but hadn't earned enough credits to apply to a bachelor's degree program. He'd probably finish his degree once he finished his career in the Navy because he was interested in getting into the FBI.

I kept quiet long enough until I became impatient.

"Ed, did Brian get back to you?"

"Yes. He called me earlier this afternoon just before I told you to come and see me after your last run to Harvester and then again twenty minutes ago."

"And," I sarcastically said.

"Brian said that he could confirm that Tommy Lupinacci is tied up in the Costello family branch in Cranston, Rhode Island according to some information he got from Joshua." That took me by surprise.

"You telling me that my Joshua, my son, told him that?" I demanded.

"Yes, your Joshua, Joshua Jonathan Sprague," he said raising his voice then, realizing his tone, lowering the last part of the sentence for me to just make out, "of the FBI".

"Shit Ed, why did you get Josh involved in this?" I demanded.

"During my first call to Brian, he suggested using some of his pull to get Josh to do some research for him. You know, he stays in touch with Josh both professionally and socially. You know that the Navy Shore Patrol and the FBI are always exchanging small bits of information about anything that's going on near any naval base, especially one as large as the Newport base is these days. Come on Sprague. You know how close they are. Josh is still pushing Brian to finish college because he wants Brian to apply for the FBI when he finishes his career in the Navy."

Josh had been two years behind Brian in school when they both played varsity soccer and baseball together. Josh had been a striker and Brian a mid-fielder. Brian was the catcher while Josh was the second basemen on the baseball team. Those were great times for all of us. It seemed just yesterday when Ed, Beth, Jean and I spent many hours watching and enjoying many of those games the boys played in. God only knew how much Brian owed Uncle Ed and Aunt Beth who kept his life normal after his father was killed.

I just sat there taking this all in. I knew one thing that I was going to do when I did see Joshua Jonathan was to ask a lot more questions about his business. I never asked Josh about his FBI work but I sure would be a lot more interested in it in the immediate future. Ed continued to say that Josh and Brian figured something had been going on at the IH plant in Newport and the one here. The plants were moving goods around quite a bit. Even though they had an IH logo on their plants they were really only vendors that supported small assembly and shipping for them.

Ed said that he told Brian that these guys had given him special gifts, like meats, cold cuts, fruit and goods of that type when he would arrange special carriers for their deliveries. He then looked at me and asked, "Where did you think that hamburger meat came from?"

I asked, "How long have you been doing this for Lupinacci?"

"Oh, just a bit on and off for about two weeks now. But when you got knocked out at their plant, some things changed. For some reason, Lupinacci asked me to make sure you were given some special treatment for getting hurt on his watch at the plant. It seemed a good gesture and a reasonable request at the time so I told him I would bring some hamburger meat over to give to Jean that day when you both had returned from the hospital. Lupinacci agreed and felt that it was a good thing to do at first. Lupinacci became irritated with you about asking all those questions but then I casually asked Tommy about some of your concerns. Tommy seemed to take no offense at the questions but he never really answered them. When you talked about the Honda and bumping into George Woodbridge and all the stuff you were getting paranoid about, I got a bad feeling in my gut. I also felt a little guilty about taking goods under the table when I knew a lot of my workers and fellow truckers were working their tails off to just make ends meet. I didn't like myself for the last few days and I needed to find out why."

I asked him what our next step was. He said that Brian would get back to him soon after Joshua and the FBI had done some more investigative work and contacted him. Until then, the both of us were to keep quiet and continue to keep our eyes open and our mouths shut. *I'd heard that too many times today*, I thought. I began to ask a few more questions when Dan Kelly came into the office and told me that my truck was ready and gave me my keys.

"How's your head?"

"Oh, it's healing okay but hurts just a little. Ed, I'll be in early tomorrow morning to get a good start on the Harvester pickup. I want to make sure I keep Lupinacci happy," I said as I looked at both men in the office. It was a comment meant for Dan. "I'll see you tomorrow too, Dan." I said directly to him. "Oh and thank you." He nodded his head as he closed the door and left.

"I think that Dan Kelly is more into this than I previously thought," Ed said. "Keep quiet around him."

That admission bothered me some. It made me wonder just how deep this Harvester thing was and just how many of the people I knew and trusted were involved. I left Ed's office, headed to my truck and impulsively drove to Melissa's house. I wanted to drop off the cooler with the meals in it for her, Joe, Jack and Lilly. I hadn't seen them in a week and I knew Jean was jealous as hell that I got to see her daughter, her son-in-law and our two grandkids more than she did. In about 20 minutes, I pulled up in front of their condo, shut off the truck, got out and walked down the sidewalk to their entrance. Before I could get half way down the walkway, Jack and Lilly were on me like bees to honey. Melissa was standing at the door smiling as Joe came up from behind her and pushed the screen door open. It was good to see all of them at home when it was still light out.

Missy, as I had always called her, yelled out, "You are just in time for dinner!" I looked at her as I dropped the cooler to pick up Jack and Lilly.

"Nope, I brought dinner. Mom sends it to you all with her love. I mean, mine too." Missy looked at Joe and told him to get the cooler while I carried the kids into the condo. Missy told the kids to be careful of granddad's boo-boo. I just looked back at her and rolled my eyes as I walked in.

Joe Harris was a big man at 6'5"and about 220 pounds. He'd been that size since Jean and I first met him at Missy's college graduation ceremony for the first time. He'd been dating her for a while before that when they had met on different sides of a security line at a campus demonstration for something that escapes me now, but was important to Missy back then. He'd been one of the state troopers assigned to the campus to keep order and she was one of the students in the demonstration. Somehow they continued their association until one day Joe showed up at our front door to ask Jean and me if he could marry Missy. He was a great son-in-law and I couldn't have asked for a better partner for my daughter.

He was dressed in his trooper uniform. He was going on duty in a few hours. He had the night shift which was the most dangerous job in the state police these days. I worried about him on that shift especially knowing that Missy and the grandkids were home alone at the condo. There were four or five other state troopers and their families living there. This put my mind at ease. These guys were smart and took care of their own. While some troopers were working, there were always others at home and only a few doors away. They all had each other's phone numbers and all the spouses had bullhorns in case the power or phones went out which usually happened two or three times a month these days. This place was like a little Fort Apache and the troopers kept it running that way.

As we all settled into the kitchen and Missy began to open up the cooler, I asked Joe if he had a minute to check out some paperwork I had received from the IH depot. He looked at me with a puzzled look but followed me to the kitchen table to review the papers I took out of my shirt pocket. I asked him if he knew anything about them. He just stared at me and then asked, "Why do you ask that, Jon?" I knew immediately that he knew something.

"Well," I began, "I just started working for the plant and I wondered what kind of an operation they were running." He listened intently to my every word. "They assemble farm machinery parts, I know, and other stuff but they seem kind of a strange lot."

"What do you mean strange?"

"Well, they don't say much at the loading dock and they don't like anyone looking over their deliveries and that kind of strange stuff."

"Did you see anything illegal?"

"No, but I have a gut feeling that something is going on. Ed McAuliffe and I found out that Tommy Lupinacci, the Harvester dock foreman, was associated with the Costello family."

Joe looked at me and said he was familiar with the Costello crime family but they ran a legal enough business in the local areas to keep the Rhode Island, Connecticut and Massachusetts State Police forces at bay. He said that the tri-state police forces had more pressing criminals to catch than the Ernesto Costello family and their associated business members.

"Joe, I know the State Police have enough things to do besides checking up on what an old trucker thinks could possibly be going on with the trucking business and the Costello family but just keep an open mind on what I am saying." Missy came back into the kitchen and stood close to the table. Joe smiled and said, "Hey, where did you get the taco dinners from?" Before I could answer, he said, "Jean called and told us you'd be stopping by today with some food that you'd gotten as a gift from your friends at work. Looks like you exchanged one gift for another." He laughed as he turned my head and studied the damage that was done.

"Aww, that just looks like a mild bump on the head," he said jokingly.

"Well it was a mild bump on the head at first but I don't remember it. When I woke up, it wasn't so mild. It still hurts a little but I have been keeping my hat away from it and following Jean's orders so that it will heal quickly."

Joe looked at me while Missy placed a plate of tacos in front of him.

"Look, I'll ask some questions of a few of my guys who patrol that area and look over some of the information we have on the Costello family that is new and interesting. If I find out anything in the next few days, I'll get back to you. It probably isn't more than some under the table or black market stuff but if it smells, I'll warn you soon enough to get out of the delivery business for them, okay?"

I thanked the big state trooper and felt a little better. I was going to inform him that Ed and I had gotten Brian and Josh involved but I figured that until I saw Josh or talked to him, I'd keep this to myself. At some family gathering someday, when nothing turned up, my family and friendly investigators would be laughing about how two paranoid old men thought that they were back in the Cold War cloak and dagger days. Missy asked if I would stay for dinner. I said "no thanks" and made up some lame excuse. Although those were the best damned tacos I've ever eaten, I wanted them to enjoy and perhaps have some left over.

"I'm going to go by the hospital and pick up Jean since I'm near this end of town."*I didn't like her taking public transportation when I could pick her up myself,* I thought. Also, the fuel station I wanted to use was next to the hospital and I had been given some information that they would have enough fuel to distribute for a while. I really didn't need too much but if I could keep my tanks full, I could be ready for any unexpected delivery that came along.

"Hey Missy, "would you keep a plate for your brother? Josh should be coming by in a day or so."*My son always visited his sister and her family especially when he was in town to see his girlfriend, Candice.

Candice Strong was Missy's friend who taught school with her at the Veterans Memorial Middle School. I didn't know how involved Josh was with Candy, as I called her, but they managed to see each other five or six times a month when Josh came down from Providence on his off days. Occasionally he would visit Jean and me but it was usually easier to see Missy, Joe and the grandkids en-route to see Candy. I hadn't figured out why they hadn't gone further in their relationship because Candy was one hell of a sweet girl and Josh was a catch for anyone. Jean always told me to mind my own business. Just because they were good looking, smart and had great careers, didn't mean that they were going to immediately fall in love with each other and marry and have a slew of kids, she always reminded me. I often remarked that if I had a woman as good looking as her, I'd be chasing that like a fly to a manure pile. Jean told me I had too much manure in my blood as it was. I kind of knew what that meant but I'd always come back and remind her that I didn't reach the manure pile until I got her. She'd always laughed and would hug me and call me some type of name that was associated with manure. I kissed Jack and Lilly and hugged my daughter as I began to leave. I turned and shook Joe's hand and told him I would call him in a few days. He told me that he would call me sooner to put me at ease or inform me to break off my contract with Harvester. I started for the truck when Missy yelled out at Jack to stay inside the house and just wave to his grandfather. I smiled at Jack and told him to listen to his mother. Lilly was there just smiling and looking as sweet as ever.

Jean and I were lucky grandparents, I thought, as I started the truck and began to slowly leave the condo complex. One of Joe's state troopers was pulling out the same time I was. He waved as he passed by. I felt secure in this part of town with guys like Joe and that trooper who just passed visible for all to see. I was headed for the hospital when my cell phone rang. I thought it was probably Jean. I pulled it from my pants pocket but realized it was Ed calling from the artery terminal.

"Hey Buddy, what's up?" I asked. The phone was quiet for a few seconds.

"Dan Kelly forgot to tell me that George Woodbridge hadn't come back for his next load. He said a substitute from Harvester came in and said that George had given him the task because he didn't feel well when he came back from Newport this afternoon. He also said he didn't think too much about it and loaded George's truck."

59

I stopped Ed for a second and said, "I saw the truck moving away from the dock when I came in this afternoon. I didn't think much of it either because I thought you or Dan knew why."

"Damn Jon, I was talking to Brian on the phone when George's truck was being loaded and you were docking for your unload."

"Oh, shit," I exclaimed.

Before I could say another word, Ed said, "George wasn't supposed to be loaded until the next morning. He's never kept any cargo in his truck overnight especially a Harvester one at that. I should fire that son of a bitch for not telling me first about George working for Harvester. And then the nerve of him for loading up the Woodbridge truck without telling me George wasn't in it. You know, Kelly said that the Harvester driver had a note signed from George authorizing it."

Shit, I thought, *that was a perfectly good reason but I knew better than to say it out loud.* Ed ran a tight schedule; always kept schedules on time and now, didn't trust Dan Kelly.

I slowly said, "Something is wrong. Where are you?"

He ignored the question. "I'm going to call Brian," he said.

"No. Not yet. Can we meet at your house in an hour? I need to pick up Jean first." He agreed and I closed the cell phone. I figured I'd put off getting the fuel until tomorrow. I needed to look for George and get some questions answered. I had a bad feeling about George Woodbridge.

Makel completed his drive from New London to Bridgeport in a little over two hours. He pulled into the CTC's parking lot and turned off his rented car. He waited about ten minutes for the day shift supervisor to complete his shift. The man walked to Makel's car, opened the door, and sat in the passenger seat. He looked straight ahead as Makel started the car and slowly drove out of the parking lot. Several minutes went by before the shift supervisor asked him the status of the units for New London and Newport. Makel reported that all was on schedule. The shift supervisor said that all the barges where the units

60

were to be installed had been loaded, checked and ready. The three other areas were to be completed tonight.

"Everything is going as planned," he said.

The man responded, "You make sure that it does."

Makel didn't smile as he nodded in acknowledgement.

Night Riders

I picked up Jean at the ER. She was surprised to see me but welcomed the ride home with me instead of riding the bus. Within 20 minutes, I'd managed to tell her about all the day's events. She just sat there and stared at me and occasionally made me repeat specific sentences when I began to cross stories and confuse her due to my excitement. The first thing to come out of her mouth was that I should be in touch with the authorities.

"I have no crime or illegal operation to report," I said. Joe said the same thing and Brian alluded to that but I hadn't talked to Josh yet to get his reaction.

"Did you call him?"

"Yes, I left a message for him to call me but I haven't heard back from him yet." I drew out my cell phone and looked through the missed calls. There were none from Josh.

"Jean, give me your phone," I asked. She dug through her bag and handed me her cell phone. As usual, it hadn't been turned on. As I turned it on I looked over at her with a look that indicated that I wasn't very happy. She just lowered her eyes as if she was embarrassed. There were four missed calls. Two were several days old, one was from yesterday and one was about an hour ago based on the time log in the phone. I chose it and sure enough it had been Josh. I quick dialed it. Several seconds later, a recording came on. It was Josh asking his mom how she was and he wanted Dad to call him when he got a chance. He wanted to ask me something but he never alluded to what it was. I was curious why he hadn't called me directly. He knew my cell phone number. I then realized that he probably wasn't calling me about the conversation I had with Ed that I just told Jean about. I had hoped to hear that Brian or Josh had found something out when they checked out the stuff Ed had told them. He always called Jean first so he could spend some time conversing with her and would always rely on her to pass information on to me. That's why I knew he hadn't been checking around and this was just a routine call. As we approached the house, I remembered that in all my excitement, I forgot to tell her about the grandkids.

"By the way, Missy, Joe and the kids are fine." She began to ask many questions.

"Did they like the tacos? What did they say about your head? Was Joe off or was he still on for one more night? Did Missy look well? You know she had a cold for over a week now. Has she talked to Josh lately? Did she say anything about Missy?"

"Jean, slow down. They're all fine. He's working another night and they loved the food. Missy looked fine to me."

I cut her conversation short to inform her that I was going over to Ed McAuliffe's to look over some shipping documents that he had brought home. We wanted to try to find out what was going on with the Harvester depot. She began to speak again when I reinforced the fact that Missy, Joe and the grandkids were just fine but I really needed to get over to Ed's house to review that stuff. I told her not to hold dinner for me, for I was sure it would go past our normal dinner time and I didn't want to rush Ed going over the shipping documents in order to make it home for dinner.

"Look honey, this will take some time. Keep the house locked. I'll be home late but I'll call you before I leave Ed's," I said as I slowed the truck and then came to a stop in front of the house. She knew I had something more on my mind as she had seen that look in my eyes before in our 40 year relationship. She knew I was preoccupied. She reached out and stroked my arm and told me to be careful on my way home.

"Give me your cell phone, please." She never hesitated and handed it to me.

"On second thought, stay with Ethel and Orin for the evening, okay?" They were our next door neighbors and were pretty good friends. "I'll feel a lot better if you would stay with them next door for the evening until I get home tonight."

"You worry too much but I love you anyway. Don't be too late because they go to bed around ten, you know. I don't want them staying up too late on my account," she said. I only nodded as I closed the passenger door and proceeded to drive on. I forgot to wave and most of all I forgot to kiss her and I knew right then she was going to be more worried than before because of that. She would now know how preoccupied I was because I had just made a cardinal sin by forgetting to kiss her good bye.

I arrived at Ed's 15 minutes later. He was outside sitting on the porch. As soon as he saw my delivery truck come around the street corner, he was up and heading for the driveway. I secured the truck, jumped off the running board and asked him a question that really baffled him for a few seconds.

"You still have Beth's Harley?" Ed looked at me and shook his head yes. "I haven't run it since a year before she died. I could never get rid of it but I haven't done anything with it, why?"

I informed Ed that he was going to get it running in the next hour or so and that the both of us were going on a biker run tonight. He looked at me as if I was crazy.

"With all the rogues and jerks out there, we are going to be riding, hell knows where, with two bikes that haven't been run for a while and with two old bikers that haven't been on a bike in years."

"Yep, that's what we are going to do," I said as I smiled at him. I took Ed by the arm and we walked into his garage to take a look at the Harleys Ed had. His was a black 2000 Harley Heritage and Beth's was a bright blue 2001 1200cc Sportster. They had ridden years ago with Jean and me although Jean preferred to ride in comfort on the back of my Harley Road King. I had sold my Road King because after Beth had died, Jean lost interest. The Harleys were a little dusty but looked relatively in good shape. Ed stopped me as I was taking off the last tarp that covered the bikes.

"What kind of idea do you have in that stitched up head of yours, Sprague?"

I explained that after we got the bikes checked out, I wanted to take a ride to Newport. I wanted to take the same route that George would have taken and I wanted a look at the address that all the documents said to deliver this farm machinery to. Ed said, "You want to do this in the middle of the night? It will be that time by the time we get these bikes running good enough to get us up to Newport you know." I just moved my head up and down to indicate the affirmative as the last tarp hit the garage floor.

"What about all the cops that might pull us over?"

"So what, let them pull us over. There is nothing wrong with riding a bike late at night, if we get stopped, hell, we're old men just getting cool on a hot summer night," I said as I smiled.

"At the price of gas these days, nobody takes night rides."

"By the way, do you have gas in these babies so we don't have to stop and bring attention to ourselves?"

"Yeah, I got enough gas in mine but we can siphon some from my Subaru to fill the Sportster. I need to take a little time and make sure that the old girl will behave herself on the way to Newport and back. These things aren't electric you know. They require a little tender care," he said as he laughed.

Ed went to work. He started the Sportster up. It came to life with little difficulty. He let her idle and proceeded to check the fuel lines, fuel injectors, lights and all the stuff that bikers are accustomed to doing. He seemed to be pleased that all was going as well as it was until the Sportster coughed and died. *Shit,* I thought, *now what?* As I began to contemplate a whole litany of reasons why the bike quit, Ed just went over to the work bench, grabbed an empty gas can and walked to the Subaru. He just glanced at me and said, "I told you it was out of gas." In less than five minutes the Sportster was running again with a full tank of gas. He looked at me and asked if I needed some time on the bike to get use to her because she wasn't an electric scooter. I just glared at him and he just smirked. He knew I had been riding bikes as long as he had and a Sportster was a piece of cake compared to the Harley Road Kings I had owned and rode over the years. I looked at him and said, "We don't want to draw any attention to ourselves. We just want to get out of town as quickly and quietly as possible."

"In that case, you better go easy on the throttle on Beth's bike because I installed a hot exhaust on it years ago. It doesn't sound too loud on an idle but you start hammering it and she will bark. Beth liked that," he said. He looked at me and for a second I could see his mind wander to a better time and place. His eyes seemed to glisten as he turned to make sure his Harley Heritage was gassed and ready to go.

Both bikes were ready. I looked at my watch; it was 6:32 p.m. I thought that was too early to leave so I asked Ed if we could wait until the sun started setting. That would also give us a chance to eat something. He looked at me with a grin and said, "I have to feed you, too? I have some frozen dinners that we can throw into the microwave." We shut the bikes down, secured the garage and went in the house and quickly grabbed those frozen dinners. By 7:35 p.m. we were done and out in the garage. Ed noticed that I had my Python stuck in the small of my back and hidden under my jacket. I expected him to protest. "You know, if we get stopped and some state cop finds that cannon you're packing, we are going to jail," he said.

"I know but I feel a lot safer having it along with us."

He looked at me and then pointed to his bike compartments.

"Put the Colt in one of these and the cops will probably miss it," he said as he began to start his bike. I looked in the right compartment and it was empty. I began to lower the Colt into the compartment when Ed stopped me. He raised another bottom separator and there was his Army Colt .45 automatic with several clips. He looked up and just smiled. I lowered my Colt next to his with about 15 extra rounds I had taken out of my truck glove box. He closed the compartment and then the top cover.

"I'll stay close to your bike so that if anything happens and we need to get to these things, we can both get to them quickly."

I hope not, I thought, as I nodded at him. Ed threw me Beth's helmet as he put on his. I immediately thought that it was really going to bother my stitches. I slowly put on the helmet and to my surprise the helmet inner webbing just missed the stitches. *That was good*, I thought. We were ready except I didn't care for Beth's pretty helmet. He looked at my expression and said, "It's the only extra I have and you look real cute with it on. It matches the bike." He laughed. It was not funny, but also not important, I decided.

Ed nodded for me to take the lead. I had said earlier that I wanted to follow the same route as George Woodbridge had taken today to Newport. I eased the clutch out and gave the Sportster enough gas to smoothly glide out of the garage, down the driveway and out on the street. Ed followed right behind me. We both passed my delivery truck and were on our way for our night ride. A few people noticed us, so we stayed on the back streets and headed for the turnpike. There was hardly any traffic until we reached one of the local fuel stations. There was the usual actively near the diesel pumps with some trucks waiting in line but nobody paid any real attention to us until I noticed a silver Honda in back of Ed's bike keeping a safe distance behind. I could see the turnpike entrance ramp coming up but I decided to pass the entrance and continue on to see what the Honda was going to do. I watched for a few seconds to see if the Honda would continue to follow Ed's bike. I could see a diner parking lot up ahead and the diner still looked open for business. I never stopped at diners anymore because I couldn't afford the meals. I was surprised that this place hadn't folded like most of the roadside diners had in the last five years.

As I came to a stop, Ed pulled alongside and yelled, "Why we stopping?"

I nodded over to the Honda slowly passing the parking lot and turning off down a side street.

"I think those guys are tailing us," I said gritting my teeth. "Let's go in and see if they surface again from the other side street. We can watch them from the front window of the diner as we get a coffee or something."

Ed understood and just followed me into the diner. Sure enough, the Honda appeared. It went down the other side of the street at a slow speed and then turned down another side street and disappeared.

I said, "Don't buy anything. Let's time it so that this bastard doesn't see us leave. When they surface again, we'll wait until they turn down another street, run out, get on the bikes and head for the turnpike. I'm guessing we should be able to do this before they make the trip around the block."

"Where do you think up this stuff?"

I thought I was going to have to try to convince him that this was a good plan.

"We got about forty-five seconds from the time they turn and can't see the bikes in the parking lot until they can see them again coming from the other street," he said.

"Okay then. We have forty-five seconds. You keep the time and I'll be ready when you say so."

Ed monitored his watch while observing the Honda from the picture window of the diner. One of the waitresses asked if we would be ordering. I shook my head "no." She said that we couldn't hang around unless we were ordering. Just as I was getting ready to say that we were leaving, Ed yelled, "Okay Jon, it's time. They've turned down the side street again." The waitress just looked at us with a confused expression. We were out the door, putting on our helmets, onto the bikes and rolling in about 20 seconds.

I hoped that we could make the turnpike ramp in time to get out of sight. I cranked on the 1200cc Sportster and she came alive. She made one hell of a racket on a full throttle and shifted real smooth. Ed was right on my tail but far enough back to maintain some safety. He was still a good bike rider and we reached the ramp in another 15 seconds or so. I leaned into the corner and straightened out as I poured on the throttle again and pulled up straight and got on the pike. Ed was right there with me. No sign of the Honda but we kept up a good speed for about two miles or so to make sure. I began to slow down to the speed limit to make sure we didn't draw any more attention to ourselves. My stitches began to ache a little because of my haste to get the helmet on. I thought, *the next time I put it on; I'll be a little more careful.*

The exit for Route 138 came into sight pretty quickly. We

now had about an hour and 20 minutes ride at the speed limit to get to Newport. I looked in my rear mirrors and only saw the tri-lights of Ed's Heritage behind and to the right of me. The night ride was a wonderful feeling. I hadn't been riding in years and it seemed odd that a developing problem had conjured up a good feeling. Beth's Harley purred and I felt that I was a young man again, just out for a ride before I had to return to tuck someone in, complete some honey do list and get ready for the next day on the job.

I relaxed a little until I noticed a sign up ahead. It read, "Welcome to Rhode Island." The state flag painted on the sign had the word "Hope" on it. *How appropriate,* I thought. Then a large yellow sign appeared almost immediately after that one. As we got close enough to it, I read the sign. "Arcadia State Park, do not stop unless for emergency." The number listed to call if an emergency happened on this stretch of the road was "911." I remembered bringing the kids up this way years ago to go swimming, water skiing and boating in the streams and on the ponds that were near and in the park. Now you needed an emergency number to inform the authorities in case you had vehicle trouble. I blocked the happier and simpler days from my mind. There was no need to get melancholy for a time probably lost in my lifetime but maybe available for my kids and their families once all these world problems had been fixed. *There still was hope, like the sign said,* I thought. Without hope, you didn't have anything.

It was quiet and now beginning to change from dusk to twilight. The fir trees that lined the road all through the park were tall and always shaded the road, even at mid-day. I was pleased to know that people hadn't been allowed to get into the forest and cut down the trees for firewood. The motorcycles seemed to hum in unison as we clipped down the highway leading through the park. Another half hour passed with no sign of any trouble. It was dark now. I thought I saw something pass my head and realized that Ed's tri-lights had swerved a little. Ed immediately pulled next to me and yelled something which sounded like, "You just missed getting hit in the helmet with a can of some kind." I slowed a little to have him repeat the statement when another can hit in front of our bikes and exploded. It was a can of beer. I could smell the spray that came over us. I wanted to tell Ed to kill his light but I knew that was impossible. The lights always stayed on when operating a motorcycle, I remembered. Just as the thought came to mind, Ed yelled, "Kill your light! Kill the light!"

"How do I do that?" I yelled.

"Hit the red toggle switch near the 'kill' button," he said as he pointed. Just then, another can hit left of the back wheel of my bike and sprayed Ed's again. We got the lights off just in time. There was just enough twilight left to see the double yellow line in the middle of the road, thank God. We were still going about 50 miles per hour, which I noticed on the speedometer just before we turned the lights off. It was dark enough though that I almost hit some son of a bitch that dared to venture out towards the middle of the road. Luckily, I saw this guy and had enough time to avoid hitting him directly. Those Harley pipes were loud enough to warn any rogue in the park that someone stupid enough to be riding bikes was coming through their turf. My right rear view mirror must have hit him in the face, or in the chest, if he was crouched as I sped by. Anyway, the force was hard enough to spin the mirror around towards me. A micro-second later, I heard an unnerving thud. I could still hear Ed's bike behind me. If he didn't swerve to the right or left, he would hit whoever it was dead on.

We continued on until we could see the lights of the next town coming upon us. Ed switched his lights on first when I noticed that one of his tri-lights was out. I realized we had been very lucky going through Arcadia State Park. Then I realized what a stupid idea it had been to even think about traveling at night, through a deserted stretch of road, on motorcycles. *I guess I was a stupid old man,* I thought as I put my lights back on. We came to an intersection that was well lit and I noticed that my mirror had only been loosened by the guy I nicked. Then I noticed some skin tissue and blood on the mirror. There was some blood spattered on my hand and right sleeve of my jacket as well. I began to point to my mirror and sleeve when I noticed Ed's bike's front left highway peg was bent and the left leg of his blue jeans was splattered with blood as my jacket was. He pulled up alongside me and said, "Close call amigo. I think we killed that guy."

He then told me to pull over to the closed gas station that was located across from us at the intersection. I followed him. Ed jumped off his bike and pulled out his handkerchief and pulled at one of the gas pump hoses. There was enough gas in the hose to dampen his handkerchief and he quickly cleaned his blue jeans and highway peg. He had a disgusted look on his face as he went to the next pump and repeated the same operation. He told me to quickly go over to the diesel pump that was there and try to do the same thing he had just done with the gas pumps. I asked for his handkerchief. He obliged and I noticed how disgusting it looked. I didn't ponder on what some of the stuff on it was but began removing the diesel pump hose. I got a few ounces of fuel from the pump, enough to repeat the same operation Ed had just performed. I fixed my mirror to make it functional again. I watched Ed attempt to straighten his highway peg. He got it close enough to look straight. He looked at me and said that he would fix it when he got back home. *If we got back home,* I contemplated. I began to ask Ed if he knew what happened to that guy we apparently hit. He looked at me before I could finish and said, "I think I killed him. After you grazed the guy, the force of your mirror had pushed him towards me. Good thing I followed some distance behind. Had I been closer, the guy could have dislodged me from my bike because he came directly in front of it. That direct hit would have probably killed me and given the rogues the opportunity to devour my person and my property. But the space between us allowed me enough time, in the slim light, to avoid hitting the stupid bastard directly. It was a glancing blow, but his head hit the left light of the tri-lights and then bounced to the highway peg and splattered tissue and blood on me and my pant leg. It couldn't have been good for the rogue."

"We'd better get the hell out of here before anyone starts to take notice," I said. We started the bikes and continued on slowly through town. There was some activity but no one seemed to think a second thought about us. Another 20 minutes passed before we saw the lights of the Newport Bridges up ahead. The toll was $8 for a motorcycle but I remembered that we wouldn't have to pay that until we were on our return route coming from the city. No matter how tough everything was these days, we were still subject to tolls which had been raised with everything else. I had enough money to cover us both but I made a mental note of it. We crossed the bridges without any incidents. The traffic was light and people were going exactly the speed limit. We followed suit and just enjoyed the scenery as we crossed the two bridges. I could see the U.S.S. Clinton in all her glory and mammoth size docked at the city cargo pier as we crossed the second bridge. The whole city was aglow from the support that the Clinton was giving. I could see why George Woodbridge was in awe at the sight of the super carrier docked for all to see and appreciate.

Ed was right behind me as I eased off the exit ramp. Immediately after leaving the bridge, we headed for the Clinton and the Harvester depot which was somewhere in the vicinity. We slowly and quietly moved through the city as inconspicuously as possible. I never once revved the throttle. We passed a few policemen on the street corners and they did not even look our way. A few local police patrol cars did appear but also chose to ignore us. It seemed that Newport was in better shape than southeastern Connecticut was. It looked like a normal city before the catastrophic world events had taken place four years before. We merged onto the road leading to the Clinton when we noticed a military check point up ahead about a quarter of a mile. I immediately pulled over into a shopping plaza parking lot and came to a stop. I kept the Harley running. I didn't dare shut it down because I felt very uneasy about the checkpoint. Ed came up beside me and kept the Heritage running also and then asked, "Are you leery about that checkpoint?"

"Yeah."

He began to speak a little louder over the idling of the two engines.

"I was going to stop you anyway up the road a piece. I knew that there was a military checkpoint before you could pass to the lower pier area. Tommy Lupinacci gave me the tip a week ago when he had asked me to begin helping his company with some of their deliveries between the terminal and Newport. I have an IH vender card on me that allows me to pass the checkpoint."

I looked at him and said, "That's great but what the hell am I'm going to do, wait for you?"

"Relax Jon, I have another one for you," he said as he handed it to me.

"This is just a generic card that says that the holder is employed for IH and has access to the depot down near the pier. This is not an identification card."

"Well, George had the same kind of card that allowed him to go back and forth so it should be good enough for us."

"George was in a goddamned delivery truck and we are two goons riding Harleys."

"I'll lead the way and do all the talking'. Ed said. "You are to just follow my lead but most of all, just sit there on your bike and keep your eyes and ears open and your mouth shut."

There was that statement again. I was getting tired of hearing it but I obliged. It was my idea for getting us into this, dumb as it was. Now it was Ed's turn to complete the journey and get us to the IH depot in Newport as planned. I did as he had instructed and slowly moved out of the parking lot following behind him slowly to the military checkpoint.

Meanwhile, an urgent call was being placed back in Norwich.
"We lost them."

"What the hell you mean you lost them? Find them now! And *do not*, I repeat, *do not* repeat what you just told me to anyone else." Then the line went dead. Ilea Adel and Mohammad Owlia looked at each other.

"Your brother, Sid, is panicking. The two old fools will show up again," Ilea said.

"He panics easily when he has to report to Makel. Start the car. We'll keep looking," Mohammad said and pointed for him to drive ahead.

The Checkpoint

We slowly approached the military checkpoint. A Navy shore patrolman was signaling a car to pass as we approached. He then signaled for us to pull over to a check area in front of a small security building. The car that was in front of us, disappeared down the road to the pier. The driver must have had some type of identification to be allowed to pass as quickly as he did. I glanced at my wrist watch; it was 8:48 p.m. We both were instructed by a cut throat signal performed by the S.P. to shut down our bikes. We did that immediately. He came over and stood between both bikes and fortunately looked at Ed first and began to speak asking the obvious questions.

"Good evening gentlemen, what has brought you two to this area of Newport this evening?" he asked most politely but with just a little sarcasm in his voice it seemed. I guess he figured that we were just two bikers that had taken the wrong turn and needed to be redirected to somewhere else. Ed began to speak with authority, at least it sounded that way to me, while producing his IH identification card. I hoped that the patrolman was as impressed as I was with Ed. He said that he was the terminal foreman and that he had come from Connecticut to check on some shipment problems at the IH plant that was reported to him today. He continued to say that I was one of his truckers that would possibly be needed to take a truck back tonight if need be. The patrolman wasn't quite convinced when he asked, "You going to leave the bikes at the plant, pal?"

Ed just looked at him as he took off his helmet and said, "Look son, bikes can fit into delivery trucks. They burn a lot less fuel and are much more convenient in getting our sorry asses up here in the middle of the evening. I really don't want to hear any shit from some twenty-something-year-old smart ass like you. Go get the officer in charge so I can talk to someone with authority, please."

The *please* was as drawn out and as sarcastic as I had ever heard in a long time. I sat on my bike and actually enjoyed the show. I had removed my helmet very gently by this time and the patrolman realized that we were probably two old truckers who were harmless unless aroused.

Another voice said, "That will not be necessary, sir. I'm the duty officer in charge. My name is Lieutenant, J.G. William Roscoe."

"Well Bill, I mean Lieutenant, my name is Edward McAuliffe and I'm on my way down the road to hopefully solve a problem for IH."

"McAuliffe? McAuliffe? Are you any relationship to Senior Chief Brian McAuliffe of the Newport Naval Base Shore Patrol?"

"Yep, the one and the same. He's my nephew. I just talked to him this afternoon about a problem I had with IH. He called me to make sure I was still breathing and looking down on the grass and not looking up at the roots if you know what I mean?"

Ed gave a fake and loud laugh. He was incredible. He was giving an award winning performance. I guess the audience thought as well because the lieutenant instructed the patrolman to let us pass and almost made an apology for detaining us.

"Sorry that the Senior Chief wasn't on duty tonight. I'm sure he would have requested that you come by to see him," Roscoe said.

"Thank you but I wouldn't have too much time to because I'm on the job right now and need to get to the IH plant as soon as possible. If I have to bring a truck back, it would be a longer night for me and my trucker." He was referring to me. I thanked God that Brian didn't know that his uncle had followed me on this night ride because he would have stopped this adventure in a heartbeat. It was bad enough to know that someone would eventually inform Brian that his uncle and another old guy had ridden through a checkpoint in the middle of the evening on Harleys. I'm sure Ed would be getting a call in the morning asking, no, probably demanding, what the hell were the two of us up to. I'd hoped that no one would have associated us with anything but I knew that was probably

76

impossible now as we were slowly moving past the checkpoint and down the road to the U.S.S. Clinton and the Harvester plant.

We went about one half mile and were out of the sight of the checkpoint when Ed pulled over and shut down his bike. I pulled up beside him and asked why he had stopped. He told me to shut down the Sportster as well and removed his helmet while straddling and balancing his bike. Before Ed could speak I congratulated him on his performance at the checkpoint. He didn't seem amused.

He said, "Do you realize that I will be getting an ass chewing tomorrow morning as soon as Brian hears that me and some guy were down here snooping around his area of responsibility? He's going to flip when he hears that I bullshitted some easy lieutenant who he probably has to deal with on a daily basis."

I didn't say any more about that. I quickly said though that we needed to get nearer to the Harvester depot as quickly as possible. We could park our bikes away from the depot and approach it by foot. I told Ed that I would go ahead and find a place to accommodate my plan. He nodded, put on his helmet and we both started our bikes.

As we approached the IH plant I could see that the depot still had several trucks lined up at the loading dock. The dockhands were busy about their work and didn't think it was unusual for us to be there. Even our Harleys didn't get their attention. I realized, while I was scouting out the terrain ahead, that there were probably many sailors with motorcycles, scooters and even on bicycles that drove or rode by this place at all hours of the day and night on this side of the checkpoint area. The road and the area were well lit and steady traffic was probably normal for the dockhands to see and hear. I found a place about one hundred yards down the road where we could park the Harleys. There was a closed liquor store that had a little parking lot as well as what looked like a delivery area immediately behind the building. I chose the rear and hoped that I didn't find someone behind the building. It looked empty and a good place to keep the bikes out of the way, but easily accessible if we had to leave in a hurry. We pulled in and stopped. It was a good decision. We were able to park the bikes close to the building, out of sight and hopefully undetected by rogue and friend alike.

"Ed, we should casually walk by the depot on the opposite side of the street to observe as much as possible." I grimaced taking off my helmet. Ed questioned that approach.

"We should get on the same side of the depot and cut behind the building to get closer to the barge that IH has tied up to the pier next to the plant. That one on the opposite side of the small bay where the Clinton is docked," he said pointing. I agreed. We moved slowly and cautiously around to the rear of the depot to observe the barge. The barge had a large sign mounted and painted with words announcing the upcoming Fourth of July fireworks display that was being planned. IH, along with the Costello Shipping Company, was listed as the two largest sponsors. The listing also included the names of the local merchants and businesses that had also teamed up to sponsor the event. The CTC, who had pulled the barge to the Newport pier, was also included.

Ed looked at me and said, "Well, we look like idiots now based on the looks of that barge and the type of sponsors that are listed on it, don't you think?" I didn't say anything because I was embarrassed a little. He continued, "The goddamned Navy is also one of the sponsors if you keep reading down the list."

"I know, Ed, I can read," I mumbled back at him. He turned and began to move back in the direction that we had come in when I saw a hatch open on the barge and several men climbed out of it. I grabbed Ed by the arm and turned him around as I put my finger to my lips to indicate for him to keep quiet. I crouched down and pulled at Ed's arm. As I pulled him down, I pointed in the direction of the men as we remained crouched, and hopefully, out of their sight. We observed them enough to see that some of them had lit cigarettes. They weren't there long before some guy came out from the depot's rear entrance and yelled over to them to get below and back to work. Then

78

he looked around to make sure nobody else was around. We hoped that he hadn't seen us. Apparently, he had not. He momentarily glared at the workers to make sure they heeded his instructions and then walked back to the rear entrance door and closed it. I looked at Ed. He didn't speak, but pointed back in the direction of where the bikes had been parked. I followed his lead. We didn't speak until we reached the Harleys. I looked at him and asked him what he thought.

"There is something obviously going on inside that barge. There shouldn't be anyone working inside. The only time there was access needed inside a barge was when it was about to be loaded and it needed barge attendants to check and prepare ballast tanks or it needed repairs."

"It must be repairs."

"Nope, all repair work is always done during the day when the port docking engineers, Coast Guard, or Navy inspection teams who rent the barges, are present to observe the repair work in process and verify compliance standards to whichever group has jurisdiction over this barge."

I asked Ed how he knew that. He explained that in some of the conversations that he had with Brian, work stuff like this came up.

"We always talk shop when we're together," he explained. Ed remembered a conversation with Brian a while back. I was happy that he did. I added one detail.

"George told me that the units he delivered were being loaded onto the barge." Ed looked at me and said, "They would have had to modify a barge hatch in order to load something that size into the barge. At the angle we were looking at, I can't see if a hatch has been modified to accommodate that." He did notice the CTC's portable barge crane that had been placed near the barge could easily reach the barge to load anything.

"Do you want to nose around the Harvester depot some more and maybe get close enough to the barge and loading dock to see if we could see anything else out of the ordinary?" I asked.

"No. We should be getting back home and we'll talk when we get back to my place." He didn't seem upset but I wondered why he couldn't spend a few more minutes and tell me what he was thinking. I looked at my watch and it was 10:12 p.m. *Shit, I thought, it will be midnight by the time we get back.* I had less than two hours to think up of an excuse to tell Jean that I had actually had a sporting chance that she would believe. I decided to call her.

The house phone rang and rang. No answer until the answering machine came on. I left a message that I was running late but that I would be home by midnight. I told her not to worry and that I was with Ed but I had a lot to tell her when I got home. We started the bikes, put on our helmets and moved out slowly from behind the liquor store and onto the access road. We passed the depot which now had only one truck left at the dock. As we slowly approached the security checkpoint with Ed in the lead, I hoped that we would not have to stop and go through all of that questioning again. The patrolman waved us through this time and saluted Ed as we passed. Ed pulled into the same parking lot that we had first stopped at before we attempted to pass through the security checkpoint. He kept his helmet on, came to a stop and straddled his bike long enough to instruct me to continue to follow him. He was going to take a different route home after we crossed the Newport Bridges. He also asked me if I had enough money for the toll. I nodded and then said that I would follow him. I knew he would be taking the interstate on the way back. It would take us a half hour more to reach home but it was much safer than trying to run the gauntlet through the Arcadia State Forest. I understood that we needed to stay clear of that place anyway. I hoped that the rogue that we hit was still alive. By the looks and sound that I had observed, and the description that Ed had given me that he had observed, I figured that my chances of hoping that was true were almost none.

We paid the toll and traveled across the bridges without any incidents. There were a few trucks and cars on the bridges but not many. Most of the traffic had disappeared as we neared Connecticut. I relaxed for a while and the ride was almost enjoyable until I sensed that a car was getting too close to the back of my bike. I was blinded by the lights and looked ahead to clear the spots from my eyes when I noticed Ed signaling that he was pulling over. I realized then that it was a Rhode Island State Trooper. I pulled alongside Ed, shut my bike off as had he had already done and pulled off my helmet.

Ed quickly removed his helmet and hung it from the bike's handle bar. I mimicked him. My stitches were getting irritated from all the rubbing and the sweating. It seemed like an eternity for the trooper took to get out of his car and approach us. As he did, another trooper came upon us and pulled up in front of us. The first trooper spoke to both of us from behind with his flash light alternating between Ed and me. As he came closer I noticed that he held the flashlight in his left hand while resting his right hand on the grip of the automatic pistol he carried. He instructed Ed to get out his license, registration, inspection certificate and insurance card. Ed obliged as the second trooper came upon us. The flashlights they carried were bright and blinding. Black spots altered my vision as I attempted to comply with the instructions that the first trooper had given us. *Ah shit,* I thought, in horror. *What if Ed didn't have the registration, inspection certificate and insurance card for Beth's bike? He admitted that he hadn't touched the bike since her death.* I hoped he had all the right documents with him and they were all valid. Ed asked the first trooper if he could dismount his bike and gather up all the remaining documentation that the trooper had requested. The trooper told him to stay on the bike. Ed complied. Once they determined that they had the situation under control, the first trooper told Ed to go ahead and get the documents that he had requested. Ed got off his bike and obtained his registration, inspection certificate and insurance card. The trooper took the documents while the second trooper kept a vigilant watch on both of us. Satisfied, the trooper handed back the documents without saying one word. Ed asked again, if he could get the documents from the bike I was riding because he was the only one that knew where they were. The trooper complied and let Ed move toward me. Ed asked the trooper if he would allow me to get off the bike so that he could fetch the required documents. The trooper nodded. Under their watchful eyes, I slowly got off the bike as Ed went to one of Beth's saddle bags and retrieved the documents and gave it to them and waited for the trooper to examine them. The trooper handed them back to him without a word and looked at me and asked for my license. I slowly handed it to him and he returned it almost immediately. I relaxed knowing we had passed that part of their request. I waited for the obvious questioning to follow.

The second trooper asked where we were going. We both began to explain to him at the same time but I quickly shut up and let Ed handle the situation. Ed explained who we were, where we had come from, and where we were heading to. He even produced the identification card to backup the IH story and told the trooper to check with the naval security checkpoint and the duty officer there that had passed us through earlier in the evening. The trooper listened, and then asked me to open up the saddle bags on Beth's bike. I obliged and there was nothing in there except some spare spark plugs, a tool kit and a few pieces of wire that Ed always kept in case of some emergency. The other bag contained similar items including a makeup kit. The trooper looked a bit confused until Ed spoke up and said it was his wife's bike and those were her personal items. The trooper actually smiled. The other trooper asked Ed to open up his compartments. I froze. I knew Ed carried both pistols in the right compartment. Ed immediately opened both to let him look in. The trooper instructed him to take out the articles like I had just done. Ed pulled out some maps, some tools similar to the ones Beth's bike had and some spare wire and stuff from the left compartment. Satisfied, he instructed him to open the right one. Ed quickly opened it and told him the compartment was empty. The trooper satisfied himself as he shined the flashlight into the empty compartment and said, "Gentlemen, you check out, okay, but I am advising you to get home as soon as reasonably possible. You gentlemen are only inviting trouble by riding bikes late at night. At your ages, you should have thought to drive here by car or truck to take care of company business." We didn't say a word. He instructed us to leave and to have a good and safe evening. We began to get ready to leave when he asked if this was the route that we had taken on our way to our first destination. Ed quickly answered that it was because this was the safest way to reach our destination. He acknowledged that and waved us on to go. The other trooper was already in his car and waiting for us to leave. We quickly obliged. We didn't talk until we arrived at Ed's house. It was almost midnight. As we parked the bikes, Jean's cell phone rang. I looked at the caller ID. It was listed as an unknown caller.

"Who was that?" Ed asked.

"An unknown caller."My stitches were throbbing now. We checked out Beth's right mirror. It was just out of alignment. Ed fixed it and I used some of his spray cleaner that I found on the bench to clean it off. Ed inspected the left side highway peg on his bike. The peg rod was not bent but the u-bracket had to be adjusted and tightened. The force of hitting that guy only loosened it making it look bent in the dark. The folding part of the peg needed to be seriously cleaned. There was dried blood and tissue on it. We grimaced as we cleaned it.

"Ed we're lucky that the state troopers didn't see what condition the peg was in." He just looked at me. I know we both hoped that the guy we hit wasn't hurt too much, but most of all, that he wasn't dead. My cell phone rang. It was another unknown number but I chose to answer it.

"Dad, you home yet?" the voice asked. It took me a few seconds to realize it was Josh.

"Hi. And no, not yet.

"Well get home. Mom is worried sick about you."

"I left her a message telling her that it would be midnight before I got home. I'm fifteen minutes away. I'll call her again." I was a bit annoyed by his tone but decided to overlook it. "How are you doing?" I asked. I pushed the speaker button so Ed could hear while I put my finger to my mouth to indicate that he should keep quiet and just listen. Josh completely ignored my pleasantry and told me that Ed and I shouldn't be riding Harleys in the middle of the night, going through navy checkpoints and snooping around the Newport Harbor. I asked Josh what he was talking about.

"Dad, I have been monitoring your little trip from the naval checkpoint, your little excursion around the harbor and your run in with the state troopers who we asked to stop and check you out. We continued to monitor you until you pulled up to Ed's house and I was assured by agents that you were safe and sound." Ed was looking around to see if there was somebody watching us.

"Josh, I need to explain"

"Dad, we'll talk tomorrow. Please get in your truck and get home. We will monitor you and will make sure you get home. I am also making sure that you stay home until it is time for work tomorrow. Mr. McAuliffe, I know you can hear me on my Dad's speaker phone."

Ed just smiled and said, "I guess Brian has been speaking to you about some things."

"He has, sir, and he will be talking to you also tomorrow. Good night gentlemen." He hung up.

"Ed, these guys had been watching us from the checkpoint on,"

"That's okay. Maybe now we can get some answers on what the hell is going on. Sprague, listen to me. We never took the Arcadia State Park road up to Newport. We went up, and back, the same way we told the troopers we did. Remember that."

I nodded. I couldn't even contemplate what that would mean if that guy was hurt or even worse, dead. I looked at Ed and I bid him good night, but before I left, I went back to his Heritage, opened up the compartment and retrieved my Colt Python. I asked Ed if he wanted his Colt .45 automatic. He shook his head "no" and commented that it wasn't a good night at all. I got into my truck and left for home. I didn't see any head lights. As I pulled up to the house, Jean was looking at me through the kitchen door window. It was 12:34 a.m., Tuesday, July 1.

Gene Moretti called Makel.

"Two bikers have been seen at the Newport plant. Based on the plate number traced from one of the bikes, one of the bikers was Ed McAuliffe. They are probably looking for Woodbridge. The other bike belongs to McAuliffe as well but the rider is probably the driver McAuliffe had hired. His name is Sprague."

Makel ordered, "Take care of Sprague. I will deal with McAuliffe myself."

Makel hung up.

Missing Persons

As soon as I walked through the door, Jean hugged me, examined my stitches, and then began to question me intensely. It seemed that she went on for two or three minutes before I could get a word in edgewise. I began to elaborate on what Josh had told her when something registered in my mind.

"You said that Anita called you looking to know if I had seen George."

"Yes. Anita called me before Josh, and then you called to say that you were on your way home and that you had been out to Newport to get some answers. Anita said that she hadn't talked to George since late this morning and that you and he had met on the turnpike and that you stopped to give him a hand with a flat tire." I nodded as she continued. "She said that George was irritated because after his Newport run, he had to go back and get another delivery for IH and back to Newport again."

"I was going to call Josh and fill him in on this."

"I already called him. He was investigating that too."

"When did you call him?"

"I called him a little after I received Anita's call." I thought that there were too many coincidences happening tonight. Jean continued, "I was very worried about you two. I was going to call Anita and let her know that the FBI and other authorities are going to look for George but Josh told me not to do that. He said that he would talk to Mrs. Woodbridge when he needed to. He instructed me to tell her, if she called again, that the FBI and local authorities would not commence any type of investigation until a missing persons report was initiated by her. I thought that was cruel. I hoped she wouldn't call me again so that I wouldn't have to try to explain that to her."

In defense of Josh, I explained that was a typical procedure of the FBI and any other law enforcement agency. I'm sure Josh did not want her to know that George hadn't become ill as reported by one of the Harvester drivers who had told Dan Kelly that. The most important fact now was the FBI was now involved and maybe they could get some answers from some of the people who had been around George in the last 12 hours or so.

"Come to bed now. I'm so tired and relieved that you are home safe. And stop acting like Sherlock Holmes with your side kick, Doctor Watson, before you both get hurt or worse. I need to be into work early and would need you to drive me to the hospital. Public transportation won't get me in early enough. My supervisor called and said that I had to get to work earlier tomorrow." I asked her why they needed her in earlier as I began to walk over to the kitchen sink to clean off some of the stains that I had on my jacket sleeve.

"Some incident occurred out at Arcadia State Park."

I froze for a second as I listened intently. She explained that some riot had happened between two rogue gangs when some gang guy was badly injured by some other gang guys riding through their turf on motorcycles.

"I guess one group went looking for the other group and some fighting took place."

"Really," I said as I continued to wash the jacket sleeve.

"Yeah. Some people really were injured in the brawl. The state police and local fire department ambulances had to go out there and bring back twenty or so people who had been hurt. It's disgusting how some people have become animals. I've been assigned to help out in the intensive care unit because they have three times as many people there than usual since this brawl occurred."

I casually squeezed my jacket sleeve to remove the excess water and placed it on a rack that Jean used to dry her unmentionables as she called them. She asked me if the jacket needed washing and I told her that it didn't. I just wanted to get some grease off that I had gotten from one of Ed's bikes when I did some adjusting on it.

"That's another thing I need to talk to you about," she said.

"My jacket?"

"No, jackass, but riding bikes with Ed in the middle of the night is what I'm getting at."

I explained that it was a lot of fun, a cheaper way to get there based on fuel costs, and actually quite a pleasant run to be on a bike again.

"Good thing you didn't run up against that riot out there," she said.

I told her that we had thought about that route but it was too dangerous and we stuck to the well used and lighted interstate on the way up and back. I cut her off to ask her more questions about some of the injured. I asked her were guns used or were there knife wounds or clubbing going on?

"I called to get an idea of what type of work I could expect when I came in. You know the extent of the injuries I would be working with. One of the guys had been reportedly injured when he was run over by some motorcycles. He wasn't in too bad of shape, though, compared to the stab wound victims she would have to nurse tomorrow morning."

I thanked God and all that was holy that the rogue that Ed and I hit would live long enough to get out of the hospital to probably die another day. I was a little sorry that we caused such a ruckus but, so far, we hadn't killed anyone. I thought of Ed tossing in bed thinking that we could have been responsible for a death tonight. I made a note to call him as soon as I left for work in the morning while I was in the security of the cab and Jean wouldn't hear me tell him. Jean told me to stay still before she got into bed. She took another look at my stitches and said that they looked red and irritated. She went to the medicine cabinet and brought out some sterile gauze to cleanse my stitches.

"Tomorrow morning we're going to wash your hair to keep all your hair oil and sweat away from that wound," she said. We went to bed.

It seemed like only five minutes had passed when the alarm startled us both. It was 4 a.m. and I was very tired. I forced myself up quickly to wash my head, specific areas and dress. I checked my jacket to see how it looked. It was clear of any blood spots and the sleeve was dry. I didn't need it today but I always put it in the truck in case I needed a little warm jacket when the summer temperature would occasionally drop in the late evening or early morning hours. Jean had dressed and was preparing some tea and toast. She must have picked up some bread somewhere.

"Where did you purchase the bread?"

"Ethel gave me a loaf that she figured would probably grow moldy before she and Orrin had a chance to eat it."

"That was a nice thing that the old lady did."

"Ethel said that Orrin needed some skin cream for his dry skin so I told her that I would see if I could get some at the hospital."

I never said another word because I knew Jean would have to cop a tube of that from the pharmacy shelf or nursing station medicine cabinet when she had the opportunity to do so. I knew she hated doing things like that but Ethel and Orrin would need a prescription for the type of skin cream Orrin needed. Paying doctor fees for creams that had steroids in them was out of the question for a lot of people these days. I told Jean, after I gulped down my toast and tea, that I would be in the truck. I handed Jean her cell phone that I borrowed the night before and turned to go out to the truck.

"Wait a minute," she said. "I want to look at that wound."

It took a few seconds and she just smiled a little as she motioned me away. I went for the door. As I jumped onto the running board, I had begun instantly dialing Ed's house. In a few seconds Ed answered and I immediately informed him about what Jean had told me about the riot out at the Arcadia State Park and the condition of the victims, especially the one that he and I were interested in.

He hesitated momentarily then said, "Good." I told him that I would meet him at the terminal and then hung up without saying another word as I saw Jean shut and lock the kitchen door on her way out of the house. As we drove off and headed to the hospital, I continued to glance in my rear view mirror looking for that Honda or any other car that could be following me, especially after the conversation I had with Joshua last night which was a little unnerving. No Honda, no nothing I observed as we drove directly to Backus. I dropped Jean off at the hospital and kissed her for a few extra seconds for several reasons. One was I was grateful that all was okay in the world now that I knew that the useless rogue hadn't died. Secondly, I saw Alice walking into the ER and I knew she noticed us. That kiss was really for her benefit to hopefully stop her from coming on to me. *Seeing me passionately kissing my wife early in the morning was a good idea* I thought, but I didn't know if it would work. Anyway, it was pleasant doing it. Jean seemed pleased.

I pulled into the artery terminal where I immediately saw Ed and Dan Kelly standing near a parked delivery truck. As I approached I could see that the truck was George Woodbridge's. They both waited until I parked my truck and jumped out.

"They left the keys with the night watchman," Ed said. Dan stood next to him without uttering a word.

"I'm checking to see if George left anything behind that could maybe tell us where he is."

Ed unlocked the door and jumped inside the cab. I went to the other side and jumped in as well. There was no sign, note of any kind or clue, as to where George could have been. I turned to Dan and asked if he knew anything more than we did. He gave no verbal inclination that he did, but the look on his face said otherwise. I stopped asking any more questions until I could get Ed alone.

"I'm sure George will turn up somewhere," Dan said nonchalantly.

"Take his truck to the loading dock and get him loaded for his trip to the Harvester depot," Ed said to Dan while Dan was starting to get busy moving my truck into position.

"I don't believe that bastard," Ed said. I had my reasons to be suspect but was curious to know what he was thinking.

"Why?" I asked.

"The bastard has been lying to me for the past week or so. I've been catching him in little lies and inconsistencies for a while now. I've been informed by several people that they saw Kelly

90

with Owlia and Lupinacci at a few of the underground clubs in the area. He's married with kids. He'd never ventured out before. Now he's doing shit like that. I'm gonna call Anita to tell her the truck is at the terminal and is being secured. I'll let her know that I'll follow up on the missing person's document as a representative of the artery terminal. At least that would be one less thing for the lady to worry about. I can file sooner than she can because George went missing on the job."

"Thanks. That will be a great help to her. She never had to do things like that. George always took care of everything."

"I also had Dan call over to the Harvester depot to talk to Tommy. He said that he left a message with Sid because Tommy wasn't in yet," Ed said. I listened to more of what he had to say until he began to express his relief that the rogue we had run over was going to be okay.

"You're relieved? I could hardly sleep knowing I needed to tell you that the rogue was going to live. It was going to be bad enough trying to keep a secret that we went that way never mind trying to cover up a death. We got lucky and thank God," I said as the phone in Ed's office rang. It was Tommy Lupinacci.

"What the hell happened to George?" Ed asked.

"I don't know. Nobody has seen him. Ed, did you call his house and speak to his kids? I got my own problem right now. I need a driver to replace him right away. As far as I am concerned, the guy lost his job driving for us if he doesn't show up."

Lupinacci was more concerned that he didn't have a driver for Newport today. I was pissed that Ed didn't pursue the questioning of his whereabouts and just succumbed to Tommy's request for him to arrange for another driver to be made available. Ed quickly responded and said, "I got Jonathan Sprague available for the run. I can get his local deliveries taken on by another driver who is just as reliable."

"Okay, you work it out, but get his ass over to the Harvester depot as soon as possible." He hung up as I just stared at Ed as he was making all these arrangements.

"Are you out of your goddamned mind?"

"No, we need to get some legitimate time to try to find out what happened to George," he said. "Don't you want to find out? You were the instigator dragging my ass around last night with all your curiosity. Now it's my turn to repay the favor. You can go and see what the operation looks like in the middle of the day when you might see something."

I knew I couldn't say "no." I was as curious as Ed and this was a legitimate way to look around. I told him to make sure that Brian and Josh knew where I was and, if needed, to call my son-in-law Sergeant Joe Harris. He looked, smiled and said, "I have a bad feeling about George but I'm sure Brian, Josh and your son-in-law will make sure you come back alive and well. I'll make sure that I tell Brian and that I placed you on the delivery list. He'll chew my ass out, but not as bad as what your son will do when he finds out what we're up to." He smirked.

He pushed his intercom button and Dan answered, "Yeah Boss."

"Is Sprague's truck loaded yet?"

"Almost. Maybe a minute or two."

Ed looked at me and told me to be careful. He made a note to call Brian in a few hours to let him know I was driving to Newport. I headed for my truck. Dan tossed my keys and never failed to say every time I left the terminal for the depot, "Jon, have a good trip." I also knew he'd know what was in my truck when I returned from the Newport run. The real question was did he know what was going to be loaded onto my truck at the depot when I headed out to Newport? Ed and I knew he probably did and we knew we would have to find out what he knew. As I slowly drove away from the artery terminal that Tuesday morning, I knew what my priorities were. I had to find out what happened to our friend George and I had to find out what Dan knew. I was inclined to believe that somehow, these two things were related. I suddenly realized how tired I was thanks to last night's events. It was 6:10 a.m., July 1. In three days, we'll be celebrating the independence of our country with old friends. *Maybe George and our families could get together again*, I thought. Then reality set in. We had to find our friend George.

As I drove along the Interstate heading for the Harvester depot, I saw the silver Honda again following a few hundred yards behind. I also noticed, what seemed to be, a mid-sized black sport utility vehicle behind the silver Honda. Could that be one of Josh's? *A black SUV wasn't too obvious*, I thought. Unfortunately, the SUV turned off and exited the highway. The Honda still continued to follow me at a safe distance. I ignored the bastards now. They were small potatoes. We had bigger fish to fry as the old saying goes. I suddenly realized that I was enjoying this. *Perhaps I should be more apprehensive*, I thought, *because I didn't know what, or who, we were dealing with.* George was missing, the IH depots were probably shipping hot merchandise, and Josh and Brian didn't want Ed and me interfering with something that didn't concern us. Well George Woodbridge did concern us and looking around to find him was the right thing to do.

I approached the Harvester depot feeling as if I had worked a full day already with all that had transpired. I was excited, a little scared, a little mad and very cautious as I noticed Sid Owlia wave me on to the Harvester depot dock. I could see Tommy Lupinacci looking out the foreman's window. The silver Honda pulled into the parking lot and as before, the two guys in it, got out and walked into the foreman's office. I could see Tommy Lupinacci through the window turn in their direction as they entered.

Newport Delivery

I waited in the truck as I was unloaded and loaded again. I never looked or spoke to anyone until Sid came over and handed me my paperwork and shipping documents. He also handed me a naval checkpoint pass to use on my way to the lower docking area where the IH plant and U.S.S. Clinton were. It was the same card Ed produced when we were stopped on our midnight run. Sid told me to obey the same rules at the Newport dock area that they had here. I just acknowledged his instructions. He looked at me and repeated his instructions but then asked, "Do you understand, Sprague?" He rested his elbow on my driver's door window opening while standing on my running board. He pissed me off for two reasons. First, he was being sarcastic and rude and secondly, his breath smelt like shit. I stared at him for a second and calmly unlocked his arm from my window and pushed him off my running board. As I said, "Yes I understand," he lost his balance and stumbled backwards. He fell directly on his behind. He stared up at me and began to get up quickly. I was out of the truck and looking straight into his face.

"Don't ever talk to me that way again or you may not be able to get up the next time." I didn't care now how big he was. "By the way, you need to go brush your rotten teeth. Your breath smells like road kill," I said as I turned to walk to my truck. A few dock workers that saw the incident never said a word as he glared up at them and told them to get back to work. I did notice one worker smirk as he turned away. He made sure that Sid didn't see his pleasure.

Tommy came out with the two goons that had been in the Honda earlier that had followed me here again. He looked at Sid and asked if everything was alright. I turned and said, "Everything is just fine now." I leaped onto my running board and got into the truck. The dock worker waved me out and I slowly moved away. I felt some personal satisfaction from that

94

small altercation. I knew that Sid was one of the last people to see George and I was sure he probably treated him worse. It made me feel better knocking him to the ground. Not knowing where George was still frustrated me.

I headed out for Newport and I knew I would have several hours to relax before I got to the Harvester plant. I still had plenty of fuel but would check out the fuel stations in the general area and maybe get a chance to fill up at a cheaper rate. It was a possibility that I could luck out and find a place where I didn't have to wait long. *This was a good plan,* I thought. I could take the time to ask around the Harvester plant while I was waiting to be unloaded and loaded again. What was wrong with looking for someone who could give me a good tip on where to get cheaper fuel?

As I drove along, I quick dialed Ed on my cell phone to see if he had heard any more news from Brian, Josh or hopefully from George or Anita. Ed didn't answer the terminal phone so I dialed his cell. No answer at that number either. I waited to hear his message and left a short one to call me on my cell as soon as he had any new information. By the time I had finished the cell message, I noticed the same signs that I had seen the previous night. Driving through the Arcadia State Park during the morning was quite an enjoyable experience. There were a few people visible on the sides of the road. Most of them looked like people in transit by the unkempt look of them. Maybe they were rogues at night, but during the day, with the constant presence of state and local police cruisers patrolling, they behaved as ordinary citizens. I came to one area where it was obvious that this had been the place of the disturbance that Jean had told me about. There was trash strewn about. The broken glass and empty bottles that littered the side of the road glimmered in the sun's rays. There were several heavily damaged trucks and a few motorcycles lying about but there were no people in the immediate area except a few police cars. I slowed down as I approached the battle zone only to be waved on by a patrolman who was walking around in the area talking into his personal radio that was attached to his shoulder.

I continued my drive but after a short time, I became bored again and decided to call Jean and let her know how I was doing and find out if she had heard any news from Josh or Anita. I planned on getting into a conversation on what I saw in an attempt to see if she knew more about the rogue Ed and I had hit last night. I dialed and waited for the ER to answer. I knew she wouldn't have her cell on and I didn't know the Intensive Care Unit's phone number. Whoever answered could transfer me to the Unit or give me the number. I hoped that Alice wouldn't answer because I wasn't in the mood for any of her lewd comments this morning. Sure as shit, Alice answered.

"Emergency Room Triage."

"Hi Alice, Jon here. Put me through to Jean will you please and I will thank you forever," I stupidly said. I immediately regretted that because I knew it would only entice her. She just said, "Sure sweetheart, I'll put you through right away."

In a few seconds Jean answered.

"ICU, Sprague here." She listened to my questions and then said, "Josh called me to say that he was investigating George Woodbridge's missing person's report that Ed filed and that he also had Brian and the Shore Patrol looking as well. He said he even talked to Joe's captain at the state police barracks."

Several Connecticut and Rhode Island barracks had been asked for their assistance in the case. All the information that Jean told me was good news. Great news would have been if they had found George.

"Jean, I'll call again on my return trip for an update. I'll be in constant touch with Ed for any information from his end."

"Be careful. How are your stitches?

"This run is a piece of cake during the day. And my stitches are fine."

I felt the urge to double check my glove box to ensure that my Colt was still there. It was of course. Maybe I was bored, or maybe I subconsciously thought that I would have reason to need it. I prayed that I wouldn't. I didn't pray much these days but I did contemplate saying a few for George to be found safely.

"What's wrong with Alice?

"The ER is really busy because most of the ER nurses are assisting other areas due to the riot last night. Alice was probably as tired as I' am."

"I understand," I said. We said goodbye and ended the call. *Shit*, I thought, *I forgot to ask her about the rogue in ICU.*

I could see the Newport bridges up ahead and double checked my cash to make sure I had all that I would need to pay the toll on the return trip. A truck could cost as much as $35 based on axle count, tonnage and length. There was a truck stop at each end of the double bridges. That had been started a few years ago by the State of Rhode Island to try to raise money any way it could to keep the infrastructure in fair repair. I could see the signs for trucks to turn off into the truck weigh station coming up. I eventually turned into the weigh station and lined my truck up as directed by a state weigh station employee. As I prepared to go through, it dawned on me that this had been an uneventfully trip and I was pleased. No sooner had the last word ran through my mind, I saw that silver Honda waiting off to the side of the line of trucks that were ahead of mine and going through the process I was about to go through. I was going to ignore them but it kept eating away at me as to why these guys needed to be following me. It was too incidental that these guys always showed up when a delivery truck was carrying cargo from any one of their depots or plants. I figured what was the harm in getting to meet these guys.

I was going to get out of my truck and go over to where they were parked when the weigh in attendant told me to drive my truck onto the scale. Introductions would have to wait. I began to move my truck and decided that I would meet these guys later on in the trip. I thought that I would pull over and make it look like an emergency stop and see if they would take the bait. Then I had the strangest thought that maybe they were hired to protect me and their company's cargo. I felt a little guilty until I remembered that guys like these were the last ones to see George before he disappeared.

97

The weigh in attendant gave me my weight slip and told me that I would be stopped and weighed again leaving Newport. He also said that my calculated average weight would include my toll fare and that the fee would be in cash. He asked me if I understood the procedure and I acknowledged that I did. He waved me on to continue my route to Newport. The two guys in the silver Honda followed. As I began to navigate the streets of Newport on my way to the pier area, I decided to do my emergency check plan. As I pulled over to stop, I pulled the Colt from my glove box and slid into the small of my back. I grabbed my light jacket and quickly put it on to hide the Colt. I pulled the hood release latch as I stopped to begin the process of opening up the engine compartment. I jumped out of the truck and moved to the front and began to release the hood latch mechanism. I stood on the truck's bumper and proceeded to look at the engine. I observed the two of them getting out of the Honda, one on either side, I pretended not to notice. I didn't feel too apprehensive because it was broad daylight and I was parked near a very busy intersection. I even was fortunate enough to see a policeman standing on the corner of the intersection conversing with someone. *The scene couldn't have been planned any better,* I thought. I acted startled when one of the guys came upon me.

"What's the trouble?" he asked.

"I think I'm getting some false reading on my temperature gage," I said as I bent over looking into the engine compartment checking for any signs of leaks in the radiator or hoses. "It indicated that I was exceeding the normal running temperature but I guess it's reading hotter than what I can see and feel. It must be a faulty gauge reading," I said to further fabricate my excuse to stop. The other one just stood on my other side and continued to look around. I said, "I don't need any help. You two can go on about your business." The guy looked at me and said, "You are our business."

I felt a chill run down my spine but threw a little more fuel onto the fire and asked, "Who are you guys and why am I your business?" One of them attempted to hold my arm to give me some kind of message when I pushed him away with my boot. I had a good leverage from that position and the bastard fell back off balance. By that time I was down from the truck and staring straight in the face of the other guy, I had reached my Colt. I had placed it at my side. They could see it but the policemen on the corner who hadn't made any attempt to observe my stopping, couldn't see it yet. I gritted my teeth and slowly talked to both of them. The one that I pushed was up and looking very angry.

"Behave yourself," I said. "If you don't, today might be your last." They both backed up. Before they could speak, I asked them, "Who are you guys and why are you following me?"

The angry one composed himself enough to speak.

"We were hired to make sure that delivery trucks like yours, working for IH, arrive at their destinations with the cargos they are carrying." I didn't ask any more questions.

"Get back into your car and go anywhere else but in my sight." They began to protest when I cocked the Colt.

"Now go tell your boss, whoever he is, that I don't need two goons like you following me for any reason. If I need protection, you're looking at it."

As they turned to go to their car, I overheard one of them tell the other that Donnie was going to be pissed. So they would know I heard, I yelled, "I don't know a Donnie, but I'll be calling Lupinacci and telling him to keep his goons off my ass or he can find some other trucker in an emergency to haul his shit! Better yet, you call him and tell him what I said. I'll save my air time. Now get the hell out of here."

I closed the hood as they drove away. I jumped into the truck just in time to conceal my pistol as the cop approached my truck.

"Any trouble here?" he asked.

"No sir, not now. Those guys were nice enough to ask too," I said as I started my truck. "I thought that the truck was heating up but it looks like a faulty gauge. I'll check it out when I reach the IH plant down by the pier." He acknowledged my explanation and smiled.

As I began to slowly drive away, he said, "The Harvester people are really going to put on a great Fourth of July fireworks display for the city. Are you carrying some of those fireworks?"

"Nah. I'm just carrying machinery. Somebody else from Harvester is doing that task." He smiled and waved me on. I reached the military checkpoint and had to wait several minutes to pass through. I showed the shore patrolman my documents and ID and he waved me on. I was glad that I didn't see anyone that could have recognized me from last night. Then reality set in and I realized, so what if they had, I was on legitimate business then as well as right now. I guess I was still paranoid from the first time I went through the checkpoint. I remembered that Ed was supposed to tell Brian I was passing through. I looked to catch a glimpse of him as I drove away. He must have been busy somewhere else or he was pissed at us. I could have cared less anyway for I was still hopped up on adrenalin from the experience with the two goons earlier. I passed the U.S.S. Clinton in her majestic setting and came upon the Harvester plant. I pulled in and arranged my truck to be the next one unloaded. I received the signal to back into position and completed my assignment. I shut down the engine and locked the emergency break. Suddenly, one of the goons that I had trouble with earlier appeared and headed for my truck. I was out of the truck quickly and ready for trouble. He slowed his pace and put his hand out indicating that he didn't want any trouble. He stood back several yards and informed me that the dock foreman wanted to see me. I told the goon to tell the foreman that he could come outside and see me. He turned around and headed for the dock office. I used that excuse to jump up onto the dock platform and walk around towards the rear of the building. My eyes were like a scanner; quickly observing all that I could in that short while.

I hurriedly checked to see if there was a big hatch opening on the deck of the barge. Damn! There were about 30 hatches on the deck of the barge. A few were open as the crane that we noticed the night before, was loading one unit down into one of the hatches. I had seen enough that I could pass onto Ed. While I casually looked over at the Clinton and took in the sights, I could sense someone standing behind me but I chose to ignore whoever it was.

"She's a beauty, isn't she, Mr. Sprague?" the voice asked from behind. I turned slowly, looked at him, and acknowledged his comment.

"I'm Donnie Costello," he said. "I'm the dock foreman you told my guy to give your message to."

"Oh," I said. He proceeded to be very nice and tried to explain that his men that were following me were doing so only for my protection.

"Well they had a real cloak and dagger way about them and I didn't appreciate their rudeness and mannerisms. They need to be taught another way of conducting business if they are supposed to be protecting people. All they had to do was introduce themselves and explain their presence at the beginning of this trip and all would have been fine. I might have bought them lunch or dinner if they had been civil. Anyway, what's so goddamned secret about these shipments?" I asked. He explained that the platforms were the fireworks company's competitive secret in the business world. IH didn't want John Deere, Kubota or anyone else assembling theses platforms for the fireworks company thereby taking business away from them. It all made sense, but I still wasn't convinced that this group was legitimate, so I pushed a little harder.

"Have you heard any news about my friend, George Woodbridge?"

"I don't know a Mr. Woodbrick," he said. Big mistake.

I looked at him and said, "Woodbridge, George Woodbridge."

"Nope, it doesn't ring a bell," he said. *What a lousy bullshit story this guy was trying to peddle,* I thought. He would have been in a better position if he had said what a shame it was that he was missing or that he hoped George would turn up somewhere or something of that nature. He obviously knew the man was my friend.

"I thought George had come up here yesterday on a delivery."

"Really? Well if he did, he must have been assigned to another Harvester plant or depot. I've never met anyone named George Woodbridge." I turned and looked away in disgust. That lying son of a bitch!

"Yeah, she is beautiful," I said. He didn't follow me for a second or two.

"What is beautiful?"

"The Clinton," I said as I noticed a piece of machinery being loaded into one of the large hatches that had been modified into the deck of the barge. The unit looked like the one I had seen just before I had been knocked unconscious by the fork lift. I looked at Donnie while he stared at me and asked, "What kind of equipment are you loading into that barge?" He stumbled for a few seconds to get his words out then began to tell me that they were special electronic fireworks platforms that were being assembled for the upcoming Fourth of July fireworks show that his father and IH were sponsoring for the city. He continued to say that there were a few more barges like this one that had been towed up from Bridgeport, Connecticut by the CTC that were being outfitted in Boston, New York City, New London, Connecticut, and Portsmouth, New Hampshire. He said that this was a real big job for his father's shipping company and that Harvester was the company building the platforms to the specifications that came from the Deutsch Fireworks Company, DFC, of Bonn, Germany. He had told the whole story in five minutes as I slowly walked towards my truck at the loading dock. I knew that I was loaded because the roll down door of the truck was being secured and locked. I was impressed with the story this Donny person told me and even said to him that I would probably attend the New London show because it was only about 20 miles from my home.

"I'll see the show at Newport," he said. "All of them should be great. I'm sure that the Boston and New York shows will be bigger than the others. The most spectacular thing, he said, is that they will all go off at the same hour on the East Coast."I asked if he knew of some possible fuel stations that were available in the area that had ample fuel supplies. He directed me to several that he knew would be able to take care of me and told me to tell them that Donnie Costello had sent me for that would get me fifty cents off each gallon of fuel. "How's the head?" he asked. I looked and said it was just fine. "Good. I heard that you'd been injured."

I thought, *this guy knows about my accident and doesn't know George?* Who did he think he was kidding? I thanked him for the fuel station directions and the favor. I also thanked him for asking about my wound but I did tell him that I did not need protection from his people.

"I must ask that you please oblige the request to insure that the shipments are protected." I looked at him and agreed to allow them to follow me.

"Just tell them that they didn't have to be so clandestine."

"That is my father's plan to assure that all shipments are protected from the competition and the rogues."

"Okay, I understand now, but this company, as well as Harvester, should inform their truckers of this situation and rule," I said.

"You are probably one of the few that know the details of my father's plan and we want to keep it that way. You and Ed are a little too inquisitive and my father felt that you should be informed so that you would understand and stop interfering with our business security plans."

I thanked him for his time and honesty. I started my truck and even waved to the two goons that pulled out behind me as I headed for the Bridges, the toll and the weigh station, the Harvester depot and eventually back to the artery terminal. I was happy that my documents indicated that I was not going to have to return here today for a second run even though I could use the money. I felt a little better but still very worried about what had happened to George Woodbridge. I reached a fuel station that Donnie had recommended. I pulled up and waited in line behind some trucks that were ahead of mine. Within a few minutes I noticed the silver Honda behind me but parked over across from the line of trucks waiting for their turn to be fueled. One of the goons in the Honda approached the fuel attendant and began a conversation. Within seconds, another attendant approached my truck and waved at me to get out of line and follow him as he walked to an open pump. I followed him. He jumped up onto my running board and asked me how much fuel I needed. I indicated the amount that I thought each tank would require and said that Donnie Costello had sent me to him with his compliments. He indicated that he knew that. Within minutes the attendant completed filling each tank. He told me the amount for the 50 gallons I had taken. I realized that Donnie had saved me about $25. I thanked him and quickly paid him. I guess the two goons had introduced my favored status to the attendant.

As I left the station and passed by the Honda, I smiled and nodded my head in appreciation. The two goons looked the other way. I quickly dialed Ed at the artery terminal to tell him I was on my way to the terminal and explain what I had been told by Donnie. Ed picked up this time and said, "McAuliffe here."

Missing Details

I gave Ed a very detailed report of my conversation with Donnie Costello. He didn't say a word as I rattled on about what I had seen and been told. When I finished, I waited for a response. None was given. I asked, "Did you hear a goddamned word I said?"

"Yes, I heard you! Just wait a minute," he barked back. "I'm online and I'm looking up something you said," he said lowering his tone.

I waited for him to find whatever he was looking for online. I heard him say, "Son of a bitch!" Then there was silence. I put the cell phone on speaker so I could free up my hands then I turned the AC back on. I was sweating and my stitches were beginning to itch like hell. I waited a few seconds more when finally, he said, "Jon, thatDeutsch Fireworks Company in Bonn, Germany is big business."

"So, it's big and in Germany," I said loudly.

"I talked to Brian an hour ago and he chewed my ass out a little for our midnight escapade. He said that the FBI and CIA and everyone else that had something to do with national security were very interested in this company and its ties to terrorist organizations."

I sarcastically asked, "Are they selling the terrorist fireworks to blow up the world? What kind of bullshit is that, Ed?"

"Look, there's some information the authorities collected on them. They have been selling explosives to some known contacts that had ties to terrorist groups. Also, the Costello Shipping Company, especially Donnie Costello, was being watched by the State Police in Rhode Island as well as Joshua's FBI office. Donnie is the head of the Ernesto Costello family now. I guess his old man was showing signs of Alzheimer's and the kid has taken on the reins of the business." Ed continued, "The old man had been, and was still, involved with shipping contraband and other illegal cargo, but the kid was moving into foreign contraband that included shipments of cargo in Jordan, Lebanon, and Syria. The CIA is now investigating shipments to Saudi Arabia."

"Wow," I said.

"The Costello family is also involved in stolen battery shipments to European and Asian auto manufacturers. Batteries are at a premium now for all the hybrids because auto manufacturers are willing to pay the high cost to anyone who can supply batteries to them."

"You got all this from Josh and Brian today?"

"No, dammit. I put shit together as Brian was chewing my ass out and letting out a little too much information that Joshua had told him." He had a higher and irritated tone to his voice now.

"Where are you now?"

"I'll be at the IH depot in a half hour or so."

"Okay. Drop off your load at the Harvester depot and meet me at my home instead. I have more to tell you but I don't want Dan or anyone else at the terminal hearing me talk to you on the terminal phone." I guess he was worried that anyone could pick up and listen in. I asked him, "What if I had to make another run to Newport for them today? George was supposed to do that when he disappeared on the second run."

Ed said, "Look, just go there, get unloaded and head for my house. Do you understand?" I was going to argue when he said, "Just tell them you will be back in an hour to get loaded for another trip if they have a second trip for you. It won't take very long for me to fill you in on what I have been up to." I acknowledged his request and closed the cell phone.

I was at the Harvester depot a short while later. I did the usual docking technique, handed in my shipping documents and waited to be unloaded. After the unloading, nobody approached my truck for a few minutes until Sid came out and just handed me the signed documents. I looked at him as he walked away without saying a word. I opened up the door and stood on the running board and yelled. He stopped in his tracks.

"Is there another load for Newport tomorrow?" I asked.

"Yes, in the morning."

"Fine, I'll be here by seven a.m., Wednesday morning," I said as I closed the truck's door. Screw him, I thought. He was being an asshole. I started the truck and headed for Ed's house. When I arrived at Ed's house, I told him that I had the signed documents from the Harvester depot. He told me to set them on the table. He then handed an envelope to me as I sat down at his kitchen table.

"What's this?" I inquired.

"Your pay from the Newport delivery," he said as he began to collect some paperwork that he had set on the kitchen table. "That was fast," I said as I counted the cash and looked at the receipt that accompanied the money. I watched Ed as he pondered the notes and prints from the internet. A few minutes passed as Ed began to organize his findings into a cohesive sequence of events that he thought could explain George's disappearance and what the Costello family was up to. He began to present his findings to me.

"George must have seen or found out something when he was at Newport."

"That's obvious."

"Please shut up and take me seriously and stop with that condescending sarcasm you have when you're scared; just like I am. You talk too much and you're sarcastic when shit bothers you." I just looked at him and smirked but he understood that I would be quiet while he presented his information. I figured that I would grab some type of cold drink from his refrigerator. He barked at me to stay still and listen. I obliged him and sat down at the kitchen table again. He repeated himself about George but said that whatever George had seen or heard the Costello family wasn't the ones who didn't want him getting a chance to tell anyone. I butted in to remind him that I probably saw the same thing George did but I was left alone to be able to return from Newport.

"You got stopped by Donnie before you could look inside the barge," he said. "Now shut up and just listen, please." I sat back and nodded. "Donnie had allowed you to get close to the barge and then gave you enough information to make you feel at ease about almost everything except he denied knowing who

George was. He could have been telling the truth because Donnie was not at the Harvester plant yesterday when George arrived with the first load. Gene Moretti was in charge. I remembered talking to Gene a few days ago when Tommy Lupinacci had asked him to call the Newport plant to coordinate deliveries and drivers. Gene was the guy in charge then and when George was delivering that cargo." I listened and made sure I didn't break Ed's train of thought. "The units that you had first been inquisitive about were supposed to be special firework units that IH was assembling for the DFC. These so called units, that were so goddamned secret to Harvester and highly protected and shipped by the Costello family, seemed too secret to me too, so I looked into different kinds of fireworks companies internationally that arranged shows like the one Newport is going to have on Friday, the Fourth of July. I couldn't find any kind or type of gadget that even remotely looked like, or, was close to the size of that unit you described being covered and loaded into your truck. I'm sure the size of George's truck and yours are almost identical as to storage capacity and only two units at a time could fit into each truck. This was a known fact. That made them about ten feet wide by twelve feet long I figured. I did some more investigating and began to look around at different fireworks systems that Deutsch had used in the past and couldn't find anything of interest," he said. "You said that Donnie explained in detail that these units were electronic units that sequenced the fireworks during the show, right?" I nodded my head. "I think he really thinks that they are some type of fireworks units." I continued to listen. "I don't think any type of fireworks have been brought to the site because there was too much work going on in the barge the night we were there," he said. I was getting a little unnerved but I wasn't sure why.

"Old man Ernesto Costello is a Korean War vet. He was at the Chosen Reservoir in Korea with the U.S. Marines. He was wounded there and returned home as a highly decorated hero. The old man received a silver star besides some other medals for his part in that campaign. Ernesto was very proud of being a Marine. Even Donnie spent some time in the Marines. He saw some action during the Gulf War in an amphibious brigade in Kuwait. Both of them are Legionnaires like we are," Ed said. "So what are you saying? Are the Costello's criminals and patriotic at the same time. That doesn't make sense." The statement interrupted his train of thought. "Think about it. The Costello family is moving goods around in mid-eastern countries, making money and Ernesto and Donnie think that everything is just fine. There are no ties to a terrorist group?" Before he answered, he got up and walked to the refrigerator, took out two beers, opened them and handed me one.

"Where the hell did you get those?" I blurted out in astonishment. I hadn't seen a bottle of beer in ages and almost thought I'd never get to taste one again. He looked at me, smiled and said, "The Costello family." He then corrected himself and said that Sid Owlia had given him a few. "I saved them for a special occasion but I need something to ease this tension and this is such an occasion. Give me the bottle when you're done so that I can smash it and destroy any evidence. If some rogue could figure out by my garbage that I had groceries like this, they'd burn my house down to get at the partially opened thirty-pack that I have stashed away in the cellar. I only put a few bottles at a time in the refrigerator," he said. I said nothing. I just listened and slowly sipped my beer. Ed was staring at the wall as if he was piecing together what he knew. "I checked out Owlia through Brian and Josh," he said finally. "Josh told Brian that Owlia was originally from Iran. He came to this country as a kid some forty years ago. He has done some traveling for Costello in some of those mid-eastern countries setting up deals for the Costello shipping business. Sid was in the Marines with Donnie in Kuwait. Another coincidence probably, but Donnie was smart enough to get Sid into his organization because Sid speaks very good Arabic and can assist him in making those business deals. Josh seems to think that from the time these guys left the Marines, Sid got tied up with some shady characters over there unbeknownst to Donnie.

Josh has information connecting Sid with some known brokers for terrorists looking for explosives and weapons. Donnie thinks he's making money moving questionable cargo for his Middle Eastern clients while Sid is knee deep in some kind of shit." Ed looked at me and asked, "Am I making any sense?" "Too much."

"So while Donnie thinks he is moving some secret cargo and probably other illegal shit for his clients, I think Sid is actually in some sub-plot and I'm not sure what he is up to. Brian and Josh are watching him, as well as a whole bunch of other people in the security business. What you need to do is keep running the loads as they want from the different docks they tell us to ship to. We were told again by Josh through Brian to keep our eyes and ears open and our mouths shut."

"Oh that statement again," I mumbled. I asked Ed, "Does Brian or Josh have any inclination as to what could have happened to George?"

"They both feel he probably got too close to something and unfortunately paid the price.

"You telling me they think that George is dead but they haven't made any attempt to shut down the Harvester plant or check out that barge or anything like that," I began to raise my voice. "Look, Jon, I think they will watch these guys for a while to see where the trail leads them. George, you or me don't mean shit. But your son and my nephew want us to keep out of harm's way and we have been instructed to stop snooping and only be observant. I already got two phone calls today from them and they were very upset with us for getting involved in something that they've been watching for a while now."

I looked at Ed and thought to myself, why hadn't Josh, my own son, given me a call to tell me this information directly. Why did I have to hear it from Ed? Something just wasn't right. As I finished my beer, I said, "There's a lot to think about. I'm pretty amazed that you figured all this out with all the players and twists and turns of this thing. I didn't have a clue what these guys were hauling or what kind of people they were working for."

Ed just sat back and finished his beer and said, "Well I'm just trying to piece this thing together with all the information I got from here and there. Not a bit of what I think I know has been confirmed by anyone of authority."

"Well, I'm going on home to think about what you just theorized."

"Look Sprague, you need to keep all these theories to yourself because they're just that, theories. I don't want to get more involved in this thing then what we already are. Jean doesn't need to know what we talked about."

"Okay," I said, nodding in affirmation. "I will keep quiet until we know what is going on and it's safe enough to tell Jean. There's no need to upset her." I shook Ed's hand and told him I was spent for the day. "All this information and cloak and dagger shit have made me tired," I said as I began to leave. "I'll see you in the morning," he said. I left his house, got into the truck and immediately called Jean's cell phone. Surprisingly she answered, "Hello."

"Where are you?"

"I'm on the bus. I'll be home in a few minutes. I got off early and I'm glad because I'm so tired. I'm heading straight home for a bath and some relaxation."

"Looks like we're in the same condition. I'm on my way but I want to run some information by you to see if I'm getting old, too paranoid or just going crazy." She paused before she said, "You have something to tell me that is really bothering you, don't you?"

"Yes, I do." I said and closed the cell phone. It was a long 15 minute drive home.

Gene Moretti was driving his black SUV from Newport to Norwich, Connecticut when his cell phone rang. Before he could utter a word, the voice on the other end of the phone said, "Make sure Sprague is taken care of." Before Moretti could answer, the phone went dead.

Moretti closed his cell phone and said out loud to himself, "He's an arrogant asshole.

111

All Alone

I could see Jean was waiting for me by the kitchen door. It was still about 85 degrees and I noticed that she had all the windows in the house open. She was attempting to cool the place down enough for it to be bearable to eat dinner comfortably in the heat. The house always became very hot but we dared not leave any windows open or unlocked while we were at work. The rogues always were casing out homes in the neighborhood to see if anyone left a window open. They usually could be in and out of a home in five minutes. They usually took your food first. If they had time, they looked for stuff that they could sell on the black market.

She had a cold drink of water waiting for me as I secured the truck and walked into the kitchen. By the look on my face, the first thing that she said was, "What's wrong?" I thanked her for the water, took a long drink and seated myself at the kitchen table. I motioned her to do the same. I went through all the details I could remember that Ed had told me. I took my time to make sure I had relayed the information to her accurately. Jean never said a word as I relayed the story to her. Before I could begin to ask her opinion, she looked at me and said, "I think Ed is lying, too."

"What?"

"He's lying to you and you know it, don't you?" I asked her how she came to that conclusion. "I can tell by your facial expressions and tone of voice that you don't believe a word he said and you are usually right." I smiled.

"The idea that he's lying has crossed my mind for one main reason. Joshua did not call me nor has he spoken to me except for a one minute call that I received on your cell phone last night in which he said that he'd been watching Ed and me."

"You are absolutely right. Your son and you might have differences of opinions but he's still your son and he would call you directly. Ed McAuliffe is not family," Jean said.

"Yet, Ed wants me to believe that my own son might have

some pertinent information involving a dangerous situation that I'm snooping around in, and he calls Ed to tell him and not me? That makes no sense or maybe he wants me to call Joshua? Shit, Ed is playing some game and I'm not familiar with the rules." I stood up from the kitchen table and said, "I'm going up to Joshua's office as soon as I can get in touch with him."

"We can't afford the fuel for the truck to get up to Providence," she said.

"We could use the 2009 Toyota Hybrid that's been sitting, locked in the garage, for a long while. I could get her fired up and running again."

We hadn't used the Toyota Hybrid very much because of the rogues. People had resorted to public transportation for two reasons: cost and safety. I realized that I would have to spend $100 or so on fuel to get up to see Josh, but I thought it was worth it. I needed to talk to Joshua directly about what I had seen, heard and what was going on with all the other people I had been in contact with. I was sure that after talking to him I'd be able to make a sound decision as to whether I needed to back out of this situation and get on with my local delivery business. She agreed the trip would be worth it. I looked at her and told her to call him and then tell him that you were putting me on the line. I always had Jean call him because he would always pick up the call if he saw her number on caller ID. If I called, he would always let it go to voice mail. I think he always figured that finding out what I wanted first, during his busy day, usually kept him from arguing with me in front of his agents. When I called, it was usually to tell him to call his mother. He'd go, sometimes, as long as a week without touching base with her. That made her a little on edge and usually ruined my day or even the whole week. So I'd tweak him, a little, to get him off his ass to call his mother. Of course, I'd do it without Jean knowing. Josh and I sometimes had some personality clashes. Well, probably, almost always.

Jean called and immediately reached Joshua. She talked about some incidentals for a short while but then told him that his father wanted to talk to him. As Jean finished her sentence, she had put the cell on speaker phone so that both of us could communicate with him. Josh began to say to Jean, "Tell Dad..." I immediately interrupted as Jean glared at me. "Joshua, I do not want to hear from anyone, including the chosen child of the FBI, that I am to keep my eyes and ears open and my mouth shut ever again, do you understand that?"

"Dad, you never do what anyone says for you to do anyway so why would an explicit order from the FBI or any other group with national security interests be any different?"

Jean cut in right away before any more salvos could be fired by the two men in her life that she loved the most and apparently knew were too much alike to communicate.

"Josh and Jon, stop it this instant. Do you both hear me?" She glared at me and waited for Joshua to respond. Joshua was quiet. When he spoke, he acknowledge Jean's request and asked me to continue. I was still his father so I said all that I wanted to.

"If you want to give me an ass chewing then give it to me directly. Why didn't you talk to me directly about all the information I had to hear through Ed McAuliffe? And why didn't you fill me in on the Costello family or about Sid Owlia's ties to Middle Eastern terrorists groups and shit?"

Josh stopped me. "Dad, I didn't chew you and Ed out for the bike escapade. I was doing mom a favor by keeping an eye on you both and I did not tell Ed any of that information that you are telling me about now. Ed McAuliffe was not privy to any information through me," he said.

"Well, Ed specifically said that you had passed information down through Brian McAuliffe."

"I did not. I'm amazed to hear some of the stuff you are saying, Dad."

This was an eye opener. If what he says is true, then Ed was lying. I decided to tell him all that I could remember that I had seen or heard in the last 48 hours. Joshua told me that he needed me to continue talking with Ed and Brian if the occasion warranted itself and to inform him on a daily basis what Ed, Brian, Sid or anyone else had to say.

114

"What do you think is going on here?" he asked.

"I don't know but there has to be a reason why Ed McAuliffe wants people to know that he knows something is going on with the Costello Family and their branches in the tri-state area and that they have ties to foreign businesses."

Joshua became quiet for a few seconds. You could hear him sigh and then he requested something that we never contemplated. Josh asked us to consider staying with Missy and Joe for a while. Jean's face turned white.

"Why are you requesting that we stay with Missy and Joe?" she asked.

"Mom and Dad, something is going on that Mr. McAuliffe feels needs to be addressed by the FBI. Until I can do some investigative work on my own and get a better perspective on this, my first inclination is safety for you both. Dad you need to…" I interrupted him by saying I knew that he wanted me to keep my eyes and ears open and my mouth shut.

"Not at all, Dad, just don't tell Ed that you talked to me. Keep him thinking that he is the only source of all this information. I'll call you both nightly. Do not tell him anything." I agreed.

"Your mom will be at Missy and Joe's tonight but I'm gonna stay home as if everything is normal. I don't want to risk any chance that some rogue would be able to get in here knowing that no one is home in the evenings and through the nights."

Josh did not protest and said, "Alright, I'll have someone keep an eye on the house during the evenings and nights."

"I'll call Joe to arrange for him to pick me up," Jean said.

"That's okay Mom. I'll take care of that. Be ready within the hour."

"Thanks Josh."

"It's okay Mom and Dad, thanks for telling me what happened. I'll be in touch daily. I love you both," he said, and hung up.

Jean didn't speak as she stood up and went to the bedroom to gather some clothing and personal items. I sat there and thought about what had just transpired. There were a lot of unanswered questions and too many unknowns. Our apprehension was pushed to a higher level after that call. The only bright spot was that I wouldn't have to spend any money on fuel for the Toyota Hybrid to go and see Josh.

I was sitting at the kitchen table when Joe pulled up to our house in a cruiser about 20 minutes after we had spoken to Josh. Jean was almost ready. Joe came in and joked like he always did when he saw me.

"How's that thick skull of yours?" he asked.

"It's real itchy and I would be glad in a few more days when Jean can pull the stitches out."

Jean came from the bedroom and said, "Those stitches will be in his head for, at least, another six days. They'll be in longer if he doesn't take better care of himself."

I just winked at him and said she knew better.

"Damn right I do," she remarked. Joe laughed and asked if she was ready. She acknowledged and then she came over to the table. I stood as she hugged me and told me what was in the refrigerator for supper.

"I'll grab a bite at Missy's, Jon." She looked at me and began to talk when I put my fingers to my lips and then to her that indicated that I knew what she was about to say and that I would come by Missy's daily or see her at the hospital on my delivery rounds. I then said that she really needed to keep her cell in her pocket and on so that I could talk to her when I was unable to come by due to scheduling conflicts. Her eyes glistened and she turned and grabbed Joe's arm and left.

"I'll make sure to have some patrol cars buzz the place during the evening hours," he said. I thanked him.

What the hell had I gotten myself into to have my kid and son-in-law instructing the FBI and Connecticut State Police respectfully to keep an eye on some old son of a bitch like me? I remembered my Colt in the truck and I went out to get it. Then I went to the closet and retrieved the remaining rounds in a box that I stored there. I also pulled out my Remington 12 gauge pump shot gun. I hadn't used the shot gun in years but it was in good shape. I had some bird shot shells but I looked for the double odd buck shot shells I knew I had somewhere in the closet. I found the box. There were seven left from a dozen shell box. I also found my Eagle Arms five shot 22 caliber derringer. It held 22 longs very nicely. My dad had passed that on to me back in 1994. It mounted on a belt buckle and looked like an ornament but it could kill very quickly in the right hands. I never used the belt buckle holder but I liked the way it fit into my sock and covered up very easily with my pant leg. Now that I had inventoried my arsenal, I was hungry. I opened up the refrigerator and began to prepare some supper.

Jean called to tell me she was at Missy's. She put the grandkids on for a few minutes. It was fun to talk with them. They were growing so fast and had more mature conversations it seemed every day. The best came out of them when Jean was around them. I guess grandmothers did that to grandkids. They seemed to have the patience that the grandkid's parents hadn't learned yet and their grandfathers had forgotten about. I told her that I was going to get to bed early, maybe watch some TV for a while until I got sleepy. We traded our goodbyes and I hung up. I watched the news in bed for a while until my eyes became very heavy. I realized that I should double check the house one more time before retiring. With all that accomplished, I slid into the sheets and immediately pushed off the top one. I was too hot for anything to be touching my skin. I laid there for a while and looked at the clock. It was only 8:45 p.m. when I must have fallen off to sleep. I awoke drenched in sweat and I had to pee. It was still hot out this evening. The clock indicated 11:52 p.m. I continued to lay there until the urge to go to the bathroom was too uncomfortable. I arose and headed to the bathroom. I completed my business and on my return, took a few seconds to open a blind to glance out a window. I noticed that there was a black four door sedan parked down the street. Now I was wide awake.

In an instant, I quickly grabbed my pants and tee shirt that I had left by the bed and quickly put them on. My stitches were tender as I slid the tee shirt over my head. I put the derringer, after I had checked it, into my sock when I had completed lacing up my shoes. I placed the Colt in the small of my back and then picked up the shot gun and put five shells into the chamber. For a second, I felt safe and invincible, then reality set in and I was scared and nauseous. I didn't change any light settings as I walked around the house. Almost all the rooms were dark except for the bathroom night light and the front and rear outside house lights. I always kept them on despite the cost to keep unwanted visitors away or, at least, discourage them a little. I didn't want to exit the house to check on the black Sedan and be seen by the outside lights. I didn't want to use the kitchen door because it led to the light and complete exposure for me. I also knew that by leaving the house through the kitchen garage door, that there was a window far away from any light from either the front or rear of the house. I quietly entered the garage, felt my way around the Toyota and unlocked the window I planned to exit from. In a few seconds I was out and slowly walking in the shadows of the garage when I heard the sound of a car approaching. In a few seconds I could see the headlights on the street as I crouched down. The car passed slowly. It was a black Sport Utility Vehicle. I thought it looked like the kind that the FBI still used. They were the only ones that used those types of vehicles because nobody wanted to pay the expense to run them these days. But then I saw the SUV slowly pass the black Sedan but made no effort to stop to check it out. The lights from the SUV clearly showed that it was a Buick Sedan and that there wasn't anyone in it. I waited to see if anyone would return to the car but it was difficult to see anyone from this distance. Another car could be heard coming down the street. I crouched again to see what this one was. Sure enough, it was a State Police cruiser. It did stop at the Buick and shined its lights directly on it.

While the Buick was lit up the trooper opened the door and walked over to the car. While shining his flash light in the Buick a shot rang out from the other side of the street and shattered the driver's side rear window of the Buick. Apparently someone had taken a shot at the trooper but had missed. The trooper immediately crouched down while drawing his automatic pistol. He was still in the light but managed quickly to get to the opposite side of the sedan out of harm's way and out of my sight. I could hear him calling into his shoulder mounted radio requesting support. There was no mistaking his request as I heard him say, "Shot fired at trooper, request immediate backup." I was pleased to know he was okay and had called for assistance but then I had a reality check. Here I was, crouched down and half hidden, carrying a pistol and a shotgun as well as a hidden derringer. I quickly decided to exit this situation and get back inside through the garage window. I was sure that there would be enough police here in the next few minutes to warrant anyone with any sense to stay inside and out of the way.

As I slowly tried to get back to the window I saw the dark outline of a person coming through the bushes that separated my home from my neighbors. I slid the safety off of the shot gun and froze to see where this guy would be going. He was coming from the direction of where the Buick had been parked and I knew this must have been the guy who took the shot at the trooper. He stopped for a second and looked in my direction. I was sure that he had seen me. Just then he waved his other hand and a second person emerged from the bushes from where the first guy had come from. They were both heading towards my house and towards the unlit area where the window was still open. I knew two things for sure. They were the ones that probably had owned the Buick when the trooper spooked them and they were heading for the open window of my garage. My third thought was that they were coming for me originally and they had to be up to no good no matter what. The seconds passed. I stood still in my crouched position and aimed. I figured at this distance, if I kept my aim low, I could injure them enough to keep them from entering the garage through the window. I pulled the trigger and the old shotgun erupted. My eyes were temporarily blinded by the flash but I immediately heard one of them scream. He continued to scream and call out to his companion for help. He yelled that his legs were burning and he needed help. His companion never answered.

As I moved away from the area that I had originally shot from, my eyes were adjusting from the flash. I could see the guy who was yelling and he seemed to be rolling around. Then I noticed that the other one was in a fetal position and motionless. Suddenly, I heard someone approaching through the bushes just as I heard sirens blaring in the distance. Still staying in the shadows and listening to my heart beating in my ears, I yelled over to the approaching person to stop where he was because I had a weapon and that he was trespassing. The voice immediately instructed me to lay my weapon down. He said that he was armed and ready. I yelled back and told him my name and I was also armed and ready. He did not come into sight from the bushes until I told him that two men were lying near the open window of my garage. One was motionless and I said that I knew he could hear the other one moaning and occasionally screaming. He commanded me to come into sight and I informed him that I would come into sight when the rest of the police cars, that were on the way, arrived here. He told me for the second time to appear and lay down my arms. I repeated what I had said about waiting. He informed me that the men that I had apparently shot were in need of medical attention and that I was wasting time. I told him that I was not concerned about their immediate medical needs and they should have thought of that when they took the first shot at him. I felt uneasy still and moved away from the immediate area but I still kept out of his view in the shadows with my shotgun pointed in his direction. I saw him stand up and approach slowly. Just then, someone else said, "Police, do not take another step or you will be shot." The guy that was talking to me froze dead in his tracks. The new voice said again, "Police, do not take another step or you will be shot." The guy that I had been watching suddenly turned in the direction of the voice. To my horror, he dropped straight on his back from the impact of the force from the flash that I saw. I kept still until the voice said to me, "Mr. Sprague, are you okay?" Still cautious and scared I answered only, "Yes." He lit his flash light and pointed in the direction of the man who now lay on his back and very still. He quickly flashed the light on the first and second individuals lying on my lawn near the garage window. The one in the fetal position was bleeding from his chest and abdomen while the other guy was still now but holding both legs with his hands that were covered in blood. Both pistols that they had been carrying were on the lawn, out of their hands but within their reach. The trooper kicked them away as I had my shotgun still pointed in his direction. The trooper walked over to the third guy who was still motionless and lying on his back. I noticed that he had a blood stain in the middle of his chest from the trooper's bullet. He was apparently dead. The trooper told me that my shot gun had hit both the other two men.

Within minutes, my yard was full of State Police. Some of the troopers assisted the wounded laying near my garage window until the ambulances arrived. I stood almost frozen in the muggy night heat and watched everything going on around me until I felt someone put a hand on my shoulder. I looked at the hand and then up at the individual who had rested it there. I recognized that it was Joe. He asked me if I was okay. I just nodded. He turned to a trooper that was standing next to him and told him that I was his father-in-law. I recognized that trooper to be the one that had shot and killed the guy that was trying to trick me into thinking he was the trooper.

"How did you know that that guy was not a trooper?" the trooper asked.

I looked at him and asked, "What is your name, son?" He couldn't have been more than 25. Joe interrupted and said, "Jon, this is Trooper Matt Smith. He's in my barracks."

"Mr. Sprague, you didn't answer my question."

"I didn't at first. But then I thought he talked too much for a cop and he didn't identify himself as a cop at the beginning of his statement to me. He also never showed any command in his voice as all cops do."

Trooper Smith smiled and said, "Lucky for you that you noticed that."

Joe asked me to give him my shotgun. I looked at him and said,

"Joe, I'm on my land standing near my home and if I didn't have this weapon you would have been calling Jean, Missy and your kids to tell them that I was shot dead. I'm not giving you or anyone here my weapon while I'm on my land. Carrying firearms is not a crime if you're carrying them on your property. I am on my property, Joe."

"Jon, you are absolutely right but I need the shotgun for evidence that you shot these guys in self defense and that the State Police is responsible for the death of the individual lying dead over there. You'll get the shotgun back," he said.

"Oh," was my only response.

Joe took the shotgun away and over to his cruiser. He returned a few minutes later and said, "One of the guys that you shot is in serious but stable condition. He was shot in the chest and abdomen but there's no vital organ damage. The second guy is in guarded condition with wounds to his thighs and shins. He'll be questioned later as to who and why he was outside your home tonight."

He looked over at the third guy that was being loaded into the body bag for a trip to the morgue and said, "He was shot through the heart and died instantly." I should have felt strange but I could care less that this guy was dead. I had no remorse for a guy that would come into my home and try to kill my wife and me. I immediately thought to call Jean but that would have to wait until all the questions from the police had been answered.

About an hour went by before I asked Joe who was supervising the troopers that were still in my yard and if I could leave and go back inside my house.

"Joe, I need to call Jean and tell her what has just happened."

"I already called Missy to tell her what did happen and that you were alright. I'm sure she told Jean. Jon, you'll need to come by the State Police barracks in the morning to fill out some more paperwork and answer some more questions," Joe said.

"I'll be there later in the morning. I have a delivery first thing and won't return from Newport until late morning."

"I'll make note of that and file it with the police barracks to let them know when to expect you. You know, the two guys that were wounded had robbed a house a few houses down from you," he said. "They'd been on their way back to the Buick Sedan when Trooper Smith came upon them. They did a dumb thing by firing at him. The guy that was killed is still unidentified. The police found a Black SUV down the road with rental plates on it. They are investigating him. They didn't think he was involved with the robbers at this time but they didn't know why he chose to get involved. Maybe he could have been on his way to your house when the two robbers got in the way," he said. "He had no ID on him so the State Police have some work to do. They're going to have to wait for the first of the two injured guys to get out of surgery to question to see if there is any connection."

I stepped into the house and called Jean. She already knew briefly what had happened. Jean's voice sounded quivery. She asked if I was okay and then started to cry. I told her I was okay now and that I was very happy she was with Missy and Joe. I also explained that I didn't think anything else would happen tonight based on all the commotion that had just taken place here. We talked for about five minutes when I told her that I would see her as soon as I returned from Newport later tomorrow morning. She pleaded for me to be in constant touch with her and to be very careful. I said I would on both accounts.

I dialed Joshua at his apartment. It rang several times before Josh's voice came on.

"Special Agent Joshua Sprague. 'I quickly explained, in detail, what had happened.

"I know. I received a call a half hour ago from some of the agents in the vicinity. Dad, did you say anything to the State Police or Joe about our conversation earlier this evening?"

"No," I said hesitantly, catching the phrase, "agents in my vicinity".

"What the hell do you mean by 'agents in my vicinity'?" Josh quietly acknowledged the seriousness of what had happened but he said that the agents had driven by earlier and were

123

keeping radio channels of the local and state police open. They heard the radio call go out from the officer who had been shot at, he explained.

"They were probably the guys in the SUV that went by just before the State Police cruiser stopped to actually check out the Buick that was parked near the house."

"Our agents do not drive SUVs anymore."

I didn't say anything more. Right then, I knew that the guy in the Black SUV was looking for me.

"I'm glad that you're okay, Dad. I'll call you in the morning. I should have a lot more information for you about what happened and anything else I can find out. You know, you're still a pain in my ass," he said. "Be careful and I love you."

I put the phone down and looked out the window one more time. The adrenaline was quickly fading away. I was winding down now and becoming very sleepy despite having the police's crime scene investigators still outside and working in my yard. I crawled onto the couch as I looked at my watch; it was Wednesday, July 2nd, 2:45 a.m.

The Next Delivery

The alarm startled me even though it was in the bedroom. It was 4:45 a.m. I walked to the bedroom to hit the snooze button for 15 more minutes. I realized I was still dressed. I was wet with sweat. Luckily, I could afford the fuel to warm the water because I desperately needed to shower. I relaxed for a few minutes as the warm water massaged my neck. I let the spray cleanse the sweat from my stitches. I used a mild shampoo and washed the wound gently. I could feel the stitches but the wound did not hurt to the touch. I thoroughly washed and was out and dressed in 15 minutes. I grabbed some of the bread Jean had received from our neighbors and toasted several pieces. We didn't have any butter but peanut butter had become one of our staples. It was cheap, filling and tasted good on toast even before we were forced to eat it regularly. I was half way through eating the toast and peanut butter when I noticed that the bread had mold on it. I lost my appetite. It was just as well because I didn't want to be late getting to the depot to pick up my main run to Newport this morning. Then my cell phone rang.

"Jon, Ed here."

"What happened at your place last night?"

"What do you mean?"

"You got to be shitting me, what do I mean? The robbers and the guy that was killed in your yard," he yelled into phone. "It's in the paper and on the local news." I told him that I had just gotten up and I hadn't read any paper or turned on the news yet. I told him I was still very tired.

"Well the news and the papers reported that three robbers were caught and shot in your yard last night by the State Police. They said two had been wounded and one had been killed and that a trooper was investigating a robbery alarm when these guys began shooting at him and they all ended up in your yard."

I continued to listen to get as much information from him as I could before I said anything. He insisted that when I got to the terminal I would have to come to his office and fill him in on all the details.

"What else is happening in this small community?" he asked in wonder. I didn't answer him but said instead that I would see him as soon as I parked at the terminal loading dock. I closed the cell and got ready to leave the house for the terminal. Within a few minutes I was on the highway. I looked into the mirror and saw my buddies. The silver Honda was behind me, keeping its distance and its occupants observing me. I pulled into the terminal lot and lined my truck up to the dock. Dan Kelly waved me back and I gently touched my rear bumper to the rubber stopper on the dock. I shut off the truck and went into Ed's office. Ed smiled as I came in and asked me if I was alright.

"Yep. All that happened to me was that I lost a lot of sleep."

"You have to go to the State Police barracks to answer some questions right?"

"They asked me to come by today after my run to Newport this morning,"

"Did the police identify any of the men?"

"As far as I knew, they were local robbers who happened to be at the wrong place at the wrong time. They made a mistake when they panicked at the sight of the trooper checking out their car."

"How'd they end up in your yard?"

I told him that the trooper must have pushed them towards my house when they first fired at him.

"That trooper must have been a good shot to get all three of them. Sid Owlia said that the whole neighborhood was awakened by all the sirens going off and lights flashing. He also said that two of them were hit with buck shot."

"The trooper had a shotgun when I saw him in my yard," I said.

"Oh." Ed changed the subject. "You have two runs to make for Newport today."

"It's going to be a long day so I guess that I should get going."

126

"Be safe and don't snoop around at Newport. I'm still searching for information on the Costello family and the DFC but so far, I haven't heard of or found anything illegal yet that they are doing." He paused and looked away for a few second as if to gather his thoughts.

"Maybe Brian will call me today with more information. Better yet, Josh might have better information to tell me."

I knew Josh wouldn't be calling him so I said, "Well, call my cell if you find out anything that supports your theory about Donnie Costello, Sid Owlia and the DFC. I actually hope your theory is wrong. I hope someone would investigate George's disappearance thoroughly enough to find out where he is. It's going on forty eight hours now and as every hour passes, I become more convinced that his disappearance is in direct response to something he had seen at the Harvester plant in Newport."

"Do you think the shooting incident at your home was related to any of this?"

I looked him straight in his eyes and said, "No. My yard was a place where three robbers got caught -- period. I don't think there is any connection." Now I was lying back to my closest friend. Dan Kelly came into the office and informed me that my truck was loaded. I looked at Ed and told him that I would keep in touch with him every few hours or so to just to let him know that I was still breathing. Ed looked at me and said, "Don't be a smart ass. Just keep in touch. I don't want you on a second trip to Newport today if you end up behind schedule on the first run for some unknown reason."

"Don't go scheduling another truck and driver for my second run if I fall behind because I really need the money and IH pays well. And besides, I'm the transportation prostitute who does it for the best price."

Ed looked up at me and waved me out of his office. He had a smirk on his face indicating that I could be a real jerk at times. He also knew from his years of experience dealing with me that I joked a lot when I was nervous.

I left the terminal with enough time to stop and grab

something to eat at the service truck parked in the terminal parking lot. I kept the truck running as I jumped out and got in line to get a drink and a bagel with cream cheese. I almost choked when Geno, the attendant, asked for $8.50. *Damn!* I thought. Four bucks for a soda and $4.50 for a lousy bagel! I quickly remembered why I usually ate a liquid breakfast at home with Jean. But Jean wasn't home and the bagel tasted real good. After all, with the shit I had been through, I thought that I should treat myself to a little piece of heaven. I really needed to forget the moldy toast with peanut butter I had partially eaten this morning. I got into the truck and realized I didn't have any napkins. I immediately opened up the truck's glove box to search for one that maybe I had left in there. I took the one napkin that was there out and placed my Colt, which was behind my back in. I thanked the heavenly stars that the thin jacket that I had on hid it. I took off the jacket after I had stored the Colt and began to drive away savoring every bite of that bagel. A few minutes into the drive I realized that I had the derringer in my right sock that was covered very nicely by my pants leg. I decided to keep that there for now.

I arrived at the Harvester depot at 7 a.m. precisely. I performed the usual maneuver and aligned my truck as directed by the dock hand. Sid Owlia watched. He slowly walked over to my cab as I rolled down the window and handed him the transport documents. No words were exchanged. I finished my soda as I sat in the truck and felt it sway a little due to the unloading and eventual loading of cargo. In a very short time Sid approached the cab with the paper work and handed it to me. Again, no words were exchanged. He jumped off the running board. I waited for his signal to be waved on. No wave. He just turned and walked into the depot office. I looked into my other rear view mirror and saw the signal wave from one of the dock hands that it was safe to leave the dock. I acknowledged his signal and slowly drove away from the dock and headed for Newport.

I was about 30 minutes into the trip when my cell phone rang. It was an unknown caller. I let it ring a few more times before I decided to answer it. With all that had gone on in the last few days, I couldn't afford not take a small chance on an unknown caller. I answered it and immediately heard Joshua's voice. "Hi Dad, where are you now?" he asked. I gave him an approximation of where I was and when I expected to arrive at Newport with the load I was carrying. Josh spoke very slowly but distinctly so I would understand every word and not have to ask questions and have him repeat things again. He was like me and had little patience for repetition.

"Dad, I have information on the characters that were at the house last night. The two wounded individuals are local low life rogues who will live to spend quite a bit of time in jail when convicted," he said. I was pleased to hear, early this morning, that I wasn't responsible for killing anyone. "I found out the name and some information of the guy that was shot and killed by the Connecticut State Trooper. His name is Gene Moretti, but better known in the Costello family as Cousin Geno Ernesto Moretti. His mother is Ernesto Costello's sister, Josephine. He comes with an interesting family history. Dominic, Moretti's father, was found face down in Narragansett Bay twenty or so years ago. No one ever knew why he ended up in the drink but we think Ernesto Costello had Dominic removed for cheating on his sister with some of the members of his prostitution ring he was dealing in outside the Costello family business. I guess Ernesto had some family pride to maintain and Dominic wasn't playing within the rules of the family and business. Anyway, Donnie and Gene grew up together in the Costello home and are or I should say, were, close."

My chest tightened as I listened to Josh. I was going to speak when Josh, interrupted. "I really think you are onto something, Dad, and I am concerned that you are in danger for some obvious reasons. I am also going to quietly speak with Ed McAuliffe when I visit him this morning outside of the terminal. He is involved, somehow, and I think he is in over his head and has used you to hopefully put two and two together to get him some help through me and Brian. I talked to Brian and we updated each other on matters we had been investigating and we agree that this is much bigger than we expected. I want you to deliver your cargo as planned today. How many loads are you expected to deliver at the Harvester plant in Newport today?"

I informed him that I had two planned based on the documents and delivery schedules I read and carried.

"What time will your second delivery be?"

"I should be completed by four or five tonight with the second delivery and be leaving Newport then. I should be at Missy and Joe's to see your mom by six-thirty or so this evening. I don't know what the plans are after that."

"Okay, for the next few days let's talk as much as necessary. I want you to make it very obvious that you are communicating with someone while you are being unloaded or loaded at any location whether it is at the artery terminal, the Harvester depot, the Harvester plant or any stop in between. Even if it is a pit stop to pee, I want you communicating with me on the cell. I am very serious about this, Dad, and I want to make sure that you do as I am requesting," he said and then paused to let me answer.

"I understand perfectly. Josh said that he was pleased that I had taken his instructions responsibly and agreed to cooperate with him with no questions or comments. He told me to be safe and hung up.

My stomach was turning and my mouth was watering. I felt as if I was going to throw up. My stitches began to ache but it was probably due to the instant headache I had just developed. I continued my drive, through the weigh station, over the bridges and into Newport without any incident which relaxed me a little enough to get rid of the headache but not the constant turning in my stomach. I figured that once I reached the Newport plant I could ask if they had some kind of a cafeteria or lunch room. Maybe I just needed some real food. The bagel didn't seem to do it. Then I realized that I couldn't do that because Joshua wanted me to keep in constant contact while I was being unloaded and loaded at the Harvester plant. Lunch would have to wait until I was on my way through Newport and before I got to the bridge toll. I would find some very public place to grab some lunch. I kept a constant watch in my rear view mirrors for that Honda that always followed me. There was no sign of it anywhere or for that matter, anyone looking suspicious that could be following me.

My cell phone rang again. This time, it was Ed McAuliffe. I immediately answered it but mentally reviewed Josh's instructions to keep Ed unaware that I had contacted Josh and I knew more details about the situation than Ed knew now. "Hey, Jon, Ed here," he said in a very low tone. "Did you find out who was the guy that the cop killed in your yard last night?"

I played dumb. "No. I don't know who was killed by the cop."

"I don't know why, but I'm scared shitless to think that those guys were looking for you," he whispered to make sure no one could hear him from his office. "Jon, I want you to turn around and come back to the terminal. We can make up some bullshit story that you had truck trouble or something," he continued. I looked into my rear view mirror and now saw the silver Honda tailing me. He must have stayed far enough back and almost out of my view for the entire trip. That was a different behavior than the usual close surveillance they maintained.

"I think you're overreacting but I see that I'm being tailed. I'm sure that if I turn around, these guys in the Honda will make every effort to keep me on track to make sure I reach my destination. If I deliver my cargo and behave like what's expected, no one will be the wiser."

"That is a better idea but we would cancel the second trip," Ed said.

"No. We should keep to the schedule and make like nothing is wrong. Contact Josh and let him know about your suspicion and all the other stuff you know."

Ed said that he would contact Brian right away. I told him that he should call Josh. I explained that this was a federal matter and not a military one. He agreed, told me to be careful and hung up the phone.

131

I had a gut feeling that Ed must be involved with these guys, trying to make a buck or two under the table. He had probably gotten too deeply involved with the Costello family and wanted out without alerting the Costellos that he wanted out. If they knew he was playing both the illegal and legal sides of this situation, he would end up like Gene Moretti. *Worst yet*, I thought, *he'd probably end up like Dominic Moretti. They'd find Ed McAuliffe in the Narragansett Bay, floating face down.* That was a thought that I quickly tried to get out of my mind.

I went through the military checkpoint and could see the Harvester plant down in front of me. As soon as I aligned my truck to the docking platform, I pulled out my cell phone and dialed Josh. He quickly picked up.

"Everything okay?" he asked.

"All seems to be normal so far."

"Good, just keep talking about anything you want and I'll feed you some more information in between some of your pauses, okay?"

"Fine, so what's new?" I asked him and loud enough for the plant attendant that had just taken my paperwork to hear. Josh explained that in a few days the FBI would be checking the plant out to see what was going in it. They were also planning an inspection of the large fireworks barge in the next several days. He also explained that Ed was involved with the Costello family. Josh said that the FBI had checked Ed's savings and checking accounts. They indicated that he was getting extra income which was a lot more than his usual income from the artery terminal foreman's salary. Josh figured that he had stumbled onto something and he was concerned for his safety. He promised me that the FBI wouldn't let Ed stay out there unprotected and scared for too long. He was concerned that the Costello family was going to be looking to eliminate him soon. I told him I was looking for Donnie Costello. I heard Josh quietly say, "Be careful, Dad."

I looked around for Costello and didn't see him. I figured that would be a good excuse to get out of the truck and try to find him. I wanted to personally thank him for the favor he had

132

given to me when I had purchased fuel in Newport. As I exited the truck with my cell phone stuck to my left ear and very visible for all to see, someone asked me to stay in the truck. It was one of the goons that usually followed me in the Honda. I looked over at him but continued to head for the plant's loading dock office. I heard Josh say again, on the phone, "Go easy, Dad."

The goon was now even with me and almost touched my arm when I turned to him in what appeared to him as a defensive posture. He said, "Look, man, get back in the truck."

I answered, still holding the cell to my ear, "I'm looking for Donnie. I want to thank him for the favor he did for me yesterday at the fuel station he sent me to."

"He isn't here today; he's got a death in the family. Get back in the truck," he said for the second time.

I heard Josh quietly say, "Dad, get back in the damned truck, will you?"

I turned to head for the truck. I looked back at the goon and told him, "I'm sorry to hear that Donnie had a death in the family. Give him my condolences, will you." The goon just stared at me and made sure I got back into the truck.

I heard Josh say, "Dad, now you know why I wanted you to stay on the phone. I knew you'd pull some shit like this. Are you in the goddamned truck yet?"

"Yes I am."

"I have to run, get out of there and head back to town. Let me know when you're approaching your next stop," he said before hanging up. I put the phone down as one of the attendants handed the shipping documents to me. He told me that they expected me back here with another load this afternoon.

"Okay, see you in a bit." I started the truck, waited for the docking attendant to wave me out and I was on my way. I noticed the Honda was already waiting for me to move out. I drove through the military checkpoint slowly. I saw a shore patrolman wave me on as I approached the checkpoint. I saw Brian standing with, what appeared to be, the duty officer near the checkpoint office. I hit my air horn and both men looked at me. I waved towards Brian. He made no effort to wave to me and seem oblivious to who I was. I drove by and thought that maybe he was doing that on purpose but then I realized that he probably didn't know that I was hauling cargo to Newport. I was sure Ed had never told him. If Ed hadn't contacted Josh with his bullshit story, I'm sure he hadn't been talking to Brian either. I was sure now that Ed was really deep in this situation and I hoped that Josh would stop his charade soon. Ed was probably getting very desperate now. I was upset that he'd gotten involved with some underhanded business practices but I knew he was honest enough to come clean due to fear and common sense. I'm also sure he was a little embarrassed too.

I was still hungry. I saw a roadside restaurant up ahead. I had seen it several times before on my travels to Newport. It was well exposed and very public. It would be a good place to stop and grab a quick bite to eat. I signaled to pull over, entered the parking lot and saw what appeared to be a takeout window. *That was better yet*, I thought. I exited the truck while pulling out my cell phone like Josh had instructed but pretended to be on the phone talking to someone. I wasn't going to use any more minutes on my cell phone when I thought I didn't need to. I saw the Honda pull in very quickly as I approached the take out window. One of the goons almost tripped as he exited the Honda before the car came to a complete stop in the parking lot. I pretended to be talking as I walked to the take-out window. I could see the goon coming quickly in my direction. I pretended to say goodbye into my cell as I quickly put it into my pocket. I focused on my peripheral vision while I asked the attendant for a ham sandwich, some chips and a diet root beer soda. As I reached for my wallet, the goon yelled, "Get back in the truck, now!" I looked at him while I was still reaching for my wallet and smacked him with my left hand squarely in the nose. It was a good shot. His eyes immediately watered and he was vulnerable for the next shot, which was a kick squarely in the balls. He grimaced in pain as he fell to his knees, not knowing whether to grab his face or privates. He was out of action as I headed for the Honda. The other goon got out of the car and just put his hands up indicating that he did not want any trouble. I kept an eye on the guy who was down on both knees now and trying to recover from the two cheap but necessary shots I had given him. The second goon said that he wanted to help his partner. I told him to stay where he was. I told him that the guy could get up by himself. I thought that I didn't need those two close together to try to overpower me. They were separated now with one out of action and other one not looking for action. The first guy stayed down as I went to the take out window.

"Is my sandwich, chips and drink ready?" I asked the attendant. He said that it would be a few seconds. I kept my eye on the injured goon who just stared at me as he slowly got up and headed towards the Honda for a place to sit down. His nose was bleeding a little now as he sniffed and limped back to the car. I waited for him to get into the car as my food appeared at the take out window. I looked over at his companion, who was now standing next to the driver's side opened door and yelled very loud for all who had started to gather now, "Tell your buddy this is the second time you interfered with my stops! Do not do it a third time!" It sounded real tough but I was sure that I had almost soiled my pants. I paid for my lunch that I didn't want now but knew I had to eat.

I thought about what Josh told me to do when I stopped and this was not in the instructions. I figured, what he didn't know wouldn't hurt him. I was curious if Ed would mention this incident to me. If he did, it would confirm a lot of our suspicions that he was involved with the Costello family. I also made a mental note to try to keep from straying away from the instructions Josh, and even Ed, had given me today. I knew that these guys would relish the first opportunity they had to get back at me. I also knew that they wouldn't do anything to me unless Donnie gave them the order. I cautiously got back into the truck, drove out of the parking lot and headed to the toll and the bridges.

My cell phone rang. It was another unknown caller but I answered it anyway. Before I could say "hello," Josh said,

"What the hell are you doing? Do you have a death wish? I told you to keep a low profile and call me every time you stopped. You didn't and you took out some goon in a public parking lot. Damn, Dad, what is wrong with you? How can I protect you when you keep doing shit like that?"

I was amused a little knowing that I had an important son who feared for my livelihood. I continued to eat my sandwich and chips while I let him go on for a few more seconds.

I just said, "I will be at the Harvester depot in about an hour and a half. I'll call you then. Call Ed and do what you said you were going to do." I hung up. I knew he would call me again and he also knew that I knew he was protecting me. I also knew he hadn't called Ed yet. Ed would have called me by now admitting he knew more than he let on. Josh's call would have put the fear of the FBI in him if they had talked.

Questions and Answers

Ed was sitting at his desk when the phone rang.

"Mr. Edward McAuliffe?"

"Yes," he said, as his heart began to race and his chest tightened.

"This is Special Agent Charles Martin from the FBI office of New London. We are requesting that you meet with representatives of our office."

Ed asked, "Why?"

"Never mind why. A car is waiting for you outside in the terminal parking lot. There will be a white Chevrolet sedan with three individuals inside waiting for you. Tell your assistant, Mr. Kelly, that you will be back in a few hours because you have some personal business to attend to." Special Agent Martin finished and hung up. Ed listened to the buzz of the dead phone line for a second or two before he slowly placed the receiver down. He gathered himself and rang for Dan on the intercom. Dan answered and listened as Ed explained that he had to leave for a little while. He gave him instructions of what he needed to be accomplished while he was away from the office. Ed walked slowly outside and looked for the white Sedan. It was where Agent Martin had said. No one paid any attention to his leaving. He slowly approached the white Chevrolet. One of the agents got out of the passenger front door and opened the rear right door for him. He got into the seat without looking at, or thanking, the agent. When he sat, he was startled to see Joshua Sprague looking at him.

"Good morning Mr. McAuliffe," Josh said. Ed hesitated, then composed himself and answered back, as the white sedan began to slowly move out of the terminal parking lot.

"Good morning, Josh."

"Mr. McAuliffe, I understand that you need to talk to the FBI most urgently. Am I correct?" he asked. Ed acknowledged with a slight nod of his head. Josh continued in a slow distinctive tone.

"My father has informed me of all the incidents that have occurred in the last, I think, almost seventy-two hours. He has gone into much detail on your theories, speculations, research, known involvement and all the information that your nephew and I have been supposedly passing on to you lately." Ed didn't say anything as Josh continued to update Ed on everything he knew. When Josh finished with the details, he asked, "Mr. McAuliffe, how long have you been involved with the Costello family and please do not lie or alter any facts or information because we have done an extensive search on all your financial records all the way back to the funeral expenses for Mrs. McAuliffe. You have collected an impressive amount of money that you not only deposited in cash amounts less than five thousand dollars, but you failed to report the extra income to our brothers at the IRS." Josh continued, "Now I'm going to sit here and listen to everything you have to say while we drive along on this beautiful summer day. Do I make myself very clear to you, sir?"

Ed sat back, looking somewhat bewildered. He swallowed and began to talk to Josh. He started telling all he knew.

"I was afraid that your Dad would take his sweet-ass time calling you to get you updated on what was going on. I knew he would eventually call you after he had discussed this with your Mom. I knew Jean would get him off his rump to call you. I also knew that you would be calling Brian to find out if something was wrong with his stupid old uncle." He continued to speak while Josh listened and made an occasional note.

"I know you guys keep in touch and I know how much respect and concern you have for each other and your families. I knew it would take a little extra time but I was getting desperate when George Woodbridge went missing. I fear the worst for him." Ed paused and shifted his weight as he tried to get comfortable in the sedan's back seat.

"I hope that son of a bitch Moretti hasn't hurt George. That piece of shit would kill anyone including his own mother, I hear. I was scared shitless that he might come for your father after some of the shit I heard he has pulled off lately. I kept in constant contact with your father to make sure he stayed clear of that guy. Your father is a pain in the ass because he won't do as he's told. He's a thick headed son of a bitch at times, you know."

"He proved that he had a thick head when he only got a few stitches from getting hit on it with that forklift," Josh said. Ed then smiled and relaxed a little. He said, "I wondered if that was an accident or some shit Owlia was pulling because your Dad saw one of those units they are so hell bent on keeping a secret. I was glad to hear that the shooting at your father's yard was just some local rogues getting what they deserved, especially after they shot at that state trooper."

Josh butted in and said, "Mr. McAuliffe, Gene Moretti is dead. The state trooper killed him in my Dad's yard. My Dad had shot the two rogues but was almost tricked by Moretti into laying his shot gun down so Moretti could murder him. My Dad was smart enough to keep out of the sight long enough for the trooper to challenge Moretti. Geno, as the Costello family called him, made a very big mistake."

Ed McAuliffe's face whitened. He gathered his thoughts after the shock of hearing that Moretti was dead and then continued to speak, "I first asked George to deliver to Newport because I knew he was really hurting to keep his delivery business going. I also figured that he could get a chance to see one of his kids who's now a naval surgeon on the U.S.S. Clinton docked at the pier next to the Harvester plant. He was proud of that ship, especially with his kid on it with a very important job. When George went missing, I got your Dad cleared through Tommy Lupinacci to begin delivering shipments to the Newport plant."

He looked at Josh and confessed, "Yeah, I didn't claim my extra income but I'm willing to pay the fines to the IRS but I am not a goddamned criminal and I want out of this shit without getting killed. Do I make myself clear, my boy?"

Josh said, "I want you to get in touch with my father and tell him that we've talked and you've updated me on all the information you had." Josh also instructed Ed to continue to take instructions from the Costello family until the FBI could investigate the situation further. Josh was explicit with Ed to maintain normalcy. He made an effort, while he looked seriously at Ed and said, "Tell my father that he is to keep his eyes and ears open and his mouth…."

Ed responded, "I know, shut."

The whole episode had taken Ed and Josh approximately ten minutes to complete. Ed asked, "What am I going to do for the next hour and forty minutes or so?"

"I'd rather have you at the terminal and visible in case Dan Kelly got suspicious," Josh said.

"What do you mean about Dan?"

"Dan is probably a mole. For who, I don't know. We know Dan had been involved with Gene Moretti for years. The FBI knows that Dan has worked for the Costello Shipping Company where he met Gene. Dan never mentioned he worked for Costello because he knew that you wouldn't have hired him. Once you started getting paid for the coordination of the Costello shipments and he saw that you were a very organized and somewhat of a legitimate cargo shipping administrator, he kept his secret so things would run smoothly and he could keep an eye on you." Josh looked at Ed and said, "Dad told me that you suspected Dan Kelly all along."

Ed just nodded and mumbled what sounded like, "that bastard." He drew out his cell phone from his pocket.

"If it is alright with you, I am calling your Dad."

Josh nodded and looked out the window as Ed made the call.

My phone rang. I could see by the ID that it was Ed.

"Yeah, Sprague here," I blurted out while finishing my drink in the truck.

"I talked to Josh and told him everything."

I stopped Ed in his tracks and said, "Did you call Josh or did he contact you?"

"He contacted me but if you don't believe me, talk to him yourself." He handed the phone to Josh.

"Hi Dad, I'm with Mr. McAuliffe now," Josh said then handed

140

the phone back to Ed.

"Are you okay? Where are you now?" Ed asked.

I told him where I was and that I would be at the artery terminal in 30 or 40 minutes. I needed to unload before I did a run over to the Harvester depot to pick up the final load for delivery to Newport today. I also mentioned that the two goons were following me. I knew I was on speaker when I heard Josh say, "Dad, we are keeping tabs on the two guys in the Honda. They are some questionable characters and you must stay clear of them at every opportunity. My agents are trailing them but they will have difficulty trying to reach you in time if these guys get violent," he explained. I acknowledged his concern and said that I would try my utmost to keep out of harm's way.

"Jon, I'm sorry for getting you into this shit, man. I'll square away with you as soon as this is over and these guys are put out of commission," Ed said.

I told him that I was pleased he'd updated Josh and also said that he owed me big time. He acknowledge that by saying, "You're right about that and I will make it up to you once I've paid up the IRS and hopefully dodge a Costello bullet."

"I'll see you in a little while when you get back to the terminal. I don't want to have to deal with Kelly."

I thanked Josh for his follow-up conversation with Ed and also told him to call his mother and explain what he was doing to protect his father's ass. I could hear both of them chuckle as I closed the cell phone.

I dialed Jean to update her on everything that transpired this morning except the altercation with the goons at that Newport food take-out parking lot. She didn't need to hear that from me. I was hoping that Joshua wouldn't say anything either but I wouldn't count on it. He told his mother everything. We carried on the usual conversation. She explained that the ICU was almost back to normal now and that all the rogues that were released were either in the custody of the police now for further questioning or back in the Arcadia Forest where they came from. Those that were still at the hospital had been downgraded and lodged in the recovery wards. She was back in the triage room with Alice. She talked about the grandkids and what I had missed last night. She told me that Lilly and Jack wouldn't let her sleep on the couch. She had to choose one of their bedrooms to sleep in. They all ended up in Jack's bed for the night. She laughed a little because she didn't get much sleep. The grandkids constantly tossed and turned throughout the night waking her almost hourly. But she enjoyed the precious little darlings while she continued to fill me in on all their comings and goings. She asked me how my stitches were doing. I told her that I was thinking of putting my baseball cap on again because it felt pretty good. She cautioned me and asked that I wait another day before I did that. I acknowledged her request and changed the subject. I informed her I would be in town in 20 or so minutes and then I would have one more trip to Newport today. I told her that the money would be very good and I looked forward to going home tonight. I hoped that Josh could figure this all out and Jean and I could go home and get our lives back to normal. I could see the terminal come into sight as I was finishing up my conversation with Jean.

"I need to get off the phone now so I can pull into the terminal."

"Okay. I love you and keep in contact with Josh as much as possible."

"Don't worry Jean. I'll obey all of your and Josh's instructions. I just want to deliver this last load, get paid and get out of whatever is going on with the Harvester people and the Costello family. I'll see you soon," I said as I hung up the phone. We parted with a better feeling in our minds than we had earlier before Joe picked her up.

As I pulled in I could see the Honda following at a distance. I never did pick up the FBI tail that Josh had put on the Honda. Those guys were either very good or Josh had wanted me to think that there was a tail on those guys. I hoped for the former. I docked and immediately saw Dan come out to the truck and retrieve my paperwork as the dock hands began unloading the cargo. I casually asked where his boss was and Dan said that Ed had stepped out on some personal business. "Oh," I remarked. I felt a little uneasy. I was hoping Ed would have returned by now. I didn't feel very comfortable around Dan anymore, knowing more details about his connections with the Costello family. Just then, Ed appeared, walking from the parking lot. He went to his office immediately and stayed there for a few minutes before venturing out to check on the unloading of my truck as well as another one that I had parked parallel to. I stayed in the truck and ignored Ed until he came over.

"Hey, old man," he said. I looked up and remarked that I wanted to get unloaded as quickly as possible because I wanted to get over to the Harvester depot and back to the Harvester plant in Newport as quickly as possible. I wanted to pick up my wife and visit my grandkids and have dinner with my daughter and son-in-law. Ed winked and said loud enough for Dan and a few dock hands to hear, "That sounds like a good plan after a long delivery day. I hope you have a good run and make those dinner plans." He yelled to Dan and asked if they were almost completed. Dan waved that I could undock and drive away. I looked at Ed and said nothing. I managed to roll my eyes at him. He looked away because he didn't want to smirk. He just yelled at me and said, "Have a good run, buddy."

I never knew where Josh dropped Ed off but the FBI was out of sight and nobody knew the better, I hoped. As I drove away, I could see the Honda roll out of the parking lot and commence its annoying, but obvious, tail on my truck. I also noticed a black Lincoln SUV Hybrid behind the Honda but never gave it a second look.

My cell phone rang again. It was Joe's personal cell number. "Hey Pop, don't forget to drop by my office and fill out that paperwork we talked about."

"Hi Joe. I have to admit, I forgot, but I will swing around the barracks and get it out of the way. I can be there in five minutes or so."

"Okay, I'll be expecting you." I immediately thought about my so called "protectors."

Those goons in the Honda are really going to be nervous when they try to figure out where I'm going. They'll wet their pants when they see me pull into the State Police barracks. I smiled a little, thinking I really have caused a little inconvenience for them. I then realized that maybe I could be really putting myself in danger if they thought that I was trying to have the State Police search the truck. Then reality set in again. If I park the truck in plain sight and those goons can watch from a distance, then nothing will happen except they will be very uncomfortable for the time I'm in the barracks. They deserved that for the irritation they had been to me. I still kept thinking, what if these crazy bastards pulled up close to the truck, pull out weapons and try to stop me forcibly? I shook my head and thought to myself that I was fanaticizing again and nothing would probably happen if I just parked in full view for them to watch and make sure nothing happened to the truck. I was thinking too much again. The interesting thing to watch will be when I turn off the State Police exit just before the Newport exit.

Unbeknownst to me, while I was driving to Newport, there was a black Lincoln SUV tailing the Honda. The driver was Sid Owlia. His passenger was a gentleman only known as Moroch. I would meet him soon enough. Both men concentrated their attention on my truck and the Honda up ahead. Sid had been very quiet since Moroch had scolded him like a child for picking two inexperienced soldiers to watch, first, George Woodbridge's delivery truck and now mine. George had apparently ended up witnessing too much at the Harvester plant and fireworks barge; and was to be dealt with before the Fourth of July based on the orders from Moroch's superiors.

Occasionally, Moroch would speak Arabic to Sid when he really wanted to drive home a point. Sid would submissively nod as the Middle Easterner spoke. Sid maintained a distant tail on the two soldiers in the Honda while they followed my truck. Sid and Moroch must have been horrified when the soldiers and I turned off the State Police exit to the barracks. They continued to drive on past the exit and only glanced at each other with apprehension about what had just occurred. Sid quickly said that he would wait at the next exit to intercept the Honda and relieve them of their duty tailing me. Moroch listened to his plan and then looked away disgustingly. Sid was very uncomfortable with Moroch's facial expression.

I pulled into the barrack's parking lot and stopped in the designated truck lanes assigned to commercial vehicles visiting or being inspected there. I made sure that I quickly pulled out my derringer and placed it with the Colt in the glove box. I imagined what would have happened when all the lights and whistles blew as I tried to enter a police building with weapons on me. No state cop son-in-law or FBI son could have gotten me out of that situation. Worst yet, I could have been shot on sight. My mind was working too hard with too many details. I just needed to fill out the police paperwork, make my final delivery and get over to see Jean at Joe and Missy's. The big security organizations were now involved and I was sure that they could carry the load and relieve Ed and me from all the aggravation we had been through in the last 72 hours.

I entered the police building. It was a small foyer where approximately a half a dozen people could sit. There were a few people waiting, but no one at the security window. I approached the policeman sitting behind the tinted security glass at a desk where I observed several TV monitoring screens that covered all access ways into and out of the building.

"What can I do for you?" he politely asked.

I explained who I was and that I had been requested to come in this afternoon by Sergeant Joe Harris to fill out some paperwork and answer some questions concerning the shooting that had taken place at my home very early this morning. He looked down at an apparent list of scheduled people and quickly acknowledged my explanation as to why I was there.

"I'll notify Sergeant Harris that you've arrived."

Within a minute, he pushed a button on his desk, and a checkpoint door opened. I entered to see Joe grinning at me with his hand extended to shake mine.

"How are you doing?" he asked.

"I'm fine but I am in a little hurry to get back on the road with the second load I have to deliver to Newport this afternoon," I said. I knew Joe knew all about my trip and I was sure he wouldn't hold me up long. He motioned for me to follow him. We entered a room where there was a gentleman in a suit and a court stenographer sitting next to him. Joe introduced me to the man. He stood up and replied, "Mr. Sprague, my name is Lieutenant William LaFleur and this Dora Harren, our stenographer. I am a special investigator for the Connecticut State Police." I noticed another gentleman come in just as I was being introduced to the Lieutenant. LaFleur turned and quickly introduced him to me. "Mr. Sprague, this gentleman is Special Agent Richard Strong. He has been assigned to be here to listen to this case."

"Mr. Sprague," he said, as he extended his hand.

"Agent Strong," I said and also extended my hand. I spoke to Joe. "This is a case? I thought I was here to answer a few questions, sign a few papers and be able to leave here quickly." I looked at everyone and said, "I assume all of you here understand my time is very important to me."

"Mr. Sprague, please relax. This will not take more than five minutes to complete," Lieutenant LaFleur said. He explained that all I had to do was answer questions that had been prepared in advance. He instructed me that I was to answer "yes" or "no" to the questions. He further explained that this was developed this way to get me in and out quickly but assure the State Police and the FBI that I gave them accurate information under oath. I listened to him as I gazed around at everyone else looking directly at me. The lieutenant looked at Dora and nodded. Dora stood up and asked me to raise my right hand and repeat after her. She also asked me, once the oath had been administered, if I understood that everything I said here would be used in court and was being typed by her onto the stenography machine and recorded as well on the tape recorder that had been placed on the table by Agent Strong.

I said, "I understand."

"Thank you, Mr. Sprague."

The Lieutenant and the Special Agent opened their copies of the statement that they had before them as Joe slid my copy in front of me. I was going to be able to read the questions as they were read and asked of me. Joe began reading the questions. After we had established who I was, where I was born, the schools I attended, my service record, my spouse and family and 20 or so more questions that were read to me telling me who and what I was, a few precise ones were asked. Did I know any of the perpetrators involved in the shooting that occurred at my home? I attempted to say that I found out later before I was stopped and reminded to say "yes" or "no." I said, "No." They continued.

To me, as I understood the questioning, they were trying to establish a base of testimony concerning the shooting, the local Harvester depot, the Newport plant, and individuals I knew that were associated with the Costello family. I completed the questions in less than ten minutes. I was thanked by the attendees and then escorted out of the meeting room by Joe to the foyer leading out of the building.

Joe looked at me while shaking my hand and said, "We are keeping good surveillance on you so relax while you finish your run. Remember to keep in contact with Josh when you stop, okay?"

I smiled, shook his hand, turned and went out the barracks door. I reached the truck, started it and slowly moved out of the parking lot. I saw the Honda parked in the rest area of the parking lot begin to move as I drove by. I opened the glove box, put the derringer in my right stocking and double checked to make sure the Colt was where it could be reached quickly in case I needed it. I entered the turnpike and could see the exit for Newport up ahead. I looked in the mirrors and the goons in the Honda were following. I approached the Newport exit and turned onto Route 138. I noticed a black SUV parked on the side of the road. One guy was out and just coming from the woods while the driver sat in the car and waited. *No problem here,* I thought. It was just someone who had been peeing in the woods. I continued on when I noticed that the Honda was nowhere in sight. *Good,* I thought. Maybe they stopped to pee too. They knew where I was going and really didn't need to be following me anyway.

The Final Delivery

Sid Owlia had been instructed by Moroch to flash the Lincoln SUVs' high and low beams at the occupants in the Honda to get the driver's attention. He complied and the Honda immediately pulled over to the side of the road. The truck was not in sight now. Sid pulled up next to the Honda and Moroch waved to them to follow his lead. The two men acknowledged and waited for the SUV to pull ahead. Both vehicles continued on Route 138 but at a much slower speed than would have been needed to catch up to my delivery truck, or, at least, maintain the same pace with it as I traveled to Newport.

One man, who was in the passenger seat, remarked to the driver of the Honda that Sid and Moroch, who they hadn't seen in a while, would lose the truck before long if they maintained this speed. The driver reminded the passenger that they all knew where the truck was going. He laughed and reminded the passenger that he didn't need to get too close to me anyway after the whipping I had laid on him. The other man said, "Yeah, I can't wait to get the opportunity to pay that guy back." The driver laughed.

"You probably won't get a chance. After this afternoon they won't be seeing that guy again anyway," he said.

They continued to follow Sid Owlia and Moroch in the black Lincoln SUV Hybrid. Sid looked over at Moroch who sat quietly and looked out the window.

"Don't you want me to catch up to Sprague's truck? At this speed it will be several miles ahead of us you know."

Moroch said nothing and continued to look out the window. Sid drove on for a few more minutes and began to ask the same question again when Moroch told him to signal and turn left up ahead. A sign that they had just passed indicated that the Pequot State Park Swimming Pond was up ahead.

Sid began to question the request when Moroch raised his voice and said, "Signal now and turn left." Sid complied and began to slow down and signal. The two men in the Honda looked at each other with confusion but also complied. Sid drove down the gravel road and never asked questions. Moroch continued to stare out the window. The SUV reached the small parking lot where earlier visitors to the swimming pond had once enjoyed the facility there. Not very many people drove to the swimming pond these days but some of the locals did walk there occasionally to enjoy the cool and mostly shaded swimming area. There were no locals there today despite the temperature being in the mid 80s. The rogues roamed the area and controlled it after dark. Moroch knew this and indicated to Sid to pull over. The Honda followed and pulled parallel to the SUV and stopped as well. Moroch immediately exited the car and approached the Honda. The driver rolled down his window and assumed that he would be given instructions when Moroch pulled out his Walther PPK and shot the driver, executioner style, in the forehead. The gray matter from the exiting bullet sprayed the passenger who froze and tried to comprehend what he had just witnessed. The driver slumped forward onto the steering column and the horn began to blare. Moroch fired a second round into the face of the passenger and the passenger door window shattered into a pink mist of blood and tissue. The passenger's head was limp and leaned out the missing window. Moroch pulled the driver off the steering column enough to stop the horn from blaring. When Sid had heard and saw the results of the first shot, he had exited the SUV and was standing outside the open door. He was frozen stiff as Moroch shot the second man. Sid, who was unable to speak at first, eventually regained control of his voice and tried to call out to Moroch to stop. Moroch turned to Sid with the automatic pistol pointed directly at him. Both men were motionless until Moroch lowered the pistol and told Sid to get back into the SUV and drive them out of there. Sid was silent and couldn't move for a few seconds until miraculously, he regained his composure.

"Mohammad is my relative. Ilea is Darish's brother," he said. Moroch looked at him and ordered him to get back into the SUV and start it. He waited near the SUV until Sid was ready to drive away. The Honda was left in the gravel parking lot with both soldiers exposed to the elements. Moroch knew the rogues had probably heard the two shots. They would be scouting the area soon. They would find the two dead men, scavenge what they could and be blamed by the authorities for the crime.

Sid was ordered to speed up and get back on Route 138. They were both silent for about 15 minutes. As Sid nervously tried to catch up to my truck, he asked, with a quivering voice, "Why did you do that?"

Moroch turned slowly, glared at Sid and said, "Because they were too casual with Woodbridge and Sprague. Woodbridge must be taken care of immediately."

He chastised Sid for keeping Woodbridge alive for the past several days.

"I kept him alive because I didn't want Donnie finding out that the old man was dead on my account. Donnie thinks that Woodbridge is old and sickly and had to bow out of his contract due to health problems. He doesn't know that he is locked up in the hold of the barge. No one except the two men that you just shot and us knows that."

Moroch looked at Sid with a smirk and said, "Now only you and I know."

"That was no reason to blow the two of them away like that," Sid exclaimed.

"They were expendable."

Sid yelled, "Expendable? What the hell do you mean? I know they weren't the sharpest tools in the shed but they didn't deserve the execution you performed on them. A simple firing without their last week's pay would have been appropriate. For God's sake, one of them was family."

Moroch continued to look out the window as Sid complained and showed signs of emotion as his eyes watered. Moroch looked slowly over to Sid and said, "You Americans are all soft criminals. Even you, who are Arabic in birth, have become soft like a woman's breast. They were useless men who performed miserably in the higher cause to strike fear in the

151

infidel. They needed to be eliminated. I do not want to hear of this anymore." Sid knew not to push Moroch because he knew firsthand what he was capable of. They continued to drive to Newport.

I had reached the outskirts of Newport when my cell phone rang. It was Josh.

"Where are you? Is everything alright?"

"Yep. The trip has been uneventful. I'm right on the outskirts of Newport. I haven't seen anything out of the usual. I haven't even seen the two goons in the Honda for the last hour or so."

"Good. Call me as soon as you begin to unload at the Harvester plant."

"I will. I'm looking forward to heading home soon. Hey, what's going to happen to Ed?"

"If Ed continues to cooperate with the authorities, the most he could get, besides a hefty monetary fine from the IRS, would be a probation period of five years or so and no time in jail. He's already talked to the federal prosecutor and the prosecutor indicated that he would heavily consider my recommendation." I was pleased to hear that.

"I don't know what I am going to do about you though."

"What do you mean by that?"

"Well, getting involved with known criminals, shooting people with banned weapons, scaring the hell out of my mother, forcing her to stay with other people, fighting in the street and wild rides with motorcycles. Do you want me to go on?" he asked, while chuckling a little.

"Look you little shit, who the hell knew that Ed was involved in this shit. I shot those bastards on my property with my legitimate shot gun. The goddamned goon was disrespectful and deserved an ass kicking or ball kicking to be exact and I enjoyed the bike ride. Your mother doesn't scare easy, but your brother-in-law and you scared her into leaving the house. I'm glad you did it and not me." I could hear him laugh and I also could hear someone else laugh a little.

"Who else is listening to this conversation?"

"Oh, it's my buddy Rich Strong; you met him today at the police barracks."

I yelled, "Hi Rich. You do keep bad company."

"Hello again Mr. Sprague. I'm used to this company."

Josh became serious and informed me that as soon as I had left the Newport city limits, I would be stopped and my truck confiscated by the FBI. Josh explained that they wanted to examine the cargo area for traces of any kind of explosives. The truck would be returned immediately if no traces were found. If they did find any traces, then the truck would be impounded until a date and time could be determined by the special prosecutor.

"What happens if my truck has shit in it and you confiscate it for who knows how long? How do I make a living? I can't afford that." I rambled on. Josh informed me that they would rent an identical truck for the duration at their expense.

"Okay and I like the way you think to take care of your old man," I said. Josh just laughed and said that he knew me too well.

Within a few more minutes I could see the harbor and the Clinton as bright as ever glimmering in the afternoon sun. I could make out part of the Harvester plant and could see the fireworks barge moored to the plant pier. I tightened up a little but felt confident that all this would be over soon and I would be on my way to see Jean and be with Joe, Missy and the grandkids. I thought that the evening would be great because I planned to take Jean home early and spend some quality time together, just she and I. This seemed to be the right way to end the day. I knew I would have to find some way to get her out of my daughter's home because once she was around the grandkids, she became mesmerized. It was like they had a spell on her. Sometimes I was a little envious, but tonight, I was going to be a little selfish and keep her to myself and leave the condo as soon as Missy and Joe began to get the kids ready for their baths and eventually bed. I knew Jean would want to assist in that evening duty but I figured I could get my daughter to convince her mother to take her old and tired father home and put him to bed. I smiled as I thought about the bed part. That really would be a great climax to the evening.

I was being signaled to stop at the military checkpoint. I slowed the truck and rolled down my window in preparation to hand my lower pier pass and ID to the shore patrolman. I stopped and performed the task that I had done twice earlier today. The shore patrolman reviewed my pass and ID and told me to pass on. I slowly pulled away. I glanced into my rear mirror and noticed the black SUV but I now could recognize the driver as Sid Owlia. The passenger he carried wasn't familiar to me. He sat there and looked out the window of the SUV while Sid was talking to the shore patrolman. I could see them being waved on. I figured that I would see Sid at the Harvester plant soon enough and maybe get a better look at the guy who was riding with him. Within several minutes, I was backing up to the dock and watching the signals of the dock hand as he guided me into the dock for my final run. Home and Jean was about two hours away. I felt the truck gently bump the rubber stopper. I set the air brakes and turned the engine off. I called Josh as I sat in the truck. There was no answer for a while. Eventually his voice came on indicating that he was not available, but would return your call as soon as possible. He went on to say that if this was an emergency, contact the number that he gave. I thought *where the hell he could be?* I realized that maybe there was poor reception and he was unable to pick up my call. I tried to remember if I had talked to him while I was docked on the previous runs but couldn't remember. Well, everything seemed to be going as planned so I decided I would contact him as soon as I was pulling away from the dock.

One of the dock hands jumped up on the running board as I rolled down the window. He asked for the shipping documents. I handed them to him but he then asked me to report to the shipping office. I inquired why I was to report there. He said that there were two men with his boss that wanted to see me. I asked the dock hand if his boss was Donnie Costello. He said "no" and that Donnie was the big boss and was out for a few days due to a death in the family. I said "okay" but hesitated as the dock hand jumped off the running board and back to his duties unloading my truck. I looked around to make sure no one could see me open the glove box as I put on my light weight jacket. I knew it was a little warm still to necessitate a jacket but it would easily hide the Colt wedged now in the small of my back. I got out of the truck and looked around for the dock foreman's office. I could see the sign with an arrow that indicated that the entrance was around to the side of the building. I walked slowly and looked around taking in anything out of the ordinary that came into my sight. I headed for the door, opened it and entered. I felt the air conditioning immediately cool my face and relax some of the tension that was building inside me. I was concerned when I was directed to the office and also concerned about my failure to reach Josh.

Sid Owlia and another man that I had never seen before were standing near a white board that had schedules and information written on it that didn't mean anything to me. The dock foreman erased some information on the board as Sid turned to smile at me as I walked in.

"I have a few questions for you before you take your last trip back to the artery terminal."

"Sure, what can I do for you?"

Sid asked, "Why did you stop at the police barracks on your way to Newport?"

"I had to stop by and fill out some paperwork for the Connecticut State Police."

"Why?" came from a man who stepped out from behind the door that was still open from when I first entered. I turned to see the man slowly walk past me and sit in the foreman's chair.

"Who are you? I asked.

"Never mind who I am. I asked you a question and I want an answer now," he demanded.

"You don't demand shit from me pal. Do you understand?" I yelled back.

Sid Owlia, sensing that trouble would inevitably commence, interjected a weak, but stalling, tactic and said, "Mr. Sprague, were you on official business at the police barracks?"

I looked to Sid while keeping the arrogant bastard in my sight.

"Yes, there was a shooting of a robber in my yard earlier this morning. I needed to make an official statement about that incident to the police. If you are worried about the ten minutes I spent there on your time, dock me," I said as I looked at the guy sitting in the chair who now seemed less interested in my story. I told Sid to check out the time I spent there with the two guys he had following me for the past two days. He was about to speak when the guy sitting said, "I'm not inquiring about the length of time you spent there; I am interested in exactly what you talked about there."

"Look pal, I told you what it was about and it is none of anyone's business what I had to say while I was behind closed doors and under oath."

The guy who was sitting stood up and walked to the window and looked out at the harbor, the barge and beyond to the U.S.S. Clinton. As he stared out the window without saying a word, my cell phone began to ring in my pocket. I turned away from them for some type of privacy which was a dumb thing to do I realized much later.

"Hey Josh, I'm…" It all went dark.

In the Hold

Sid yelled as Moroch followed through with the blackjack that he had taken out from the desk of the foreman. Moroch had managed to hit me over the head while I was preoccupied with the call that I'd just received. The blow to the head was almost exactly where the two days old stitches were. The gash on my head was now almost a third open and bleeding very heavily. I was motionless and face down on the floor. The floor was concrete and it was quickly absorbing the blood. Moroch saw the cell phone on the floor and realized it was still activated. He smashed it with another blow from the blackjack. Pieces flew in every direction in the office. Sid immediately checked to make sure I was alive. By the sound of the blow, Sid thought that Moroch had definitely cracked my skull. Once he realized that I was still alive, he positioned himself between Moroch and me.

"You care for this person?" Moroch asked.

"I care enough for you not to kill anyone else today."

Moroch looked at the dock foreman who still was frozen and wide eyed.

"Take this thing to the hold of the barge with the other one. Get help from the one you have been using to feed the black person. He can be trusted. And get the floor cleaned now," he barked. Sid watched as Moroch barked his orders. The dock foreman began to move slowly, his face frozen with fear. He was still in shock because of what he had just witnessed. Moroch yelled and the foreman came to life and exited the office to perform his duties.

I was still lying on the floor, breathing smoothly as Moroch looked down at me.

"He will be alright. You look worried," he said looking at Sid.

"For Christ's sake, you could have killed him," Sid said, while trying to apply some pressure to the wound to slow the bleeding. "This guy is a harmless truck driver and all we had to do was let him finish his last delivery and go home. He is an old man."

"This old and harmless man has been trouble for us since we allowed Lupinacci to make hiring deals with the one you call McAuliffe. The whole Costello organization is full of fools who rely on friendship and family. They do not function in ways that I am accustomed," Moroch said to chastise Sid for allowing me to remain in the delivery service too long.

"As soon as they found out that he had a son in the FBI they should have taken him out. They should have sent one of their own instead of that idiot Moretti who failed and paid with his life."

Moroch continued to slap the blackjack in his hand. His hand was turning very red as he rambled on.

"The McAuliffe person will be the next to feel my wrath because he has been involved with the navy police. Kelly has kept me informed of his phone calls to this person he calls Brian," he said.

Sid Owlia found some paper towels in the closet and began to apply more pressure to my still bleeding head. Moroch looked and said, "It will congeal. Stop and go see where that idiot is and the help he was told to get."

As Sid began to rise and go search for the foreman, the man entered with the helper he had been instructed to get. The foremen carried some cleaning supplies with him and attempted to remove my blood from the floor. The men laid down a canvass tarp used to cover the units that they had been shipping, on the floor next to me as I became more conscious. I felt them lift me up and place me on the canvas cover. They gagged me first, tied my hands and feet with nylon rope and then wrapped me as if I was cargo. Moroch searched me and found the Colt. He looked at Sid and said, *"Old Man?"* They took me to the barge while Sid and Moroch watched. I heard Moroch remind the foreman to return to the office as quickly as possible to finish cleaning it. He gave him specific instructions on what he expected to be completed when he returned in 30 minutes. He instructed Sid to gather up all the soiled paper

158

towels and bring them with him. Moroch emptied the Colt and kept the bullets and pistol in his hand.

My truck had been reloaded with cargo headed for the artery terminal in Connecticut. Sid jumped up into the driver's seat, threw the bloody paper towels on the floor of the passenger side and started the truck. Moroch took a few seconds to circle the truck, looking around before entering on the passenger's side. He nodded to Sid to slowly move away from the dock. "Drive past the shore patrol imbeciles and head for the center of the city," he said to Sid. Moroch wiped the Colt and put it into the glove compartment and threw the bullets out the window into a grassy area before the checkpoint. I could feel the dock foreman and his assistant carrying me onto the barge. No one paid any attention while they worked wiring up the 30 or so units to receive the fireworks that were scheduled to be delivered the next day. The two men came to the hatch in the first deck of the barge and slowly, with a great amount of difficulty, lowered their covered package down the hatch. Within a few minutes they were ready to descend down the next hatch to the second deck where they had to repeat the same difficult maneuver. They eventually entered the third deck. Both men were dripping with sweat and the foreman was nauseous from the sweltering heat that they had to pass through to get to the last deck in the barge. The foreman must have signaled to his assistant that he needed to stop and rest before he proceeded on the last leg of their journey. The assistant turned the dogged hatch and opened it very slowly. It was very rusty and squeaked when he opened it. There was no light in the small, damp but cool room. It was cooler than the third level deck had been but it still remained warm. It smelt of human excrement. They uncovered and carried me into the small room and placed me on my back. I heard them as they left immediately. I could hear the assistant tell the foreman that he would return in a few hours and provide some water for me and the other one.

Joshua Sprague redialed his cell phone to hear the same

message that he had heard four times before.

"Hi, you reached Jon Sprague. Leave a message and I'll get back to you as soon as I can."

"Shit, I can't get him and I'm sure he was on the phone when I dialed the first time," Josh said while pacing back and forth. "He'll get back to you. Just give him a few minutes," Agent Strong said although he too felt a little uncomfortable about the situation. Josh looked at Richard Strong and instructed him to contact the Naval Shore Patrol and the Agents that were in Newport that had tailed and lost the Honda today.

"See if they have a visual on the Sprague delivery truck leaving the plant or passing through the security checkpoint," he said.

Agent Strong immediately began the task while Josh continued to pace back and forth in his office. Strong returned in a few minutes to inform his boss that the delivery truck had passed the security checkpoint a few minutes ago as reported by the Shore Patrol. They identified two men with Harvester ID cards. "Shit," was the only thing he could utter from his mouth. Josh gave a myriad of orders to a few of the agents that had begun to gather at the control desk near Josh's office. One was to get the Shore Patrol into their military vehicles and try to catch and stop the truck. He notified the agents that were waiting at the weigh station to check my truck for explosives residue when I arrived, to break camp and immediately start searching to intercept the delivery truck as soon as possible. The agents that had lost the Honda still had not been contacted, but he instructed his agents to continue that task. The most important task at hand was to find his father before he had to tell his mother that he had lost him.

Sid and Moroch continued into the city. Moroch ordered Sid to take different side streets until they were well hidden off the main route and into the old section of Newport where the truck could barely fit down the narrow two way streets. He told him to stop. Sid complied. He told Sid to smear some of blood that had almost dried inside the cab's driver side.

Sid said, "What about wiping off our finger prints."

"You are a stupid man. Do you realize how many times different people handle these trucks at the docking station? Let these morons tell us that they found our fingerprints in and on the truck. Who would care?" Moroch said.

They left the truck but not before Moroch moved to the driver's side and opened the door and left it open. He looked for anyone walking on the seemingly deserted street. He then drew out his stiletto and punctured a small hole into the tread of the left front tire. An immediate hiss could be heard. The tire would be flat in less than five minutes. Both men would be far away by that time, he thought. Moroch dialed his cell phone as he still held his stiletto in his hand. In a few seconds a voice answered. Moroch asked, "Have you completed hiding Sprague with the other?"

"It is done."

He instructed the foreman to send a car to America's Cup Avenue to pick him up as soon as possible. He closed his cell phone, turned and stabbed Sid in his abdomen. Sid's eyes widened in horror as the pain reached his brain. Moroch surged again and stabbed him a second time but twisted the stiletto while holding his hand over Sid's mouth to muffle the scream. Sid's eyes closed as his knees buckled and his muscle control ceased. He slumped to the ground. Moroch quickly observed that no one had witnessed his violent act. He dragged Sid a few feet and placed him under the truck. It would be several minutes before anyone would suspect anything was wrong and he would be out of sight before anyone would be able to identify him as being associated with the truck. He headed for America's Cup Avenue, on his way far from the scene.

Moroch walked quickly and reached America's Cup Avenue within ten minutes of eliminating Sid Owlia. He began contemplating which way his ride would be coming from when a red pickup truck approached and stopped across the avenue from him. He recognized the driver. He was the dock foreman who had been obedient to all of his demands. Moroch jogged across the street and entered the truck. He commented that he was pleased with the driver for his punctuality and choice of vehicle. The red pickup truck suited the plans for which he had for it in the next few days. The driver asked, "Where do we go?"

"Drive to I-95 South and I will instruct you on the details when we get on the interstate," he said. The foreman acknowledged him without looking at him and drove as instructed. He asked where Sid was. Moroch said that he was with the truck now. The electronic clock in front of the Greenwood Credit Union indicated it was 81 degrees and 5:32 p.m.

I felt the pain in my head the instant I became fully conscious. Prior to that, my head had been numb from the blow. My face was cool and I could smell rusted iron. I tried to move but realized my hands and feet were bound with something that kept me from moving them. My head ached terribly and I could feel the dampness in my shirt collar and back. My jaw was aching because material that had been put in my mouth had spread it like I had been in a dentist's chair for hours with my mouth wide open. It was pitch black wherever I was. I almost panicked when I thought that I had lost my sight from the blow to my head but then I caught a glimpse of light. I could see a glow from what looked like a watch. It was glowing and I guessed that it read 5:33 p.m. I relaxed for a few seconds realizing I had my sight. Whose watch was that I wondered? I heard a sound and saw the watch move. I froze. I didn't know what it was but then began to realize it was a person mumbling something. I couldn't make out what was being said to me so I attempted to move in the direction of the mumbling. I inched closer to the sound until I touched something with my head. I moved my face in the direction of what I had just touched and felt what seemed to be cloth material. The material smelled of sweat and was damp to the touch. The cloth moved away and then toward me again. It was like it was rocking back and forth and occasionally the person mumbled. I mumbled back and the mumbling increased as well as the rocking. I inched along until I was parallel to the other person. My nose was pressed against what seemed to be the back of this person's head. The hair smelt sweaty and stale. I could still see the watch and guessed it was even at where my belt would be. I used all my strength to turn myself around so that we were back to back. After I rested a few minutes to regain any strength I had left in me, I reached out and could feel this person's hands. They were bound like mine. I could feel the knots and began to untie the knots with my fingers as best I could with the limited use of my bound hands. It took a long time to get the knots loosened in the complete darkness. Eventually, I was able to free the hands. The hands, then arms began to move and the body turned to the side. Another minute passed as I felt the individual rock and bump me. Very quietly and with a whisper, I heard the individual ask, "J.J., that you?" I recognized the voice now. With the watch and now the voice, I was relieved to know my friend George was alive. I mumbled to indicate that I needed my mouth gag removed and my hands and feet untied. I felt the scratching and sting in the back of my neck as my mouth gag was untied. As soon as I was free I said, "George, you old son of a bitch?" I felt my eyes moisten a little with the relief and emotion I felt.

"George Woodbridge in the flesh," he said.

"Jon Sprague here," I whispered.

"I figured that could be you J.J. when they brought you in here. They talked too much before they left you and checked on me to see if I was still alive in this hell hole. I asked George to finish untying my hands and I would get my feet as soon as he finished. George said that they came by every few hours to check on him. I asked him how he knew that. He reminded me that he kept his wrist watch attached to his belt and not on his wrist. I remembered that he had done that for years because wrist watches irritated his wrist and he couldn't afford a nice pocket watch."

"I could see the glow from your watch when I first came fully to."

I finished untying myself and sat up next to the bulkhead I could now feel that my outstretched hands had found. I could feel George move to where I was and he too sat up.

"My head is killing me."

"Your head still bothering you from that accident you had?"

"George, the bastards hit me on the head in the same goddamned spot. Can you believe that?"

I told him by the feel of it that it would need to be closed again at the hospital. George said that we had first better find a way to get out of there alive. I asked George to make sure I heard him correctly, "You said they come here every two hours or so to check on you?"

"Yeah, he comes in about every two hours. Only one guy though and he comes in long enough to untie me to piss if I have to and drink some water which he tells me that I must. I haven't eaten since I got here. I feel kind of weak and sick to my stomach. I even had to shit in a bucket over in the corner while the bastard watched me. I used my handkerchief to wipe my ass. Now I know how my ancestors must of felt like coming over on those slave ships," George said and with no humor in his voice.

"Yeah, I could smell the waste when I woke up," I said. I explained to George that when the guy came again in an hour or so, we are going to break out of here. I couldn't see him but he fumbled to grab my arm and said, "J.J. the guy had a gun pointed at me all the time." I asked him if he could see if anyone else came with the guy when he checked on him. "No, but it takes a few minutes for your eyes to adjust to the light and I can't guarantee anything that I saw man," George whispered.

"Well, big guy, we are going to die in this shithole based on the guy I ran into in the foreman's office. He was an evil looking bastard. Had you ever seen him before?"

"I'd seen him twice before. I didn't know his name but I saw him talking to Tommy Lupinacci once on the first day I had starting hauling from the Harvester depot. I also saw him in the Foreman's office at the plant when he was having an argument with the foreman there. I heard them arguing so I started walking around to the barge to kill some time. I saw these guys

164

loading the units I had been carrying for them. They used the crane to load the units into the barge. I sat there for a while and watched what was going on. I lost interest and walked back to the foreman's office and all I remember was looking at the foreman and the lights went out."

He stumbled for my hand to place it on his head and said, "I knew I had an egg on my head. As I feel it now the size of a golf ball was probably an understatement. It's gone down a bit."

"The evil bastard hit you on the head too?"

"It must have been him. I thought there were only two guys in the room when I walked in."

George grabbed my arm again. "How do think you are going to overpower this guy?"

"Well, in their haste to knock my ass out, they failed to check me over," I explained to George in a tone a little above a whisper. "I lost my Colt but I still have my derringer stuck in my right sock. It's a five shot twenty two caliber one. If he gets close enough to me, I'll jam the steel into him and hopefully he'll drop his gun when he realizes I have a pistol. You can grab it and we can get out of here."

"Okay but aren't we going to have to lay here and pretend to be tied up when he comes in?"

"We'll loosely wrap up our feet and lie on our backs to hide our free hands. We'll act like we are semi-conscious and very docile. He won't expect a thing. It will work providing he is alone."

I figured we had a half hour until the guy came back but we would get into position now to be safe. I could see by my watch now it was 6:37 p.m. and my head was throbbing again.

Moroch said nothing while he sat in the passenger's seat of the red pickup truck. The foreman glanced occasionally at Moroch due to fear of the unknown. He drove the truck at the posted speed limit and passed only when absolutely necessary. He didn't want any run in with the police or a traffic ticket especially carrying this man. The signs for Providence came into sight. The foreman got up enough courage to ask Moroch where he wanted to be driven. Moroch stared out the window for ten or fifteen seconds before turning to the foreman and telling him to keep driving.

"I will tell you when it is time to leave I-Ninety-five," was his only statement as he turned back to look out the window of the red pickup.

Rich Strong called Joshua Sprague on his cell phone. Joshua picked up immediately as he looked at his watch.

"Agent Sprague," he said.

"Boss, I have been in touch with the two agents that lost the tail on the Honda that had been tailing your Dad."

Joshua listened to Rich as he informed him the agents backtracked on their tail of the Honda to a place called the Pequot State Park Swimming Pond. They had been directed there based on some local residents hearing pistol shots and reporting it to the local authorities. When they arrived, they spotted the Honda in the dirt parking lot with several rogues going through the car. The rogues ran into the woods with whatever they had taken from the Honda as the agents slowly approached. They found the two guys they recognized as the ones his father had the run in with. Both were shot execution style.

"Rich, you sure about the type of execution?"

"I am sure, boss. Both guys had a precise close range shot to the head. They were probably unsuspecting and knew their killer. If it had been rogues, I'm sure there would have been evidence to indicate some kind of a shootout. There wasn't according to our agents."

"Anyone see anything at all?"

"Yes, the agents interviewed one local who said that she had seen two cars go down into the swimming pond but only saw a black SUV come out after she reported the shots. We got a partial plate number from her and we are searching as we speak."

"Good, let me know," he said as he closed his cell. He knew he couldn't wait any longer as he opened his cell phone back up again and dialed his mother's number. As it rang he glanced at his watch. It was 7:10 p.m.

"Hello?"

"Mom," was all Josh could get out of his mouth.

"What's wrong? It's your father, isn't it? Is he alright? He's late and he won't answer his phone. Josh, tell me what is going on."

"Mom, we are looking for him," was all he could say.

"What do you mean, you are looking for him. For God's sake you had him under surveillance. What are you doing about it?" She continued to rant and rave.

"Mom, please calm down and I'll explain," was all he could say this time before she cut him off.

"Calm down? Calm down you say? I'm your mother Joshua Jonathan, and you asked me to calm down?" She was yelling now.

"Mom, if you don't calm down and be quiet, I'm going to hang up and you won't know anything," he yelled back. There was a pause and then she said, "Tell me Josh, quickly, and in detail. Explain to me what happened and what you are doing about it."

He told her all he knew and told her he would get back to her as soon as he had more information.

His mother said, "You call me immediately on any changes, do you hear me? Find him Josh."

The phone went dead. Josh closed his cell phone as Agent Strong was entering the office.

"That was your Mom, right?" he asked.

"Unfortunately, yes," he said as he picked up his office phone.

The Search Begins

Josh began notifying agents in the Providence and Boston area of his plan to search the IH plant and depot as well as the central artery terminal. He notified the Rhode Island State Police that he was requesting a SWAT team be made available. He had his office contact the Newport Naval Base Shore Patrol Office and was in direct contact with Senior Chief Brian McAuliffe's commander. Josh kept the affiliation of Ed McAuliffe from Commander Bob Arsenault who was in charge of all base security. Josh did explain that the Commander should notify Lieutenant Commander Woodbridge on the U.S.S. Clinton that his father was one of the individuals that were missing in the vicinity of the base along with another individual named Jon Sprague. He made no mention of the relationship. He also informed the Commander that the two individuals in question were harmless, but their lives were in danger from persons of interest that had been associated with the Harvester Plant and the fireworks barge moored in the harbor. Josh requested that no signs be made to alert the individuals working or otherwise associated with the Harvester Plant and fireworks barge until he presented and reviewed his plan with the Commander. The Command complied and said that he would alert key individuals in his command but would not proceed to do anything until he consulted with Josh and had reviewed his plan. Josh thanked him and told him he would be in Newport within the next few hours.

Rich Strong called Josh on his cell to give him an update.
"Boss, the guys in the Honda were illegal aliens. We traced their ID cards through IH and they were not employed by them. Harvester said that they were never part of their organization. We also searched the FBI database's physical facial features and identified one guy as Muhammad Owlia. This guy came from Iran through Kuwait. Owlia had been involved with the Costello family until Ernesto became concerned about Middle

Eastern employees after nine-eleven. Ernesto purged the company of them despite the protest from his son, Donnie. We don't have any further information why Ernesto purged his organization of Middle Eastern types but my thought is that this ex-marine may still be patriotic in some sick way. Ernesto forced Donnie Costello to fire Sid Owlia about the same time. I also suspect that the dead Owlia could have been a relative brought over by Sid. I assume, boss, that Sid regained favored status again with the Costellos once Donnie started running Middle Eastern cargo. He knew Sid's expertise and used him to his advantage to take over the majority of the business from the old man as he started to fail in the past several years. We are still searching for information on the second guy."

Josh thanked him and instructed him to keep updating him as he found out more information.

The Shore Patrol and the Newport Police found the Sprague truck about 7:30 p.m. The Newport Police were advised that a truck was blocking the road on Vine Street and that the local residents who investigated found a person lying under the truck who had been seriously injured. The Newport Police had the Newport Fire Department Ambulance Service bring the injured man to the hospital. The Shore Patrol called their Commander to inform him that they had found the truck that the FBI had asked them to search for. Commander Arsenault immediately called Josh on his cell phone.

"Special Agent Sprague, this is Bob Arsenault at the Naval Base."

Josh acknowledged and listened to the Commander as he informed him of the injured man that they were told by the Newport Police, was taken to the hospital in serious condition. Josh swallowed as he asked, "Did they identify the injured man yet?"

"No, but I understand that he had been stabbed several times in the stomach and had lost a large amount of blood."

Josh thanked him and asked the Commander to call him as soon as he found out any new information.

Josh wanted to relax but he couldn't just yet. He knew his father carried his identification with him all the time. He was sure that the Newport Police would have identified his father very quickly. The once registered Colt in his glove box that he kept there at all times would confuse the cops because he knew it was registered last to Joshua Jonathan Sprague and not Jonathan Sprague. He thought quickly of when they use to target practice together. It was a moot point now.

He called the Chief of Police in Newport. He explained what was happening and asked him to contact his people and report immediately on the identification of the individual that was taken to the hospital who had been stabbed in the vicinity of Vine Street. The Chief said that he would be in contact as soon as he had updated his people on his request. Josh thanked him as he walked to the door of Chief Agent John DiStasio. He knocked and John signaled him to enter through the glass door that separated DiStasio from the rest of the office.

"What's happening Josh?"

For the next five or six minutes, Josh updated him on the situation. He detailed what had been accomplished to organize the Naval Base, Newport Police and both the Connecticut and Rhode Island State Police concerning the disappearance of two independent truck drivers as well as the FBI's plan to deal with illegal persons, illegal cargo and known murder victims. Chief DiStasio agreed with Josh's plan and suggested a broader investigation to ensure that this situation was not bigger than first anticipated. Josh left with new orders from his superior that he definitely agreed with and welcomed.

George and I waited for the next half hour expecting our incarcerator to appear so we could try to make our way out of the hold and escape. It was 8:15 p.m. and the bastard hadn't shown up yet. As we lay on the rusty floor in our fake condition, I asked George, was he sure that the guy came every two hours or so. George responded that he did and that he had kept track of the visits since the first time he awoke. I asked George if he could remember how long he could have been out.

170

George thought a few seconds and said, "J.J., I got knocked out about 4p.m. and woke up about eight."

"Eight at night or eight in the morning?"

"Shit, it had to be eight a.m. because I had to pee and take a morning shit now that I remember. Damn, we will have to wait here until Wednesday, no Thursday morning, before we get that prick to check on us. Son of a bitch!"

"It'll be Thursday morning, the third of July, before we can make an attempt to get out of here. Should we try to bang on pipes or something to get someone above to hear us?" I asked. George reminded me that it would only bring down the bad guys. I agreed. We both decided to stick to our plan and jump anyone who opened up the door. I felt my head and it was damp. I realized that it had to be still bleeding a little.

Josh's cell rang. It was Rich Strong again.

"Yeah, tell me what's going on," Josh said.

"The other guy in the Honda was Ilea Adel who was a Lebanese gentlemen and an associate of Muhammad Owlia. He's got the same background and that's all we know about him right now."

"Okay, but keep searching their contacts and see if you can dig up someone common to the both of them in the Costello family, any terrorist group or anyone associated with the DFC."

As soon as he hung up, his phone rang again.

"Special Agent Sprague, this is Chief Donald Dowd of the Newport Police Department. The man we found under the truck and now have in the hospital is a person called Sid Owlia. We found a Connecticut Drivers License and a Harvester ID card on him. This guy must work for Harvester."

Josh asked, "Did your police officers notice if Mr. Owlia had a recently stitched wound on his head, by the way? I am curious."

"The report only indicated two stab wounds to the abdomen.

"Why do you ask?"

"I was curious about another incident tied with this guy, but it doesn't matter. Thank you, chief."

Josh pushed end on his cell and pushed number two on his speed dial. He glanced at his watch and it read 9:43 p.m. "Mom, we found Dad's truck. He was not in it but a questionable gentleman was found stabbed and lying under Dad's truck. The man is alive and we will question him as soon as he is able to talk. He has just come out of surgery. I will call you as soon as I know more. I have to run. I love you."

Josh realized that he'd never spoken to his mother so quickly before. Jean turned to Missy and repeated what Josh had just told her. Missy listened to every word and then called Joe to give him the update.

George said, "I need to get up and use that bucket again."

"Okay, I'll get by the door in case our attendant returns," I responded as I slowly maneuvered my way towards the direction of the door, sliding on the floor. George used the facility. He crept back to what he thought was the center of the hold.

"Thanks man, I hope I didn't miss the bucket. I can't see anything and I refuse to feel around for it. That thing is nasty!" George asked if I needed to pee or anything. I told him "no" and I hoped in my mind that I would never have to pee in the bucket based on the smell of it. I'll try to hold mine. I'd rather piss on the attendant before I attempt to use that thing.

Moroch told the driver of the red pickup truck to turn off on the next exit and follow whatever road was going north until he told him otherwise. The driver said that he needed to get back to Newport tonight because he was expected by his family over two hours ago. Moroch said nothing as he stared straight ahead. The driver waited for a response. Moroch looked at him and told him to pull over before he got to the exit. The driver immediately pulled into the emergency break down lane on I-95 South, stopped the truck and was looking to put on the emergency flashers. Moroch instructed him to take the truck out of gear and slide over to the passenger side of the truck. He then informed him that he would drive the remaining miles to their destination.

Moroch rolled down the window on the passenger side as he exited the truck. The driver slid over and fixed his seat belt and waited for him to walk to the front and then the other side of the truck to enter the driver's side. For just a second or two, the former driver thought about getting back into the driver's seat and leaving this crazy bastard here in the middle of nowhere. As Moroch walked around to the driver's side he drew out his Walther PPK and kept it in his left hand, sheltered from his companion's view. He entered the driver's seat and began to engage the truck and drive off. His passenger looked ahead and was unconcerned. Moroch switched the Walther quickly and pointed it to the head of the passenger. He pulled the trigger and the left side of his newest victim's head exhibited a perfectly round dark red spot as the right side of his head exploded with pink brain tissue and blood. He quickly stopped the slow moving truck. He bent over and unlocked the door and pushed his latest victim out of the truck and onto the breakdown lane. He left immediately and checked around quickly to see if anyone had noticed what he'd done. The few cars that were out in the opposite direction were too far away to see anything. In the rear view mirror he noticed two cars approaching as he attempted to gain speed and leave the scene.

State Trooper Richard Longo had been a Connecticut State Trooper for six years. The Norwich, Connecticut native had just been married and returned from his weekend honeymoon to Block Island, Rhode Island two days ago. Block Island had become a big honeymoon resort during the spring, summer and fall months in the last five years due to the price of fuel and lack of transportation to go anywhere. Trooper Longo could see the red truck signaling back on the Interstate. He caught a glimpse of something as he concentrated on the red pickup. As he passed, he recognized that it was a human body. He jammed on his breaks and came to a screeching halt. He backed up and immediately put his search light on the apparent victim of a hit and run incident. He called on his radio to inform his dispatch operator that he had come upon a possible hit and run victim and that he was exiting his cruiser to investigate. The operator acknowledged his call and said that she would stand by. Longo checked the victim and, to his horror, recognized an execution style head wound. He'd remembered from earlier in his shift, the two guys they found 25 miles from here that had met a similar fate. He checked the road side mile marker and radioed his position. He then requested an ambulance to be sent to that location. He was also requesting back up as he was in pursuit of a red pickup truck seen leaving the scene.

Moroch wasn't sure that the car that he knew had stopped was the police but he didn't want to take any chances. As soon as he exited I-95, he immediately began his plan to re-enter I-95 North using the corresponding entrance ramp. While he maneuvered to accomplish this, Trooper Longo was just exiting the Interstate. The State Trooper hadn't turned on his emergency pursuit lights in the hope of being able to catch the red pickup unsuspectingly. He caught his second glimpse of a rear tail light entering the opposite entrance ramp heading north. Based on a clear view of the road ahead, and no tail lights in sight in an area he was very familiar with, he chose to do a quick turn and pursue his hunch. He chose to keep his pursuit lights off until he visually confirmed he had the red pickup.
Moroch kept nervously glancing in the rear view mirrors of the truck. He was exceeding 80 miles per hour when he noticed a set of head lights behind him. He slowed a little so not to draw much attention to himself in case it was a cop. He looked down and he had reduced his speed to the speed limit. He kept the Walther on the seat and easily accessible if need be. Trooper Longo could see a vehicle up a head and waited a few seconds as he gained on it to positively identify the vehicle as the one he saw leaving the scene of the crime. He got closer and realized that it was the pickup. He identified his position to the police dispatcher and crept slowly closer to the truck to

read the plate number. He called in the number, Rhode Island commercial plate number LJW 025. He maintained his position behind the red pickup, still with no pursuit lights on yet. What seemed to be many minutes to Trooper Longo, the police dispatcher identified the truck as belonging to Leo Lupinacci of Westerly, Rhode Island. The dispatcher said that there were no arrest warrants out for this man and that he had only a few breach of peace incidents on record. The dispatcher said that he should proceed with caution.

Trooper Longo immediately put on his pursuit lights and siren simultaneously in an effort to stop the red pickup truck. Moroch clutched his Walther on the seat next to him as he slowly obliged the request of the State Trooper. Both vehicles came to a stop on I-95 North. Trooper Longo radioed that he had stopped the truck and he was investigating. The trooper left the driver's side of his police cruiser and approached the red pickup from the passenger side. His flashlight was firmly held in his left hand while he held his right hand close to the handle of his automatic pistol. Moroch kept still with both hands in plain sight on the steering wheel. He knew the drill from experiences he'd had in previous situations like this. The trooper flashed his light into the truck and illuminated Moroch's head and the right side of his face. Moroch turned slowly and politely asked through the open passenger window, "What seems to be the problem, Officer?"
"Please exit the driver's door slowly," the officer said as he slowly moved up to the passenger side window. Moroch kept his hands in full view but did not exit as requested.
Moroch asked again, "What seems to be the problem, Officer?"
Trooper Longo slowly spoke again that he wanted him to exit the driver's door slowly. Moroch still refused to move and appeared, to the trooper, to be scared by the changed tone of voice. This should have been a signal to the Trooper that the nervous driver was about to do something. It was a mistake the trooper would find out the hard way. He bent down and looked into the truck cab with his flashlight shining through the rear

175

sliding window and on Moroch. The trooper slowly un-holstered his pistol with his right hand which was not in view of Moroch and began to request, for the third time, for him to exit the vehicle. Moroch waited until the face of the trooper was clear and in full view of the window. It was then that the trooper noticed the blood spatter on the upholstery of the tan interior fabric of the truck. As Trooper Longo reached and pulled out his pistol, Moroch grabbed the partially hidden Walther and fired point blank into his face. The trooper was pushed back by the force of the blast and fell straight onto his back on the emergency lane concrete. The video camera in Trooper Longo's cruiser recorded the entire incident. Moroch put the red pickup in gear and quickly drove away. A few minutes later the dispatcher called Trooper Longo and asked his location and status. The dispatcher repeated her request three times before alerting troopers in the area of the no response situation.

Joe Harris got the call while he was in route to investigate the body of Leo Lupinacci that had just been found on Interstate 95 South. Joe realized the two incidents were connected by the name of the victim and now the victim's truck was involved in a routine pullover with a no response situation from the involved officer. He felt a cold chill run down his spine as he pressed down the accelerator of his state police cruiser.

Trooper Longo twitched and moaned for a few minutes until he became conscious. His left temple was bleeding and he felt excruciating pain. He realized that the man in the red pickup truck had attempted to kill him. He thanked Jesus that he was still alive and would be able to see his new bride tonight. He got up slowly and headed for his state cruiser. The video recorded his slow walk back to the car. He immediately radioed that he had been shot and requested assistance. The dispatcher could be heard asking him questions with excitement in her voice. She was happy to hear his voice even though he had been shot. Trooper Longo looked at himself in the rear view mirror. He had a perfectly straight gash in the left side of his head. If he hadn't moved his head the instant he saw the Walther he would have been dead.

Joe Harris heard the radio report coming from Longo. He could now see Longo's cruiser up ahead and he knew he would be the first on the scene to assist the injured officer. Longo saw him coming and waved him on in the direction that the red pickup truck had fled. Harris understood him but he stopped to make sure Longo was stable. Longo approached Joe's cruiser and yelled, "Get the bastard, I'll be okay Sergeant." Joe acknowledged and began his pursuit of the red pickup truck.

Moroch knew that he could not stay on I-95 North so he headed south into Connecticut. He also knew that every State Policeman would be looking for him in a red, of all colors, pickup truck, and that they had probably figured out that he shot and killed Leo Lupinacci. He turned at the next exit. He turned right towards the lights of a few houses he had seen from the Interstate before he exited. He drove slowly in search of another vehicle that he could confiscate. There were none to be found. He entered a small town. There were very few lights on as it was now approaching 10:30 p.m. and suddenly he noticed a car approaching in the opposite direction. The car signaled right and turned to enter a driveway as the automatic door opened and lit the way for the approaching vehicle. Moroch slowed the truck and timed himself almost perfectly to enter the same driveway exactly behind the Green Toyota Hybrid. The operator of the Toyota became terrified as he drove his automobile into the garage with glaring lights from a vehicle directly behind him. Moroch placed the red pickup truck in a position so that the garage door could not be operated to close. He jumped out of the truck quickly and was at the driver's door pointing his Walther in the face of the Toyota's driver in a matter of seconds. He quietly waved to the driver to get out. The driver began to talk loudly that he didn't want any trouble but Moroch signaled for him to be quiet. He made the gesture as if he would cut the man's throat if he continued to talk. The driver understood. He made the driver get into his truck and whispered into his ear to back the truck up and pull over enough so he could exit the garage. The driver slowly did as he was directed as Moroch trained his pistol at the man the entire time. As soon as the pickup was far enough away, he signaled the scared driver to stop. He casually walked over to the driver and told him to exit the truck. He complied. Moroch hit him over the head with the Walther. The man went down to his knees but was still conscious. He hit him a second time to render him unconscious.

Moroch got in the Toyota and slowly backed it out of the garage and courteously, he thought, closed the garage door behind him with the remote control. There were no lights or movement from the house he noted as he laughed, thinking how easy it was in this country to steal as one needed. He was back on Interstate 95 South and guessed that he would not be bothered by the police until the man woke up and reported his car stolen; that is, if he did wake up from that second hit on the head. He looked at his watch and figured he would arrive in New London in time to supervise the final tasks to get the barge ready for towing. He would send Darish Adel from New London to Newport and have him supervise the same. Darish would be finished with his task before he ever found out that his relative, Ilea, was dead. He would never know that he was one of his victims. He pleased himself at the thought that he would be near McAuliffe's home and be able to neutralize him at his convenience.

Josh looked at Rich and said that he should catch some sleep in the lounge. It was going to be a long night coordinating this case and he figured they should alternate commanding the control room as information came in. Rich obliged and untied his tie and removed his sports jacket to lie down. He slipped his loafers off and placed one foot at a time on the lounge. Josh hit the light switch in the corner of the room to aid in setting the condition of sleep. He glanced at his watch and calculated that his father had been missing about six hours and that

Woodridge had surpassed seventy two hours. They had to be somewhere near the plant, barge or harbor. He hoped that neither man was in the harbor.

Josh kept reviewing his notes about the DFC in his head. He reviewed his notes on the Costello family as well as a few of the Middle Eastern gentlemen they had encountered in the last twenty four hours. He knew that the key to breaking this case was to see the Costello family first thing in the morning, and, leaving no stone unturned, observe and question everything. They would have an excellent chance of questioning all the main players of the family. Ernesto would be with Donnie as they attended Gene Moretti's funeral. Josh thought that he would be able to put a little pressure on them when they were vulnerable. He could also inform Donnie in front of Ernesto that Sid Owlia was in critical condition, maybe even dead. After that shock he would gladly inform them that Sid's brother, Muhammad was also dead. It got better he thought, because he would have Rich Strong with him and he could have Rich tell Tommy Lupinacci in front of his bosses that Leo, his brother, was now dead as well along with a middle eastern gentlemen identified as Ilea Adel. His next statement to all these men wouldn't be condolences but the threat of action from the FBI, CIA, Military Police, two State Police departments and the Newport City Police.

The Funeral

July 3rd was going to be another warm day. Not as hot as the previous five or six days but the meteorologist predicted the temperature would reach the low eighties. Mr. Guillot of Guillot Brothers Funeral Homes was busy planning the services for Gene Moretti. He was nervous thinking that the head of the Costello family would be in his establishment mourning the killing of his nephew at the hands of the State Police. It was bad enough when the police were present when the rival mob families killed each other, but to have the police, who were responsible for the killing present, was unnerving to Mr. Guillot.

He barked orders at his subordinates to check various things that were important to have a successful funeral with no obvious glitches. He knew the Costello family had requested to be at the funeral home at 8:30 a.m. to begin to welcome their guests prior to viewing the body before the service for Gene Moretti at St. Patrick's at 10:00 a.m. Donnie Costello had been emphatic that he alone would be the lead mourner for his cousin. He didn't want his father embarrassing the family in front of everyone. The old man had a tendency to get confused and repeat himself to the annoyance of everyone around. Mr. Guillot glanced at his watch again for the fifth time in less than a minute. It was approaching 8:20 a.m. and the rented limousines would be delivering the entire Costello family momentarily. The state police were stationed all around the funeral home already.

Across from the funeral home, agents Josh Sprague and Rich Strong waited to observe the limousines they knew would be approaching. Josh yawned while Rich tried to subdue his yawn as they waited. They both looked very tired because they had only been able to sleep several hours due to the constant updates being given to them at the control point office during the previous evening.

"Here comes Donnie boy and the old man. I'll take those two," Josh said, as he stepped out of the car. Rich looked at him and nodded while he observed the second car and identified Tommy Lupinacci. As the procession began to form in front of the funeral home, Agents Sprague and Strong sought out their assigned individuals.

Donnie noticed Josh approaching him while he assisted his father out of the car. Several Costello strongmen quickly moved close to Donnie and Ernesto on seeing the approaching FBI agents. Josh spoke while presenting his badge.

"Mr. Costello, I am Special Agent Joshua Sprague. I need to ask you a few questions." Donnie looked at the strongmen and by his facial expression they knew to back down and allow the conversation to take place.

"This is a private funeral, agent, and I would appreciate it if you would allow us some privacy as we mourn one of our family members." He stared at Josh, never blinking or moving his eyes at all.

"I assure you that what I have to say won't take very long." Donnie continued to stare without saying a word.

Josh began, "Mr. Costello I need to inform you that one of your employees, a Mr. Sid Owlia, is in critical condition at the hospital. He had been stabbed by an unknown assailant and is not expected to survive the day."

Ernesto said, "I fired him years ago."

Donnie looked at his father and then back at Josh and said, "Please continue."

By this time Tommy Lupinacci had been informed by Rich Strong that his brother was dead.

He walked to Donnie and said, "Leo was killed last night." Ernesto looked confused and couldn't figure out the magnitude of what had just happened to one of his captain's brothers. Donnie shook his head in disgust and asked Josh if he knew who Leo's killer was. Josh answered that he had suspected someone who was tied up with either the DFC or the guys Donnie Costello said were employed with IH.

Josh continued. "We also have more victims that you are

181

associated with. You know Muhammad Owlia, Sid's relative? He was killed. Do you know Ilea Adel who was with Muhammad?"

Donnie said nothing at first. He told the people in the procession to begin to enter the funeral home and he would talk with the agents. No one protested as they filed pass. Josh had Donnie's full attention. Josh detailed the past 80 hours as Donnie listened. Josh finished with asking Donnie two clear questions.

"When was the last time you saw George Woodbridge and Jon Sprague?" Donnie paused and said that he never met Mr. Woodbridge but he did meet the Sprague guy only once during a delivery. He explained to Josh that it was just after meeting Sprague that he left Newport to make funeral arrangements for his cousin. Both he and Tommy had been involved at the Newport plant but he had left Sid in charge at Newport and another guy in charge down here.

"Why do you ask me about these guys?" Donnie asked.

"Because neither of them have been seen since they delivered their cargo to the Newport plant. Mr. Costello, we think that the DFC is a front for a possible terrorist group. Some of the employees that you say are Harvester employees have been found out to be illegal aliens from Iran and other Middle Eastern countries. We suspect that this terrorist organization has used your shipping company to front some secret activities that involve Newport and probably other cities in this country. What they are planning is unbeknownst to the FBI and other authorities at this time." Donnie listened intently as Josh spoke. "Agent, I will do all I can to assist you with your request as soon as I have completed the business at hand. I'm sure the FBI can wait several more hours until I am free. Where shall I meet you?"

"We will be here after the service." Donnie left him there as he walked into the funeral home.

Woodbridge looked at his watch and said, "J.J. that son of a bitch has left us here to die. He ain't coming back, is he?"

"He'll be back for us, George. Either he has to make sure we are dead or he will have to kill us. Perhaps he has to take us out of here," I said realizing how my first statement sounded. I had no clue what these guys, whoever they were, were going to do to us. We hoped and waited. I even did a little praying to ease some tension as we sat in the damp, stinky and dark hold. We could hear noises from people working on the barge above us. I was sure it was in preparation for tomorrow's Fourth of July celebration and fireworks.

The mass for Gene Moretti at St. Patrick's Cathedral ended at 10:50 a.m. and the trip to the cemetery began. Josh and Rich watched from a distance. There were other agents assigned to watch different employees of the Costello family. The state and local police were standing watch also to ensure no one interfered with the service. Josh looked at his watch and remarked, "This shithead is going straight to hell so why are they wasting time putting on a show that he was a goddamned angel or something. They should stick him in a crematory and burn his ass to ashes."
Rich chuckled a little but kept his mouth shut. He reminded his boss that no one was under arrest so they would have to wait and bear the torture of waiting for Moretti to be planted.

Moroch woke just before 11 a.m. He had parked the stolen green Toyota Hybrid two blocks from the apartment he rented with Darish. He had already sent Darish to Newport. He was to supervise and protect the cargo that had been placed in the barge while the fireworks were being loaded by the representatives from Deutsch. He had gone over the plan twice. The fireworks installation by the Deutsch representatives would take place work on the first level of the barge. Darish was to ensure that he armed the already loaded explosives on the second level deck. They had been cleverly loaded into the ballast compartments that were contained and out of sight of anyone venturing down below. His task was to ensure that the last section of fireworks that were designated to go off during the grand finale would trigger a sensing device in the barge. All the ballast compartments that were filled with explosives were to remain dry. In order to accomplish this, the ballast status board on the barge had been rigged to indicate red if the compartments were flooded to assist in ballasting the barge. If it indicated green, it meant that the ballast compartments were dry. The CTC took care of those details. The ballast status board had been rigged that way so that anyone observing the status board would think the compartments were flooded, but in reality, they were dry and full of explosives.

As the barge was towed past the U.S.S. Clinton by the CTC tug, Darish would activate an electronic trigger that would detonate a small charge he had placed on the cable to sever it from the tug to the barge. This would be the signal for the tug pilot to begin his task. He had been trained to position the tug so it looked like he was attempting to take control of the loose barge. The Coast Guard and Security in the harbor would observe the tug pilot ordering his deck hands to fasten the tug to the barge, secure the barge, and begin to push it back to its berthing at the pier. The pilot would then radio the proper authorities that he had the barge under control. The bumping of the tug to the barge would not trigger the sensing device. The tug pilot knew from his training that he would have to push the barge as quickly as possible into the hull of the carrier. The pilot knew the location of the reactors on the carrier. The collision of the barge into the hull of the carrier would set off the motion sensors on the barge. They would ignite the loaded ballast compartments to produce an explosion destructive enough to rupture the hull of the carrier and scramble the reactors. The blast and concussion would kill anyone within a hundred yards of the explosion. The radiation exposure from this catastrophic event would eventually kill anyone in 24 hours, who had been within two miles of the blast. In all, the terrorists expected to kill, by exposure to radiation and the blast, some 50,000 people. They estimated that 25,000 people would show up for the fireworks and die in that first 24 hours.

It would be a great day, they both agreed, before they parted.

Moroch showered and dressed. He ate some fruit that he found on the kitchen table. He looked around and spotted the picture of Darish and his brother Ilea in a happier time. He knew he would never have to tell Darish that he had killed his stupid brother. Darish himself would be dead in 24 hours. Perhaps he'll meet his brother in heaven, he laughed. Moroch left the apartment and walked several blocks until he could see the barge docked at the New London City pier. He looked across and could see the U.S.S. North Carolina anchored down the river supplying electrical power to the Electric Boat Ship yard and the surrounding cities of New London and Groton, Connecticut. His plan and timetable was identical to Darish's. He felt confident that the other three would be as successful as they were going to be. He presented his Deutsch identification card to the security guard and walked across the brow to the barge. It was noon, Thursday, July 3.

Darish entered the foreman's office at the Newport Harvester plant and found the barge attendant sitting at the foreman's desk. The attendant stood up when he entered. Darish asked him where Sid Owlia was. The attendant replied that he didn't know where anyone had gone. Darish asked, impatience obviously showing, what the attendant meant by that statement. "I helped Leo take the driver to the hold and I have not seen him since. He left in his truck to pick up a man he called Moroch," he said, looking uneasy. Darish asked him his name.
"They call me Scooter, mister," he smiled. Darish never smiled or made any attempt to ease him.
"What do you do here?"
"I help around the pier and do odd jobs for Leo."
"Where do you live?"
"I have a room in the plant near the men's shower room."
"Have you seen Ilea or Muhammad?" Scooter said that he didn't know who they were. Darish kept his patience.
"They drove a silver Honda. They were security guards who

185

checked deliveries to and from the plant. Did you see them?" he asked while raising his voice a little.

"Oh yeah." Scooter said that he hadn't seen them since yesterday. He couldn't remember when exactly. Darish moved past Scooter and opened up the foreman's desk and recognized keys that were identical to the ones he had left for Moroch to pick up in his New London apartment. He told Scooter to wait outside. Scooter looked confused.

"Get out, now," he demanded. Scooter moved quickly and left. Darish dialed his cell phone. It rang only once and Moroch answered. Darish informed him what he'd found and that he was concerned that there were no men he could trust to supervise the Deutsch fireworks workers when they started loading the fireworks into the first deck of the barge in approximately one hour. Moroch listened. He was also concerned that Adel and Mohammad were not there yet to assist in the security duties that had been planned for today.

"I don't know where your brother or his companion is," Moroch said. "I'm disappointed that they had not fulfilled their duties. Ask Leo to supply two men to make sure the Deutsch workers do not enter the second deck."

"He is not here," Darish answered. Moroch assured him that no one knew what was in the second deck except Ilea and Mohammad. He corrected himself.

"The imbecile Scooter has been to the second and third deck but he is unaware of the material stored there. I know he has checked on the two in the hold. Do not say anything more to him. He is harmless and not worth the effort to eliminate. He will go with all of us when the time is right," he said as he hung up.

Darish held the cell phone to his ear a few seconds more than he needed to while he thought of the duties he must carry out. He left the foreman's office and observed the DFC logo on three delivery trucks that slowly drove into the Harvester parking lot and close to the pier crane. Scooter stood off to the side near the foreman's office door. Darish looked at him.

"Come here." Scooter jogged over.

186

"Listen carefully because I will not repeat this to you again, understand?"

Scooter stammered, "Yes sir."

"I want you to go into the barge and make sure that no one enters the second deck for any reason. If someone requests access to the second deck, you tell them to come and find me. I will be on the first deck observing the workers loading and installing the fireworks for tomorrow night. Do you understand?" he asked looking straight into Scooter's face. Scooter was frozen with fear. When he was finished, Scooter only shook his head up and down quickly and turned and left. Darish thought how someone like this would not survive in his country. Someone would have eliminated him long before he reached adulthood.

The services at the cemetery ended and the Costello party entered their cars at the Maplewood Cemetery for the drive back to the reception hall where they had planned to dine for lunch. Donnie Costello assisted his father, mother and aunt into the lead limousine. He explained to his parents and aunt that he would meet them at the reception because he had some business to attend to. He closed the door and the auto procession slowly drove away and out of the cemetery. Donnie entered one of the other captain's cars with Tommy Lupinacci and headed for the Guillot Brothers Funeral Home across town. Agents Sprague and Strong were already waiting in the funeral home parking lot.

The stolen green Toyota Hybrid was parked on Bank Street. People passed it without taking any notice. It was another car parked in a bus pickup point which would get towed soon if the owner didn't move it. Officer Al Kinsal walked the Bank Street beat every morning and afternoon for years and knew every place where traffic violations occurred and where he could contemplate potential trouble areas in the city. He recognized the parking violation immediately. He walked to the green Toyota and wrote down the plate number. He waited for a few minutes to allow the owner to notice him near the car so that he or she could claim it, give some lame excuse and move it before he would have to call to have it towed. Parking violations usually warranted a ticket but this car was parked in the bus stop area where signs clearly said that violations would result in towing at the owner's expense. The officer waited. No owner appeared after several minutes. He called the dispatcher and reported the plate number, location and auto description. He requested a tow truck be sent as soon as possible. He waited for the usual acknowledgement when the dispatcher replied, "The auto description and plate number indicated a stolen auto. Proceed with caution. Backup is in route to your location." Officer Kinsal stepped away from the car and back onto the street. He walked away from the car just in case the owner returned. He did not want to cause an altercation until backup arrived. He walked approximately 25 yards away and proceeded to act as a routine cop on the beat. He heard the sounds of several sirens approaching. He timed his arrival back at the stolen car as a New London patrol car and a State Police cruiser arrived.

Moroch entered the fireworks barge moored to the New London City pier. He showed his identification card to the one of Darish's men who wore a Deutsch Security uniform. He called to one of the security guards and asked him if the Crescent tug had arrived. The security man nodded to Moroch as he passed and pointed over to the opposite side of the pier where the bright green and black tug was moored. A large white crescent symbolized more than just a tug company to him. The Deutsch fireworks workers were busy loading fireworks onto the barge. The identical units that had been trucked to the Newport barge had been strategically placed on top of the deck of this barge. Moroch noticed how easy it had been for Darish to load this barge. All the units were topside and did not require the deck modification that the Newport barge had needed. He knew the Deutsch engineer assigned to the Newport job had been an idiot. All those days he had to work with the moron to cut holes in the Newport barge's deck to keep the units protected from the elements while the engineer here at New London and probably at all the other locations had allowed the units to be covered with canvas. He envied Darish for the easy task he had here in New London. Moroch was afraid that the explosives stored in the second deck of the Newport barge would explode with all the cutting torches and sparks working just a few feet above them. He did credit Mohammad and Ilea for keeping workers away from the second deck during the evening hours when most of the cutting of the deck took place. It didn't matter now, he thought. All had worked out except for the two drivers that Sid had mistakenly kept hidden in the barge. He should have eliminated them but he realized that their missing was better than their discovery dead somewhere. Again, he thought, it didn't matter. They would all be casualties tomorrow night.

Donnie Costello and Tommy Lupinacci got out of the car that had taken them back to the Guillot Brothers Funeral Home parking lot. He walked to the FBI agent's car with two strong men following closely behind. Josh called out to Donnie and Tommy to sit in the back seat. Donnie waved off the strongmen and told them to wait in the car. Both men entered the agent's car. Josh proceeded to first give his condolences to both men for their losses. Rich Strong kept a straight face as he thought of Josh's comments earlier that had made him chuckle. Josh proceeded to inform Donnie of the dealings that Sid Owlia had with known Middle Eastern terrorists groups. He also explained that he was not interested in the Costello family's black market deals but was interested that his organization was probably being used as a front to carry weapons or explosives to specific locations in an effort to cause destruction of the United States and her allies. Donnie began to protest when Rich cut him short.

"The DFC of Bonn, Germany is a legitimate fireworks company but they too have probably been used as a front because of their ties to known terrorist groups," Agent Strong interjected.

Josh cut back in and said, "IH had contracts to build the units for the DFC and the units were considered highly competitive by Deutsch. They were checking all their records to see where the units were shipped to besides Newport."

"The Deutsch representatives that we did business with said that they would provide security at the Harvester depots and plants as we shipped the units. Tommy made contact with the union guys at IH and the central artery terminal to make sure we were the only ones that supplied the dock hands to load the delivery trucks. We couldn't get the artery foremen to agree to let us use our own delivery drivers and trucks in and out of his terminal. We had to convince the Deutsch people that it was safe for the artery terminal to pick drivers and use local trucks. They weren't happy but eventually they agreed to let the artery foreman supply the drivers and trucks so the terminal foreman picked locals who needed the work. In the old days, my father would have convinced him to use our drivers and trucks but I don't do business like that agent," Donnie said. Lupinacci sat there and just nodded in agreement with Donnie.

"Hey Tommy," Donnie said. "Were the units delivered?"

"The last units were shipped to Portsmouth last night."

Donnie looked at Josh and said, "Agent, I'm an American just like you. I run a business and sometimes that business crosses people that you don't consider welcome in your circle if you get what I mean. I was a Marine. Just like Tommy, Sid and my Dad. We served in some hot spots during our tours with the Marines. My dad is a decorated Korean veteran. I don't know what you are getting at or what is going on here except that we have now lost two people and I don't like to be made a fool of by anyone. I will help in any way that I can."

Josh acknowledged his apparent cooperation and began to ask details as to why Gene Moretti was where he was the night he was killed and why Sid Owlia would have been stabbed in Newport. He wanted to know when any of Donnie's dock workers had last seen Woodbridge or Sprague. Tommy Lupinacci's eyes lit up for the first time and he asked, "Jon

Sprague related to you?"

"He is a relative." Josh left it at that. Agents Sprague and Strong continued to gather information from the two men for the next hour. As information was made available, it was forwarded to Chief Agent DiStasio's office.

Smooth Talker

Chief Agent John DiStasio had made a career in the U.S. Army for 20 years and retired as a Lieutenant Colonel before entering the FBI. He now was approaching 20 years of service in the FBI. The 65-year-old New York City native was looking forward to retirement on Long Island in a year or so. He listened to the reports being submitted by Special Agent Sprague and was looking at his greater New York and New England plot board in front of him. He used a grease pen to circle the city locations of Newport, RI, New London, CT and now Portsmouth, NH on the plot board. He had names of individuals and associated notes and details pertaining to each one as he pondered the connection. He glanced down at his watch and decided to ask one of the agents outside his office if anyone was going for pickup. The time was 1:04 p.m.

I had been forced to relieve my bowels into the bucket that my friend had used several times before me today. The stench, heat and atmosphere in the hold were becoming unbearable. George Woodbridge had been quiet for over an hour now. I didn't know if he had fainted or was just resting so I decided to crawl back into the direction where I thought George would be. I couldn't see the glow from George's watch which meant the man had to be lying down. I crawled and felt my way along. I touched George.

"Hey, J.J., you getting familiar in your old age?" I was happy that George seemed okay.

"No, I'm not, you old coot. I was just making sure you weren't dead and adding to the stink you already had given to the place."

George chuckled and said that he was resting and keeping still. He told me it was getting hard to breathe, he was feeling light headed and he was really thirsty. I felt the same way. I looked at his watch. It was 1:16 p.m. I thought to myself, *where is that guy?* I tried not to think of what could happen to George and me.

Darish spent the afternoon watching the Deutsch workers loading and hooking up the fireworks. All was proceeding as scheduled. Scooter appeared only once asking him if he could get something to eat for lunch. He disappeared for a half hour, returned and didn't bother Darish for the rest of the afternoon. Darish checked on him a few times and saw him sitting near the closed second deck hatch watching the Deutsch people do their work. Moroch spent a similar afternoon. He occasionally toured the barge and nodded to the two security men he trusted to keep guard on the two entrances to the lower decks of the New London barge. No incidents occurred except one. A Deutsch worker had requested that he check a section of the lower decks to make sure some electrical panel located there was functioning properly. Moroch was made aware of the request and he accompanied the worker to the next deck. The worker made his check and didn't notice anything there. The explosives, like the explosives at Newport, were hidden in the auxiliary ballast tanks that were indicated as flooded by the red light that was lit on the control board. Those tanks were only needed when heavy loads were anticipated to be used on the barge or in very rough seas when extra weight was added to help stabilize it. To the untrained eye, no one would notice the ballast control board indication lights and what the closed and sealed doors contained. Moroch thought about the two drivers held in the third level deck of the Newport barge hold. They must be close to death now with lack of water and food and the extreme heat.

Joe Harris received the word that the New London Police had recovered the green Toyota Hybrid that had been stolen at gun point from a North Stonington, Connecticut resident. The individual that had been accosted was in stable condition at the Westerly Hospital in Rhode Island and recovering from a severe concussion inflicted by what appeared to be a pistol whipping. The description of the assailant fitted the one that State Trooper Longo had given. The Trooper was resting in the

Norwich Backus Hospital with a concussion brought about from a grazing nine millimeter bullet missing its mark. The trooper's video camera had provided a good picture of the killer in the pickup truck who had failed to kill Longo and the owner of the green Toyota Hybrid. Joe had called in the Connecticut State Police CSI unit to go over the car to gain as much evidence as possible from it. He thought about his missing father-in-law, the shooting at Jon's home, the wounded trooper assigned to his squad, and the links that seemed to be developing.

Josh called Chief Agent DiStasio and asked permission to get search warrants for the Harvester depot, Harvester plant and Newport Barge. The chief agreed to the requests and advised that he would supply the necessary agents along with the local and state police to assist. DiStasio ordered his assistants to initiate the proper communications to these agencies to get things started. He notified the special prosecutor's office to initiate the search warrants. Josh thanked him and notified Senior Chief Brian McAuliffe of the Newport Naval Base of what was happening. He didn't need his support but he didn't want any shore patrol men questioning the agents and policemen that would be descending upon his military checkpoint within the hour. Brian understood and hung up. He immediately notified the officer of the day. He suggested that the duty officer notify the Base Commander of the situation.

Josh called his mother and informed her that the search for his father was in progress and that he would notify her as soon as he had any information to relay back to her. She thanked him and hung up. Josh knew that his mother was very upset when she acted like that with him. He called his sister again. He had been talking with his sister several times during the day to see how his mother was doing. Besides being calm and sitting quietly, she had gone to church for an hour while Missy and the kids visited the Sprague home. On her return, she played a little with the kids but did not act as she usually did with them. Missy had mentioned that when she updated Josh. She also said that Joe had been at their condo getting a few hours sleep before returning to his barracks so that he could stay abreast of the shooting of one of his troopers that had taken place.

"Josh is there any connection to your case?" she asked.

He ignored her and said, "I'll call you and Mom as soon as I have anything."

Darish saw the line of local, state and unidentified police cars quickly entering the Harvester plant parking lot. He did not panic. He slowly walked to where Scooter was. He told Scooter to go below and go into one of the ballast compartments and stay there while he talked to the police. Scooter looked at him very oddly and asked why. Darish smoothly smiled at the obviously slow individual and said, "The police are looking for you because you are keeping men below. You are responsible for them being locked up and if you do not do what I say, they will find you, arrest you and take you to prison for a long time." When he spoke, he put precise placement of emphasis on certain words. Scooter looked petrified. Darish instructed Scooter to quickly go below, find the first open ballast compartment he could find and quickly enter it. If someone were to enter the one he was in he was to stay behind the open door and out of the light of the flashlight that would be used to illuminate it. He encouraged Scooter when he said that he would make sure that they never found him. Scooter disappeared.

The FBI agents were approached by the foreman of the DFC who met them in the parking lot.

"What's this all about?" he asked. The agent in charge produced a signed search warrant for the plant first and then the barge. The foreman looked at the papers and said, "This area is dangerous to be in with all the fireworks that are in various stages of installation for tomorrow's celebration. I have no objections with the plant because I don't have jurisdiction there, but I do object to your searching the barge because of the danger involved. Your officers could damage the many electronic wires that have been placed on the deck and are in various stages of being hooked up. Any damage to those electronic wires could result in the delay and even possible cancellation of the fireworks planned for tomorrow night."

The agent assured the Deutsch foreman that there would only be a few agents assigned to the barge and that he could accompany them. The foreman pointed to Darish as he slowly walked over to meet the agents and stand by the Deutsch foreman.

"I am Daryl Adams," Darish Adel said. "I am the security representative for the plant and the loading of the barge. What seems to be the problem?"

"We're here to search the plant to investigate two missing persons who were last seen delivering to the plant," Agent Howard Bruckner said.

"Well, I don't know anything about the two missing individuals but we will assist you and your men in any way we can."

"Thank you," Agent Bruckner said as he turned to his men and advised that since he was near the barge, he would search the barge while his men searched the plant.

"I'll assist you," Daryl Adams said. He felt that there was no need to have too many men interfering with the fireworks installation that the Deutsch foreman was concerned about. "It'll be easier for the two of them to search the barge while the rest of the men searched the plant."

Adams smiled. He even laughed when he said he didn't want any agents being rocketed into the harbor for setting off some of those larger fireworks. Agent Bruckner wasn't amused but he followed Adam's advice. The Deutsch foreman thanked both the agent and the security guard for their understanding of the potentially dangerous situation that existed on the barge while his men installed the live fireworks and electronic devices on board.

Agent Bruckner assigned his men to the search as he began towards the barge. The local and state police guarded the area to ensure no one came in or left during the search. Agent

Bruckner glanced at his watch. It was 3:18 p.m. He and Daryl Adams searched the top deck carefully as the Deutsch Fireworks workers went about their business. Eventually it was time to inspect and search the second deck. Adams climbed down to the second level and waited for the agent. The agent immediately noticed a board of red and green lights that were lit. The lights were depicting compartments in the barge. Agent Bruckner began to ask questions about the board.

"I assume that this is some kind of a status board for the fireworks?"

"No sir, it is the ballast compartment indication board for the barge," Adams said.

He explained that the red indicated that the compartment was full of water and that the green indicated that the compartment was empty. The agent asked why there were more green lights lit on one side than there was on the opposite. Adams explained the Naval Architects were responsible for the calculations of weights and ballast and that they had indicated what compartments were designated to be empty or full based on the weights that the Deutsch people had given them before they began loading the barge. Adams said that Agent Bruckner could see the calculations and the signed paperwork at either the topside control office on the barge or with the Newport Coast Guard Office that had control of all barge inspections and moves. Agent Bruckner understood and accepted the explanation. He approached one green lit compartment and asked if it could be opened. Adams complied and opened it. The agent couldn't see much even using his flashlight but only smelled the foul and stale air that rushed into his nostrils. The agent backed away and Adams closed the compartment. Behind the door was a very scared Scooter. The search and inspection continued through the second deck to all the green indicated compartments. The agent was satisfied not only with finding nothing but with the professional help from Daryl Adams.

Adams closed the last compartment on the second deck. He stood by the hatch to access the third deck. He stood there and waited for the agent to ask to see the third deck. The agent looked around and asked, "Is that the entrance to the third deck?"

Adams acknowledged that it was and began to open the hatch when the Agent Bruckner asked, "Is the same type of status board on this deck that we saw on the third deck?"

Adams said that there was no status board on the next deck. He explained that the second and third level ballast compartment statuses were shown on the board that the agent had seen. Agent Bruckner was convinced he was wasting time furthering his search. A voice was heard coming from the forward end of the second level deck. One of Agent Bruckner's agents informed him that the Harvester plant was thoroughly searched and no traces of explosives or any contraband had been found. He also said that there were a few Harvester plant workers in the plant now. No one here has seen the two men that were missing. Agent Bruckner instructed Adams to close the hatch and to accompany him back to the Harvester plant parking lot.

As they walked, neither man said anything until they reached the parking lot where most of the police cars had left and only several agent cars were waiting for the lead agent. Agent Bruckner thanked Adams for his professional courtesy and cooperation.

Daryl said, "You're welcome, Sir."

The agents left. Darish waited until they all had left the parking lot before he called Moroch and explained what had happened. He was distracted from making the call when he heard the whistle of the Crescent Tug as it approached the pier to where the barge was moored. The bright green and black tug with its white crescent painted on the smoke stack, relaxed Darish a little because the plan was working well.

Chief Agent DiStasio and Special Agents Sprague and Strong listened while Agent Bruckner updated them on what he had not found. All of them were disappointed but were still convinced that something was wrong and it would take more investigative teamwork to crack this case. Josh called his mother to state that the FBI, State Police and local police forces from one end of New England to the other were updated on the missing men and certain individuals of interest connected with the case. All the FBI mumbo jumbo didn't impress Jean Sprague at all even if it did come from her son.

The Connecticut State Police CSI unit didn't get a match on the fingerprints that had been taken from the red pickup truck or the green Toyota Hybrid. They couldn't match them to any finger print data base shared by the U.S., Canada or Mexico. Sergeant Harris had asked for assistance from the FBI to approach Interpol and bump the prints with them. That would take a few hours he was told. Joe decided to stop by the hospital to visit Trooper Longo and go over some questions he thought of during the day. He headed to the hospital. He couldn't keep from thinking about Jon Sprague.

Scooter stayed hidden until he thought it would be dark enough to leave the barge. It was only 6:10 p.m. when he exited the second level deck and ran into full sun light and Darish.
"You did well," Danish said to him. "Don't worry, I sent the police away. You will not have to go to prison because I saved your sorry little ass." Scooter asked if he could go to his room now. Darish dismissed him.

I woke up. I was weak, thirsty and hungry. I called over to George, "You okay?"
George answered, "I'm alive."
I asked George if he remembered if the attendant could have left any bottled water anywhere when he had last checked on him. I reminded George that he had said that the attendant pushed him to drink water when he did visit.
"Do you think that he could have left some when he last checked on you?" I asked. There was no word from George. I asked again.
George finally spoke up and said, "The only way we are going to answer that question in the complete dark is to search the

compartment hand over hand. You prepared to do that J.J. because I can't. I'm spent."

"I am going to start to feel my way around and see if I could find anything," I said.

George warned me to stay away from the shit bucket. I told him that I could smell where that came from. My eyes became heavy as I looked at his watch before moving very cautiously in the compartment that was in complete darkness. It was 7:17 p.m. I felt my head and it was still painful to touch. I could feel dampness in my fingers. I thought it was still bleeding. My hand smelled and I knew I had developed an infection.

More information came into the FBI office in Providence from other offices throughout the United States. Information was forwarded between offices if they thought it could be connected to the information that the Providence FBI office had supplied them to date. Chief Agent DiStasio pawed over every bit of information even remotely connected as he made marks and notes on his status board in his office. Besides, New London, Newport and Portsmouth, now he had circled New York and Boston based on contacts and information received involving people that they were interested in talking to, finding out more about or were gathering information based on their past because they were dead now. What were the connections, the links, and the commonalities he asked himself over and over again? He thought it was right in front of him and he couldn't see the forest for the trees, as the old saying went. Agents Sprague and Strong were looking at the same board and thinking similar thoughts that evening.

The disappointment at the Newport Harvester plant was evident on their faces. Josh decided that he would talk with Agent Bruckner face to face and see if there was anything he missed. He would see him in the morning and Josh made a note of that. He looked over at Rich Strong and said, "Give your sister a call and tell her what's going down. I haven't seen or talked to her since my mother called to ask us to check on my father and Mr. McAuliffe."

"You call her, boss. Orders that involve my sister and her relationship with you are not responded to by me," he said. Josh acknowledged that Rich was right and that he would take a few minutes to call Candice Strong and update her on why he had not seen her in a while. He loved Candy and he realized that after this case he would take some time off to be with her. She was off for the summer except for some summer school morning classes she taught to earn some extra cash but otherwise she was free most of the day and best of all, the entire night. He opened his cell and called. It was 8:07 p.m.

Cities in Peril

Interpol contacted the FBI about the finger prints they lifted. They'd found a match in their international database. The prints matched a suspected terrorist named Moroch Makel. He had been involved in transporting explosives that were seized by the Spanish authorities back in March of 2013. They identified him as one of the drivers of the vehicles that was confiscated but Makel managed to elude the authorities at several checkpoints out of Spain and into Morocco. He eventually was seen in Iran and Pakistan this year. Over the last several months, he had been tracked in and out of those countries and surfaced in several other European countries. He is suspected of killing several Spanish authorities and at least one Moroccan policeman. He was quite adaptable and apparently highly educated. He possessed a degree in mechanical engineering and spoke English, French, Spanish and Arabic fluently. Most importantly however, he was considered to be extremely dangerous and had been reported to have uncontrollable mood swings when provoked.

Joe Harris called Josh to see if he had read the report on Moroch Makel. He'd seen the report a few minutes before Joe was presented with the information.
Joe asked, "What kind of guy have we got ourselves tied in with?"
"Based on what we both read, I would say that we are on to something that is bigger than shipping contraband and illegal cargo, big guy."
"You visited Trooper Longo today, didn't you?
"Yep."
"That kid is going to be all right. He was resting comfortably. I expect the doctors to release him in the next day or so but he'll be out of work for six weeks. The doctors want to make sure his skull mends and that he's physically and mentally ready for patrol duty again," Joe said.

"What about Sid Owlia? Is he still alive? If he is, did they question him yet?"

Josh explained, "He's still alive. He lost a lot of blood before the doctors could stop the bleeding and begin to put his insides back together again. They said that he lost part of his stomach and several yards of his small intestine. He has a temporary colostomy until his bowels heal. The loss of blood induced a coma and they are hoping he wakes up so that they can question him, but they can't say when he will become conscious."

"The Rhode Island State Police CSI unit and the FBI explosives unit worked together on your father's truck and found his blood all over the cab and on some paper towels that were left in it. The blood was dried and they estimate that it was used to wipe his head first before it was spread in the cab."

Josh responded, "Someone is trying to cover up something different than what they figured we would surmise. There were no signs of any explosive residue found in the truck. The Norwich, Connecticut Police investigated the Woodbridge truck and found nothing out of the ordinary there either. Everywhere we turn we come up with shit."

Josh's words were said with obvious frustration. Joe thanked him for the information and said that something would turn up because a lot of people were involved trying to figure out what was going on.

Joe called Missy to check on her and the kids and to ask how Jean was doing.

"Mom has said nothing since Dad's disappearance. Can you please send someone over to her house to pick her up and drive her over here? I hate the thought of her sitting in that house all alone."

"Okay, I'll send someone over immediately," Joe said before hanging up.

He called into the dispatcher to send a cruiser over to the Sprague residence. He instructed the dispatcher to inform the responding officer to call him immediately if Mrs. Sprague

203

refused to comply with his request to be moved to the Harris condo.

I slowly inched my way on the floor. I kept asking George to make a noise so that I could determine my proximity to him. This went on for about an hour until I was completely exhausted. There was no water to be found. The only place that I had not searched was near the waste bucket. I had to try because I knew that George would probably not be able to maintain consciousness much longer and needless to say, I wasn't far behind him. I inched along closer to the waste can until I touched the can. There was nothing. I was upset and turned to be rid of the smell of the waste bucket when my hand touched plastic. It was a bottle left on its side with the cap still intact. I quickly grabbed it and then I felt a second bottle. This one seemed heavier and I yelled over to George. George only mumbled. I opened the warm water and took a small sip. It tasted like plastic but it was drinkable. I took several mouthfuls and quickly scampered into the direction of where I had last heard George's mumble. I actually bumped George, who still had enough strength to ask me if I was still sweet on him for bumping him in the dark again.

"Shut up you foolish bastard and take a sip," I said. George moved quickly to grab my hand and search for the water bottle. I cautioned him to be careful as I released the water bottle. I could hear George gulp the water. I cautioned him to go a little easier.

"I guess that simple kid left water for me after all."

"What do you mean by simple kid, George?" He explained that Scooter was a nice kid who didn't have anyone to watch over him. He had been kind of adopted by the workers at the IH plant awhile back. They had supplied him with a room and enough pay to maintain himself. George knew, from talking to some people there, that Scooter's job was to keep the supply rooms neat, clean the showers and men's rooms and perform any duty the plant foreman wanted him to do if he thought the slow kid could handle it. George sipped one more drink of water and said that he was harmless.

"So if the kid comes in with some more water and points a gun in our direction, remember that he doesn't know what he is doing, okay?" George said.

"J.J., I remember that Leo held the gun at me when Scooter untied me to use the bucket. The kid came again to deliver water but he just left it I guess and you just found it. He's harmless so don't hurt him if he comes alone."

"I hope the little shit does come back."

My scalp was dry in the area where the stitches were but there was some moisture developing. I smelt it and realized that an infection was festering.

Darish called Moroch and told him that his job was complete. He had attached the severance device to the towing cable where no one would be able to observe it. The Deutsch Fireworks people had completed their work and would be back in the early morning to finish testing. The Crescent tug had arrived and was moored at the pier. They had left and had put security in his hands. He laughed as he told that to Moroch.

"I've been home for an hour already. The New London barge and tug were ready as well. I left my two men to secure the barge for the night also," Moroch said.

"Can you send one of your men to Newport?"

Moroch agreed that he would send one guard.

"Have you seen my brother Ilea, or Muhammad or Sid?"

"I haven't seen any of them."

"There has to be a problem." Moroch did not answer at first while he gathered his thoughts.

"I will contact the Lupinacci brothers, one of them should be able to get in contact with Sid Owlia. Sid acts as an American now and he could have assigned the two of them to another job that came up and hasn't attempted to inform us of the change," he said. Darish didn't think that happened but was relieved a little that Moroch was attempting to find his brother.

Josh talked to Candy for over an hour. Occasionally he had to keep her on hold while agents and other law enforcement agencies updated him on the case that was growing bigger by the hour. Candy was used to communicating with Josh this way. She was a patient girl. They decided to spend a few days on Block Island after Josh was free to take a few days off from the case. He definitely could not take off before the two people he was looking for were found. Candy was not irritated or upset at Josh for not telling her what was going on personally. Rich and Missy had been updating her on the situation as it unfolded. She would have liked it better if Josh had informed her of the details but knowing how busy Josh has been was understandable. She did tell Josh of the information she possessed. He was amazed at the details that she remembered. He felt like she was an agent working with him to solve the case. She asked pointed questions that he had to think about. Josh wished that he had spent more time with her. His love for her was growing and he missed her more each time they conversed. They both agreed that Josh would update her as often as possible to solve two problems that they agreed that they had as a couple. One was that they didn't talk much and two was that he was always too busy to spend more time with her. By talking over cases, they developed a good technique for Josh to pass ideas and hunches past Candy and it temporarily served problem number two which was the lack of time they spent with each other. It was just then that Candy stumbled onto something that hit a nerve in Josh.

He told her what Chief Agent John DiStasio had said to him. The link, the commonality, was the terms going over and over in his boss's mind as well as her brother's and his as he explained certain details to her. Candy said something very common to the entire situation when she casually said, "Josh, all the areas you told me about have nuclear generated electrical power."

"Say what you just said, again."

Candy repeated that all the cities that have ports deep enough had received electrical power assistance from the U.S. Navy. The New London-Groton area had a nuclear submarine assisting with generating electrical power was one place she knew for sure. She remembered that from a report a kid did in her sixth grade class on producing energy. She remembered that Newport had the aircraft carrier Bill Clinton to assist in supplying power and she knew for sure Boston and New York had a few ships docked at the piers to assist with their needs. She told Josh that he could check it out quickly by calling his friend in the Navy that he always talked about.

"Call him," she said. Josh told her that he loved her and that he would call her back. Her line went dead. It was 10:29 p.m.

Josh was back at his boss's white board. He double circled the five cities that Candy had mentioned. He typed some information into his secured computer and began to search the FBI database. Within seconds he had a current list of all the nuclear capital ships of the U.S. Navy that had been docked at piers of major American coastal cities. Twenty three cities had been utilizing assistance from the U.S. Navy. There were five listed that were very interesting to him. The Navy had stationed the U.S.S. Arleigh Burke at Portsmouth, NH, the U.S.S. George W. H. Bush at Boston, MA, the U.S.S. William Clinton at Newport, RI, the U.S.S. North Carolina at New London, CT, and the U.S.S. Seawolf and U.S.S. Connecticut at New York City. He was surprised to see that New York actually had two nuclear submarines to assist in power support for that metropolitan area.

The East Coast report also identified, Newport News, VA, Jacksonville, FL, Biloxi, MS, New Orleans, LA and Corpus Christi, TX. The Great Lakes area had nuclear submarines docked at Chicago, IL, Erie, PA and one at Montreal, Canada to keep the Canadian link to the U. S. supported. He gazed over the list of the ships involved. The West Coast had ten ports with 12 nuclear ships and submarines in support. San Francisco and Los Angeles were the two cities with two each, he noted. Josh read additional information that indicated that these ships and submarines were on standby. In a moment's notice, they could break power support and head out to areas of concern by the commanders in the Pentagon. The information also included the expected completion of nuclear power plants under construction in the areas the capital ships supported. The United States had undertaken a massive nuclear power plant construction effort in the past four years and the plants were going to be completed and operational within the next year. He made more notes and realized how tired he was. It was now almost midnight. He needed to catch some sleep for a few hours. John DiStasio would be in the office by 4 a.m. and asking him and Rich Strong what progress they had made this evening. DiStasio had mentioned that he was going to take off by noon. He wanted to spend some time with his wife, kids and grandkids and enjoy the Fourth of July festivities. It was one day that he still cherished besides Christmas and Easter. Everything else to him was a full workday. Josh thought about the holidays he had spent with his family and friends. He thought of the holidays that the McAuliffes and Woodbridges spent at his parent's home. That was a long time ago, he thought. It would be nice to just be with his parents and sister's family. Most of all, it would be nice to be with Candy he thought as he slipped off to some much needed rest.

Moroch returned to the apartment. It was now 12:19 a.m., the Fourth of July. He relaxed and mentally went over his tasks for the day. He wondered how the Portsmouth, New York and Boston plans were proceeding. His main task was to supply explosives and make arrangements for the fireworks units for all the leaders while he personally lead the Newport and New London task. He did not know the other leaders but he knew that one controlled Boston and Portsmouth and the other New York City. He hoped that they would be as successful as he had been at New London and Newport. He made one more call. It was to Darish.

He was resting in the foreman's office. He couldn't sleep thinking about the events that were going to take place in New England and New York today. He had hoped, from some of the talks that he had with Moroch months ago, that more areas in

New England and New York could be affected by the results of their plan to cripple the region. His concentration was broken by the startling ring and vibration of his cell phone. He answered then listened to Moroch's questions and orders. When Moroch was done, he reported that all was well but he mistakenly mentioned his experience with the agent that had searched the barge and the Harvester plant. Moroch screamed into the phone.

"Why did you not call me immediately when you observed the FBI and police coming to search the Newport area?" Darish began to answer but was cut off by Moroch's displeasure. "You are an idiot like your brother!" Moroch shouted.

"I have the situation under control," Darish said calmly as to not further enrage his immediate supervisor. Moroch continued to scream into the phone reminding him of past instances when he or Ilea had disappointed him. He screamed about how stupid the Owlia men had been during this operation. Moroch was beginning to lose his voice, Darish noted, due to the yelling and sometime uncontrollable screaming. He waited for Moroch to calm down. It took a few more insults before he stopped. When he did, Darish cautiously asked if he had been in contact with his brother Ilea. Moroch lied. He said, "Your brother Ilea and Mohammad have been assigned to the Portsmouth area. The idiot Sid brought them with him. They have been requested by the Boston and Portsmouth group leader. I did not find this out until just recently that your brother has been assigned to go there. They will remain there for obvious reasons."

Darish thanked him for the information and said that he would see him in heaven and ended the conversation. Moroch was relieved that he did not inquire further of his brother's location. By now he was in some morgue somewhere. He didn't care. It was 1:02 a.m., the Fourth of July.

Moroch heard a pounding on his door. He froze at first and then reached for the Walther. He positioned himself so as he opened the door with his right hand, the visitor would not notice the Walther in his left hand which was behind the door. There was no peep hole to view a visitor so he made sure the chain lock was in place. Moroch asked, "Who is there?"

"I'm your pissed off neighbor one floor above you. What's all the screaming about?"

Moroch slowly opened the door enough to see the man standing in his bath robe before him. Before the man could speak, he apologized and said that he was having an argument with his girl friend and he had gotten a bit out of control. The man asked where Daryl was. Moroch quickly remembered that Darish's alias was Daryl Adams.

"Oh, Daryl is out on a date and will probably not return tonight. You know how it is," he said. The man continued to look at him as Moroch cocked the Walther behind the door.

"I am Mark. I am a cousin of Daryl's. I am here until tomorrow," he said as he smiled. The man only grunted and mumbled for him to keep it quiet. He left. Moroch closed the door and uncocked the Walther. He undressed, set the alarm for 6 a.m. and tried to get some sleep. His mind continued to go over details when he realized that he had not instructed Darish to eliminate that retarded Scooter. He began to dial him and then realized it was not worth his time. He did not want to risk Darish killing someone that close to the operation site. The drivers must be dead by now and the Scooter person was harmless. He went to bed.

Scooter woke up at 4 a.m. He awoke like clockwork every day since he had been given a chance to live and perform assignments at the Harvester plant. He grabbed his towel and face cloth that had been placed neatly on a hanger to dry. Both were stiff but smelt slightly of the soap he used. He started the shower and waited for the warm water. He slipped off his underwear and walked into the running water. He first washed his underwear with the soap. He placed it on a peg that was near to the shower. His plan was to wear them the following day after they had dried on the hangers he kept near his bed. He routinely did this with the two pair of underwear that he owned. The other would be dry now because he had repeated the same task yesterday morning. He quickly washed as to not be scolded by the men who used the shower. Those men that worked at the plant sometimes yelled at him for using too much hot water. He dried quickly and slipped on his stiff, but clean, underwear. He dressed in soiled jeans and a tee shirt that he reminded himself to wash tonight. He headed for the plant cafeteria. He would purchase an apple and some dry cereal there, return to his room and eat it. He would then brush his teeth and be ready to report to the foreman's office before 5 a.m. when his work day started. The routine was easy for Scooter to remember although he had been diagnosed with an extreme case of Attention Deficit Disorder. He never received any proper treatment as a child and never had been on any medications. With no parents living to care for him, he had bounced around until he was given some semblance of normalcy at the plant.

I was awake most of the night. I prayed a little that someone would find George and me. I was thinking about some of the Vietnam Veterans that died over 50 years ago and weren't found until years later. It was finally in 2011, that the U.S. Military buried the last remains of the Missing in Action for that time. I hoped it would not be 50 years before they found two skeletons in this steel shit hole we were stuck in. I called over to George. He answered, "I'm still here J.J. That water kept me going but I'm almost out now."

"I'm in the same condition. We're going to have to start making noises as soon as we hear anything or think anyone could hear us."

"I don't think anyone will ever hear us but I'll support you as long as I can."

"Well, I'm going to empty that shit bucket and use that to hit the side of the hold. Metal hitting metal might alert someone above. I just hope that it's not someone that's trying to kill us." He laughed.

"You are going to cause a shit storm, literally, aren't you J.J.?"

211

I had to laugh a little at that. We waited quietly and strained our ears to listen for noises we could identify that were made by people working on the barge. I fell off to sleep for a few minutes.

Scooter reported at the foreman's office at 5 a.m. precisely. There was no light on inside the office. The dawn light was getting brighter by the minute and the sun's orange glow could be seen breaking over the horizon. Scooter entered the office building and froze as Darish was standing and staring at him. "What do you want?" he asked.

Scooter froze and couldn't speak for a second or two. He slowly explained that he always cleaned the office at this time of the morning. Once he was finished in the office, he went to the plant to clean the showers and men's room there.

Darish said, "Leave here and go to the plant. You may return here at a later time." Scooter stood for a few more seconds until Darish yelled, "Leave now!" He didn't realize that Scooter had a set schedule and changes to the schedule confused and upset him. He returned to the foremen's couch to rest and Scooter withdrew to the plant parking lot and walked in circles deciding what to do. He walked to the cafeteria and got some water. As he drank the bottled water he remembered that he had not checked on the one in the hold that he had helped Leo carry down there. No, he remembered, there were two now. He grabbed two bottles and walked back past the foreman's office and onto the barge. Only one of the Deutsch fireworks technicians was on the barge and he was busy testing electronic hookups. He didn't pay any attention to Scooter.

As he approached the first hatch that led below, a voice yelled over to him from topside.

"Where are you going?" The night security officer asked. He had been sent by Moroch from New London to assist Darish at Newport. He had driven up from the New London barge in the early morning hours. He'd seen Scooter leave the Foreman's office earlier but he wanted to know where Scooter was going now. Scooter looked at him and said that he was going to give water to the two in the third level hold. The security guard couldn't quite make out what Scooter said so he waved for him to come towards him. Moroch had mentioned to the security guard that Scooter was like the village idiot here. The guard told Scooter that he was not allowed on the barge unless he had written permission to board the barge. Scooter said nothing. But before he left, he gave the security guard a bottle of water. He left with the other bottle of water.

Josh woke and looked at his watch. He overslept. John DiStasio was busy making notes and looking at the white board. Josh entered his boss's office and asked, "Why didn't you wake me?"
"Because you are dead on your feet and need some rest to function properly," DiStasio remarked. By this time, Rich Strong was up and looking at both of them. John DiStasio requested that both men take a few minutes to freshen up and have some breakfast down in the cafeteria before returning to work and putting in another eighteen hour day again.

Chief Agent DiStasio looked at the information Josh had put on the white board in black grease pen. The circled cities were interesting. He looked at the list of nuclear ships and submarines listed supporting specific cities on the coast and Great Lakes. He wondered what interest Josh had in looking at the electrical grid of the country. DiStasio typed into his computer and reviewed the latest security write ups from the Nuclear Power plants in the country. Besides the usual animal trespassing episodes and an occasional rogue who tripped the security alarms, all seemed to be normal in that area of operation. No reactors had been shut down or emergencies declared. He reviewed the naval ship status report available to him from the Pentagon. No incidents at sea has occurred, no alerts had been issued from anywhere. The North American Aerospace Defense Command was not in any elevated DEFCON status. Everything seemed normal. He looked forward to a happy Fourth of July picnic at home this afternoon and anticipated some excitement for his grandkids when they viewed the Newport fireworks that he had first watched in the early eighties when he was a young man and had watched almost every year since then.

The Village Idiot

Josh and Rich were finishing their breakfast in the Providence FBI Office cafeteria when his cell phone rang. It was Agent Howard Buckner returning Josh's message.

"Howard, I need you to come into my office when you get settled. I want to go over some information about the Newport Harvester Plant and barge before your trip to Connecticut to search the Harvester depot," Josh said. He was still pissed about the extra time it took to get a Connecticut State Judge to authorize and approve the Harvester depot search. It took much less time for the Rhode Island State judge to authorize and approve the Newport Harvester plant and barge search. He thought it was stupid the way the Federal Prosecutor dealt with interstate warrants these days. He knew that someday, maybe, he would be the one that got that issue resolved.

"I'll be there in thirty minutes. I just have a few things to finish up."

"That'll be fine," Josh said, ending the conversation.

Rich Strong looked at him and asked, "Do you want me to listen in on the conversation?"

"No, why do you ask?" Josh retorted stiffly.

"Because you can't stand the little son of a bitch and you just showed it the way you answered me," he said as he smiled.

"Maybe you should," was all Josh said as they both headed for Josh's meeting with Howard Bruckner.

Josh thought Howard was a nice guy but he questioned his abilities. He had worked with Howard years ago when they first entered the FBI. He'd seen Howard botch a few cases that almost cost a few agents their lives. He did not trust the man's ability to prosecute a case thoroughly. Howard always missed obvious things and had to be questioned extensively to make sure all the angles of a case were covered. Josh knew from experience that Howard would look you straight in the eye while you questioned him and fail to recognize where you were going with your thoughts. Rich Strong always pointed out that it was like he was a deer looking into the headlights of a car. Howard arrived at Josh's office at 7:45 a.m.

"Good morning gentlemen," Howard said as he took a seat at the table in front of the white board that Josh and Rich were looking at. They acknowledged his greeting in unison. Josh began immediately.

"Did you find out anything on this Adams guy?"

"No, not yet but we are working on that."

"What was the barge like when you inspected the decks? And what were the results of the background check on the Deutsch foreman that you spoke with?"

Josh started to ask another question when Howard slowly answered, "Boss, could you slow down a little and let me respond?"

Josh waited as Howard began to describe the barge and the top and second levels he had inspected. Josh listened to all the bullshit about what each compartment looked like and how professional the security guard had been. Then, he stopped him cold.

"Howard, we don't know shit about the security guard. This Daryl Adams guy, the security guard you reported as very professional, doesn't show up anywhere. A few agents and I double checked that last night. I hope you find more on him than we did," Josh said looking at Rich.

"Howard, I want to go over one small point I just picked up when you were describing your search in detail," he said smiling through his gritted teeth.

"The third deck, Howard, you made no mention of the details of the third deck," he said raising his voice.

Howard went into detail about the ballast compartment control panel and all the green and red lights indicating empty or full compartments and that the panel controlled the two decks from one location. Josh looked at Rich and had to walk away to regain his composure. Rich took the sign very well and simply said to Howard that he would have to initiate another search at the Newport barge and physically have his team search the third deck. Howard disagreed.

216

"And besides," he said, "I'm heading to Connecticut with orders to search the Harvester depot." Josh told Howard that he agreed with Agent Strong and that he would have to return to Newport as soon as possible to follow up on the search of the third level deck and any other area below that.

"Boss, I still have the Connecticut Harvester depot to check and revisiting the barge at Newport is unnecessary work for me to have to repeat," he protested.

Josh looked at Howard and said, "I want you to recheck the second deck. I want you to search the third level deck, and if need be, I want you to check the fucking barnacles on the outside of the goddamned barge. Do you understand that request, Howard?"

Josh was almost screaming now. Howard got up and left. Chief Agent DiStasio heard the commotion and politely asked Special Agent Sprague to come into his office and close the door behind him. It was 8:45 a.m.

"What the hell was that all about?" the chief inquired. Josh explained, in detail, why he had lost patience with Agent Bruckner. The chief agreed but he also knew that screaming at his subordinates would not help them solve cases. He advised that he would look into Howard's personnel jacket and see if maybe he was more suited for administrative duty than special investigations.

"But for now, Special Agent Sprague, he is assigned to you, so make him work smarter. Do you understand?" he said.

"Yes sir."

"I know you are frustrated and I know it is harder when it is a family member. Get control of yourself or I may have to release you from this investigation," the Chief Agent said as he opened the door and patted Josh on the back.

The pat was more of a show for the other personnel in the room. It was important that they saw their Chief take immediate action of a situation while still showing confidence in one of his men. Personally, he agreed one hundred percent with Josh but he had to also be concerned that perhaps, because it was a family member, Josh may not be able to handle it.

What if the outcome was disastrous? Besides, he didn't want someone writing to the personnel office describing the scene they had just seen and heard.

Howard was gathering his belongings when Josh approached and apologized to him. He explained that there was no excuse for his behavior. He was tired and this case involved his father but that was no excuse for his unprofessionalism. Howard accepted his apology and said that he would return to Newport as soon as possible after the Connecticut search. Josh just nodded and returned to his office. Many people witnessed the apology and moved on about their business. Most of them understood the stakes at hand for Josh. Rich said very quietly, "One of these days the Chief is going to wake up and bounce him out of here. He really is the village idiot."

Scooter finished his chores in the Harvester plant. He looked for anyone familiar to give him work to do. The place was very quiet except for those working on the barge where he could not go. Why was no one here today? The cafeteria was empty this morning when he took an apple and some cereal. There was no one to pay so he left the money near the cash register. No one came to the shower room to wash and no trucks came to deliver and leave with cargo today. Scooter was confused. He walked to the foreman's office and opened the door to see Darish just getting up from his sleep.
"What do you want?"
Scooter explained that he needed someone to assign him work and Leo or Tommy weren't around and he hadn't assigned him anything. Moroch could not believe how imbecilic the boy sounded and acted.
"Go and do anything you want. Get out of my sight. The next time I see you, I will turn you over to the police," he said, motioning him away.

The dispatcher for the CTC notified his supervisor that all of the five tugs had reported ready to be underway from their respective piers at 10 a.m. The dispatcher also reported that all the pilots reported that they would be in position to commence towing their respective Deutsch Fireworks barges into position by 11 a.m. The holiday supervisor sat at his desk and put green push pins into a map indicating the tugs were at their respective locations. Hussein Adel sat back and relaxed knowing that his brothers and companions had almost accomplished their tasks. The dispatcher called to Harry Adams, as he was known, that there was a call for him on line number one. Hussein picked up the phone.

"Crescent Tug, Adams here." The voice on the other end asked some questions. Hussein answered every one with one simple answer, "yes." The line went dead and Hussein put the phone down. It was just a matter of waiting about nine more hours for the greatest attack every planned and executed to take place. The Fourth of July would not be associated with the birth of this country but with the beginning of its death.

The CTC of Bridgeport had been contracted by the DFC to handle all their fireworks barges since 2013. They operated in Bridgeport, New Haven and New London. On occasion, they had been to Boston, New York and Portsmouth harbors towing and pushing various types of barges in and out of the ports. Several times they had been contracted to assist in docking carriers, destroyers, cruisers and submarines for the U.S. Navy. The bright green and black tugs, with a white crescent on the smoke stacks of all the tugs, were a familiar sight on the New England and New York coastlines. The tug company was owned by a Saudi Arabian oil distribution company and incorporated in 2012. The tug company had been successful in the area due to its easy access to fuel supplied by the parent oil company.

The CTC had been able to eliminate competition in some of the harbors in the last two years. They also bought up the available tugs from the companies they had eliminated. The CTC wasn't disliked too much by the American tug companies that still maintained business in the harbors and on the docks because Crescent rehired those tug pilots and union deck hands that became unemployed and paid them fair wages and also holiday pay.

The Fourth of July schedule had been developed by Harry Adams and he had hired five temporary pilots and ten deck hands to fill in for the Crescent employees who welcomed the holiday off. The union looked the other way as they unofficially welcomed the ten dock workers to fill in for them on this one special day. None of the pilots complained either. A paid day off was one they looked forward to.

Scooter kept thinking of what Darish said, "You can do anything you want." He thought of the two men in the hold and went to the cafeteria and took several bottles of cold water from the cooler. He carried one in each hand and walked past the foreman's office and began to walk onto the barge past the Deutsch Fireworks representative who had completed his testing and was leaving the barge to orchestrate the fireworks show from a small boat. The Deutsch boat was clearly identified and was cleared to be in the harbor and next to the barge by the Coast Guard.

The security guard saw Scooter approach but was too busy assisting the deck hand removing the barge lines from the cleats on the pier. The Crescent tug's smoke stack billowed with diesel smoke as the tug applied power to hold the barge while the lines were removed. By the time the security guard remembered Scooter, he had disappeared below.

Darish watched Scooter head for the barge and thought of eliminating him but knew that the tug would have the barge well into tow and out in the harbor before Scooter would realize he was on board for the duration. He walked onto the barge topside. He climbed down into the first level deck and saw the hatch that Scooter had left open behind him. He closed it and dogged down. The hatch was the only way to the lower decks. Darish knew that with the hatch dogged down from the first level, Scooter would never be able to get out. He then walked off the barge and over to tug and jumped onboard and entered the pilot house with a small suitcase he was carrying.

The tug pilot did not say a word as Darish sat in the empty co-pilot seat. One dock hand was ordered to leave the tug and join the security guard and the other deck hand on the pier. They knew to leave the area immediately and head towards the Canadian border and cross wherever possible. The five groups of deck hands and security guards from the five cities were to stay in Canada as long as possible and slowly migrate back to their points of origin.

Moroch answered his cell phone as he watched the undocking activities from the pilot house of the tug he was on in the New London harbor. He listened for a few seconds at the questions that had been asked of him. He answered with a simple "yes" to each question. The phone conversation ended and Moroch gazed out at the New London harbor. The tug pilot continued his task of steering the tug into position.

Hussein had already updated the status of his board. The five tugs and their pilots were engaged in towing the undocked barges. The tug co-pilots were now on board each respective tug and reported all tasks had been completed and that all suitcases had been placed in the pilot houses of the tugs. The five groups of security and temporary deck hands were in route to their Canadian destinations. The only minor issue was that the two security guards from the Newport group had failed to communicate their location to their group leader. It was a minor glitch but was reported as not a problem from the group leader Moroch Makel. Hussein told the dispatcher to call him if there were any problems. He instructed him that if he could not contact him, he was to leave a message and he would periodically check his messages. He explained that he had some company business to attend to and that he would return his calls as soon as possible. He reminded the dispatcher that the second shift would be here to relieve him at 4 p.m. and he only had four hours to remain alone.

"Can you handle that?"

"Sure Harry," was the reply as Hussein left the building.

Hussein entered his vehicle and drove north. He estimated that he would be close to their designated place at the Canadian border by 8 p.m. where he would rendezvous with the five groups of men. He would direct them again, he thought, when the time was right to strike this country again. If all went well, he would be able to plan that sooner than later.

I thought I felt the barge move. I thought I was dreaming and I felt it again. I looked at my watch and it read 11:13 a.m. I called over to George but he did not answer. I figured this was the time to make noise so I inched over where I thought I could find the bucket. Again, I felt the barge shudder and knew that it was being moved. I finally found the bucket, flipped it so that its contents would hopefully exit in the opposite direction from me. The stench made me gag but I had no food in my stomach to vomit up. I inched back towards the bulkhead I was familiar with and propped myself up so that I could bang the bucket and make enough noise for someone to take notice. I didn't care if it were friend or foe because I knew I was going to die in this place. I banged and kept banging the bucket on the bulkhead until I was tired and had to stop. George had awakened and kept still until I had stopped.

"Good try J.J., but I don't think anyone will hear you." The barge shuddered again.

"Did you feel that?" I asked.

"Yeah, I did, but do you think the people outside are going to hear you banging when they are banging the damned barge themselves to make it shudder like it is. They must be moving it with a tug," he said as he surmised the situation. I banged again a few more times but the smell, heat and my general weakness overcame me. I heard a bang on the door.

"I heard that," George said very loudly. I drew out my derringer immediately and crawled towards the door which was being un-dogged and would be open in a few seconds. My heart raced as I crawled much quicker towards the squeaking and metal scraping sounds. I could see a thin line of light that outlined the edges of the door as the pressure was being relieved on the seals. I positioned myself in time so that when the door opened, I would be out of sight of the person opening the door and hopefully would have enough time for my eyes to adjust. The door opened slowly but squeaked loudly. The light seemed brighter then staring into the sun. I squinted and tried to adjust my eyes as I pointed the derringer towards the light. I heard the person who opened the door say, "I have water for you. Are you there? I have water in bottles. Can you hear me?" The person did not enter but he stayed just outside of the opened door. I heard George say but weakly, "Is that you Scooter?" Scooter replied that it was. George asked, with a little more pitch to his voice, "Are you by yourself, Son?" As soon as Scooter replied, "Yes," I moved around the door and grabbed the kid by his shirt and touched the derringer to his forehead. My eyes were hurting but my severe squinting allowed me enough sight to apprehend the kid and hold him down. He kept telling me that he had water over and over again. I heard George yell at me to leave the kid alone as he struggled with all his strength to stop me from hurting the kid. I yelled to George to relax. I wasn't hurting him. I immediately asked Scooter where the guards were. He didn't answer but remained frozen in my grip with the derringer touching his face. I asked him again but he was frozen. I looked down the third deck passageway and nobody was coming and I relaxed enough to loosen my grip on the kid as George appeared at the doorway. He looked at the kid and then at me and said, "Leave him alone, you are scaring the shit out of him. Can't you see that?" as he too was squinting and adjusting to the light.

"You're welcome, you old coot," I said.

"Never mind being a smart ass, just let the kid go so he can tell us where the bad guys are, Jon," he said.

I relaxed my grip on the kid. He immediately went to George. George explained that everything was okay now and he was happy to see him come back and open the door for us. I noticed the water and could feel the cold on my hands as I cracked the seal on the bottle. The water was nice and cold and I downed one third of it. I tossed the other bottle to George. He attempted to open it but was fumbling. The kid noticed it, took the bottle and opened it. George thanked him and began to gulp the cold water. I looked at George and observed that he was the dirtiest that I had ever seen him. I looked at myself and realized I was as dirty and smelled probably as bad. George looked at my wound and told me that it was very infected. He got close to me and said, "J.J., that wound is nasty looking. It smells too. You're going to need some medical attention and soon." Scooter was looking at both of us and not saying anything. I instructed George to ask the kid questions because I knew I had scared him and it would be a little while before he would respond to me. George asked, "Is there anyone on the barge with us?" Scooter said that he didn't know for sure but he didn't think so. George asked him several other questions and the kid answered to our satisfaction.

"Okay, we are on a barge that is apparently moving to who knows where," I said. George reminded me that the barge wasn't going far.

"It's the fireworks barge for Newport, remember? It will stay in the harbor until late tonight." I looked at him and realized how dumb that must have sounded. I told him that I was going to snoop around and see what was going on while he regained his strength.

George said, "Hold on J.J. and give me a few more minutes to get myself set and I'll go with you."

"Look, you're still too weak. I'll be careful and come back for you and Scooter soon.

"J.J., I spent too long of a time with you in that shit hold and I want to be close to you from now on just in case you need some help. Now wait a goddamned minute, will you?"

In ten minutes George was up and walking slowly as all three of us checked the barge. The third deck was empty as well as all the 16 ballast compartments. I checked the eight starboards and George and Scooter checked the seven on the port side. We ascended the ladder to the second deck. We noticed the ballast compartment panel board and observed the green and red lights. I figured the green lights out for the 16 third level deck ballast compartments. They indicated that they were empty ballast compartments.

"What do the red lights indicate, George?" George shook his head and said that it was either water or some ballast material to stabilize the barge.

"Are those lights for the units we saw being loaded that heavy?" George indicated that he didn't think so based on the size of the barge.

Scooter spoke up, "They hold fireworks."

George and I looked at him. George explained that the fireworks were already top side and must be hooked up for the show. He told Scooter that they would not keep extra fireworks in the barge. It was too dangerous. Scooter said again, "They are fireworks, Darish said so."

"Who is Darish?" I asked.

The kid answered that he was a friend of Moroch's who had left. I remembered that bastard. I looked at George and said, "I have a feeling that the shit in the red lit compartments is not fireworks." He nodded in agreement.

We decided to un-dog one of the red compartment doors and see what was inside. If water came in, it would not make much difference to the stability of the barge and we really didn't care. I un-dogged the door slowly in the anticipation that water would begin to seep out past the seal. There was no water seepage. I opened the door completely and looked in. I could see that the compartment was three quarters full with plastic bags. They looked like bags of cement but were full of something I couldn't make out at this distance. I looked back at George and said that I think I know what is going on here. I explained that this must be illegal contraband that these guys were using to store in the barge.

"No wonder they didn't want us around, we'd screw up their operation," I said.

George slowly moved past me into the compartment enough to touch the closest bag. He reached into his pocket and pulled out a very small pocket knife that he used to pick at everything including fingernails and food. It was a nasty habit he had never broken. Anita had always tried to break him of it. The goons had missed his pocket knife as they had missed my derringer. George slit the bag and felt the material. He froze and slowly removed the knife and backed away from the material. He never spoke a word. Despite his brown skin and the dirt that was on it, he turned grayish and pushed me away and closed the door.

"Dog the door."

I complied and turned to him and asked, "What is that stuff?"

He looked at me, and then Scooter, and said, "That material is plastic explosives. We are in deep shit."

George limped over to another compartment that was indicated as a red lit one. I helped him un-dog it. He confirmed the same material again. I glanced at my wrist watch; it was 12:35 p.m. We tried to move up to the first deck but the hatch was shut and most likely dogged down from the other side. Someone didn't want Scooter to get out either. We could see and recognize, from some of the deck drain holes in the overhead of the barge, the special units that we had shipped in our trucks to the Harvester plant. From what we could see, they looked very different now with the fireworks loaded into them and all the electronics hooked up. The Units were evenly spaced and all the cabling that had been attached to them were banded and laid neatly in metal troughs. The troughs lead to central point topside where a large metal container, we could only partially see, must have been a control point or computer for the fireworks display. I could make out a small antenna and realized that, with no one aboard; the fireworks display was remotely controlled. I turned to George as we strained to see through the second deck overhead holes trying to see into the first deck and topside and remarked, "We are the only three on this barge by the looks of it." We all sat down and agreed that we would case out the second deck and hopefully find another way to the first deck and then topside. I looked at George and asked, "Are you thinking what I am thinking?"

"I'm afraid so J.J. These guys, whoever they might be, are going to blow this barge up to get at something. Based on the

226

fireworks and all the attention they will be getting from the people who will be watching, they plan to kill a lot of them."

"That's not what I'm thinking George."

He looked at me strangely because he thought his idea was credible.

"The people will be secondary, George. The target is that brand new carrier you keep talking about. If you rupture its hull, there will be enough radiation to kill everyone for miles."

We sat there for a few minutes and didn't say a word.

Agent Howard Bruckner and two other agents had arrived at the Harvester depot around 9:20 a.m. There were only two security guards on duty as the agents entered the depot. The security guards explained that the plant was closed for the holiday. Agent Bruckner still insisted that he be allowed access to every space in the building. The three agents and several State troopers combed the depot from one end to the other. One CSI detective was swabbing different areas of interest in the storage rooms and terminal shipping areas. Copies of schedules were copied on the Harvester's own copy machines by Bruckner and some of the agents so that they could further study the deliveries, drivers, dock workers and products shipped over the last six to seven weeks. It took the agents and troopers about ninety minutes to complete the task. Bruckner felt satisfied that he wouldn't get questioned or second guessed again from that hot headed boss of his. He ordered the withdrawal of the group and instructed the State Police to return to their barracks. Bruckner planned on getting in touch with the Rhode Island State Police when he was close to Newport to assist him in the search of the Newport Fireworks Barge.

The agents made the trip in just a little over 70 minutes. As the agents reached the outskirts of Newport, they radioed ahead and requested backup at the Newport Harvester plant pier to search the fireworks barge moored there. The Rhode Island State Police dispatcher acknowledged the request. The dispatcher told agent Bruckner to stand by. A minute later, the dispatcher said that the barge had been moved from the pier according to the troopers stationed at the harbor to patrol the activities that had started for the Fourth of July.

Agent Bruckner said, "Repeat radio broadcast please, say again." The dispatcher repeated the same message. Agent Bruckner called into the Providence FBI Office requesting further instructions after he informed the office of the changed situation. Chief Agent DiStasio listened to the message he had received from the dispatcher. He walked over to the dispatch office and spoke directly to Bruckner.

"Howard, find the supervisor of the fireworks company and get the status of the timetable for the event tonight. Next, contact the Coast Guard and find out if the barge can be approached by one of our small crafts safely and make sure you are on it. I don't want you to disrupt the festivities tonight but you need to coordinate with the events chairperson who has all the event information and contact names as fast as you can. I will work with you on my end. Keep in constant communication with me. Do you understand?"

Bruckner acknowledged and told the Chief he would update him hourly. Chief DiStasio asked the office in general where Sprague and Strong were. Someone informed him that they were somewhere in the building following up on some leads they had. DiStasio said, "Find and update them on the status of Bruckner at Newport."

Agents Sprague and Strong were contacted within minutes. Josh knew to call Brian McAuliffe immediately and get him to inform his superior officers of the situation. Commander Bob Arsenault took immediate action to notify the U.S. Coast Guard to contact the Crescent tug pilot to inform him that the Coast Guard would be assisting the FBI to search the barge. The Coast Guard contacted the Crescent tug pilot who responded that he would need permission from the Deutsch Fireworks supervisor on the small cabin cruiser that was accompanying them to the final position for the barge in the Newport Harbor. The DFC supervisor immediately contacted

228

the Chairman Richard Cugini of the Newport Fireworks committee.

"Mr. Cugini, any delay in the barge positioning would be critical. It needs to take place as scheduled. I do not have adequate workers to recheck the electronics onboard the barge after a second search nor can I now guarantee the success of the fireworks display with rush to complete that recheck. Furthermore, any inexperienced persons on board the barge would be in danger. Lastly, the fact that the barge had already been searched will cost extra time and money for the Deutsch Company. I will recommend to my immediate supervision a void of contract and withdrawal of sponsorship immediately."

This put the committee chairman into a panic at first and then into a rage that the FBI was causing unnecessary strong arming and displaying poor tactics in their investigation. The chairman first contacted Agent Bruckner who immediately forwarded his rage and insults to Special Agent Sprague. Josh explained the need for the re-check and said that he was not going to delay the search. The chairman screamed that he wanted his immediate supervisor to be contacted and informed of this cock and bull story the FBI was orchestrating to delay or even cause a cancellation of one of the most important civic display of patriotism in America. Josh stalled until the chairman said that if he did not give him the name of his immediate supervisor, he was contacting Senators Michael Cedrone and Patrick Dority of Rhode Island who were planning to be in attendance tonight as well as Governor Richards and his State Cabinet. Cugini screamed, "If you want a shit storm, Sonny, then you are going to have one! Do I make myself clear? I want the name and number of your superior and right now!" By then, Chief Agent DiStasio had entered the control room. Josh had put his phone on speaker phone so that his boss could listen in on the last two sentences of Cugini's conversation.

"Mr. Cugini, this is Chief Agent John DiStasio. May I be of service to you?" he asked as politely as possible seeing that Josh had gotten the FBI into a worse predicament than Howard Bruckner could have ever done. He knew Bruckner side stepped the responsibility and walked Josh right into one mad Richard Cugini who now threatened the wrath on the FBI from every Senator, Congressmen and Government official in Rhode Island.

"Mr. Cugini I understand your concern but this search will not take very long. We are looking for two individuals that maybe on board," he said and then realized he just left himself wide open for criticism.

Cugini said, "Possible, maybe, could be, what kind of bullshit story is that? Who was the judge that signed the search warrant?" DiStasio relayed the information to him. Cugini laughed and said that Judge Marco was on his committee.

"Chief Agent, the judge is here so I will give him the phone so you can explain to him why this search hadn't been apparently performed the first time correctly. Hold, please," he said.

Chief DiStasio rolled his eyes as Judge Marco said, "Chief Agent, I'm listening." Chief DiStasio quickly, and with a tone of importance, relayed exactly what had happened and why a second search was needed to verify that no one was on board that had been reported missing. The Judge quietly said that the FBI had botched the search; the FBI did not have any a reason to re-search the barge when they found it to be satisfactory with the help of the Deutsch Fireworks and Security persons assigned to the barge. Judge Marco said that the barge could be searched when the FBI had proof that the two individuals were on board.

"Have the Bureau contact the State Prosecutor's Office when you have more proof. When you have convinced him he will contact me. If he can convince me that the Bureau's information presented is reliable, then I will issue your search warrant. Chief Agent DiStasio, do I make myself clear?" he asked.

"Yes, your honor. Very clear," the chief responded. The line went dead.

"Josh, get several groups of agents in boats in the harbor to closely observe the tug, barge and the Deutsch cabin cruiser. Keep a safe and unsuspecting distance away. Tell the agents to dress like sightseers and act like they are enjoying the festivities. Get the groups using listening and observation tools to pick up any cell phone activity and watch for any human movement on the barge or tug or even the cabin cruiser. If something looks out of the ordinary, contact me immediately."

Darish had called Moroch to inform him of the situation with the FBI's request. Moroch informed Darish to sit and wait because he had a hunch that the City of Newport would fight the movement and search of the barge. Darish hung up and waited for the tug pilot to be contacted by the harbor security, Coast Guard or FBI

Josh reminded the Chief of the temperament and orders of Judge Marco. The Chief said that the Judge didn't say we couldn't search it as soon as the fireworks were gone. We'll do that as soon as the barge is docked. "In the meantime, we will obey the Judges orders that reasonable proof from reliable sources is required. What else were the agents in the harbor assigned to be?" he said smiling to Josh. Chief DiStasio said that after Josh assigned Special Agent Strong to lead Bruckner and the other groups that were to be assigned in the harbor, he wanted to go over information that had been accumulating in his office over the past several hours. The Chief said that he needed to show Josh the information because he wanted to skip out to attend his family function this afternoon. Both men looked at their watches in unison. The time was 1:12 p.m.

The Story Board

Josh contacted Missy and passed information onto his mother who was staying at the condo.

"How's mom doing?"

"She's hanging in there. She called Anita Woodbridge to update her as much as she could about the search for Jon and George. She wanted her to know that the search was still on and now in full swing. They talked for quite awhile. I guess they were trying to cheer each other up. It sort of gave them a chance to feel some normalcy for a moment."

Lupinacci and Costello went to Kelly's house after the talk with the Special Agents. The Kelly family and their guests were in the back yard having a holiday get together when both impeccably dressed men arrived in a car with two Costello soldiers. They walked to the rear of the yard to meet Dan. Dan was surprised to see the two men and quickly went over to them to welcome them to his house. Donnie shook Dan's hand while Tommy stood next to him and smiled at the family members and guests that had turned and were looking with curiosity. Dan gave his condolences to both men. Donnie nodded and then asked if they could talk somewhere private. Dan immediately invited them into his home, through the kitchen and into his study in the front of the two story colonial home. He offered refreshments. They both declined. Donnie spoke in a clear, low, but distinctive tone as Tommy got up and closed the study door and stood by it.

"Danny boy, you need to listen to what I have to say. You will not interrupt me nor say anything at all until I ask you a question or two, got that? Your answers should be the truth or I will have Tommy escort you out of your home and into my car outside and your family and friends will never see you again."

Dan's face drained of color as he stood motionless and hinged on every word Tommy was about to say.

"Dan, who is the guy you have been contacting from the

232

depot?"

"What guy, Donnie? I contact hundreds of guys for the depot every day." Tommy slapped Dan in the back of the head to remind him of the conditions that Donnie had first said.

"Don't let me have to remind you again how Donnie told you to answer his questions." Dan rubbed the back of his head as Donnie waited for an answer and Tommy was poised to hit him again.

"I talk to a guy Sid Owlia told me to contact to earn a little extra cash under the table. His name is Moroch. That's all I know of him. Sid gives me an extra few hundred bucks a week to do this for him."

Donnie looked at Tommy and nodded. Tommy slapped him harder now. Dan caught his balance and began to talk a little quicker, "Sid told me to call this guy every time a shipment left the depot or artery terminal that had to do with IH and the shipment of the those secret fireworks units." Dan looked at Tommy to see if he was going to hit him again.

Donnie asked, "What else did Sid and this Moroch guy want you to do?"

"They wanted information on what kind of guys Woodbridge and Sprague were. I got that information from Ed at the terminal. Ed knew them both real well. They asked me to keep an eye out on Ed because he was the one that you and Tommy had to negotiate with for drivers and Sid said that this Moroch guy didn't like the way you negotiated and I could earn a little more money just letting him know if any changes took place. That's all Donnie, I swear," he almost pleaded. Donnie asked if Sid ever said anything else that could be of interest to him. Dan thought for a few seconds and said, "Yes, I heard Sid talk to Moroch on one occasion about making sure that the CTC was the only tug company to deliver the fireworks barges, if that helps you boss."

Donnie stood up and told Dan that he should not report to work tomorrow at the terminal. He looked at him and said he was disappointed in him and that he should not seek employment in the shipping industry in the area. He advised him that he should move away as soon as possible and enjoy his family while he had the chance.

"You do not realize how close you came to never seeing them again. Enjoy your life and your family," he said before signaling to Tommy to open the study door through which they left. Donnie nodded his head to Dan's wife as she held her two year son in her arms while the four year daughter tugged on her barbeque apron. He smiled and told her to have a great Fourth of July. Tommy followed Donnie to the car without saying a word. Dan sat on a chair in the study motionless. He felt nauseated and weak. His wife asked him what the matter was. He looked at her and tried to speak but his mouth was too dry.

Donnie called Josh. Josh pondered the information he had before him as he spoke with Chief DiStasio.

"Special Agent Sprague here."

"Agent," Costello said. "I just found out that you may be interested in the CTC. One of my guys confessed that a guy named Moroch had talked with Sid Owlia. He told me that the CTC was the tug company contracted to service the firework barges. Kelly said that they were the only ones allowed. I hope this helps you. I will be in touch." Before Josh could respond, the phone went dead.

"Costello says that the CTC was involved with Moroch Makel. I need to get more information on the company," he said to DiStasio. Josh began to look up the company and cross reference any new information he could obtain from his sources in the FBI.

Dan Kelly called Ed McAuliffe at his home. Ed immediately picked up hoping that he would get good information on Jon Sprague and George Woodbridge.

"Ed, this is Dan Kelly. I need to tell you something and I need a favor." Ed listened as Dan told him what had happened when Donnie Costello and Tommy Lupinacci had visited him a few minutes ago.

"I knew you were into something, kid. What can I do for you?"

Dan asked if he could stop by the terminal very early in the morning to pick up whatever wages he had left to collect for the week. He explained that he would be selling his home and moving away. He told him that he was not allowed to be in contact with anything or anyone associated in the shipment business ever again. Ed suggested that he could bring the cash home with him; that way, Dan could pick it up and not risk any confrontation with the Costello family. Dan thanked him. "Dan, did you know anything about Sprague and Woodbridge?"

"Ed, I swear on my life that I do not know anything about them."

"I hope you are telling the truth because if you're not, the Costellos and the FBI won't need to look for you. I'll find you myself. Do you understand?"

Dan acknowledged his threat and hung up.

Darish was concerned about all he had to accomplish. He had to board the barge, kill that imbecile Scooter and dispose of the two drivers who were probably dead now. Darish figured that he could move the bodies onto the tug and hide them there. The FBI was looking to search the barge, not the tug. He contemplated how he could manage moving the bodies during broad daylight when the radio announcement came on from the U.S Coast Guard that there would be no search from the FBI. Darish relaxed and looked at the tug pilot and said, "Keep your eyes on the lookout for private crafts that look like they are getting too close. I don't think that the FBI will give up that easily." They began to closely watch any boat that seemed remotely interesting in the harbor.

Darish called Moroch immediately after the second call indicated that there would be no search warrant granted for the FBI to research the barge. Moroch said, "If anything changes again you are to signal to the boat with the DFC supervisor in it. Have him come alongside the tug. You will kill the supervisor and launch the fireworks yourself."

He figured that the crowds would be confused. In their

confusion, the tug pilot could be building up speed as he headed for his target. He was prepared to have all the tugs and barges at the other cities follow the same procedure if the Newport Barge was forced to be searched. Darish said that the FBI would search the barge after the fireworks display. Moroch reminded him that the search would be useless by that time because the task would be complete.

Sid Owlia could feel his lungs expand and contract. He could hear the strange noises around him that included strange voices. He went to move and felt extreme pain in his abdomen. He was groggy but instantly remembered what had happened to him. Moroch Makel had tried to kill him. He tried to focus his eyes until he could see the clock on the wall. It looked like it was 4:03. He could see light through the windows so he knew it was daytime but that's all. He drifted back to sleep. The charge nurse in his room thought that maybe he had opened his eyes but she wasn't sure so she turned her attention back to her charts and continued logging Sid's vital signs.

Hussein Adel was traveling on Interstate 91 North at the normal speed limit. His Gold Honda Hybrid was an easy car to drive. Hussein relaxed as he drove. Sometimes he became excited as he pondered how he would be treated when he returned home to a hero's welcome. He thought of how his brother Darish would be elevated as a martyr for his international cause. He thought of his sacrifice and how his mother would be so proud of him after her initial sorrow that she had lost one of her three sons. He didn't know that Moroch had killed Ilea and his mother would now grieve for two sons. Hussein looked at his watch and noted that in five hours or so, the biggest attack ever on the United States would take place and far exceed anything known up to that time. Hussein wasn't concentrating on his driving because he failed to notice the smoke coming from the rear tire of a tractor trailer truck up ahead of him carrying steel girders in route to some construction sight.

The driver of the tractor trailer truck tried to control the rig as the trailer began to swerve back and forth on the travel lane of I-91 North. The driver over compensated causing the trailer's blown tire rim to dig into the asphalt and force pressure to flip the trailer and disengage the hitch from the cab. The trailer began to roll over and over breaking the steel chains that had secured the steel girders. The dislodged girders bounced over the Interstate as Hussein's gold Honda quickly approached. One girder smashed onto the roof of the automobile as a second one crushed the engine compartment. Hussein was killed instantly as the roof collapsed and crushed him. The Honda was almost stopped dead from the force of the girders and their weight. The Interstate was completely blocked with the mangled trailer, Honda and steel girders. The driver in the truck cab had managed to survive the accident. He climbed out the truck's window shook up but alive. Several cars had stopped now and the occupants began to approach the gold Honda. All those that approached were horrified at the gruesome sight of Hussein still in the Honda. Someone called 911. It was 4:20 p.m.

Twenty minutes later, several Massachusetts State Troopers had arrived with emergency medical, fire and towing assistance. The tow truck that first arrived at the scene was instructed by the medical technicians to use its towing winch to pull off the steel girder that had crushed the roof. After several minutes, it was removed. The fire department used hydraulic steel jaws to separate the crushed steel roof from the body of the car and exposed the body of the accident victim. The medical technicians were able to remove the body and retrieve the wallet of the individual that had been killed. The wallet was delivered to the closest Massachusetts State Trooper at the scene who called into his dispatcher that the rented Honda had been driven by a Mr. Harry Adams of Bridgeport, Connecticut. The other papers found in his wallet indicated that he worked for the CTC of Bridgeport. The trooper also reported that a Canadian Passport was found in his personal belongings which indicated that he had been to Pakistan and Syria over the past several years. A plane ticket for Bonn, Germany, by way of the United Kingdom, had been found as well as a Walther PPK automatic pistol. The personal bag also had $15,000 in 20 and 50 dollar bills. Several other identification cards found in Mr. Adams bag indicated that he was also identified as Hussein Adel but did not indicate his country of origin. The information was sent directly to the CIA, FBI and Homeland Security.

George, Scooter and I began looking for an alternative exit out of the second deck. George was too weak to walk any distance so we placed him near the dogged hatch and began our search through the second deck again. We hoped that there was another hatch leading to the next deck that was open. Even if the first level hatch was dogged we figured there was enough room for us to squeeze in between the fireworks units and the open spaces directly above. We combed the second deck and found the other access hatch. It was dogged like the other one was. It was useless; there was no way out of the second level. Scooter and I returned to George who was resting comfortably propped up against a bulkhead sipping the remains of the little water he had left. I explained to George our dilemma and he didn't answer and then smiled.

"J.J. we'll take a little of the plastic explosives down there and blow the goddamned hatch," he said, still smiling.

"You're out of your mind."

George explained that he would take just a little of the plastic and cut a light fixture wire somewhere that would be long enough to keep us out of harm's way when it exploded. I asked George where he was going to get electricity to ignite the plastics. He looked at me and said there has to be a source of auxiliary power on board to keep the ballast compartment lights on and to run the electronics for the fireworks. He explained that all we had to do was find it. I looked at my watch. We didn't have a lot of time to engineer this idea George had. I looked at him and asked where he learned about plastic explosives. He answered that he watched a program on explosives once and that he himself was a half-assed electrician. I knew he was crazy now.

Moroch relaxed in the tug pilot's cabin. He spoke very little to the pilot who controlled the tug positioning the barge for the fireworks display. Both men searched the surrounding waterways to make sure the Deutsch Fireworks boat was close by as well making sure harbor security stayed more interested in small crafts getting too close to the fireworks barge than to their tug. All seemed on schedule and Moroch seemed pleased.

Darish was a little less nervous. The security boats stayed away and he could also see the Deutsch cabin cruiser slightly rocking in the smooth harbor waves. No FBI boats were in sight and the Coast Guard never came close to the tug or the barge. They hoped that the harbor security enforced keeping sightseers from getting too close to the Newport barge. In both harbors, the crowds were filling up all the coastal spaces in anticipation of a great show. The weather was perfect as the sun inched down the sky towards it daily rendezvous with the horizon. The time was 5:35 p.m.

Special Agent Josh Sprague was very hungry now. He had gone over all the latest information with Chief DiStasio who left two hours later than he anticipated. He was looking forward to being with his family and getting ready to attend the Newport fireworks. Josh saw the incoming messages from Langley FBI headquarters forwarding the news of a Mr. Harry Adams, also known as Hussein Adel, had been killed on Interstate I-91 in a car accident in Massachusetts. Josh skimmed the information and saw that Mr. Adams was a CTC employee. He remembered the call that Donnie Costello had made to him recently. Josh checked further into the CTC and its history. He called the company to find a second shift dispatcher on duty. He identified himself and the dispatcher was very cooperative. Josh asked why the company was open today on the Fourth of July. The dispatcher said that they had tugs out all over Long Island Sound involved with transportation contracts and a dispatcher was always on duty.

Josh asked to speak with the foreman in charge. The dispatcher told him to hold a few seconds while he transferred the call over to his desk. Within a few moments the Crescent foreman was on the line. The foreman answered all of Josh's questions without any hint of cover up or evasiveness. Josh asked if there was a Harry Adams working for the Company and he was informed that Harry had left early today on personal business but could be reached at his cell phone number in case of emergency. The foreman asked Agent Sprague if he needed to contact Harry Adams. Josh said that if he needed additional information he would contact Mr. Adams directly. Josh thanked the foreman for his time.

Josh called Langley and asked if the CTC was under any investigations by the FBI. Langley reported that it did not have any cases pending against the tug company. They did have some dead leads of individuals that had been associated with the tug company as deck hands and tug pilots but they weren't under investigation at this time. Josh asked for the tug company's file to be sent to his office electronically. His request was granted and in 15 minutes a six page report was available to him on his computer. Josh studied the information and reviewed the names on the report. One named that popped up that was interesting was Daryl Adams. Josh checked Howard Bruckner's report and recognized the same name, Daryl Adams. This was the same security guard that assisted Bruckner in the search of the Newport fireworks barge. Too much of a coincidence, he thought. Josh requested two New London agents be sent to Daryl Adams's apartment immediately.

Josh then contacted the Connecticut State Police to hear if Joe Harris had anything on the identification of the guy who killed Leo Lupinacci and tried to kill Trooper Longo and the owner of the green Toyota hybrid. "Sergeant Joe Harris," he said as he answered his phone. Josh asked him if he had any luck identifying the gunman. Joe reported that they were still running an identity search but they thought that it could be several individuals that matched the facial characteristics and description the computer was analyzing. Joe went through a list of the four possible identities. The last one was a Moroch Makel who had been wanted in Spain, Morocco and some other countries. The description of his known assassinations and his ability to perform executioner style killings was of much interest to the authorities. Josh asked for as many different pictures of Makel as possible.

The New London and the Connecticut State Police lifted finger prints from the green Toyota Hybrid and they were sent by the State Police through the FBI to Interpol. Josh called to see if Interpol had matched the prints and they had. The Langley report, which had been delayed for some unknown reason, had identified the prints from the red pickup and the green Toyota Hybrid as both belonging to the same person. They were waiting to confirm the identity of the prints from Spain and Morocco from the crime scenes allegedly committed by Moroch there.

A half hour later, the two agents at Adams's apartment found no one there. They did manage to talk to one resident above his apartment. The resident said that Daryl had not been home all night but that his cousin Mark was there having a loud argument on the phone and he had to go down there and tell him to be quiet. The agents called Josh to inform him of their find. Josh asked the two agents what the cousin looked like. Josh faxed a photo of Moroch to one of the agent's cell phones. Josh contemplated the names of Moroch and Mark; easy enough to be an alias, he thought. It could be that same guy. It took ten minutes for the agents to return and confirm that the resident identified the person in the picture as the guy he was calling Moroch. He had a lot more links now. It was 5:54 p.m. and he needed something to eat. Before he hit the cafeteria he called Rich Strong in Newport to get an update on the agents on duty there.

Scooter and I helped George get into one of the loaded ballast compartments. George skillfully extracted some plastic explosives from the first plastic bag that he saw. He took about a golf ball sized piece from one of the large bags that had been placed there. We slowly closed the door when I asked George a question.

"What if we went around and just cut all the power lines to the plastic explosives and render them useless?" I asked.

George looked at me and said the there was probably a device implanted that if someone broke a circuit then an electrical charge would be sent to the other ballast compartments and the hole barge would go up killing anyone trying to disarm it. I removed that idea from my head immediately and followed George's original one.

George split the plastic explosive into four smaller pieces, rolled them and placed them carefully on the four corners of the hatch. George said that he still needed to get back down to the third level deck and find a non-essential wire he could cut without blowing up the barge. He explained that he needed it long enough to keep us away from the explosion and be able to find a hot wire to attach it to detonate the plastic explosive placed on the hatch. It took several minutes for us to get George down to the next level. He searched until we were standing outside the open door to the hold where we had just come out of hours ago. There was a switch on the outside of the door leading into the hold. George turned it and a light went on in the hold. George traced the wire back from the switch to a junction box about 75 feet away. He looked at me and said, "This is a good one." I was glad because I didn't want to go back into the hold because of the stench of human waste. We used George's pocket knife as a screwdriver and a cutting tool to free the wire from the switch and junction box it was attached to. George had enough electrical knowledge to keep from getting hit with the low voltage. The hard part was freeing the wire from the many steel wire clips that were attached to the steel in the barge. The clips had been painted many times which added to the difficulty of loosening them to free the wire. It took us over an hour to free the low voltage wire. All three of us were drenched in sweat. I was pleased that Scooter was with us because he had the youth to keep pulling and working to loosen the painted over screws to free the wire. I looked at my watch and it indicated that it was 7:10 p.m.

We ran the wire from the hatch to another junction box that George knew was powered. The junction box was right next to an empty ballast compartment hatch. George opened the hatch to the compartment. He stood in the doorway and reached for the open junction box. His arm reached it and the opened door shielded him enough from the blast, he thought. We secured the wire as best we could by looping it around a few dogged hatches to hold it in place. George attached the wire to the plastic explosives stuck to the hatch. He walked to the open power source and told Scooter and me that it was ready to blow. I told George to hold that thought for a little bit. He looked at me a little confused. I explained that it was only 7:30 p.m. I asked if we wanted to blow this thing now or wait until we had the advantage of twilight in an hour or so.

"J.J., I don't know how much longer I can stay on my feet. I'm thirsty and dead tired from lack of sleep and food. I don't know if I can get through the hatch after and if we blow it," he said.

I asked him, "So you want to blow it as soon as possible?"

"Yes." I nodded in approval and told Scooter to get into the open ballast compartment. I followed and allowed George enough room to get inside and be partially protected by the door while his arm was exposed to make the exposed wire connection to the active power in the junction box.

"Everyone ready?" he asked. He turned and touched the wire to the junction box. Nothing happened. "Shit," he said. He repositioned himself which meant he was a little more exposed, turned to us for acknowledgement. I nodded. He touched the junction box again and the explosion was deafening. The open door tried to push shut from the force of the explosion squashing George's arm. It almost broke it but his arm kept the door from slamming and possibly locking and keeping all of us in the empty ballast compartment. George was moaning, holding his left arm and lying in the doorway while I pushed the door back open, picked up George and placed him away from it. Scooter and I checked to see what had happened to the hatch. It was not in our way anymore. It was nowhere to be seen. I scampered up the ladder to the first level, crouched down and kept my derringer ready.

Darish heard a muffled explosion. He looked around 360 degrees with his binoculars. He called over to the tug pilot who was doing the same while checking occasionally on the gauges of the tug. Darish could hear some fireworks being set off by the people waiting on shore as well as some brave individuals who occasionally lit a firework off from their boat. The noise he heard was different so he decided to investigate by leaving the pilot's house and looking around the deck of the tug.

Agent Rich Strong watched Daryl Adams through binoculars three hundred yards away. He observed Daryl but did not see any reason to report his movement on the tug. He radioed other agents to observe from their angle if they could see anything different than what he was seeing. No one reported back after acknowledging his request.

I told Scooter as he came through the hatch to go back and help George get to the hatch as soon as possible while I kept watch from the first level deck. He obeyed and within minutes popped his head up through the hatch again to inform me that George was ready to climb the ladder. We both struggled to get George through. We tried to open the first level deck hatch to topside but realized that it was dogged too. We moved through some of the wired units and realized that we could squeeze up between the firework units loaded with live fireworks and access topside. It would be difficult but we knew we could get topside now.

Josh looked at the board and all the information strewn out on the large table in the control room. He recognized the name of Ilea Adel again on the board that had been killed with Mohammad Owlia, Sid's relative, execution style just like Leo

Lupinacci had been. Leo was Tommy's brother. He'd been seen with a man of whom he wasn't sure of his identity.

Donnie Costello paid his respects at the home of Leo Lupinacci's wife. He dreaded going to another funeral in a few days but his best captain's brother had been killed by someone the FBI had some leads on. Leo's wife, Doris, hugged Donnie while Tommy and his wife looked on. They had gathered to begin making arrangements for Leo's wake and funeral. Donnie asked if he could ask Doris some very important questions concerning anything that she could remember Leo saying to her about his job at the Newport plant. Doris looked at Donnie a little confused. Tommy asked his boss if this was necessary at this time. Donnie could have ordered the response but he was too respectful of Tommy and his entire family.

"Tommy, I wouldn't ask but I feel that we might gain some information that could lead us into finding who killed Leo and why. Please let me ask these questions," Donnie asked.

Tommy was taken aback because his boss, and leader, had asked permission to do something. Tommy nodded to Doris and then to Donnie. Donnie asked several questions concerning names of individuals that Leo could have mentioned. He went through the ones that Special Agent Josh Sprague had informed him of. One name did stand out to Doris. She said that Leo didn't like working with a tug company guy.

"Leo called the guy Moron," she said. She also said that Sid Owlia didn't like this Moron guy either. He told Leo to keep away from the guy if he could. Leo said that the guy was always coming up from New London to the Harvester plant checking on the deliveries even though he was employed by the tug company out of Bridgeport. Leo told Sid that he was going to ask Tommy to check him out because he was a weird sort of an individual.

"He never got a chance and neither did Sid to ask me to check this guy out," Tommy said.

Donnie called Special Agent Sprague.

"Sprague here."

"Agent Sprague, a guy Leo called Moron was employed by a

245

Bridgeport tug company. He came up from New London quite a bit to check on the Harvester unit shipments. Both Sid Owlia and Leo Lupinacci were going to ask Tommy Lupinacci to check the guy out for them. Neither ever did.

"I'll call you if I get more information."

Donnie hung up and turned to Doris and hugged her. They all sat down to plan Leo's wake and funeral as a representative from the Guillot Brothers Funeral Home rang the door bell.

A Hunch

Candace Strong contacted Missy Harris to find out any new information she could on the search for Josh's father and family friend George. Missy updated her and said that the FBI, CIA, Homeland Security, the Newport Naval Base Shore Patrol and the tri-State Police Forces were working together. Josh even had mentioned to Joe that the Costello Family was helping in the investigation by gathering information from their ranks. "All that information still doesn't soothe my mother's worries and anxieties. The longer my father and Mr. Woodbridge are missing, the colder the trail will become based on my experience listening to my husband when he discusses cases he's worked on. My father has been officially missing over 80 hours now. The old saying that no news is good news doesn't apply in this case."

"Is there anything I can do for you your mother or the family in general?" Candy asked.

"You can call Josh and give him as much support as you can." Within a few minutes after her conversation with Missy, Candy reached Josh at his office. Just as she was about to hang up, his voice came on the line.

"Josh Sprague here," he yelled into the phone.

"Hi Josh, are you okay? Should I call back?" she said in a voice that was the sweetness voice he could hear in his ear.

"Yes, I'm okay and I'm glad that you called on this line. My cell phone is constantly ringing with updates on the Newport and New London situations."

"Is there any new news on your father and Mr. Woodbridge?"

"Unfortunately there hasn't been any encouraging news."Candy listened to some of the details that Josh gave her. She was confused by all the details but she kept most of the main points in her mind while Josh talked shop a little longer. He apologized to her for going on and on about this difficult case.

247

"Hey, I miss you. As soon as I can get away from this office, the case and the FBI, I'm going to take you on a vacation like we had talked about."

"Well, I can't wait to be alone with you and I'll make my best effort to relax and just love you."

He felt a little aroused and told her that she was interfering with a government investigation by distracting one of the Special Agents in charge.

"I'm sorry. I guess Special Agent Joshua Sprague will have to punish me for being a distraction and a *bad girl.*"

"I guess I'm going to have to send agents out to your apartment and have you apprehended and brought in for questioning right away," he slyly said.

"Well, I would only come in if you personally came for me and handcuffed me to make sure I wouldn't fight back."

Josh said, "Wow, you are a bad girl, Candace Strong. I'm appalled that you would stoop to this level to trick an agent of the FBI."

"You don't know how much I will stoop for you Special Agent Joshua Jonathan Sprague," she said and giggled into the phone.

Josh laughed as well. The banter and sexual arousal put him a spirited mood. That was Candy's plan and it had worked very well.

"Thanks, sweetheart."

"For what?"

"For getting me into a better mood to help solve this case and loving me."

"You are most welcome and I love you too," she said returning his affection. "Now go solve this case and find out why all these situations are leading you to the East Coast Harbors, tug companies and evil people who are not who they say they are."

Josh laughed, said good bye, and hung up.

Josh looked back at the white board and called Chief Agent DiStasio. He wanted to run the latest information by him and some of the thoughts he had in his head. Josh looked at the story board and began to connect the links while he waited for the Chief to answer his cell.

"DiStasio here."

"Boss, I hate to bother you but do you have a few minutes?"

"Sure, Josh, what do you have? We just found an open spot to watch the fireworks and placed several blankets down with a cooler for the kids and grandkids to enjoy the show."

Josh began to talk very seriously. The tone of his voice disturbed the Chief. Josh began to revisit all the information that he had compiled that was pertinent to the case, in his opinion, to present to his boss before he gave his recommendation. DiStasio looked at his watch, the setting sun and the activity around him. It was 8:15 p.m. Josh began to explain that Ilea Adel was Ike Adams. He was employed at onetime by the CTC of Bridgeport and supposedly employed by IH. Their records did not indicate he was one of their employees. Muhammad Owlia was also known to work at the Bridgeport based CTC. He was either Sid Owlia's brother or cousin and was brought here through contacts Sid had while working in the Middle East for the Costello family setting up shipping contracts there. Both Adel and Owlia were killed, execution style, as the Chief knew, at a remote location off Route 138 which is the secondary road used heavily by truckers to Newport, Rhode Island. A car that they were driving was described by his father several times as a silver colored Honda Hybrid.

"Okay Josh, I'm familiar with that," the Chief responded.

Josh continued talking and noted to the Chief that Sid Owlia was in a coma from stab wounds incurred from an unknown assailant. The assailant was probably Moroch Makel or Moron as Doris Lupinacci said Leo described him. He updated the Chief on the new information that had come in from Donnie Costello.

"I'm pleased the mob boss is cooperating with the FBI," the Chief said.

Josh continued, "Leo probably died at the hands of this guy based on the video recording by Connecticut State trooper Richard Longo who had stopped him in Leo's truck. Remember, this guy tried to execute the trooper but failed. The

249

prints of this guy were found in the green Toyota Hybrid he stole from a North Stonington, Connecticut man that he almost killed by pistol whipping him. The car was found in New London and the prints matched the prints found in the Lupinacci pickup truck. The prints also matched the prints found in the Sprague delivery truck along with Sid Owlia's prints. Jon Sprague's blood was found in the truck but the CSI technician said it looked like the blood was staged in the truck's cab to look like he had been taken from the truck. That meant that Sprague was probably still in Newport at that time. Whether he is dead or alive, we don't know, but Newport was the point of origin for Leo and Moroch or Moron."

The chief said, "Go on, please."

Josh acknowledged the chiefs intense interest and said, "Daryl Adams was employed at the CTC of Bridgeport at one time and also claimed to be a security guard for the DFC. He was probably the relative of Ike Adams who was also known as Ilea Akel. I now know that Moroch had stayed in New London with Daryl Adams. Darish Adel and Daryl Adams are the same individual. I guess he's related to Ilea Adel." Josh looked at the newest FBI report on Harry Adams who also was known as Hussein Adel.

"I think that Adel is a common Middle Eastern name such as Jones or Smith is in this country. I also realize that there was too much coincidence in this story board to indicate that. Hussein Adel was the supervisor for the CTC. Most of these people were or are associated at one time or another with the tug company. The supervisor told me that they had tugs working all over the East Coast today. I thought that there was nothing working on the Fourth of July."

"Shit," the Chief exclaimed.

"I called the tug company again to make sure of my hunch. The dispatcher said that they had tugs supporting the Newport and New London fireworks shows. They also had tugs in Boston and New York. It was a very busy day for the tug company today. I followed up with it and all the tugs that were being used today are from the CTC. It had been contracted by the

DFC to do this work for the third year in a row. I also contacted Portsmouth and found out that they had hired the DFC as well and the CTC to tow the barge for their festivity. This was the first year that Portsmouth had a Fourth of July harbor fireworks display in years and Deutsch had been contracted to perform the fireworks display."

Rich Strong called Josh while he was updating the Chief.

"Chief, can you hold on while I take Strong's call?"

"Okay, I'll hold," he said as he processed all the information Josh had relayed to him. Rich Strong reported that he had a visual on one individual that he had not seen before.

"Josh, I have a photo for you to check out and put through the system," he said. Rich had one of the agents take a photo of the person walking around on the deck of the tug. Josh told Strong to hold while he viewed the picture and went back to the Chief. Within seconds, the picture was coming through to the photo printer that was hooked to his FBI desk computer. From the distance the photo had been taken, it was difficult to confirm an identity. Josh had one of his technicians enhance the picture and run it in the features identity software. Within a few more seconds, the computer identified a 95 percent chance that this photo was of Daryl Adams.

Josh said to the Chief, "The picture Strong just sent me is a ninety five percent likeness of the Deutsch security representative that bullshitted Howard Bruckner. He also has been connected to the CTC and is also known as Darish Adel." Josh flipped back to Rich to tell him to watch this guy because he was bad news but he couldn't arrest him just yet.

"We need to watch him very well," he said and hung up the phone. Rich was surprised at the immediate closure to the conversation but realized Josh was running on fumes lately. *They all were*, he thought.

Chief DiStasio told Josh that based on the information he had provided, he would bypass Judge Marco and call FBI Headquarters at Langley to get the FBI Director's Office up to speed and let them deal with the politics.

"I'll get orders from the Director's Office to intercede and stop the fireworks starting at Newport and encompassing New London as well," the he said.

Josh knew that the new orders coming from the FBI Director in Langley would allow him to get his chance to search the barge and apprehend Darish Adel.

He said, "I'll contact Chuck Martin in New London and I also have some other leads that might contribute to the arrest of these guys."

"Get back to me as soon as possible. I'll begin the process to notify the staff of the Director and eventually get to converse with the Director personally."

Josh called New London and asked Special Agent Chuck Martin if he or any of his men could get close enough to the Crescent tug in the New London harbor to identify anyone sitting in the pilot's house. Agent Martin told him he would get him some photos and get them to him as soon as possible. Josh went back to the story board and information on the table and looked further into Hussein Adel's information. Fifteen thousand dollars in small bills jumped out at him. He pondered why this guy was heading north with a ton of cash on him. He thought that amount of cash would signal too many law enforcement authorities that this guy was up to something if he paid for something that would cost that much money to purchase. He was heading north to Canada, maybe, he thought. He had enough identification on him to get across the border. If he were to buy a ticket he would need, maybe, $600 to $1000 and that wasn't a big amount to pay for a one way air flight these days, he pondered.

"What if Hussein Adel, aka Harry Adams was paying for multiple tickets?" Josh said out loud to himself as he looked at the board. He continued to talk out loud to himself as a few agents turned his way to see if he was talking to them. Adel would have had to carry that amount of money to divvy up if he met up with others who might need a ticket or what? His mind contemplated his own sentence. He realized this guy would never be able to meet up with anyone if that was a true statement. Adel had been killed on I-91 North. He looked out

252

through the entrance of the office. A few agents were standing looking at him.

Josh took the opportunity while he waited for Agent Martin, to complete his task of notifying U. S. and Canadian Customs and Security on the Canadian border. He also had to notify the International Air carriers in Quebec, Montreal and Ontario that there was a high probability that individuals associated with the CTC of Bridgeport, Connecticut, the DFC of Bonn, Germany or the IH Company of either Connecticut or Rhode Island, may be passing through any or all of these major cities in route to other locations in Europe. They would probably have purchased flights destined for the United Kingdom or Spain in route to other European and Middle Eastern countries.

Agent Chuck Martin called Josh back to say that he had sent photos they had taken and down loaded them to his laptop on board the FBI boat of the pilot and co-pilot of the Crescent Tug in the New London Harbor.

"Check your laptop and run the photos I just sent you from our digital camera. We developed a scheme of distraction to get close and take the photos. Maybe these photos will get us and the New London Harbor Patrol permission to intervene and search the tug and the barge."

"How'd you get close enough for the picture?"

"We acted like overzealous local boat owners trying to get as close to the barge as we could to observe the fireworks. The charade worked boss. When the co-pilot came out to observe us zealous boaters, we got what we wanted until the U.S. Coast Guard pretended to whisk us away. Josh, we didn't get great shots of the pilot but the co-pilot came out real good," he said.

Josh never answered Agent Martin. Josh looked at the pictures that appeared on his computer. He was looking at the likeness of Moroch Makel.

"Why was that son of a bitch on board a Crescent tug in New London?" he asked out loud.

Before he called the Chief back, he decided to review all the latest information he had just received again. He wanted to be absolutely sure of all his information now that the FBI

253

Director's Office was involved when it hit him and a cold chill ran down his spine. His stomach began to turn and that made him nauseated for a few seconds. He realized that some type of attack was underway and he began to put the pieces of the puzzle together very quickly.

The DFC, the IHC, the CTC and some members of the Costello Family had been used as a front for a terrorist group that was planning some type of attack. They were towing and pushing barges into the Harbors where hundreds of thousands of American citizens were standing by innocently preparing to watch the Fourth of July fireworks displays. New York and Boston would have millions of people watching. There were, at least five major ports in New England and New York involved. Each harbor had a naval vessel docked at its pier assisting in generating electrical power to the respective areas they were assigned to. All the naval vessels were nuclear. Josh almost froze thinking that if these guys were able to knock out the vessels and cause nuclear shutdowns or worse yet, a nuclear catastrophe, this area would be a waste land for ten thousand years and millions of people would be dead in less than a month. His hand shook as he dialed the Chief. Josh informed him of his findings and his theory. DiStasio listened carefully and decided that his theory made sense and this could potentially be the greatest catastrophe America could ever witness.

He paused before responding.

"If your theory is correct, and I think it is, we are in the midst of the greatest catastrophe of all times. I'll immediately notify the Director and give him the update," he urgently said. "He will decide whether to involve the Pentagon. Josh, thank you and good work."

"Chief," Josh said before disconnecting the call. "I have no proof that there is anything in those barges except fireworks. It is only a theory, a hunch, or whatever you want to call it but someone is trying very hard to get close to these barges and take control of them."

"I understand. But great observations," he said. "Stay near all your phones and direct all your people here in Newport and those that are in New London and get this information to all agents in the other cities you suspect. I want our agents to be able to board the Newport and New London barges at a moment's notice. I will notify Homeland Security to notify the Coast Guard and the Navy in the respective harbors to prepare to assist. If we get our New London or Newport search and our find produces explosives, the Air Force will be called in immediately to eliminate the barges in the other harbors. Put out a nationwide alert per my direction now," he commanded and ended the call.

Chief DiStasio looked at his wife and children who heard bits and pieces of the conversation he'd just had with Special Agent Sprague. They asked if they should be leaving now. The Chief looked around and just nodded. The grandchildren objected at first but their parents quickly and skillfully kept them under control for the trip back to the parked cars. Upon arrival at the parked cars, the Chief stood in their midst and quietly explained what had transpired and that they must all leave as quickly as possible and without any reservations. As soon as the last car, with his wife safely inside departed, the Chief headed for the FBI Office. In route, he contacted the FBI Director's Office in Langley. His watch indicated that it was 8:29 p.m. At precisely 8:30 p.m. the tug pilots knew to untie the tugs from the barges and position the tugs far enough away for safety reasons during the display. The tug would maintain control of the barge in the harbor by the towing cable now. Upon completion of the fireworks display the tugs were to tow the barges back to Bridgeport where the fireworks units would be unloaded by the DFC. The temporary tug pilots had a different plan than returning the empty barges to Bridgeport. They had trained to blast the cable free and make it look like the barge had become free. In their fake attempt to bring the barge under control by swinging around and pushing the barge, the Coast Guard would think the pilots had the barge back under control. At that point they would be able to complete the

255

plan and push the barge loaded with explosives into the side of their targeted vessel killing themselves and initially hundreds of people. If the blast ruptured the nuclear reactor, the hundreds of deaths would immediately climb to the hundreds of thousands.

I could feel the barge move slightly so I began my move through one of the units, trying very carefully not to snag any wire or loosen any fitting. I really was trying to keep from blowing us up. I was able to squeeze up and get my torso through enough to look around topside. The tug was partially visible as it backed away from the barge. I kept low so that the pilot or any deckhands would not see me. I called down to George to keep low as soon as he was clear of the units and wires. Scooter kept behind George to assist in pushing him up as George was very weak and dehydrated now. It took five minutes to get George up to the top deck. I realized that we had to jump off and swim to shore to inform the authorities but I also realized that George would never make the swim. I thought of waving frantically but the chances of anyone seeing us were almost next to nothing. I also worried that the tug pilot or that mean bastard would see us and return. It was getting dark now. The time was 8:45 p.m. and the fireworks would commence at 9:15.p.m. I remembered. I discussed the choices we had with the other two. Scooter said nothing as he clung to George.

George said, "Once the fireworks are done, it would be too late to jump off and warn anyone. We need to get off this barge and head for the closest boat and try to get on board and have them notify the authorities."

I reminded George that he was weak and that it would take a lot of effort to stay afloat and try to swim to the closest boat.

"J.J., look over there. I'm going to float over to those boats while Scooter here holds on and pushes me along."

I looked where he was pointing and could clearly see a white life preserver hanging.

"Scooter, move down and see if there is another one on the

barge," he directed.

Scooter crouched down and searched the barge. He found another one. George explained that it was time to jump into the water.

My plan now was to jump in with both life preservers. George would follow with Scooter's help. I would swim over and give the life preservers to George and Scooter. The plan seemed easy enough, the water was warm and we should be able to get to anyone of the boats in the harbor. The closest boats seemed to be about 500 yards away. I went over the plan twice to make sure Scooter understood. We all decided that we were ready to go. I jumped off the barge carrying the two life preservers. The fall was about seven feet into the relatively calm harbor water. The temperature was cool so there was no worry about hypothermia. Besides, I hoped that we'd be in the water for only a small amount of time. My head began to sting. The salt water was burning my open wound but I forced myself to concentrate on the next jumper. When George jumped, I panicked for a few seconds. I swam to him as quickly as I could and gave him the other life preserver. Scooter had already jumped in and was almost touching the life preserver as I secured George to it. I looked around and headed away from the barge. I planned to paddle away keeping the barge in between us and the tug. So far, the plan was working well. It was 9:05 p.m. according to my wrist watch. My head didn't burn anymore. It was numb. The salt water was cleansing my infected wound.

Josh had notified all the lead agents at the Newport and New London Harbors. Rich Strong and Chuck Martin had contacted all their agents and they were poised in the inconspicuous boats. They were ready and could head for the tugs and apprehend the pilots and co-pilots in a relatively short time. Josh had informed the naval bases at the affected harbors of the situation. He instructed them to be on alert and to be in contact with the harbor security organizations and the Coast Guard. They understood to keep their radio correspondence to a bare minimum as to not alert any of the Crescent Tugs or any other tug in the area what was developing.

Chief DiStasio had contacted the Director's Office emergency staff and they were in direct contact with the FBI Director at all times. The staff agent questioned Chief DiStasio on every detail of the investigation until the Chief requested direct communication with the Director. The staff agent said, "Chief, we understand your concern but there are some details that are conjecture and not factual. There has been no confirmation of explosives and the repercussions to the FBI Director for stopping five major fireworks displays where two of them are being nationally televised would be catastrophic for the FBI's credibility."

The Chief asked to speak to the Director directly. The staff agent said that until the Chief had more creditable information he was not authorized to contact the Director. There was a pause and the Chief said, "Sir, I have twenty years in military intelligence with the army and another twenty years in the FBI and I am wasting time explaining my life history to you who's afraid to contact the goddamned Director. It's my ass on the line if I piss this guy off and it's my career for bothering him during the Fourth of July. If I'm wrong, the laugh and consequences are on me. If I'm right and I survive this catastrophe, I will personally come down to Langley and shoot you dead. I won't have to wait to be tried and executed for shooting an agent for the fucking radiation I will be exposed to will do it for me. Do you understand, sir?"

There was a pause and the staff agent said, "Hold on Chief."

A few clicks could be heard and a few more seconds went by. Chief DiStasio waited and glanced at his watch. It was 9:10 p.m. and in five minutes the shows would begin.

"Director Kirk here. What is it, Chief, that is so important this Fourth of July?"

Check

The Chief informed the Director, as quickly as possible, of all the pertinent information that Josh had presented to him a few minutes earlier. The Director did not say a word for the approximate two minutes it took Chief DiStasio to present a precise outline of the situation. It was important for him to emphasize the urgency of the situation. When DiStasio finished, he waited for a response. Several seconds went by.

The Chief finally asked, "Director, are there any questions?"

"Hold Chief. I have my staff agents on the line so you and they can respond as I direct. Instruct your agents to board the tugs as soon as possible after the fireworks displays have been completed in New London and Newport and apprehend the operators. Instruct your staff to contact the harbor security at New London and Newport and have them immediately assist you as required. I want you to search the barges after the tugs are under your control. My staff will notify the other respective naval bases, Coast Guard and harbor security groups to be ready to follow your lead. We will also notify the respective State Police Forces to begin preparations to control the evacuation of the civilians from the harbor coast lines if confirmation has been made that there are explosives on board these barges. If the situation elevates, I will have already informed the Pentagon to have aircraft scrambled and circling the areas you say are targeted. Chief, I hope you are correct on this," he said as he hung up.

Darish looked at his watch. It was 9:15 p.m. The Newport Fireworks display commenced. Darish looked over at the tug pilot and their eyes met. No words were exchanged but both men knew their time on this earth would end before 10 p.m. The fireworks continued to light up the harbor while synchronized music played over thousands of radios tuned into the local FM stations that had the musical score that the DFC timed their new fireworks units to. Everything was working perfectly as the crowd relaxed and enjoyed the show.

Moroch continued to look out through his binoculars at the surrounding moored boats to make sure everything remained normal. He looked down at his watch and was startled when the first fireworks commenced. It was 9:16 p.m. Moroch also looked at his pilot who ignored him while he concentrated on keeping the barge in the relative position the Coast Guard and Deutsch people wanted it at.

George, Scooter and I continued to paddle towards a white cabin cruiser that seemed to be taking forever to get to. We could see the occupants standing and watching the fireworks display. I yelled over but they were preoccupied with the brightness and colors displayed in front of them and the sound of the music that was playing. The sound was almost deafening on some boats. We continued to paddle and yell. Eventually one boater on the white cabin cruiser happened to spot us heading towards the boat. He pointed and several others that were with him began to gather on the side closest to us to observe what he was pointing at. We yelled louder and they responded. The boater pulled his anchor, started his boat and slowly moved in our direction. It was 9:21 p.m. when I was plucked from the water.

While the occupants of the white cabin cruiser pulled George and Scooter from the water, I asked the owner if I could use his radio. I told him who I was and that I needed to contact the Harbor authorities immediately. He responded that he would call them for me. He said that I had a very nasty cut on my head. I told him I knew that. It wasn't important now. I told him he needed to pick up the radio and call in. He did as I instructed.

"Coast Guard, this is RI 132351. Come in please." He repeated, "Coast Guard, this is RI 132351, the White Swan. Come in please."

A few seconds went by as the thunder and fizzing of the fireworks continued and the loud music played. He was about to repeat his call for a third time when a voice came on.

"This is the Coast Guard, RI One-three-two-three-five-one. What is the nature of your call?"

I grabbed the microphone from the owner and pushed the button.

"Coast Guard, I'm Jonathan Sprague. Please call the Providence Office of the FBI and contact Special Agent Joshua Sprague immediately. The number is four-zero-one-five-four-three-one-two-one-two." I waited.

"RI One-three-two-three-five-one, this is the Coast Guard. Please repeat."

"Coast Guard, this is Jonathan Sprague. I was picked up by this boat from the harbor waters. I was on the fireworks barge and had been kept there under guard. I am with two other individuals the FBI is probably looking for. The barge is loaded with explosives. I repeat the barge is loaded with explosives. Contact the FBI at four-zero-one-five-four-three-one-two-one-two immediately."

"RI One-three-two-three-five-one, this is the Coast Guard. Please have the owner of RI One-three-two-three-five-one, Mr. John Paige take over the radio." The owner grabbed the radio.

"Coast Guard, this is RI One-three-two-three-five-one, John Paige speaking." He had a concerned look as he waited for the Coast Guard to answer him.

"RI One-three-two-three-five-one, this is the Coast Guard. Please explain the current situation."

John Paige explained in detail what had occurred and what he understood the situation to be. The Coast Guard asked for the location of the cabin cruiser. John Paige explained his approximate location so that the small pontoon patrol boat could approach his location. Jon Paige was instructed to put on his running lights as soon as he had a visual on the approaching Coast Guard pontoon boat. Approximately three minutes later, a small patrol boat with blue lights was approaching their location. John Paige lit his running lights.

Josh Sprague waited in the control room with ten other agents manning the computers, monitors, phones, and harbor radios.

His cell rang.

"Special Agent Sprague here."

"Agent, this is the Newport Harbor Coast Guard Patrol. We have information from a man stating he is Jonathan Sprague. He is with George Woodbridge and another unidentified person who were picked up in the Newport Harbor several minutes ago. He said that he was onboard the DFC barge and that it contains explosives. Do you copy that message?"

"Coast Guard, I do copy, I do copy. Pickup the three men and take them immediately to the Newport Security Tent. Do not contact the tug or barge. Coast Guard, I repeat, do not contact the tug or barge. I have agents in the area that will proceed to the tug immediately. We have them under surveillance as we speak. Please notify your command to be prepared to assist the FBI as requested on channel six in your area. I repeat that communications will be on channel six. Do you understand?"

"Affirmative, affirmative, channel six, the Coast Guard is standing by."

Josh's eyes were glossy. One tear slowly moved down his cheek from his right eye. All the agents in the control room were happy that his father was alive. Josh immediately called Chief DiStasio.

"DiStasio here."

"Chief, we have confirmation of explosives on board!" He almost yelled into the phone.

"What or who is the source?" the Chief requested.

"Jonathan Sprague and George Woodbridge," Josh said.

"They're alive? Thank God," he said.

"Yes Sir they are. I am bringing them in as we speak."

"Okay, go get these bastards with all that is available. I will concentrate on the other cities."

Chief DiStasio notified the Director that his agents had individuals in their custody who were eyewitnesses who confirmed explosive had been loaded into the Newport barge. The Chief said that there was a very high probability now that the four other barges had the same condition. The Director rescinded his previous order to wait until after the fireworks

262

display was completed.

"Chief, have your agents board the tugs and barges immediately."

"I'll do so immediately."

"Good. I'll initiate the Naval and Air response immediately for New York, Boston and Portsmouth. Newport and New London will be handled by your agents who were already poised for the assault. I'll also organize Naval and Air support for the two cities as backup and under your direction. Where are you located now?"

"I'm just entering the Providence FBI control room."

The Director kept his line to the Chief open while the Chief began to bark orders to his immediate subordinates. He saw Josh as he entered the control room and said, "Board both tugs immediately, I repeat, board immediately."

Josh instantly yelled to the FBI dispatcher to initiate the new orders to Newport and New London. Agents Strong and Martin revved the engines of their boats and headed for their respective barges and tugs. Naval security forces within the entire United States went on Code Red for terrorist attack imminent. The Connecticut Air National Guard scrambled ten F-16 Fighters in five groups of two to cover the respective cities. The jets would take less than 20 minutes to be on station over all the affected cities. Other Air Force units were also scrambled to cover the entire eastern seaboard while the Connecticut Air National Guard approached the barges for possible destruction.

Darish noticed, through his binoculars, the Coast Guard Security pontoon boat move up to a lit up white cabin cruiser a few minutes earlier. It looked like a routine investigation of the Coast Guard of a civilian boat that had a problem. The boat raced away with some additional occupants and headed for the emergency area on the opposite side of the harbor. He assumed it was some injured, drunken or obnoxious individuals being hauled to the emergency services area in the harbor. A few minutes later he noticed the blue and white lights of several approaching boats. Despite all the commotion and flickering lights and flashes from the fireworks that continued to go off, these lights indicated trouble for him and his plan. Darish told the pilot that there was trouble approaching and that he was initiating the explosive device to sever the cable from the tug to the barge immediately. The pilot acknowledged, while the spectacular fireworks display continued, and the crowd applauded and whistled. A small explosion went unnoticed as it severed the steel cable from the tug to the barge. The tug pilot immediately swung the tug around to position it to begin pushing the barge in the direction of the U.S.S. Clinton. Off-duty officers and men enjoying the festivities could be seen lining the carrier's flight deck. The tug pilot knew he had to maneuver the tug cautiously. It took a little more time than expected for the pilot to maneuver the tug into the proper position to initiate the attack without setting off the sensors on the barge.

Darish calculated that that the security boats would be upon them before the pilot had attained a reasonable speed moving the barge towards the Clinton. He realized that he needed a diversion to hold off the approaching boats long enough to gain the speed they needed to be successful. Darish opened the opposite side of the suitcase he had brought on board. One side contained the activation device he had just used to sever the tug's cable to the barge. The other side contained the machine pistol that he possessed for unforeseen emergencies like this. He slapped in one of six clips he had available for the Israeli machine pistol. He waited for the boats to come in range.

Moroch observed two boats approaching the tug and barge from his observation point on the tug in the New London harbor. He too, realized that the operation was in jeopardy now. He immediately called over to the tug pilot to begin his maneuver to come about while he activated the cable explosive device. The device went off without anyone noticing anything during the flashing and booming of the fireworks that people in New London and on the Groton side of the harbor were enjoying. He told the pilot that he was going out on the deck to keep the boats away as he drew out his Walther PPK and grabbed a small bag. The pilot did not answer as he began his immediate turn about. Moroch waited and jumped just as the tug made its turn. The pilot never noticed that he was not on board now. He kept underwater as long as he could and then surfaced. Under the flashing of the fireworks and the noise of the blaring FM radios playing the synchronized music, he headed for the closest boat he could see as he swam.

Darish began to fire his machine pistol at the oncoming FBI boats flashing their blue and white security lights. The tug pilot maneuvered the tug to slightly touch the barge and immediately began to push the barge with all the power the diesel engines in the tug could produce. The black smoke poured from the bright green smoke stack with the white Crescent painted on it. The smoke looked gray from the fireworks illuminating it. Flashes could now be seen from the deck of the tug and approaching boats.

Agent Rich Strong was hit by one of Darish's machine pistol bullets in the left shoulder knocking him down and temporarily putting him out of commission as the firefight began. His accuracy took down another agent who died instantly from a head wound. The other two agents in the boat continued to return fire at the flashes that could be seen coming from the deck of the tug. The operator of the FBI Security pontoon boat continued to steer directly at the tug in response to Rich Strong's orders he continued to yell as he lay on the deck, wounded in the shoulder. The second FBI Security pontoon boat veered slightly to get a better angle on the tug pushing the barge now towards the carrier. The crowd cheered as they realized the barge was moving to a different location. It was a little closer to the spectators now and some thought it was part of the show. Everyone seemed to be enjoying it. No one knew that one agent was already dead, one was wounded, and the tug was still under the control of the terrorists.

Moroch continued to watch as the blue and white lights of the FBI Security pontoon boats circled the barge and began firing on the tug. He continued to push his body by half swimming and half floating closer to the boats in the harbor, closer to where spectators were enjoying the show. The grand finale was beginning and he could hear the crowd's pleasure over the sounds of the exploding fireworks. The FBI marksmanship was better at New London than at Newport. A FBI bullet founds its mark and instantly killed the tug pilot of the New London tug before he could reach the barge to push it towards the U.S.S. North Carolina docked at the Electric Boat Shipyard on the opposite side of the harbor. The pilot was hunched over and his dead weight forwarded the throttle of the single engine tug. His arm was wedged in between the throttle and the pilot wheel as the tug headed straight towards the barge which held the final displays of the fireworks show and the ballast compartments full of plastic explosives.

The FBI control room personnel listened intently to the reports coming in from Agents Strong and Martin from the Newport and New London harbors. New York and Boston agents were just getting organized and were beginning their assault on the tug and barges. The Portsmouth response was lagging behind and there was concern in the entire FBI control room. The Portsmouth fireworks display had ended five minutes earlier. The display had been pushed up due to weather reports indicating that low clouds and heavy rain was imminent and would obscure and dampen the fireworks display.

The Newport firefight continued for several more minutes until Darish Adel ran out of clips of bullets. He died in a hail of bullets while pumping his hand in the air. The pilot was killed as the grand finale concluded to the cheer of the Newport crowd who was still oblivious to what had just happened in the harbor between the FBI and the terrorists.

Within minutes, the barge and tug were surrounded by Navy, Coast Guard, Harbor Security and the FBI boats. The barge was secured and demolition experts and bomb squads were cautiously brought on board to begin to disarm the barge in the middle of the harbor. The bright green Crescent Tug could be seen approaching the fireworks barge as the last fireworks of the New London grand finale made its mark over the harbor. People were cheering and applauding the show's conclusion as Moroch swam to a small speed boat with a couple sitting and applauding the exhibition of a superb fireworks show they had just witnessed. He threw his small bag into the boat then pulled himself onto the speedboat and laid face down in the rear of the boat to the surprise of the occupants. They immediately stood up to approach the intruder when the fireworks barge exploded. The force from the blast immediately knocked the occupants into the dark water. Moroch felt the concussion but was shielded enough in his face down position in the rear of the speed boat to get up to witness the aftermath of the explosion.

Pieces of the barge fell back to earth in a non-stop shower of jagged projectiles that tore at anything they landed on with the force and speed of Mother Nature's gravity. There were no visible signs of the pursuit boats of the FBI or of the bright green tug that had rammed into the barge. A four foot wall of water had begun to spread out in every direction from the explosion and was gaining height and speed for every second it moved. Moroch tried to start the boat when he noticed some people lying in the water motionless and apparently affected by the concussion from the blast. Some smaller boats had capsized and were in the process of sinking while some people, who were able to function after the blast, threw life preservers or jumped into the water to save individuals. Moroch managed to start the speed boat, pull up the anchor and speed upriver from the carnage of the catastrophic blast. He powered the speed boat over the five foot tidal wave that had now reached the anchored boats that remained and began to take its toll of damage on some of them. There was carnage and confusion all over the harbor but that did not affect Moroch Makel. He thought of the other locations and hoped that he would stay alive long enough to hear how successful those teams had been.

Chief DiStasio immediately updated the Director of the New London explosion. The Director ordered the jets to strike the remaining targets in New York, Boston and Portsmouth as soon as the FBI reported the assault forces were away. Chief DiStasio waited several seconds and shook his head and looked at Josh.

"Director, the FBI agents are reported clear. Proceed with air craft assault." The Chief heard the Director give the order to fire at the barges.

The New York barge had just finished its display. The approaching jets could see the tug attempting to hook up to the barge. It had not begun its run in the direction of the U.S.S. Seawolf and U.S.S. Connecticut moored at the New York piers to assist in the generation of electrical power for the New York area when the lead F-16 Fighter launched two missiles at the barge while the second fighter aimed and fired on the tug. All four missiles struck within micro seconds of each other and directly on their mark. Another explosion similar to New London shook Manhattan and surrounding skyline. The catastrophic explosion damaged windows on sky scrapers a mile away as well as upturning all types of vessels in the harbor from the concussion of the explosion and from the four foot tidal wave that had been generated from it.

Chief DiStasio and Special Agent Sprague sat quietly as they began hearing the reports from the agents in the field. Josh said nothing to the Chief who he knew had made the correct decision to inform the Director that all the agents were clear of the blasts. Josh knew that if he had waited the five to ten minutes for the agents to react to the order maybe some of the barges would have found their mark and caused further mayhem.

The Boston barge was still in the final stages of the grand finale when it erupted into another catastrophic explosion similar to New York and New London. The force of the blast rendered many people unconscious or dead. The tidal wave that was generated hit the side of the U.S.S. Constitution with enough force to cause considerable flooding as water poured into the open cannon ports. The crew was able to control the situation with emergency pumps and the Navy's oldest ship had survived the country's newest attack.

There was still no report from Portsmouth until a voice message was heard from one of the pilots of the F-16s over Portsmouth. He reported that he was in process of lining up his approach and confirming his shot when the barge rammed into the nuclear destroyer U.S.S. Arleigh Burke. He reported that the destroyer was on fire and had a large hole mid-ship. She was listing to starboard approximately 15 degrees and except for the fire, there were no lights on coming from the immediate city which indicated to him that the reactor had been damaged and wasn't generating power to it. He reported that some emergency lights could be seen in the harbor through the smoke from the initial blast and from the nuclear destroyer. The control room heard orders for all fighters to stay on station until further notice.

Jean Sprague, Missy Harris and the children had heard the sound of the explosion from the New London barge 20 miles away when it occurred. Only fear and exasperation was felt until Joe Harris had reached Missy to tell her briefly what had occurred and that he was okay but didn't know when he would be able to see her at home due to the emergency procedures that had to be executed by the law enforcement authorities after a terrorist attack. He told her he loved her and hung up. Jean looked at Missy as she explained what she had been told by Joe. Jean sat there and knew that her husband had an idea something was happening but couldn't have known something of this magnitude. She slowly got up and went to Lilly's bedroom and closed the door. Jean knelt in prayer and asked for blessings for the soul of her husband and dear friend. She drew out her rosary from her pocket and began to pray.

Josh sat with the others in the FBI control room listening to the radio chatter amongst the different emergency groups at the scenes in the Newport and New London harbors. They had other communications open to the New York, Boston and the Portsmouth sites. Chief DiStasio got direct communications from the medical team that was treating Special Agent Richard Strong for a gunshot wound to the left shoulder. He was in stable condition and would be taken to the hospital shortly. The Chief was also informed that Agent Howard Bruckner was killed in the line of duty. He had been shot through the head and killed instantly. He was being taken to the morgue at the same hospital that Special Agent Strong was to be treated. Josh heard the conversation and had mixed emotions. His friend was alive and he had lost a group member. He thanked God that his conscience was clear. He had left Agent Bruckner on a civil note after he had accepted his apology for yelling at him. If Bruckner had only pushed a little harder maybe none of this would have happened, he thought. It was pointless to think about that now. His colleague was dead.

Chief DiStasio listened for the New London report. There was no word from Chuck Martin and his team. A message from the remaining agents on land reported that Special Agent Martin and three other agents had not been accounted for after the explosion. Based on their proximity to the blast, they were considered casualties. The Chief looked at Josh and stared into space. He slowly rose from his chair and walked to his office. He closed the door softly behind him and sat at his desk. No one bothered him until he returned a few minutes later to resume his position as leader of the Providence FBI Office. Then Josh remembered and said out loud, "My God, my father and Mr. Woodbridge." He picked up his phone and dialed his sister's house. *It's taking forever*, he thought, *for Missy to pick up.*

"Hello."

"Dad's alive! Did you hear me? Dad's alive!" he almost yelled into the phone. Missy screamed and called to her mother. Jean's first reaction was that the final bad news had arrived until she realized Missy was smiling as tears streamed down her face. They were happy tears as Missy handed her the phone and hugged her at the same time. She managed to get the phone to her ear.

"Hello."

"Mom, Dad is alive and under the protection of the FBI. Mr. Woodbridge is with him! That is all I can tell you but he is alive and well enough to walk on his own! Call Anita Woodbridge, please. I'll call you back later."

"Yes," was all that she could manage to say. The phone went dead. Jean just smiled as she dialed Anita to inform her that George and Jon were alive.

More information began to flow into the FBI Office on the casualties in the Portsmouth Harbor. The U.S.S. Burke had nuclear reactor damage that had caused radiation to be released into the atmosphere. Luckily for the Burke, its crew, the naval facilities and the City of Portsmouth, the destroyer had taken on water and had settled upright in the harbor, covering the reactor and maintaining the core from a compete meltdown. The radiation that did escape into the atmosphere was quickly pushed out to sea from the violent thunder storm that had occurred thirty minutes after the explosion. The storm that caused the fireworks display to be hastened forced the escaping radiation from the ship out to sea quickly and away from the heart of the city and surrounding population.

There were an estimated 3000 people that had been within 300 yards of the ship when the explosion occurred rupturing the hull and causing the reactor to be exposed. Approximately 20 percent of those people were reported killed by the explosion; some ten percent were estimated to die from wounds received from flying shrapnel from the barge, tug and portions of the hull of the U.S.S. Burke. The radiation would start to take its toll in 24 hours as the radiation began to affect the blood, organs and bones of the victims that had survived the explosion. The authorities couldn't estimate yet what percent would die from radiation.

New York had estimated some 900 people had died from the barge explosion and twelve hundred more had been injured.

Boston was estimating 250 killed and almost 300 injured. New London had the most casualties due to the size of the harbor and the close proximity of the crowd to the event. Approximately 1000 people had lost their lives with another 1500 injured. Property damage was in the billions of dollars including one nuclear destroyer of the U.S. Navy. Josh looked at the data with Chief DiStasio.

"What would have been the cost of lives and property if we hadn't accomplished what we did, Chief?" Josh asked in a monotone voice staring at the incoming data.

"Son, we wouldn't have been able to ever know that. We wouldn't have lived long enough to see that cost. The radiation concentration would have killed tens of millions and no one in this area would have been around to know. Right now we are dealing with 2800 dead and as many or more injured. The radiation will take its toll and we will exceed what happened on nine-eleven," he said.

The Chief sounded cold as he compared statistics. But Josh realized that we had been lucky. The Chief said that he had just developed a plan to begin handling the office and workload while the Bureau got through the aftermath of the largest terrorist attempt to inflict damage on the United States. Josh's group would be the first off for 24 hours. Josh was relieved because he had been at the office for 36 hours straight and he needed to rest. He was going to drive to Connecticut and stay at Candy's. He could be with her in 50 minutes. He planned to be with her when she went to see Rich in the hospital. He could visit his parents and sister's family while he was there. He could see the Woodbridges. He could be home. That sounded very good but he would sleep next to Candy for as long as he needed.

It was 5:11 a.m. and the sun had just started to peak over the horizon as Moroch Makel ditched his boat near the gaming casino that had been built on the Thames River 25 years ago.

The Aftermath

On July 5, 2014 at 5:26 a.m. Jon and Jean Sprague, and George and Anita Woodbridge, met at the Naval Hospital at the Newport Naval Base. FBI Special Agent Joshua Sprague was on the phone, while on his way to Connecticut. His call had been to George Woodbridge's son, Flight Surgeon and Commander Thomas Woodbridge of the U.S.S. Clinton. He had called the flight surgeon to get updated on the condition of his father and Mr. Woodbridge. Josh remembered Tom's athletic records and feats posted in the gym of the high school they both attended. There was a bit of small talk about the high school and about when Tom came home from college. The families would meet sometimes for holidays or just weekend barbeques. They both never thought their paths would cross in a manner such as the one that had just occurred.

"You're missing one hell of a great time here, Josh," he said, as he watched Josh's and his parents hug each other in the Emergency Room. Josh was pleased to hear his mother cry and then scold her father for scaring her to death. He could hear her ask about the bandage Jon had on his head and then she scolded him again for taking on that job for the Harvester people. Tom Woodbridge told Josh, in a low tone, that maybe he was better off in his car on his way to Connecticut then seeing this. Josh laughed out loud over the phone.

Anita Woodbridge hugged George for a long time and never said one word to her husband. Her smile and touch were enough for George. Anita turned to Tom and asked, "Dr. Woodbridge, have these men of mine been properly treated and are they ready to go home now?"

"Yes Mom, they are."

"Good, then. Give your mama a kiss and we'll be off, son."

"You take them home now and I'll be home as soon as I can. I still have a lot of work to do here."

Anita turned to Jean and said gleaming, "That's my son, the doctor. I know he did a good job on your husband."

Jean laughed and said, "I'm sure he did but too bad the doctor couldn't have put some common sense back in this old man's thick head."

Both women laughed and then Anita said, "He's a medical doctor, not a miracle worker." They both laughed again but a little louder. I looked at Thomas and went along with their banter. George could have cared less. He wanted to go home. George turned and looked at Scooter who stood there watching the group move away. George stopped walking and said, "Scooter, you come home with us. We are going to find you a good job and your own place to live in. Aren't we Anita?"

She smiled at the boy and said, "Come on with us child."

I realized Joe Harris had a Connecticut State Police Van and two officers waiting to take Jean and I and the Woodbridges to our homes. We had been instructed by Chief Agent DiStasio to be ready in a few days to be picked up and brought to the FBI Office in New London for a debriefing. We were told that we were to be questioned under oath as to what had taken place in the 90 or so hours we had been involved in this national case. The press was waiting outside the Naval Base Hospital Emergency Room for the three of us.

"Here we go J.J.," George turned and said to me as we exited the ER door. The press was upon us in an instant. Multiple questions were being asked at the same time while some individuals kept shoving microphones and cameras into our faces hoping for some comment or statement they could publish. We were having difficulty getting to the police van until I spoke up and said, "Please stop this." The press seemed to expect an interview. What they received was something different.

"We will talk to you in the morning when we have had time to rest. There are many stories for all of you to cover out there tonight, aren't there? Get the story from the people who are out there helping the people that still need help. Please, leave us alone," I said as I assisted Jean and Anita into the van. George and Scooter had already been seated by the two troopers. A few in the press pursued some additional questions only to be ignored by the other press members who had enough on camera to show their audiences within the hour.

The Connecticut State Police van left the hospital under the guard of four Rhode Island State Police cruisers. Chief DiStasio kept in contact with the Directors Office which was now in a nationwide pursuit of members of the terrorist groups that were thought to be trying to or had crossed over to Canada in the last four to five hours. The Chief mulled over the casualties of the FBI, State Policemen, Coast Guard, Navy Shore Patrol and local police officers. The list was in the hundreds causing a major shortage of different law enforcement agencies in the New York and New England area. The list included types of injuries, organizations affected and various statistics of estimated percentage strengths of the units. Names and ranks were being added by the minute. One name that caught his attention was Senior Chief Brian McAuliffe of the Newport Naval Base Shore Patrol who had been seriously injured from gunshot wounds. The Chief knew of the man from Josh, and his name had been presented as a possible FBI candidate when he retired. He also knew his connection to Ed McAuliffe who was still under investigation in this case. He thought to call Josh but decided he would find out soon enough in a day or so. Let the kid relax for a few hours and get some sleep, he thought. This news would hinder that and he needed Josh sharp and ready for the days and weeks ahead finishing up this case.

The Mohegan Sun Casino was still doing business despite the economic turndown. The numbers of gamblers and amounts of money the casino took in were 60 percent down from the peak years. The casino still employed the locals but it was in the gaming portion of the casino only. The great shows and vacation stays at the 11 story hotel were not held or booked anymore. The hotel was vacant and minimal maintenance crews made sure the building was ready for an upturn in the economy. The casino management hoped that they would be able to open the hotel portion up again within the next few years once the economy improved.

Moroch was wet and did not have much money on him. He possessed his Walther and the clothes on his back. The casino was a good place where he could get quick cash from an ATM machine, he thought. He still had almost $1000 in an account and he still possessed his ATM card. He walked for a short distance and found himself in the almost empty employee parking lot. There were a few people in the dimly lit parking lot. The lights flickered as Moroch walked toward the casino entrance. A large sign over the entrance way said that he was entering the "Winter Entrance." The lights for the sign and everything in the building as he entered were dim and occasionally flickering. He saw a men's room and entered. He dried his hair under the hand blow dryer and fixed his damp clothing as well as he could to look presentable. There were a few people playing black jack and a few crap tables open. There was no one playing any of the slot machines, he noticed. He asked one of the attendants why the lights were so dim. The attendant looked at Moroch and said that the lights were running on the emergency generators because the power had been lost. The attendant said that there had been an explosion in New London that affected all the power in the area. Moroch nodded and moved on to find an ATM. He found one and realized that the machine was down due to the power outage. He moved to the cash office to see if he could be advanced money on his credit cards or maybe even process his ATM Card in the cash office. The attendant said that all he could do was exchange chips for cash. He couldn't get cash this way. He looked around and noticed several people playing black jack. He watched from a distance and noticed one individual with a decent stack of chips in front of him. He found a seat and observed from a distance. He figured that he could stay at the casino and dry out some more and watch the game across from him.

By 6:00 a.m. the guy with the stack of chips decided to cash in. Moroch watched the man leave and approached the cash office and present his chips to the attendant. He walked past the man to eavesdrop on the casual conversation going on between the attendant and the man. He was fortunate enough to see the attendant count enough twenty dollar bills to get his attention. The man held the money in his hand, folded it and put it in his right front pocket and walked slowly over to a breakfast bar for some breakfast. He sat down to order some food. This irritated Moroch but he followed and casually sat down on the opposite end of the breakfast bar. The man ordered a quick drink and some kind of pastry. Moroch ordered a drink of juice. Before he could sip his drink, the guy grabbed the drink and pastry and started to leave towards the exit. Moroch waited until the man had completely exited before he left the bar. The man continued to walk towards the parking lot but turned to enter the overhead parking garage. Moroch had to move quickly but cautiously as to not make his intended victim aware he was stalking him. The parking garage was four levels and the man chose to take the elevator. He had to pass the waiting man to get to the stairwell. He smiled as he passed the man and looked as if he was in a hurry to get somewhere. He noticed that the guy had pushed the third level. He climbed the stairs as quickly as possible to the third level. He reached the third level he could hear the elevator coming up. He quickly placed himself directly in front of the door and looked around to see if anyone was approaching the seemingly deserted parking garage. It was empty. The bell rang as the elevator alerted potential passengers of its arrival to that floor. The door opened and Moroch hit his victim squarely on the top of his head with his pistol. Blood instantly spewed from the gash on the man's head as he went down back into the rear of the elevator. He hit him again to make sure he was out, closed the door and hit the stop button. The man was still alive but groaning. Moroch rolled him in the elevator. He had keys to some type of vehicle that had a remote attached to the keys. He checked his wallet and found several hundred dollars in cash. He left the credit cards. He searched the right front pocket and extracted a roll of twenties that he had observed the man receiving from the cash office. He flipped through the cash and realized he had another

277

$600 or so. Eight hundred dollars from this guy was a good hit. He opened the door, looked around, and dragged the moaning guy out of the elevator over to some litter cans that had been placed near the elevator entrances for patrons to use. He hid the guy behind them. No one would find this guy for awhile, he thought as he walked back to the elevator and released the stop button. His one mistake was forgetting that casinos had multiple security video cameras. Most of the incident had been caught on tape. He walked away quickly and pushed the panic button on the key remote. A blue Nissan Maxima's horn and lights were blaring and blinking. He quickly shut them off and went to the car. Moroch left the overhead garage at 6:23 a.m. according to the clock in the dash board of the Maxima.

He drove for a few minutes and found an open truck stop diner. He pulled over and thought he would get a real breakfast. He tucked the Walther into the small of his back. His soiled thin kaki jacket hid it well enough. He locked the car and entered the diner. He noticed a newspaper stand and grabbed the two papers that the stand carried. He scanned the Norwich Bulletin and the New London Day. Both newspapers headlines were about the explosion in New London last night. Other articles, pictures and illustrations of what the FBI had found out, with the assistance of other law enforcement agencies, were on every page. The death toll was mounting and the radiation levels in Portsmouth were being analyzed as to what affect they had on the general population and life forms in the area. The President was to speak on national television and on the internet today about his plan to find all the terrorists involved. He continued to scan until he found what he was looking for. A waitress interrupted him and asked for his order. He quickly ordered and resumed reading an article on the three men that had been held by the terrorists on the Newport Barge that had escaped and notified the FBI that the barges had explosive in them. Moroch smiled and thought the black man, the arrogant driver and the idiot did survive. He thought how he would never make that mistake again. He should have killed all three of them when he had the chance. He realized that he

278

did it again, just this morning. He should have killed the man in the parking garage. Too many loose ends, he surmised. He would have to remember Hussein Akel's training to leave no loose ends. He finished the article about the three men and wrote down their addresses. Maybe he would visit them one last time. He thought of Ed McAuliffe who he knew was the fourth person. He already knew where Ed lived and he definitely planned to visit that one tonight. He froze when he read a small article about an accident victim, suspected of having links to the terrorist, who was killed in an accident on I-91 in Massachusetts. Hussein Akel was listed as an employee for the CTC of Bridgeport, Connecticut and was carrying a large amount of money on him. The FBI had confiscated false identification cards, credit cards, passports and other incriminating information. He stopped reading the article. Hussein had become careless and paid for it. Moroch smiled because he realized he could probably return to his country now. Akel and his brothers were dead and martyrs now. He thought about how he would be a hero for returning after partial success when the waitress interrupted his thoughts and placed his breakfast in front of him.

Ed McAuliffe was ecstatic of the news that Jon and George were alive and being considered heroes. He read the newspapers and gleamed at every bit of information they reported on the two old fools. He envied them and wished that he had been with them during their captivity and escape. What a trio they would have made he thought, then reality set in. He still had to explain his involvement with the Costello Family and their involvement with the three companies that were being investigated. People would probably look at him with more suspicion now. He still didn't care about that. Two good friends of his were alive and he helped to solve this plot indirectly. That had to be a plus for him in the eyes of the FBI. The IRS, he thought, he could deal with later.

The phone rang and Ed listened to his sister explain to him

that Brian was in serious condition at the Newport Naval Base Hospital. She explained that he had suffered multiple gunshot wounds during the firefight with the terrorist that had been on the tug. She asked him if he would come because Brian had been asking for him as he went in and out of consciousness. Ed said he would be there as soon as he could and hung up. He finished dressing, called the terminal to inform his new assistant that he was going to see his injured nephew at the hospital. He told the assistant to call Dan Kelly and tell him to come to his house later tonight to pick up his last wages and hung up.

I was happy to be home. I immediately looked for my truck and then asked Jean where it was because I didn't see it. She explained that the FBI had it in Providence and that it would be returned in a few days. I then remembered that Josh had told me that they were prepared to rent me a truck if they needed to hold it for investigation of explosives residue. Jean then told me that I wasn't going anywhere in the next few days anyway so I relaxed. My head still throbbed and it really wasn't worth getting into it with as to when I would or should return to work. We had no sooner entered the house when Missy called, crying and carrying on about how she had been worried to death, that she, Joe and the kids would be over after I had some sleep, whether I needed anything, that she loved me, etc., etc., until I had to stop her and say, "Sweetheart, I thank you, I love you, I'm so happy you took care of Mom while I was a captive and I can't wait to see the kids but I am dead tired and my head is killing me. I want to get a little sleep, okay? Here, talk to mom." I handed over the phone to Jean as I walked to the bedroom and collapsed onto the bed. I guess I fell asleep in less than a minute.

Josh reached Candy's apartment and knocked on the door. He knocked again and waited. He could hear the peep hole cover move and then heard the door begin to be unlocked. Candy opened the door in her bath robe and said, "How is Rich? Will he be okay? We have to see him as soon as we can." Josh explained that Rich would be in pain from the shoulder wound and he would need to rest for awhile before they could see him. Candy relaxed a little and said, "You must be dead tired and want to go to sleep?" Josh acknowledged that he was.

"Well Special Agent. I have been waiting for you and I think I have your best interests in mind."

She backed up enough for Josh to enter her apartment and lock the door behind him. He stared at his petite beauty and said, "I missed you," She opened up her bathrobe, pulled it off her shoulders and let it drop. She stood there in the morning light naked and said, "Well, are you going to just look at me because you are tired and sleepy or do you have a little bit of strength left in you to make love to me?"

He never answered her as he picked her up and moved towards the bedroom.

Ed McAuliffe rode his Harley Davidson motorcycle as fast as he could to reach Newport in an hour. He arrived at the Naval Base hospital and found the information he needed to get to the Intensive Care Unit. The hospital was already full to capacity and in some areas; beds were in the hallways and in any open space available for the attending to care for the victims. Ed could see the ambulances lined up and waiting to take the over load of patients to other hospitals once they were checked through the triage center, given immediate emergency care to stabilize and place in other hospital facilities. Ed found Brian with the assistance of a navy corpsman. Brian was awake when Ed entered the ICU. Brian smiled and asked, "How you doing?"

"How am I doing? How the hell are you doing?"

Brian explained that he had a bullet pass completely through his right lung and out his back. He continued to explain that his lung had collapsed but the doctors had gotten it inflated and working properly. Another bullet had gone through the inside of his right arm. It missed the bone but his arm pit hurt like hell.

Brian said, "Uncle, I'm glad that guy was moving his machine pistol in the other direction when he caught me with two rounds. If he had been going the other way, who knows what the results would have been." Both men said nothing after that observation. Ed finally said that Brian should thank his surgeon.

"Who is your doctor here, anyway?"

"I was lucky enough to get Commander Woodbridge."

Ed smiled and told Brian to sleep now and he would come up as often as possible to see him. Once he was well enough, he wanted Brian to stay with him during his convalescence. Brian smiled when he heard that comment come from his uncle

Moroch Makel was getting very tired as he drove along after the large relaxing breakfast he had just eaten. He observed a motel up at the next exit and decided to get a room and sleep until night. He exited I-395 in Norwich, Connecticut and pulled into the parking lot of the Comfort Motel. He opened the glove compartment and read the name of the individual on the registration form. He was going to be Thomas Morin for the day and longer if he could get away with it. He entered the motel lobby and proceeded to rent a room.

George Woodbridge slept like a baby as Anita checked on him every hour or so. He needed plenty of bed rest. Anita was told by her son Thomas that he needed to be hydrated constantly. Scooter wasn't as tired and he sat on the edge of his bed with the bedroom door open. Anita noticed the young man was awake and asked if she could get anything for him. He said that he didn't need anything right now. She told him that she was very thankful that he had helped her husband and Jon escape from the barge. Scooter did ask her if George would be able to find him a job like he said he would earlier this morning.

"Child, if my George says he going to get you a job then by golly, he will. Don't you fret and loose one hair in your thick auburn head about that. Now you get some rest before George starts bothering both of us," she said. Anita knew George had a plan for this boy but she would have to wait until he told her of it. Scooter smiled and seemed to relax.

"Mr. Morin, I hope you enjoy your stay here with us," the motel clerk said. Moroch smiled and headed for his room for some much needed rest. He passed the motel clothing shop and stopped to look. He purchased a new shirt, pants and underwear. He saw a lightweight zip up jacket and some toiletries and decided to purchase them as well. He paid in cash and continued up to his room. It was almost 9 a.m. He set his watch to wake him at 6 p.m. He thought of the last few tasks he had to complete. Ed McAuliffe would be visited tonight as he drew down the covers to his bed. He visualized how he was going to eliminate Ed McAuliffe as he laid down on the bed. He started to plan the elimination of the other three but sleep overcame him.

Checkmate

Josh woke up and looked at the time. It was almost noon and he needed to get over to see his dad and then head up to the Westerly, RI Hospital where Rich had been taken for his wounds. Candy lay on her side completely exposed to his view. He looked at her for a few minutes and thought about ravaging her again but decided to slip quietly out of bed to gather up some toiletries and clothes that he kept at Candy's apartment. He looked forward to standing in the shower and relaxing for a short while. He gathered what he needed then slipped into the hot shower. He just finished rinsing the shampoo from his head when he felt her hands wrap around him, her breasts pushed against his back and her pubic area push against the back of his thigh. *So much for a relaxing shower,* he thought.

Chief Agent DiStasio was tired now. He had just finished an hour long telecom with the Director, his immediate staff and several high level pentagon officials about the incidents that had occurred. The Chief was pleased to hear that Josh's hunch about the terrorist heading for Canada had paid off. The Canadian authorities had arrested seven suspects attempting to use traced credit cards to purchase plane tickets to the United Kingdom, Spain and Portugal. Three suspects had been apprehended driving back into the United States after they suspected that their credit cards were being tracked. They had watched their comrades being arrested for presenting them at some of the ticket counters and decided to leave. The three failed to stop at the border checkpoint and were chased by federal and state authorities and stopped at gunpoint. The Chief needed some rest. He retreated into his office, cleared the leather couch of Sprague's investigative paperwork and lay down. He was asleep in a few minutes.

Josh and Candy arrived at the house for lunch. Missy, Joe and the kids had already arrived a few minutes earlier. I was happy to see my son and his pretty girlfriend as well as my daughter, son-in-law and grandkids again. Jean had fixed a nice lunch and after hugs and kisses were exchanged, we settled down for a well needed family gathering and a meal. Anita and George did the same.

Ed McAuliffe returned to his home after visiting with his nephew. He parked the Harley Davidson in the garage. As he dismounted the motorcycle and remembered to take the automatic Colt .45 pistol out from the secret compartment and bring it into the house. He thought he would place the piece in his bed stand drawer in case he would need it some time. But tonight, he'd keep it on top of the refrigerator again where he had always put his keys and wallet as soon as he entered the house. Although it used to drive Beth crazy, he never broke the habit.

Ed decided not to go to the terminal and finish the rest of the workday. He was tired and decided to stay at home, follow the news on the TV and relax as much as he could. He had been stressed during the time he had been questioned and mostly while George and Jon had been missing. He blamed it all on his greed to make a few bucks on the side and look the other way. A lot of people had been doing that just like he did and we were all now paying a very high price for all that greed now, he thought. The terrorists knew that there was always a taker when money was involved and took advantage of it. They had proved that less than 24 hours ago. Three thousand people were reported dead now and the numbers were expected to rise over the next weeks and months as the radiation sickness took its toll.

Moroch Makel woke up before 6 p.m. He felt rested and laid in bed looking at the ceiling and contemplating his next move. He switched on the local news and waited to see if there was any mention of the guy he rolled at the casino. He watched the advertisements until he was about to scream when the news came back on. The terrorist attacks, pictures of the explosions, the sinking of that destroyer, the people floating in the water, the hospital rooms filled with crying kids and women, and officials grandstanding and stating what they were going to do about this. He laughed. He thought that as long as Americans were greedy and in need of something, they were vulnerable. It would take time but the Americans would fall in due time with the right plan. This plan came close and they had learned much from the attacks but the next time would be better and hurt America even more.

He could head south and cross into Mexico in a few weeks and work his way to Venezuela and back to Europe, he thought. Canada was being watched too closely. He liked his idea but he would need more cash. Once he killed McAuliffe, he could drain his accounts and use that money to get to Mexico. It was time to wash, pray, eat and then find McAuliffe.

Candy and Josh had finished their visit with Rich. He seemed in good spirits and was in a little pain. The medications they had given him had eased the pain but also had made it difficult for him to stay awake and converse with his visitors. After about 40 minutes of watching him try to stay awake, Candy and Josh decided to head back to her apartment for a quiet evening before Josh had to return to the FBI Office. He also wanted to hear the President speak at 8 p.m. on national television about the New England attacks.

The TV played in Ed McAuliffe's living room. CNN was reporting that the New England attacks casualty lists was growing to over 3200 dead and 3900 injured. The list included 1000 law enforcement casualties. Ed watched and decided to call me to see how I was doing. He wanted so desperately to see me but he knew Josh was probably here and he knew he would feel uncomfortable. He also knew he would have to face Jean which disturbed him more. He dialed and the phone number and tensed up instantly when Jean answered.

"Hi Jean, this is Ed McAuliffe here." He asked sheepishly if it would be okay to talk to me. Jean didn't say anything and handed over the phone.

"Hello."

"Jon, I just wanted to check on you and say how pleased I was that you and George were okay," he said as I heard the emotional cracking in his voice.

"Thanks."

"In a few days, you can come over and visit, have lunch or something and we can talk about what happened."

"You think Jean would mind me being in her house after what happened?"

"Jean is mad at me and she doesn't dislike you anymore than she does me. She's mad at the two of us getting into this situation. Look, when you come over in a day or so, you will see I'm right and that Jean will be back to her old self again."

He was happy to hear that and said, "I'll make it up to you both as soon as I can."

"All you have to do is keep being my friend and stay clear of quick ways to make a buck," I stressed.

He laughed a little and said, "I will. Thank you again for being the friend that you are." Before he hung up he said, "You know, Donnie Costello had threatened to kill Dan Kelly if he didn't leave town. I have Dan's last pay here at my house and I'm waiting for the kid to show so that I can pay him before he leaves town with his wife and kids. He's trying to sell his house while he looks for a new job and home. Donnie doesn't want him at the terminal or anywhere involved with cargo and trucking."

"Wow," I said. "The Costello's are getting soft. If Dan was a mole during the Ernesto days he wouldn't have been found."

I told Ed that it was better that Dan get away and get a new start somewhere with the young family he had. Ed bid me a good night and said he'd be in touch. I hung up the phone.

Jean looked at me and said, "I don't want you anywhere near that man for what he did to you and George."

"Jean, he's my friend who made a mistake and tried to correct it the best way he knew how. Let's leave it at that."

She was going to argue the point but I guess the look on my face indicated that she would do that another day. She smiled and asked me if I needed anything before the President was to speak.

"Yes I do. I need to have a little quickie before the President's address."

She smiled and said that I should be more concerned about my new stitches. She said she would be afraid that I would pop them. I asked why?

"Because your head is swelling thinking you can make love to me after what you have just gone through, you old fool."

"I guess that's a 'no' then." I smirked. She never gave me another look or an answer.

Josh left Candy's apartment to head back to the Providence FBI Office and pick up where he had left off. The office had been a beehive of activity and everyone stationed there needed some relief time. Josh was the first to get relief after the attacks but was ready to resume his duties and allow others some needed relief. He still had hours more to be with his loved ones but he wanted to get back to the office and continue the action his agency was doing to get the terrorists. As he drove along, he called into the office and was immediately in contact with the Chief. He had remained in the office to direct the activities to assure that all the terrorist objectives had been protected from any additional attacks. Some cell groups were found in Charleston, SC and Jacksonville, FL but were broken up immediately. The West Coast seemed to be free from immediate terrorist activity and the Gulf Coast was being searched and any suspects arrested.

Law enforcement authorities in Coastal European cities began the same sweep as the American authorities were doing. More information was being collected and compared, cross referenced and double checked to see if there was any correlation between the groups of individuals that had been involved in the New England attack in America with European cells they knew of.

The DFC of Bonn, Germany was now occupied by the

German Military. All assets had been confiscated and all the operations officers were in custody by the German Military for questioning. Any Deutsch representatives on travel were hunted down by the local authorities and were brought in for questioning. Some individuals that disappeared were assumed armed and dangerous by the world community. The borders of Afghanistan, Pakistan, Iran and Iraq were being closed by order of the United Nations in anticipation that protection would be given to these escaped employees. The remaining American Special Forces stationed in Afghanistan were on alert to be sent to anywhere in the region that the escapees were reported to be fleeing to. A net was being spread over a very large area in the world and many nations were cooperating this time because all of them realized that the terrorists were taking advantage of the world's present circumstances.

Josh arrived and reported in to the Chief. He was updated on the recovery activities being undertaken in Portsmouth, NH as well as the situations in the rest of the affected cities. The death toll had now reached 3500 known dead and 4300 injuries. The radiation toll was still expected to rise but it would take another week or so for those statistics to be reported. In all, the terrorists had succeeded in executing the worst attack on American soil ever.

The President was in the process of addressing the attack that occurred last night and was assuring the American people that all was being done to assist the injured. He said that the U.S. Military was assisting all law enforcement authorities throughout the country. The Military would be used to hunt down any suspects and all questionable individuals would be placed in confinement and processed with due process of American law as soon as possible. The President mentioned that the Providence FBI Office had broken the case with the assistance from several brave American citizens. No mention of names was given to protect these individuals from harm until the case had been completely solved. The President was deeply sorry for the loss of life and resolved to help all those that had been injured until they had completely recovered. Food and medical assistance was being made available from the military to assist the American Public. The New England Attacks casualties were being treated as combat casualties. The President had mentioned that a day of mourning and prayer was being planned nationally for July 11. He also said that the United Nations would be asked by the United States to assist in their effort to rid the world of these types of terrorist organizations for good. He hoped the United Nations would supply the resources to track down the terrorist organizations that threatened the world's civilized and industrial nations. The United States would supply and share all intelligence information on these groups and hoped that similar information would be shared with the United States. The United States would wait for full cooperation from the other members of the United Nations for a certain amount of time to be determined in the next several weeks. If no United Nations action was taken in a reasonable amount of time, the U.S. would act on its own initiative and seek out the terrorists in any country where they had been identified to be in. Force would be used if the circumstances presented it. Nuclear force would be considered to be used on any country that was considered friend or foe if it was harboring known terrorists. Very few countries were going to criticize the President's speech and most were expected to cooperate with the United Nations as quickly as possible.

Josh was informed of the final FBI casualty list. Arrangements were being made for the services of the deceased agents. He wondered if the families of the deceased FBI agents would be willing to wait for July 11th for a national honoring of their fallen family members. He settled down and began to review the latest information that was being presented to him through the Chief's office. One bit of trivial information that popped out and stirred his curiosity was a pistol whipping that had occurred in the overhead parking lot at the Mohegan Sun Casino in the early morning hours. The report indicated that a video likeness was being processed at the time the report was made. He asked a control room agent if the videos had identified anyone of particular interest to the FBI. The agent said that he hadn't followed up on the video due to the amount of work that had come through the office in the last twenty four hours. Josh ignored the agent's slight sarcasm and asked to see the videos from the Sun Casino. In a few seconds the agent had the video on his computer screen. Josh watched the video and couldn't make out the assailant for about ten or fifteen seconds until the altercation was completed and the unconscious body of the victim was dragged in an attempt to hide him. The face of the assailant was none other than Moroch Makel. While he watched the remaining video he immediately contacted Joe Harris's barracks and informed the duty lieutenant that Makel was in his jurisdiction and that he would probably be driving a Nissan Maxima. Josh was able to get the license plates numbers from the report and video as well as the identity of the John Doe that had been taken to the Backus Hospital in Norwich in critical condition. The identity of a Mr. Thomas Morin from Dayville, CT was made from the Connecticut license plates.

Moroch Makel had left his motel room, paid his bill in cash and walked to his car almost two hours earlier. It was 8:40 p.m. and that infidel was still blabbering on national TV and radio about the attacks. Moroch thought that if he had been a better Commander In Chief, he would have seen the weakness in the Great Satan. The lowest class of Americans was easy to infiltrate, bribe and take advantage of. There wasn't any patriotism in this class and they looked the other way to get a buck. Even the middle class people from IH, the Costello family, the union officials, and drivers were almost as easy he thought. He drove by Ed McAuliffe's house in the Maxima and looked to see if there was any activity. It looked like someone was home but he would case out the place again on the next drive by.

Several minutes later Dan Kelly knocked on Ed McAuliffe's door. Ed acknowledged the voice he heard from the other side, opened it and let Dan into the house. Both men commented on the President's speech that was going on and viewable on Ed's TV screen. A little small talk ensued until Ed asked Dan into the kitchen where he had his money. Moroch drove by on his second sweep and noticed a car parked in front of the house. Moroch contemplated another drive by but realized he could be noticed by other neighbors in the area so he decided to pull up, stop a few houses up from McAuliffe's and slowly walk down to the house and into the back yard unsuspectingly.

Ed and Dan continued to talk in the kitchen about the sketchy plans Dan had to leave the area and start another job out of harm's way. Ed mentioned that he was a lucky individual to be standing here talking about another start away from the Costello family now that he had crossed Donnie Costello. Ed went to the top of his refrigerator and grabbed the cash envelope he had for him. He noticed some movement through the glass of the kitchen door. As he grabbed the envelope, he also grabbed the Colt on top of the refrigerator. Moroch saw the slick move as plain as day through the door. As Dan approached Ed to grab the envelope, the glass of the rear kitchen door exploded and Ed McAuliffe's upper left chest was painted in red. While Ed was pushed back onto the door of the refrigerator from the shock of the bullet, he slid down the door. A small hole was visible in the refrigerator and a red streak of blood marked the decent of Ed's body. Dan stood there in complete shock for a second or two before he felt the sting of something hitting his right upper back that took the air completely out of his lungs and threw him forward next to Ed's unconscious body. Moroch contemplated another shot but decided against it. As Dan lay face down on the kitchen floor gasping for air, he observed an individual out of the corner of his eye come into the kitchen. Dan lost consciousness for a few seconds but awoke to see the individual checking Ed's body for signs of life. He could see that the shooter was picking up the envelope of money that was still in Ed's hand when he went

292

down. The shooter opened the envelope and removed the cash. He stuffed the cash into his pocket as he rose. Dan was able to breathe a little but realized that he had been hit in the lung with a bullet. The shooter left the kitchen and apparently was looking for something or someone but gave Dan enough time to reach and obtain his pistol he kept with him ever since Donnie Costello and Tommy Lupinacci had roughed him up at his house the previous day. He managed to sit up and prop himself enough to hold the loaded and cocked pistol in the direction of the kitchen exit to the living room where the shooter had gone. He could hear the shoes of the shooter clicking on the hardwood floors during his return to the kitchen. Moroch thought that he needed to leave the house quickly now that two pistol shots had been fired. He was sure that someone would have heard the two shots. As he rounded the entrance way into the kitchen from the living room he felt, but never heard, the pain of the bullet passing through his forehead. He was dead before he hit the floor. Dan Kelly found his cell phone and pushed 911. Within seconds, the emergency operator came onto the phone and asked, "What is your emergency?"

Dan answered with Ed McAuliffe's address and then fainted.

Joe Harris was on duty when the call came through to the barracks to investigate the scene as emergency vehicles were being sent there. He knew McAuliffe's home address and immediately responded. During his drive to McAuliffe's, he contacted Josh Sprague at the Providence FBI Office. Josh requested several New London FBI agents to the scene. Within 20 minutes, emergency vehicles from the Norwich Fire and Police Departments were also at the scene. The first trooper to enter the McAuliffe home found Ed McAuliffe shot through the chest and sitting up propped against the refrigerator unconscious. Dan Kelly was laying on his side breathing heavily and semi-conscience. He responded to the first trooper by pointing to Ed McAuliffe and whispering to him to take care of him. The trooper retrieved Dan's pistol and found the body of a man in the living room entrance to the kitchen. The Trooper observed a small hole in the man's forehead and the parts of his devious brain spread over Ed's living room floor. The trooper searched the body and found some cash and a wallet with a considerable amount of cash money placed neatly by denominational order. The Nissan Maxima was found a few houses from McAuliffe's that contained a satchel which held passports, money, false identification cards from the DFC, CTC, Newport Naval Base check point cards and employment identification papers from the IH Company. Several Bank accounts from the Chelsea Groton Bank identified several aliases that Moroch Makel had used. One artifact of particular interest was a well used copy of the Koran found inside a small bag with ammunition for his Walther PPK pistol.

Josh informed us that Ed McAuliffe was in the hospital with a gunshot wound to his chest. I wasn't able to contact Brian McAuliffe to inform him of his uncle's condition but was able to get in contact with Dr. Woodbridge who did. Dan Kelly was also in guarded condition at the hospital but was able to inform the authorities of what had happened at the McAuliffe residence. The Connecticut State Police and Norwich City Police informed the FBI Office of the death of the alleged assailant in the McAuliffe home. Josh, in particular, was upset a little that he hadn't gotten a chance to interrogate this terrorist. I, myself, was glad that this guy was humping the 12 or so vestal virgins he was promised in heaven.

The Fight Continues

Dan Kelly awoke to a considerable amount of pain but was glad to see his wife hovered over him. After a few emotional minutes, both he and his wife settled down to hear the doctor inform him of the surgery that he'd undergone and told them that his prognosis was excellent. He should be out of the hospital in a week or less and that four to five weeks of convalescence at home would be needed for a complete recovery. Dan looked at his wife and they both understood that they would need to be out of the area as soon as possible. He realized he would have to risk his health and a speedy recovery in order to save his life from the threat from the Costello family.

Ed McAuliffe lay four rooms down from Dan Kelly and was informed that he would need several more weeks in the hospital before he would be released to convalesce at some senior center until he could be discharged to take care of himself again. When Jean and I heard that, we offered our home as the place for him to convalesce until he could be self sufficient again. We also knew that Brian would be discharged from the hospital in a few more weeks according to Dr. Woodbridge and that Brian had decided to retire from the Navy within a year. He still had his eyes set on the FBI and Josh was doing all he could possibly do to support that plan. Brian also said that he wanted Ed to live with him once he retired from the Navy so he could keep an eye on the old man. That idea pleased both Jean and I, but mostly Ed.

Dan Kelly was eventually paid a visit by Donnie Costello and Tommy Lupinacci the day he left the hospital. He feared that they were coming to make sure he left as soon as possible. The head of the Costello family must have become melancholy because he granted Dan clemency and allowed him to stay in the area with his wife and family in the same home that he threatened them in. He wasn't lenient enough to allow Dan back into working for the Costello family but all of us who knew the Kelly family, knew that they were much better off not being involved in the Costello family business anymore.

Donnie Costello and Tommy Lupinacci were questioned many times by the Federal Authorities and were under indictment for a multitude of illegal activities that would take the United States Federal Prosecutors Office months to prepare and prosecute. Some leniency was being considered for both men for their last minute cooperation with the FBI. Ernesto Costello was committed to a nursing home within months of the New England attack for progressive Alzheimer's disease. Sid Owlia eventually recovered from his injuries sustained at the hands of Moroch Makel. He was questioned by the FBI and other law enforcement authorities and was eventually put in a witness protection program by the Federal Government. The information Sid possessed was being cataloged for use against the Costello family. Terrorist contacts and arms cargo deals that Sid had information about were also of great interest to the authorities of many other countries besides the United States. Sid would be returned to the Middle East someday after a lengthy stay in the witness protection plan.

The FBI, CIA and Homeland Security were able to trace numerous banking transactions and cell phone records of Daryl Adams, Ike Adams, Harry Adams, Sid Owlia, and Mohammad Owlia which lead to several more arrests of illegal aliens who were detained in connection with the New England attacks. Further investigation of the IH Corporation's employment records weeded out the false employees that had begun to penetrate other depots and plants on the West Coast. They were rounded up, incarcerated and were being quickly prosecuted.

The DFC's assets were frozen by the German Government and the company ceased to exist approximately six months after the attacks. Four of the seven board members of the company had direct terrorist contacts. The CTC's assets were frozen as well. Investigations revealed that the CEO of the company had escaped to Canada but had not left the country according to Canadian intelligence. There was a large manhunt under way to find this guy who was originally from Saudi Arabia. The CTC left a large void in the tug business for Long Island Sound but many independent tug owners who had been hired on by Crescent were allowed to continue to work the coast line as independent tug owners. They eventually unionized again and formed as the New England Tug Company. The bright green and black tugs with the white crescent were now bright red with navy blue hulls. NETCO was painted in white letters on the red stacks.

The final death toll six months after the attacks had reached 3612 dead, 4847 injured. This was America's most severe attack in its 238 years of existence. The President and Congress swore to uphold the protection of the citizens of the United States against another attack by terrorists but no one in the country could be expected to believe that. The citizens of the United States learned from this experience that its citizens could be as corrupt as any other when forced to live a sub-standard lifestyle. The mightiest military and the strongest civil form of government in the world were not enough to keep its own citizens from becoming corrupt at any cost to survive.

The United States entered into an era of social stability. Medicare, Social Security, public works projects, mandatory military service requirements and border control were revisited by the American Government and its citizens. Green projects became priorities for all industrial manufacturing in this country. America withdrew its sons and daughters from foreign soil but maintained their presence in every corner of the world where nuclear powered fleets patrolled the seas. Humanitarian aid was their main objective as they sailed the seas. But all countries were now well aware of the New England Doctrine that had been passed by the United States Congress unanimously and signed into law by the President. The doctrine informed the United Nations that the Army, Naval and Air forces of the United States would be on constant standby and ready to assist them if so required. No U.S. land forces would be allowed into any country unless authorized by the United Nations. There was one condition that the United Nations did not approve that was said in the doctrine, "The United States reserved the right to use tactical nuclear weapons if the host country of known terrorists were not making an assertive effort to remove them from their country by any means necessary including requesting U.N. or U.S. ground forces.

Within six weeks of the introduction of the New England Doctrine on January 1, 2015, the Philippines, Malaysia, Saudi Arabia, Iraq, Pakistan, India, Spain, Morocco, Libya, and Palestine turned over suspected terrorists to the United Nations for prosecution under the World Court. Afghanistan and Iran continued to insist that terrorists were not being harbored in their countries. The proponents of this twisted Jihad belief continued to think that if they continued to inflict terror and death on the West, the West would abandon the fight and leave. That twisted belief fueled the great New England Attacks of July 4, 2014 and nearly succeeded in bringing the United States down on one knee. The belief that "The Fight Will Continue" was ending quicker than anyone who believed in the Jihad could imagine. Complete nuclear obliteration was the only answer the West would have now and that would be executed quickly if required.

On December 13, 2014 the President of the United States awarded the Medal of Freedom to Jonathan Joshua Sprague and George Thomas Woodbridge at the White House, Washington, D.C. Standing next to both men as the President put the medal on each one were two equally proud teary eyed women who looked over to all their family members watching the event take place. All those who watched the ceremony at the White House and on National Television were grateful to the two old men that risked all to save all, as the President had said in his speech minutes earlier when he addressed the crowd there and those watching on television.

Also watching the ceremony on TV, were two illegal aliens sitting in a Silver Springs, Maryland condominium.
"Hussein was unlucky and should have prayed more. God was not pleased with him to have him die in such a way," one said.
The other one simply said, "He gave Moroch too much rope to hang himself. We will not make that mistake the next time."

About the Author

Thomas Michael Coletti has lived most of his life in the Norwich, Connecticut area. He has been married to his high school sweetheart, Donna Jean, for 37 years. He has four grown children, Jennifer, Kimberly, Crystal, and Michael and two grandchildren, Katie and Sean.

Tommy graduated from the Norwich Free Academy in 1967. He enlisted into the United States Air Force during the Vietnam War and spent four years from 1968 until 1972 as a medic. He was honorably discharged as a Staff Sergeant. He attended college on the GI Bill. He received an Associates Degree, with highest honors, in Science from Mohegan Community College, Norwich, Connecticut in 1974 and a Bachelors Degree, with Cum Laude distinction, in History from Eastern Connecticut State University, Willimantic, Connecticut in 1976.

He applied and was accepted to law school but declined admission to work for one year at the Electric Boat Shipyard (EB) in Groton, Connecticut until his wife gave birth to their first child. He remained there as subsequent children were born every three years after that and has now been there for 33 years.

Special Delivery is one of four novels he has written, the first to be published.

CPSIA information can be obtained at www.ICGtesting.com
Printed in the USA
BVOW030832061011

272919BV00001B/11/P